ACCLAIM FOR RACHEL HAUCK

The Wedding Shop

"I adored *The Wedding Shop*! Rachel Hauck has created a tender, nostalgic story, weaving together two pairs of star-crossed lovers from the present and the past with the magical space that connects them. So full of heart and heartache and redemption, this book is one you'll read long into the night, until the characters become your friends, and Heart's Bend, Tennessee, your second hometown."

—BEATRIZ WILLIAMS, *NEW YORK TIMES*
BESTSELLING AUTHOR

"*The Wedding Shop* is the kind of book I love, complete with flawed yet realistic characters, dual timelines that intersect unexpectedly, a touch of magic, and a large dose of faith. Two breathtaking romances are the perfect bookends for this novel about love, forgiveness, and following your dreams. And a stunning, antique wedding dress with a secret of its own. This is more than just a good read—it's a book to savor."

—KAREN WHITE, *NEW YORK TIMES* BESTSELLING AUTHOR

The Wedding Chapel

"Hauck's engaging novel about love, forgiveness, and new beginnings adeptly ties together multiple oscillating storylines of several generations of families. Interesting plot interweaves romance, real life issues, and a dash of mystery . . . Recommend for mature fans of well-done historical fiction. "

—*CBA RETAILERS AND RESOURCES*

"Hauck tells another gorgeously rendered story. The raw, hidden emotions of Taylor and Jack are incredibly realistic and will resonate with readers. The way the entire tale comes together with the image of the chapel as holding the heartbeat of God is breathtaking and complements the romance of the story."

—RT BOOK REVIEWS, 4$^1/_2$ STARS AND A TOP PICK!

The Wedding Dress

"In *The Wedding Shop*, the storyline alternates between past and present, engrossing the reader in both timelines. There are certain elements that are more obvious to the reader than to the characters, and it can get slightly frustrating waiting for the characters to get a clue. However, this is short lived, and the ways that God's provision is shown is heartwarming and can even increase the reader's faith. The weaving in of characters and plot points from *The Wedding Dress* and *The Wedding Chapel* adds depth and meaning to the gorgeously rendered tale."

—RT BOOK REVIEWS, 4 STARS

"Hauck seamlessly switches back and forth in this redeeming tale of a shop with healing powers for the soul. As Cora and Haley search for solace and love, they find peace in the community of the charming shop. Hauck succeeds at blending similar themes across the time periods, grounding the plot twists in the main characters' search for redemption and a reinvigoration of their wavering faith. In the third of her winsome wedding-themed standalone novels, Hauck focuses on the power of community to heal a broken heart. "

—PUBLISHERS WEEKLY

"*The Wedding Dress* is a thought-provoking read and one of the best books I have read. Look forward to more . . ."

—MICHELLE JOHNMAN, GOLD COAST, AUSTRALIA

"I thank God for your talent and that you wrote *The Wedding Dress*. I will definitely come back to this book and read it again. And now I cannot wait to read *Once Upon a Prince*."

—AGATA FROM POLAND

The Royal Wedding Series

"Perfect for Valentine's Day, Hauck's latest inspirational romance offers an uplifting and emotionally rewarding tale that will delight her growing fan base."

—*LIBRARY JOURNAL*, STARRED REVIEW

"Hauck writes a feel-good novel that explores the trauma and love of the human heart . . . an example of patience and sacrifice that readers will adore."

—*ROMANTIC TIMES*, 4 STARS

"A stirring modern-day fairy tale about the power of true love."

—CINDY KIRK, AUTHOR OF *LOVE AT MISTLETOE INN*

"*How to Catch a Prince* is an enchanting story told with bold flavor and tender insight. Engaging characters come alive as romance blooms between a prince and his one true love. Hauck's own brand of royal-style romance shines in this third installment of the Royal Wedding series."

—DENISE HUNTER, BESTSELLING
AUTHOR OF *THE WISHING SEASON*

"*How to Catch a Prince* contains all the elements I've come to love in Rachel Hauck's Royal Wedding series: an 'it don't come easy' happily ever after, a contemporary romance woven through with royal history, and a strong spiritual thread with an unexpected touch of the divine. Hauck's smooth writing—and the way she wove life truths throughout the novel—made for a couldn't-put-it-down read."

—BETH K. VOGT, AUTHOR OF *SOMEBODY LIKE YOU*,
ONE OF *PUBLISHERS WEEKLY*'S BEST BOOKS OF 2014

"Rachel Hauck's inspiring Royal Wedding series is one for which you should reserve space on your keeper shelf!"

—*USA TODAY*

"Hauck spins a surprisingly believable royal-meets-commoner love story. This is a modern and engaging tale with well-developed secondary characters that are entertaining and add a quirky touch. Hauck fans will find a gem of a tale."

—*PUBLISHERS WEEKLY* STARRED REVIEW
OF *ONCE UPON A PRINCE*

THE WEDDING SHOP

THE WEDDING SHOP

Rachel Hauck

 ZONDERVAN®

ZONDERVAN

The Wedding Shop Copyright © 2016 by Rachel Hauck

This title is also available as a Zondervan e-book.

Requests for information should be addressed to:
Zondervan, *Grand Rapids, Michigan 49546*

ISBN: 978-0-310-35080-4 (mass market)

Library of Congress Cataloging-in-Publication Data
Names: Hauck, Rachel, 1960-author.
Title: The wedding shop / Rachel Hauck.
Description: Grand Rapids, Michigan: Zondervan, 2016. | ?2015
Identifiers: LCCN 2016008490 | ISBN 9780310341543 (softcover)
Subjects: LCSH: Bridal shops—Fiction. | GSAFD: Christian fiction. | Love
stories.
Classification: LCC PS3608.A866 W44 2016 | DDC 813/.6—dc23 LC record
available at http://lccn.loc.gov/2016008490

The author is represented by MacGregor Literary, Inc.

Printed in the United States of America

17 18 19 20 21 / QC / 5 4 3 2 1

To the friends of my youth, with whom I dreamed, rode bikes in the street, and created make believe worlds in our basements and bedrooms, pretending to be Mary Tyler Moore or dating an Osmond brother. We may not have seen each other in decades, but the echoes of our laughter rebound in my heart, still.

PROLOGUE

HALEY

SUMMER 1996
HEART'S BEND, TENNESSEE

The scent of rain laced the afternoon breeze as it shoved through summer-green trees, ramming ominous black clouds together like a craggy mountain ridge. Haley scanned the heavens as she dropped her bike on the edge of Gardenia Park, a swirled chocolate-vanilla cone in her hand.

"Gonna rain, Tammy. Hurry!" Haley glanced over her shoulder toward their "fort," an abandoned building once known as The Wedding Shop.

The wind kicked up and a bass rumble thundered through the park. Haley shivered, curling her toes against her flip-flops.

"Tammy!"

"Hold your horses. He's making my dip cone."

Haley liked Tammy, the prettiest girl in their class, from the moment she met her in first grade.

"Just get regular chocolate." A thunderclap approved Haley's words, adding a lick of lightning for effect.

"But I like the dipped ones."

"We're going to get wet."

From the ice cream stand, Tammy shrugged, grinning, reaching for her cone as Carter Adams finally handed it through the window. Haley couldn't stand Carter. He was friends with her oldest brother, Aaron, and every time he came over to the house he teased and picked on her until she screamed.

Then Mama would burst into the room. "Haley, for crying out loud, be quiet. What's with all the screaming?"

Did Aaron defend her? Or Carter confess he'd been teasing her? Noooo . . . That would be too much to ask. When she grew up, she was going to defend people. Help others. Stand up for the picked on.

A girl learned a lot about self-defense when she was the youngest of four brothers. She liked them all right, except when they were being *boys*.

"Where do you want to go?" Tammy sat down on a bench, motioning for Haley to join her, careful with her cone, catching the vanilla dripping through chocolate cracks with the tip of her tongue. "Your house? We can play Mario."

"Naw, we did that already. Besides, one of my brothers is bound to be playing on it." Haley glanced back at their fort, the old wedding shop. "What about your house?"

Haley preferred the neat, quiet calm of the Easons'. An only child, Tammy had the run of the place, *including* her own bathroom.

Her very own bathroom! Haley had to share with Seth, two years older, and Will, four years older. They had what Mama called a Jack and Jill bathroom. More like a Jack and Jack with no room for a Jill. One of these days Haley was going to defend others, yep, and have her own bathroom. And that's that.

"I think your brothers are nice."

"Nice? Try living with them." Haley wrinkled her nose. "They're loud and they smell. Bad too."

More thunder rocked overhead, this time with a sprinkle of rain. From her bicycle basket, Tammy's beeper went off.

"That's Mama," she said, working hard on her ice cream to keep it from dripping down the sides and soaking the napkin wrapped around the cone. She reached for her beeper. "It's a three."

Ah, a three. Which meant "Be safe." Usually Mrs. Eason sent a one, which meant "Get home."

Darkness hovered over the large town-center park, over Heart's Bend's center square, as the wind blew sprinkles of rain. Lightning whipped through the black-and-blue sky.

Tammy shivered. "Better get someplace safe. Mama will ask me later."

"Want to go to the fort?" Haley motioned over her shoulder toward the abandoned place.

As if on cue, the heavens burst open with buckets of rain. Tammy dropped her ice cream as she skedaddled for her bike, screaming, laughing as water poured from the clouds.

"Let's go!"

"Wait for me." Haley gripped her cone as she hopped on her bike and pedaled down First Avenue for all her life. "Wooooooo!" She ducked against the spiking rain, the water cooling her hot, sticky skin.

Dashing across the avenue as the light turned red, she bounced up on the Blossom Street curb, dropped her bike in the shade of the old oak tree, and ran her hand under the dripping Spanish moss, racing Tammy for the back porch.

The clouds crashed together, declaring war, wielding their swords of light and showering Heart's Bend with their battle sweat as the girls tumbled onto the wide-board floor.

Haley jumped to her feet, hanging out of the door, her arm hooked around the weak screen doorframe. "Ha-ha-ha, you can't get us now!"

"Come on, let's go inside." Tammy slipped through the shop's back door by jiggling the doorknob, weakening the lock.

Haley followed, pausing just inside, next to what Mama called a butler's pantry, shaking the rain from her stick-straight blonde hair. The shop's stillness settled on her, speaking something Haley couldn't understand but definitely felt. And like every time before, Haley felt as though she'd walked into a place like home.

Daddy called it a sixth sense. Whatever that meant. But somehow Haley understood time and space and anything that might be beyond the world she could see. The notion excited her. And scared the living daylights out of her. Let's just be honest.

"Look, I can't get it off." Laughing, Tammy flicked her hand in front of Haley's face, pieces of the cone's white paper napkin stuck to her sticky fingers.

Reaching up, Haley yanked the piece free, wadding it up in her pocket. She didn't want to trash the place—like everyone who'd tried to run a business here once it was no longer a wedding shop. A shame, a crying shame, how folks could disrespect a building and all it stood for.

Haley may be only ten, but she'd heard the stories of the shop's brides, of Miss Cora, and all the good she'd done. The place needed respect.

"Let's play bride." Tammy ran up the wide, thick grand staircase. The carved and curved banister put Haley in mind of a great palace. That's what this shop was to Heart's Bend. A grand palace. For girls getting married. "You be the bride this time, Haley. Walk down the steps from up there—"

"The mezzanine."

"Yeah, that place." Tammy licked the chocolate from her fingers and wiped her hand on her shorts. "How do you know it's a mezzanine again?"

"I heard Mama say it when we watched some documentary." Haley made a snoring sound. Mama was all about education, and just about everything in the Morgan family had to be "educational." Even Christmas gifts. Praise be for Daddy who drew a line at Mama's educational obsession during the holidays.

See, Mama was a doctor and Daddy an engineer. They worked long hours and employed a maid-slash-cook, Hilda, and a nanny, Tess. They were all right. Kind of cranky. Last time Haley asked either one of them to help her bake a cake, they tossed her out of the house.

"Go swim. Got that big ole pool out back and you kids all hang around inside. Crying shame, I tell you, a crying shame. In my day we'd have . . ."

Hilda's "her day" stories shot Haley and her brothers out of the house faster than a greased pig.

Anyway, that was routine around the Morgan house. Daddy and Mama were home for dinner every night, though, because Mama believed in families eating together. But they had to discuss something intelligent. Mama always reiterated, "There's nothing *more* important than education."

Yeah? Except goal setting. That was Mama's other bugaboo. Everyone had to set goals come New Year's Eve. She made the family sit and write down what they wanted to accomplish. Even Daddy. So there was no way of ever getting out of it.

For the past three years, Haley wrote, "Get a puppy." So far, she never got one. What was the point of a goal if her parents never helped her achieve it?

"Are you going to be the bride or not?" Tammy said. "I was the bride last time. It's my turn to be the shopkeeper."

Haley jogged up the stairs. She preferred shopkeeper to bride. "Okay, but who am I going to marry?"

"Who do you want to marry?"

"No one. I told you, boys smell."

Tammy made a face. "Pretend they don't. Now who?" She twisted the knob on the closet door under the dormer eaves. They liked to pretend the wedding dresses were inside.

But the door was locked. Like always.

Haley could only think of one boy at school who didn't annoy the heck out of her. She peered over at her friend through the light falling through the mezzanine windows. "Cole Danner?"

"Cole?" Tammy sighed, making a face and planting her hand on her hip. "He's mine."

"I don't really want him. Geez. This is just pretend. He's the cutest boy in class and, as far as I can tell, stinks the least."

"Okay, I guess it's all right since it's just pretend. But when we grow up, I got dibs."

"On Cole? You can have him. I'm not getting married until I'm old, like thirty, maybe even forty."

Tammy laughed. "But you have to be my maid of honor, promise?"

"Promise." Of course she'd do anything for her bestie Tammy.

Overhead, the thunder rumbled. But the old wedding shop walls remained steady.

Haley's Grandma Morgan and her friend Mrs. Peabody bought their wedding dresses here. Mama was in medical school in Boston when she met Daddy, who was at MIT. They got married in a courthouse or she'd have bought her dress from Miss Cora too.

At least Haley liked to think so. Even at ten, she had a strong sense of tradition.

Daddy and Mama moved back to Heart's Bend when Haley was two, wanting to be near family, wanting out of the cold. And Mama started her own sports medicine clinic. She was pretty famous as far as Haley could tell. Athletes from all over came to see her.

"You need a veil." Tammy claimed a discarded piece of newspaper, smoothed it out on the floor, and folded it over Haley's head.

Haley laughed, ducking away, the black-and-white veil slipping from her head. "If I come home with lice, Mama will have a cow." She inched toward the third-floor stairs. "Let's explore up here. Maybe we can find something to use."

But the third floor was cluttered, full of boxes and old computer equipment. Paint peeled from the walls, the floor was covered with rotting carpet, and the bathroom was torn apart.

Tammy shivered. "This creeps me out. Let's go back to the mezzanine."

But Haley spied something peeking out from the edge of the carpet. She stooped, pinching the edge of a black-and-white photograph.

Tammy squatted next to her. "Hey, that's Miss Cora. I saw her picture in the paper."

"I know. I remember." Haley looked up at the dank quarters. "Do you think she lived here?"

"I hope not. It's gross."

Haley stared at the haunting reflection in the woman's eyes, like she longed for something. A strange twist knotted up Haley's middle. Taut prickles ran down her arms. Her sixth sense again. Running into something she could feel but not see.

"Look, clothespins. And a piece of tulle. This can be your veil." Standing next to a bookshelf, Tammy held up her treasures.

"Let's just pretend I have a dress and a veil." Haley stared at the face in the picture. Miss Cora was not very pretty, but kind looking with old-fashioned hair, like in Granny's pictures, a curiosity in her expression. And sadness. She was definitely sad.

But she'd heard only happy things about Miss Cora. Did she like running a wedding shop? Did she have lots of brothers like Haley? That can make a girl sad. Or was she an only child, like Tammy?

"Hal, come on before Mama beeps me home."

Thunder let loose a boom of agreement. Haley tucked the picture in her shorts pocket and hustled down the stairs.

"I changed my mind. You be the bride. I'll be the shop owner, Miss Cora."

"Miss Cora?"

"Why not? It's pretend, right? Besides, if Cole's the groom, it's best you be the bride. You'll marry him before I ever will."

Back on the mezzanine, Haley hurriedly moved into pretend mode jogging down the stairs to the foyer. "Oh, hello, Mrs. Eason. Your daughter is putting on her veil right now." She mimed opening the shop's front door because the real one was dead bolted. "Please, have a seat."

Overhead, Tammy shuffled across the mezzanine, then hummed the wedding song as she descended the staircase, one slow step at a time. Haley breathed out, blowing her bangs from her forehead, the stale, hot air of the shop making her sweat, causing dust to stick to her skin.

"Isn't she beautiful, Mrs. Eason?" Haley jumped an imaginary line and pressed her hands to her cheeks to play the role of Tammy's mother. "Oh my stars, I'm going to cry. I'm going to cry." She fanned her face with her fingers. "Darling, you are beautiful, so beautiful."

Tammy modeled her newspaper veil, held out the skirt of her imaginary gown, and cooed how she couldn't "wait to marry Cole Danner."

Upon her words, lightning cracked, so bold, so loud this time the windows rattled. Tammy jumped into Haley's arms.

Then they fell to the floor laughing, hooting, popping their hands on the splintered hardwood. When they quieted down, Haley stared at the high ceiling.

"Let's own this shop one day, okay?" She gripped Tammy's hand in her own. "We'll go to college, then maybe join the Marines or something—"

"The Marines! I'm not joining the Marines." Tammy's protest was sure. "But I'll run this shop with you."

"But first we go places, see people, visit Hawaii, *then* buy this shop."

"Best friends forever." Tammy hooked her pinky finger around Haley's.

"Best friends forever."

"We'll come back here one day and own this wedding shop."

"Pinky promise."

"Pinky promise."

The lightning flickered, kissing the front window

again. Haley jumped up and ran screaming around the shop with Tammy in pursuit.

Because make-believe was what best friends did. But make-believe ended.

Best friends were forever. And pinky promises could never be broken.

CHAPTER ONE

CORA

The morning began like every other weekday, with Cora making her way up the back walk to the shop, unlocking the door, and clicking on the lights.

But today the spring sun's brightness drifting through the trees stirred a sense of hope. A vibrant anticipation.

Let today be the day.

Hanging her sweater and hat on hooks in the mudroom, Cora entered the small salon and stood at the nearest window, pushing the lace sheer aside. She gazed toward the cut of the Cumberland River visible through the trees and wished for *him*.

While she treasured spring's green and gardenia perfume, she missed the unobstructed view provided by leafless limbs. In the winter, she could see for miles from her shop's perch on the hill. Despite the cold gray days of winter, its barrenness enhanced her perspective.

But now spring had arrived and, still, he had not. She so ached for a glimpse of his long, lean stride coming up from the port, boldly taking the avenue with his broad physique, his mass of blond hair tangling about his face while the loose sleeves of his white blouse billowed about his thick arms.

Come today, darling.

"Cora?" The back door slammed, drawing her away from her post. "I'm here." Odelia, Cora's shop assistant and seamstress, entered with a gust of cold wind and the scent of cinnamon. "Sorry to be late. The buns were still in the oven." She chuckled, shifting the weight of the garments in her arms. "The buns . . . get it? I should've been in vaudeville. Anyways, couldn't get the old car started so Lloyd drove me in on the wagon."

Cora leaned over her shoulder. "Hmmm, those smell divine. And no rush. We've an hour before they arrive. Mama's on her way."

"Good, good. Ain't no hostess like your mama." Odelia set the hot buns in the first-floor pantry, where Mama would set up a service of tea and coffee along with pastries from Haven's bakery. She'd have to delicately decide what to do with Odelia's buns. "Even your Aunt Jane said she couldn't out hostess Esmé. Now, let me get the rest of the dresses out from the wagon. Lloyd has work back at the farm and he don't cotton none to being held up."

"I'll help you." Cora followed Odelia out of the shop and down the walk to Blossom Street. "Morning, Lloyd."

"Cora." He jutted his chin her way, then lowered his hat over his eyes, handing her several dresses swinging from hangers. "Got work to do."

"Now, shush. What do you think we're doing here

all day, playing tiddlywinks?" Odelia anchored her toe on the wagon wheel and lighted into the bed, taking the dresses from her man. "Don't hold them against you. They'll go smelling like horses and pigs."

"Odelia, here, hand them to me." Cora reached for three more dresses.

The woman was a backbone to the shop with her seamstress skills, yet a constant mystery. Part Irish, part Cherokee, she was a workhorse with smooth brown skin that defied her age. Mama said she'd stick a needle in her eye if Odelia was a day under sixty.

When they'd unloaded the dresses, Lloyd took off. Odelia called after him, "Come get me, you old coot, or there won't be no supper."

"How long have you two been married again?" Cora said, falling in step with her assistant. Odelia was an Aunt Jane find. Hired her when she first opened the shop in 1890.

"Since Jesus was a baby." She examined one of the white satiny dresses. "If Lloyd's old blanket left a mark, I'll crown him."

But in the light of the mezzanine, the dresses were perfect, the white skirts shimmering with purity and beauty. No one in Heart's Bend could work a needle and sewing machine like Odelia.

"I'll get the display cases set up." Cora headed down the stairs. The grand staircase with the carved, glossy, wooden spindles divided the shop in two—the grand salon on the left, the small salon on the right.

The grand salon Cora treated like a Hollywood living room, at least from what she could tell from the movies and magazines, covering the hardwood with plush carpet and the walls with bold paper.

In the light of the front display window, she positioned ornate chairs around the long, curved davenport made of a polished wood and covered with heavy gold upholstery. Here she sat her clients and their mothers, grandmothers, sisters, cousins, friends, aunts, and nieces. Here they waited for the bride to descend the staircase in her wedding gown.

If the bride was so inclined, the bridesmaids also descended the stairs, modeling their gowns for the other women. Once in a while, a father insisted on joining the party. After all, they protested, weren't they the ones footing the bill?

In the small salon, the display cases housed a variety of veils, gloves, sachets, clutches, stockings, and every other sundry a bride might desire. Dress forms and mannequins modeled wedding gowns, going-away dresses, and a very modest style of lingerie.

At the bottom of the stairs, Cora paused. What was she setting out to do? Oh yes, the display cases. And she needed to run and get the pastries from the bakery. But she paused at the front door, peering through the etched glass, unable to quell the stirring in her heart. It moved from taut anticipation to a burning restlessness.

Rufus, where are you?

In his last letter, he said he'd be on the Cumberland this spring. "Look for me in March." But it was already the first week of April, when the dogwoods bloomed in Gardenia Park and down First Avenue.

She feared he'd been hurt, or fallen ill. Or worse, his

boat had hit the snags and sank, a swift current trapping him beneath the surface.

"Do we have time to dawdle at the window?"

Cora turned to see her mother crossing the small salon, patting her hand against her hair, then smoothing her hand down the front of her skirt. "I was just checking the temperature." Cora rapped her knuckle on the cool glass in the direction of the thermometer. A blessed coincidence.

"Checking the temperature? Or watching the river?"

Mama liked to think Cora was an open book. One she could read well.

"I'm fixing the display cases before going to the bakery. Can you open the top panes of the windows, let in the fresh air? When the Dunlaps arrive it will get warm in here. They are a large party."

"You know, staring out the window pining for him won't make him arrive any faster, Cora. Or make him a man of his word." Mama unlocked the window next to the door and pulled open the pane.

"You're being unfair. He is a man of his word."

"Well, when he can change it at will and convince you it's the truth, then I suppose you're right. Did you say something about the bakery order? I glanced in the pantry and only saw Odelia's cinnamon buns."

"Yes, after I set up the cases I'll head over to Haven's. Will you start the coffee and tea at five till?"

"I've been hosting this shop since before you were born. I know when to start the coffee and tea. What I don't know is what to do with Odelia's buns. The woman can sew dry grass into a beautiful gown, but her baking leaves much to be desired. No wonder Lloyd never smiles."

Cora bit back her laugh. "Shh, Mama. She'll hear you. You can't deny they smell wonderful."

"They do, but I've told her to her face her sweet buns are like rocks." Mama moved to the bottom of the stairs. "Isn't that right, Odelia?"

"What's that, Esmé?"

"Your baking could break the strongest teeth."

"That's what you've been telling me for twenty years, but Lloyd don't seem no worse for the wear."

"Except he never smiles." Mama turned to Cora, whispering behind her hand. "'Cause he ain't got no teeth."

"Mama, stop." Cora muted the laugh in her chest. "You taught me better. Now act like a kind Christian."

"Telling the truth is being a kind Christian." Mama moved to the remaining windows, slipping down the top panes. In the grand salon the grandfather clock chimed the hour.

Eight o'clock. Cora must get herself together. At the display cases, she retrieved the head forms from the bottom drawers and adorned them with veils, curving the long tulle around the glass and splaying it across the polished hardwood. On another set of heads, she stuck ornate combs into the coarse, fake hair.

Next she set out long, silky white gloves with pearl buttons and arranged a pearl set on a blue velvet runner.

The shop had an important client this morning. A Miss Ruth Dunlap from Birmingham, a society bride who also happened to be a shop legacy. Her mother, Mrs. Laurel Schroder Dunlap, born and raised in Heart's

Bend, bought her gown and trousseau from Aunt Jane in 1905. She would expect the royal treatment for her daughter. As well she should.

Jane Scott cut her bridal fashion chops in Milan and Paris in the late 1880s, bringing them back home to Tennessee when her mama, Granny Scott, died. Never in all their born days had the women of Heart's Bend—farmers' wives, mountain women, half-breeds, and former slaves—seen the likes of what Aunt Jane brought to town.

But they loved it. Aunt Jane's elegant style made the small-town shop a legend in middle Tennessee and northern Alabama, launching an unlikely small-town tradition and becoming Heart's Bend's darling.

"Cora, I know you don't like me nosing into your business," Mama said, returning to the small salon. "But—"

"No, I don't. I'm not a child." Cora examined the last display case. Everything seemed to be in order.

With a smile at Mama, she headed up to the mezzanine and her desk. She shuffled the papers, shoving aside a large box of mail. All work for tomorrow after Miss Dunlap returned to Alabama.

Mama followed her up.

"You are *not* a child. Which is precisely my point." Mama anchored her hands on the side of the desk and leaned over Cora. "You're thirty years old, darling. I'd been married, given birth to two children, and become president of the local Tennessee Equal Suffrage Association by the time I was twenty-eight."

"Cora, you want to choose a veil for Miss Dunlap?"

Odelia popped out of the wide, long storage room. "I think gloves would go well with her gown too."

"I set out the veils and gloves on the display cases in the small salon. She can choose when she tries on the dress."

Aunt Jane skimped on nothing when she hired Nashville architect Hugh Cathcart Thompson to design The Wedding Shop. It was the height of high class.

A place of business *and* a place of residence. Though Cora had yet to occupy the third floor for herself, Aunt Jane had lived atop her beloved business for thirty years.

"What about a leaving dress? Casual wear? We have the samples from Elsa Schiaparelli's knit collection."

"Yes, of course, let her choose. We can order what she wants. The knitwear is still popular."

Cora liked Schiaparelli's styles. As if she knew women were real people, with real work to do.

"Odelia, help me out here. Tell Cora not to close off her heart." Mama brushed her hand over Cora's dark hair. "That's all I'm saying. Walk out with another man. Don't just stand at the window waiting for the captain. You run a wedding shop, yet have never been the bride."

"Thank you, Mama. I hadn't noticed." Everyone in a town the size of Heart's Bend noticed the thirty-year-old wedding shop owner had never been a bride. "Weren't you the one who taught me to follow my heart?"

"Yes, but I sure didn't know it'd lead to a dead end." Mama started down the stairs. "I'll say no more. I don't want you upset when the Dunlaps arrive. Shall I go for the pastries? I have time before the coffee and tea."

"No, Mama. I said I'll go." She needed the escape,

the fresh air, the walk to straighten out her thoughts, to dream of *him* for a moment without Mama invading.

In the four years she'd known and loved Rufus St. Claire, he'd never lied to her. Ever. He'd been delayed, hampered by shipping schedules, and hindered by the rule of the river, but he always kept his word, walking up First Avenue with his rogue smile, his arms laden with gifts, his kisses more sweet and passionate than the time before.

Then he'd press his silky lips against her ear. *One day you're going to marry me.*

Cora shivered, collapsing in her chair. She missed him so much she ached. She'd been fine all winter and spring, satisfied with his letters, until this week, until she saw the back end of March but not the face of the man she loved.

Leaving the mezzanine, with its three oval, cherry-framed mirrors used to dress and style the brides, Cora felt nothing like the brides she loved and served. But oh, she longed to walk where they walked.

She'd dreamt of her day in this shop since she was a girl. Of descending the grand staircase to the musical ooh's and ahh's of Mama and Odelia, her groom's mother—if she was alive—her friends and family.

She'd sip sweet tea and nibble on a butter cookie with sugar sprinkles, full of joy and life over her coming day.

She fought feeling dull, old, and left behind. But *he'd* promised. And until she knew otherwise, she'd follow her heart, believing and waiting.

"Esmé, help me out here, will you?" Odelia said, motioning to the mannequin she styled with the dress

Miss Dunlap chose during her first trip to the shop a month ago. Miss Ruth Dunlap had selected a dress from a Butterick pattern, and Odelia worked her magic.

Cora anticipated Ruth's first glance at her gown. It was always a thrill, the bride's face a sight to behold. *It's happening. I'm truly getting married.*

When the clock chimed eight thirty, Cora fluffed the sofa pillows in the grand salon and made sure the curtains were opened wide. The shop was ready.

"Miss Dunlap is going to be swept off her feet," Cora said, heading to the stairs. "Mama, Odelia, I'm off to get the pastries. Mama, remind me to put a record on the Victrola when the Dunlaps drive up." Aunt Jane always liked the brides to enter with music playing, and Cora wanted to carry on the tradition. Because, after all, wasn't love the truest song of all?

Collecting her hat and sweater, Cora ducked into the first-floor powder room to fix on her hat. Seeing her reflection, she paused.

Thirty. She was thirty years old. Not a girl. Nor even a young woman. But a grown woman, a working woman. Where had the years gone? Where had she spent her youth?

She had been in love with her high school sweetheart, Rand Davis, until the war. Then he returned home and married Elizabeth White.

Good luck to them. May they be blessed. Cora had been so grieved over the death of her big brother, Ernest Junior, at Somme that she never found the heart to pine for Rand.

She leaned closer to the mirror, gently touching the

corner of her eyes where one thin line drew toward her cheek.

In the twenties it seemed everyone was marrying. The shop was busy. But the door just never opened for her.

Because, she liked to believe, she was waiting for Rufus. Oh, seeing him the first time . . . He walked into the shop bold as you please to personally deliver a shipment. *"This was left behind on the* Wayfarer. *Thought I'd deliver it myself."*

His blue eyes locked on her and never let go. She yielded without hesitation to their beckoning. His voice nailed her feet to the floor, and for the life of her, she couldn't utter one intelligible word.

Aunt Jane had to step in, direct him where to drop the bolts of cloth, and apologize for Cora.

Now she angled away from her reflection, smoothing her hand over her bobbed hair. She wasn't a beautiful woman. Handsome, Mama liked to say. Tall and lean, with the figure of a teen girl rather than a mature woman of thirty. But she kept herself dressed in the latest fashions and managed to keep what little shape she possessed without the aid of cigarettes or dieting.

Stepping out of the shop, down the front walk, Cora headed toward the center of Heart's Bend. The small but affluent town in the shadow of Nashville was alive with morning commerce.

Shop owners swept their front walks, calling to one another. And she was one of them.

No one counted on Aunt Jane dying five years ago, at seventy, from a malaria outbreak the authorities claimed was contained. Robust Aunt Jane never saw it coming. No one did.

So Cora took over the reins of the shop. Proudly.

Down the avenue, the air twisted with the aroma of baking bread along with the sour odor of horse droppings. Rosie, the milk cart mare, swished her tail at the biting flies.

Cora crossed Blossom Street, heading along First Avenue, trying to take in the beauty of the day to break free of Mama's comments. She spotted Constable O'Shannon across the wide avenue, at the entrance of Gardenia Park, talking to a giant of a man with blue leggings tucked into black leather knee boots and a loose blouse billowing about his arms, the breeze shifting his wild golden hair about his face.

Rufus?

"Rufus!" She shouted his name through her cupped hands, forgetting decorum, forgetting the gossips with their ears to the ground. "Darling! You're here."

Running into the avenue, Cora avoided a passing car. The driver sounded his horn, but she didn't care. Her Rufus was here.

The breeze kicked up as she ran to greet him, her heart racing with love.

So her morning tingle of anticipation was correct. He *had* returned. Just like he said. "Rufus, darling! You're here."

CHAPTER TWO

HALEY

The pad of paper resting on her lap was blank. At any minute Mom would call up the stairs, "It's time!" and she'd have nothing.

Yet across her childhood bedroom, another piece of paper on her dresser said everything. It dictated her future. Filled her achieving parents and brothers with pride.

The Kellogg School of Management and Marketing at Northwestern University.

But she'd already given four years of her life to college. Then six years to the United States Air Force. Earned her captain's bars. Three years ago she spent six months in Bagram.

Being in a war zone changed her. She was grateful to spend her final years in the air force in California. Near surf and sun.

But nothing prepared her for last year. First, the whirlwind, crazy-love, destructive relationship with

Dax Mills. She'd lost her mind to the power of his charms. It was like she'd stepped outside of herself and become a different woman.

She was locked into his swirl and almost lost herself until the phone call came that woke her up. Tammy Eason, her best friend since first grade, was dying from an aggressive form of brain cancer.

How could it be? She was only twenty-eight, four months from marrying the man of her dreams, Cole Danner. Haley was to be her maid of honor.

Instead of a wedding toast, she spoke a funeral eulogy.

Haley tossed the pad of paper across the room. What did any of it matter? Goals? Dreams? Notching achievements? Making a name for herself? Landing a Fortune 100 job?

In the end, wasn't it all just wood, hay, and stubble? A stray bullet from life could steal it all.

After the funeral Haley filed the papers to end her military career, broke up with Dax once and for all, ending the dysfunction and despair, hopped on her Harley, and drove across the southwest, struggling to find her sense of right and wrong, her faith and hope.

That's when she heard God speak. Like a strange echo from her Jesus-freak teen years. His gentle voice was a soft rain over the dry, craggy terrain of her heart.

"Go home."

It was easier to yield to His whisper than she imagined. Because His voice came with the love her hungry heart and thirsty soul desperately needed.

But home? With the parental units? It would be challenging.

Once home, Mom insisted she apply to grad school and, well, here she sat. In her old bedroom, facing another Morgan family New Year's goal-setting event, and she had bupkis. Mom's admonition slithered through her thoughts.

"If you have no goals, you will achieve nothing."

Know what? She didn't want to achieve anything. She wanted to find the pieces of herself she'd lost—not to war, as so many of her fellow airman had, but to so-called love.

"Knock, knock." Mom peered around the door. "How's it going up here?"

Haley pointed to her pad of paper. "Great."

Mom leaned against the doorframe. "You could always write what you wrote in high school. 'Wear a bikini to school,' or 'Drive around the square at midnight on my birthday in my birthday suit.'"

Haley laughed. "I only wrote those things to irritate you." Her sports medicine doctor mother needed a little controversy now and then. Haley was more than happy to oblige.

Mom would get all flustered, claiming Haley just wanted to "vex" her (true!), while her four brothers guffawed. Then Dad, the mechanical engineer, who tried really hard *not* to burst out with his own laugh, sided with Mom. *"Hal, come on now."*

"I can't help but think of Tammy." Mom made her way over to the window where a soft white light hit the glass, the glow of Dad's Christmas lights flooding the room with a bright warmth.

"I was thinking of her too." Haley moved to the

window, peering out and down, seeing the tip of Dad's slippers as he stood on the porch, staring toward the street.

With him, she'd known safety in this house her whole life. When she embarked on her own adventures, she never grasped that men like Dax existed. She'd only known the kindness of her father and the teasing, sideways love of her brothers.

"I saw Shana Eason the other day," Mom said. "Looked like her soul had left her. Eyes vacant. Moving like she had no purpose."

"She and Harm lost their only child, Mom."

"I can't imagine. I can't." Mom retrieved Haley's notepad and handed it to her. "When you were in Bagram, I woke up many nights, saying prayers."

Haley glanced around at her mother, intrigued by her confession. "I thought you didn't believe in prayer."

"Can't say as I do, but it's true, there are no atheists in foxholes. There are no atheist mothers with children at war."

Picking up her pad of paper, Haley returned to her spot on the floor. "Is everyone here?" The brothers all returned to Heart's Bend for the big goal setting. Two from Atlanta. One from Nashville. Another from Orlando.

"Seth and Abigail just arrived."

"In their new Mercedes?" One was a lawyer and the other a psychiatrist.

"Yes." Mom grinned. "That'll be you one day. You're going to outshine them all. You have the smarts of Seth and Zack combined."

Then why was she sitting on the floor with absolutely no vision for herself?

Her brothers were achievers just like their parents, David and Joann Morgan. Each one married an achiever. Among the four couples—she was the only one not married—there were six PhDs. The remaining two slackers only had law degrees.

She was just a lowly captain. Captain Morgan. Like the rum. Didn't that gain her some notoriety in the military? It was good for a few tricks.

In fact, that's how she met Dax. When her friend Rick Cantwell baited him into meeting his friend "Captain Morgan."

Dax thought he'd find a golden-brown liquid in a bottle. Instead, he found a "hot blonde with gorgeous blue eyes."

A shout rose from the first floor. "Football," Mom said.

"Who's winning?" Haley didn't have to ask who was playing. Some SEC team.

Dad had posted the post-season bowl schedule on the wall in the media room, and the alma maters of the Morgan household played today—Alabama and Tennessee.

"Last I looked, Bama. The work I did with their quarterback after his accident last year paid off. He's a seventy-percent passer right now."

Haley shifted her gaze to her mom, who returned to leaning against the doorframe. She was so intense about her work, such a medical geek, she had absolutely no awareness of her legend among college athletes.

Coaches and athletic directors had her number on speed dial.

"Does it ever occur to you how successful you are, Mom?"

A brainiac and introvert, Mom grew up the only child of a World War II widow and her much-older second husband.

"Not really. Just that I'm good at what I do. And I love it."

Haley sat up. "That, right there. That's what I want this year. To do something I'm good at, to do something I love."

She'd loved the air force, but it was more like a duty, giving back to her country, helping others. Now it was her time. Find what she loved and do it.

Mom reached for the university letter. "Go to Kellogg. You excelled in management and marketing in college."

"I guess . . ." Haley stared at her blank notepad.

College was seven years and a lifetime ago. Was she still the girl who wanted to build a career telling people what to buy or sell?

"Does your hesitation have to do with Dax? What happened between you two? Your dad and I liked him."

She'd been waiting for this question. "We broke up. End of story."

A shout pierced through her answer, followed by male voices cheering in unison and the distant pop of high fives.

"I think the goal setting tonight will help you, Haley," Mom said.

"So you've said since I was seven."

"And? Goals led you to college, the air force, to the rank of captain. Now you're home again with grad school ahead. Weren't you the one who always wanted an adventure?"

"I had my adventure. After the air force I was supposed to come home and open the old wedding shop with Tammy." Haley smiled at the memory of playing in the shop with her best friend. "Man, I don't think I've really thought about that since high school. But if she were alive now, she'd be begging, 'Let's open the shop, Hal. Now's the time.'"

"The old wedding shop? What? I never heard this before. Why would you want to open that old place? The city owns the property and, last I heard, was about to tear it down, thank goodness." Mom opened the bedroom door and hollered down, "Dave, is it almost halftime? We can do our goals."

Haley was on her feet. "Tear down the shop? Why?" Her dream with Tammy woke up, stretched, and rattled around in her soul. "They can't tear it down. It's part of Heart's Bend tradition, the center of bridal lore."

"I say good riddance to the place. It's an eyesore. Why would you want to reopen the old wedding shop? There are all kinds of great bridal boutiques in Nashville. Petra Cook's daughter bought her whole trousseau online. Haley, you're too smart and talented to be chained to a shop, catering to picky brides."

"When did the town decide to tear it down?"

"Well, it's been in the works for a long time, but the old brides . . ." Mom shook her head, surrendering her hands in mock exasperation. "They come out of the woodwork, protesting, calling the shop a historical place in town. But it's not part of the historical district. Besides, Akron Developers needs that space for parking. They're renovating the old mill into loft apartments and building a shopping center to go with. They purchased the old cow pasture for it."

"Where we used to play home run ball in the summer? Football on Thanksgiving and Christmas?"

"Yes, finally Heart's Bend comes into the twenty-first century."

The conversation boiled in Haley's chest. She'd lost a lot in the last year. Herself by way of Dax, her identity as an air force captain, and her best friend.

She didn't want to lose her dream too. *Their* dream.

Haley snatched up her notepad and pen. "I know what my goal is for this year."

Mom angled forward to see what Haley wrote. "Really? Well, okay, good. I look forward to hearing it." She started out the door. "You coming?"

"In a minute." She wanted to think this through. If she set a goal, she'd need to have some steps in place.

Yet the more she thought about it, the more she wanted to resurrect the wedding shop. She scribbled on her pad of paper. "Reopen the wedding shop!"

Haley set the pad on her bed and stood over it, staring down at her New Year's resolution, the words coming alive, whispering to her, telling her *this* was what she came home to do.

CHAPTER THREE

COLE

Change required courage. Even the smallest steps. Like meeting a friend of a friend for dinner. Casually. Not a date. Just a prearranged meeting with a woman he barely knew.

He'd determined to make this year a good one. Shake off guilt, doubt, the lingering stench of death, and move toward his future. Build his business. Maybe find love.

Besides, what else would he be doing on a Sunday evening other than watching football with his brothers if not meeting a friend of a friend for dinner?

His head told him it was time. Though his heart still lingered at the weigh station.

He snatched his keys from his dresser and headed downstairs, exiting the bottom steps into the living room where his middle brother, Chris, a Georgetown MBA student home on break, sat in a Barcalounger with a large cheese pizza on his lap.

Baby brother Cap was a Vanderbilt sophomore and was working tonight at their mother's diner, Ella's.

Cole flicked his hand against his brother's foot, his fingers landing against a wet, soggy sock. "Dude, seriously?" Cole made a face, wiggling his fingers in the air. "Where've you been?"

"Playing a game of touch in Gardenia Park with Kiefer and some of the guys. I texted you about it." Chris worked his way out of the chair, carrying the pizza into the kitchen, offering Cole a slice. "Where you been? And where are you going?"

Cole hesitated, washing his hands at the sink. Tonight's venture was private to him, something he needed to explore on his own without Chris, Cap, or Mom butting in.

"Meeting a friend."

He'd wanted to meet this friend of a friend in Nashville where she lived, away from the prying eyes of his hometown, but she'd insisted on coming here. Said she loved Heart's Bend and hadn't visited in a while.

"A friend?" Chris shoved the last bite of his pizza into his mouth. And continued speaking. "What friend?" Little brother leaned forward, sniffing. "Wearing cologne? You're going on a date."

"No, no, not a date. I'm meeting a friend of a friend."

"A date." Chris hooted, reaching for another slice of pizza. "Bro, this is good. Tammy's been gone nine months."

"Hey, a little respect." Cole yanked a bottle of water from the fridge.

"I'm showing respect. But you can't hole up here forever. Tammy wouldn't want it." Chris gestured to the glass-encased guitar hanging on the wall over the dining table. "Unless you want to do your heart like you did that guitar."

"*That* guitar is a classic. Worth a lot of money." Cole didn't have to tell Chris it was a rare Fender Stratocaster. Purchased with his dad when Cole was thirteen.

"How'd you meet this girl? Which friend is setting you up? Are you taking her to Ella's? 'Cause you know Mom will be all over it."

Their mother, Tina Danner, owned the old Heart's Bend diner, Ella's. Worked there as a waitress after Dad left . . . by invitation of the FBI.

"I'm going on a blind meeting, okay? And not to Ella's. You think I've lost my mind?"

"Blind *meeting*?" Chris said, his face lit with a sloppy grin, an arrogant grad student glint in his eyes. "Bro, it's a *date*."

Of course he was right. But Cole couldn't quite admit it yet. That being said, he should've insisted on a Nashville location. The trouble with living in small-town Tennessee was everyone knew your business, your name, how cute you were in the first-grade Christmas pageant when you sang "Away in a Manger" too loud and off-key.

"I'm meeting her at the Burger Barn." Cole reached for a napkin and flicked it toward his brother. "You have sauce on your chin."

Chris snatched the napkin with swagger. "Are you kidding? Everyone in town goes to the Burger Barn on the weekend."

"Technically, this is Sunday night. Not a weekend. And the Barn is on the edge of town, on the other side of that old wedding shop. Tucked away. Less likely to have foot traffic."

"Oh, right, the church crowd goes right home after Sunday-night services. I *forgot*."

"They'll be cleared out by eight."

"Reverend Smith closes the place down with rounds of root beer and a medley of 'The Old Rugged Cross' and 'This Is My Story.'" Chris shoved the pizza box toward Cole. "Take a piece. You look like you need some sustenance."

Cole eyed a small slice. Now that he was ready and waiting to go, his empty stomach played ravenous notes against his ribs. He'd been too busy to stop for lunch, working on Sunday to finish a remodel that was over schedule and over budget.

The holidays had put his crew behind, and he wanted to finish up lingering projects to get ready for new business. He had a lot of bids out, and he expected a full work queue by the middle of the month. He had to because Danner Construction was running out of jobs and out of money.

He bit into the pizza with a glance at his brother. "Does Mom know you're here? She might have fixed dinner."

"She's working. She and Cap are both covering a shift for someone out sick." Chris moved between Mom's house and Cole's like a flowing river. "I thought I'd hang here, watch football. You're on for the bowl games tomorrow, right? I've got some guys coming over. Oh, hey, you remember Jason Saglimbeni? He's back in town. We were thinking of getting up a jam session before I go back to DC. I haven't played drums in over a year."

"You guys go ahead."

"Come on, Cole. Take that Stratocaster out of its glass tower and jam with us. You know that's what Dad—"

"I don't need you to tell me what Dad would want." Cole checked the time. "'Cause I don't really care what Dad would want."

"You can't hide from him forever."

"Who says I'm hiding?"

"I do. When was the last time you played? Talked to Dad?"

"Hey, look at me." Cole stretched his arms wide. "I'm going on a date nine months after my fiancée died. I think that's accomplishment enough."

Actually, she was his ex-fiancée, but no one really knew that. Except maybe Haley, Tammy's best friend. The breakup and her diagnosis happened at the same time. And the whirlwind took over. Then death and grief. He didn't have the emotional bank account for "jamming" or talking to his deadbeat dad.

Cole paused at the door leading out to the breeze-way and garage. "Don't leave your pizza box out. Clean up when you're done."

Into the cold evening, the air doused the heat of Chris's random confrontation. Dad and music. He hadn't jammed since Dad's incarceration.

After his arrest, the FBI took years to bring their case to court. Meanwhile, Mom, Cole, Chris, and Cap grew hopeful. Maybe the charges of fraud wouldn't stick.

But a new trouble brewed. Dad lost his construction company, so he took to drinking, wrinkling the family name with a new kind of shame.

Sitting astride his Harley 750, Cole fired up the engine, shifting his emotions away from the conversation with Chris. The past was the past. Dad's reputation was not his.

Old things have passed away . . . all things become new.

Shifting into gear, snapping on his helmet, he breathed in the night, the air pregnant with snow. The *Farmer's Almanac* predicted a lot of winter precipitation. If so, it would be bad for business, and Cole didn't have the bank account for a long, lean winter.

One shift of the clutch and a little gas, he'd be out of here, off on a *date*.

Yet he didn't have to go. He could cancel, go inside, watch bowl games with his brother, and order another pizza.

Wait, that's exactly what he'd been doing the past year. Hiding. Retreating. This was a *new* year. Time to move forward, get on with life.

He eased out of the garage, closing the door behind him. He'd be warmer in his truck, but he felt the need for speed. For the cold to press through his leather jacket and jeans, to wake up his dull, sleeping self.

Down the street, past golden windows where families gathered, past the festive flicker of a few remaining red, blue, and green Christmas lights, Cole turned right on River Road, heading for town and First Avenue.

He eased off the gas as he drove past the old wedding shop, a three-story brick construction sitting alone under a sentry of shading elms. The large front windows were dark, a pair of sad eyes watching the world go by.

He'd always liked the charm of the place, appreciated the shop's role in Heart's Bend's history. Both of his grandmothers and a great aunt bought their wedding dresses from Miss Cora.

But the shop's days were numbered.

"Sorry," he whispered against his helmet. "But you had a good run, no?"

A wind gust happened by and the no-good For Sale sign, barely visible under the amber street light, swung from its white post.

The city had tried to sell it to a business-minded person who might finally turn the space into a viable part of the downtown commerce, but so far only Akron Developers ponied up any money. But they wanted the land. Not the building. They needed a parking lot for their new lofts and outdoor shopping mall.

Demolishing 143 First Avenue was one of the jobs Cole had bid on for the winter.

It was time. The old shop had stood empty more than not in the past thirty-five years. Whatever it once stood for—brides flooding in to purchase their trousseaus from noted Heart's Bend citizen Miss Cora—had long been forgotten.

Tammy had some emotional attachment to the shop. Something about playing there with Haley as kids. How the two of them decided, at age ten, they were going to reopen the old wedding shop someday. Return it to its former bridal glory.

But Cole had doubts. Tammy talked about law school and Haley was off with the air force, fighting a war. And frankly, he couldn't see *that* girl running a wedding shop for nothing.

He'd been beaten up twice in his life. Once in first grade by Jeremy Wayne for calling him a cheater. And once in fifth grade by Haley Morgan—the more humiliating of the two—for telling her she looked pretty.

Cole gunned the gas, moving on. The time for reminiscing had passed.

When he pulled up to the Burger Barn, he saw a woman waiting on the front bench, her slender legs peeking out from the hem of a pink, fur-trimmed coat. She stood as he rolled up.

Cole cut the engine and removed his helmet, smoothing his hair in place. "Betsy?"

"Mariah told me you were hot, but I didn't know you rode a Harley."

"Mariah likes to exaggerate." But he'd take the props.

Joining Betsy at the bench, Cole could see her face in the restaurant's light. She was beautiful with her raven hair and full lips. A subtle, wild fragrance bounced in the air around her.

"No, I think she was right this time." She beamed and slipped her arm through his. "Maybe you could take me for a *ride* later?"

"Yeah, maybe." Bold, this one. "You hungry?"

"Starving."

Her breath brushed over his cheek and she squeezed his arm. Yeah, she was starving all right, but for what?

Cole stepped to the front door, holding it open for

his lovely, if not racy, date. This was good, right? A change of pace. A woman very different from his last. This was so much better than staying at home with sweaty-socks Chris.

He ordered a table for two at the hostess stand, then eased back, giving his nerves a rest.

Betsy may not be the one for him, but here she was, in the moment, wrapped in a beautiful pink package. The first moment of Cole's new tomorrows started here and now.

. . .

Cora

She stood eye to eye with him. A riverboat captain. But not *her* riverboat captain. Not Rufus St. Claire.

"Hello?" he said, a spark of amusement in his eyes.

Constable O'Shannon stepped up. "Captain Riske, may I introduce Miss Cora Scott. She runs the dress shop at the end of the avenue there."

"Wedding shop," she said, her eyes still locked with the captain's—who seemed rather delighted at her discomfort. "I operate a *wedding* shop."

"Well, you have dresses too, don'tcha?" O'Shannon insisted on being right. After all, he was the *law* around town.

"We do, yes, for after the wedding. For the honeymoon." Her skin blushed with embarrassment. "The bride's trousseau, you see."

"Honeymoon?" Riske's voice teased her and her

embarrassment. "I like the sound of that word." The captain leaned a bit too close, bringing with him the spice aroma of beef jerky.

Cora took a giant step back. "I'm terribly sorry to have disturbed you." She wanted to run but feared stumbling over her trembling legs.

"A pretty woman is never a disturbance." Captain Riske was a flirt.

Cora knew better than to yield. She'd never inspired the word *pretty* from a man. Except for Rufus, who called her his "beautiful coral."

"Is there something you need?" The captain's amusement bordered on mocking.

"Of course not," she said. Except to be away. Her pulse throbbed in her ears as she spun around, her heels crunching over the concrete sidewalk, her disappointment loud in her ears.

Rufus had not come.

Cora pressed toward the shop, through the rising pockets of sunlight, forcing down her tears, willing her heart to go numb. Why had he *not* come? What was the delay?

He said he'd see her in the spring. And she believed him.

Ever since he'd declared his love for her and asked her to wait for him, Cora had set her heart like a flint to do as he asked, to be true to him, courting no other man. No matter how long it took for him to marry her.

No man had ever whispered words of love before. Besides Daddy. And even he didn't say them often.

The shop was only two blocks away, but the distance

felt like miles. Would she ever reach the front steps? Her safe haven?

The incessant sound of her heels against the gritty sidewalk filled her head, irritating her thoughts. Yet the *crunch-crunch* was the only way to escape the constable, the captain, and her embarrassment. The only way to escape her disappointment.

Sweat beaded along her neck, under the wisps of her dark waves. She quickened her steps, yet the shop seemed no closer.

Cora clutched her skirt and kicked into a run, her muscles yielding to her demand. Faster. Faster. Past the shops. Bumping around the morning pedestrians and their blurred faces, their disembodied voices.

"Cora, where you going in such a hurry?"

"Cora, honey? Are you all right?"

She tripped over Mr. Griggs's broom as he swept the walk in front of his haberdashery and nearly toppled to the concrete. She caught herself in time and pressed on, her pulse resounding, her lungs burning.

About to cross Blossom Street for the back of the shop, Cora darted from the curb without looking and smashed into something firm and gripping, corralling her about the waist.

"Let me go . . ." She swung her elbows high and wide, trying to wrench free.

"Cora, it's me, Birch. Simmer down. Shoot, girl, where's the fire?"

She exhaled, releasing her tension, and peered into the bright glint of Birch Good's sky-blue eyes. His ruby lips curved into a smile above his square, dimpled chin.

"Birch, I'm sorry. I didn't see you." Cora pushed out of his arms. This time he gently let her go. "I-I'm late, you see, for the shop. I-I had to get the morning pastries."

He glanced at her empty hands. She made no pretense, no attempt, to hide them. "What happened back there?" He motioned toward the park.

"I-I don't know, really." She pressed her fingers to her forehead, averting her gaze, trying to work up a jolly laugh. But her voice remained weak and quavering. "A case of mistaken identity."

She glanced back to where the captain stood, but he was gone. Had she not panicked like a scared child she might have asked him if he'd seen her Rufus on the river. Was he well? Was he on his way?

"Look at you. You're trembling." Birch's hands slipped down her arms, pulling her to him. "Shh, it's going to be all right." His strong arms wrapped her against him.

Cora propped her cheek against his checkered shirt, inhaling the familiar fragrance of lye soap and hay. "How badly did I embarrass myself just now?"

"I don't know. Was anyone looking?" Birch Good, farmer and friend, was as solid as the Tennessee limestone.

She raised her head with a soft laugh. "Apparently you were."

"Only because you 'bout ran me over."

"Mercy me, I didn't even see you," Cora said, patting his full, farmer-built chest, then smoothing away the wild ends of her hair flitting over her eyes. "I *can* get so focused." Her adrenaline ebbed, taking the shaking with it.

"Who was it, Cora? Who did you think was over there?"

"Maybe another time, Birch. I really must get going. We have customers from Birmingham this morning." She tried to hold his gaze, but her eyes drifted toward the park once more.

Birch followed her sight line. "The riverboat captain?"

Cora chose not to confirm or deny. "This is a special customer too. Her mama grew up in Heart's Bend, bought her dress from Aunt Jane twenty-five years ago. It's exciting to outfit the daughters of our former brides." Cora turned for the shop, checking the traffic before stepping off the curb.

"Rufus St. Claire?" Birch fell in step with her. "You thought you saw him, didn't you?"

Cora faced him right there in the middle of the street. "Well, if you know so much, why are you asking? What are you doing in town at this hour, anyway? Don't you have a farm to run?"

She'd known Birch from eons ago—their fathers were school chums—and it really irked her how familiar he was with her. And how comfortable she felt with him.

"I had some business with the bank. Thought I'd treat myself to breakfast at the diner. Old bachelor farmer gets tired of his own cooking." Birch moved with her, across the street and toward the shop.

"Then why don't you get married?" Birch, five years her senior, farmed his family's vast lands, and he could have any number of women as his bride.

"You applying for the job?"

"Aren't you humorous? I believe there's a line of women every Sunday after church just waiting to invite you to supper."

"Well, I got my eye on a girl. Only trouble is, she ain't looking back."

"Then find one who's looking."

His words burned, carving out truth she suspected for a long time. But she was hopelessly in love with a man who lived on the river. The predicament was both exhilarating and terrifying. Either way, she would not let go. She'd made up her mind. Given her word.

Marching up the back steps, Cora reached for the door. "It's good to see you, Birch."

"Who do you recommend for a fella who might be looking?"

"For Pete's sake, Birch, you can figure that out for yourself."

"You thought you saw Rufus St. Claire, didn't you?"

She started inside, but Birch gently gripped her wrist. "I don't see how it's your business."

"Am I wrong?"

Cora regarded him for a moment, reading his eyes, his expression. "You disapprove?"

She wished the question back. Because if he did, it would bother her. She didn't like Birch's disapproval. It was enough she had Mama's.

Birch had been there for the family during the '14 bank panic when Daddy disappeared for a while. Helped out her brother, Ernest Jr., with things around the house.

Then in '18 he came home from the war when EJ

didn't. Came around the house almost every evening to see how Cora, Mama, and Daddy were doing.

"I don't like that he hurts you."

"He's not hurting me."

"Then why the blinding run? The dark expression? The panic?"

The slam of car doors popped the air and Cora peeked inside the shop. Mama was waving her in. "Birch, I've got to go. My customers have arrived."

"What about your pastries?"

"We'll have to do without. Odelia brought in her cinnamon rolls."

"Those rocks?" He made a face and Cora pressed her hand to her lips to hide her laugh. "Surely you can't offer your special customers, all the way up from Birmingham, Odelia's cinnamon buns."

"She is so proud of them."

"Maybe so, but ole Dr. Walsh is out of town fishing, so if they break a tooth—"

Through the open windows Cora heard the Victrola and Mama's sweet, "Welcome to The Wedding Shop. Welcome."

"What would your aunt Jane say?" Birch whispered.

"She'd say just serve tea and coffee and forget the pastries."

"No, about you pining for that no-good riverboat captain."

"She'd have said, 'Follow your heart, Cora Beth.'" Her old aunt regretted choosing work over love and marriage. She died an old maid. Cora refused to follow her fate. "She would want me to be happy."

"I'm sure she would. But with a man who was true."
Birch backed away. "I'll pick up your order. I assume
it's at Haven's."

"Cora!" Mama appeared at the door. "Why are you
dawdling? They're here. Morning, Birch."

He tipped his cap. "Mrs. Scott."

"Darling, where are the pastries?" Mama gestured
at Cora's arms, her eyes wide and wild. "Mrs. Dunlap is
about to spend a small fortune on her daughter's trousseau, and the least we can do is offer her a cup of tea
and a petit four. Otherwise, Odelia will offer her buns,
and we don't need an emergency trip to the dentist. I
think the doc's out fishing."

Cora rolled her eyes, peering at Birch. "Did you two
arrange this conversation? Fine, Birch, will you fetch
the pastries? Charge them to my account. Bring them
around back. Mama will be setting up tea and coffee in
the pantry."

"What about the kisses?" Mama said. "We're out."

"Kisses?" Birch echoed, a chuckle in his tone. "Yeah,
how can I help with the kisses?"

"Oh, you," Mama said with a naughty giggle, turning away and heading inside.

"Mama means Hershey's *chocolate* kisses, Birch,"
Cora said. Goodness, were they children, giggling over
the word *kisses*? "You can get a tin at Kidwells."

"Kisses?" he said again, his grin taking on a teasing
swagger. "For a wedding shop? A bit on the nose."

"Go on now. For a farmer, Birch, you're acting
mighty highbrow."

Cora started inside, but he reached for her, gently

holding her arm. His nearness stole her breath and filled her with a sudden and disarming sensation. She swallowed, pressing her hand to her chest, trying to gain composure.

"You want chocolate kisses, right?"

"Yes, w-why do you keep asking?"

"I wouldn't want to get the wrong ones. I've never had chocolate kisses before." The wind of his words brushed her cheek and fashioned an army of tingles down her spine.

"W-well then, try one when you get here."

"I think I will."

Cora fell against the door as Birch released her and headed off to do his errand, whistling.

The ardor of his tone when he said, "*Kisses*," still fired against her skin. Wait until she saw him again. She'd give him a piece of her mind. And what was that tune he whistled as he trotted off?

Cora went inside, musing over the melody, searching for the words. Ah! That silly Helen Kane melody, "I Wanna Be Loved by You."

I wanna be loved by you / nobody else but you.

Cora gave the back door a good hard slam. Birch Good could just sing that song to another gal. Because she belonged to Rufus St. Claire.

CHAPTER FOUR

HALEY

Sunday evening Haley fired her Harley 750 out of the garage, into the cold night, and headed north, toward town. Toward First Avenue, passing under the streetlights, needing a break from the house.

As the youngest, she was used to being home alone with the folks. But ever since college she'd been on her own, and now it felt weird to live with her parents again.

They clearly had a routine. A way of living that fit their lives, and Haley felt like an interloper. But after Tammy's death and the breakup with Dax, coming home gave her the reset she needed.

Riding under the shield of night, twilight long gone on the horizon, Haley's thoughts took on a motor of their own.

The family goal setting three nights ago went well. Until Haley said, "*Open up the old wedding shop.*"

At first everyone just stared back at her. Silencing the Morgan boys was an accomplishment in and of itself.

Sister-in-law Jodi from Chicago wanted to know what the wedding shop was, and the boys sputtered over their explanation. But boy howdy, they were against it.

They took their cue from Mom, who spoke loudly in her silence.

"You were a captain in the air force. How can you be a huckster for the bloated wedding industry?"

"An MBA from Kellogg will set you up, Haley. A buddy of mine landed a job with a nice six-figure salary when he graduated."

"From fatigues and logistics to lace and tulle? I can't see it."

Finally Dad stepped in, said to let Haley make up her own mind. She'd done a good job with her life so far. *Thanks, Dad.* *"After all,"* he said, *"Aaron was a really nice boy growing up, then he decided to be a lawyer. The family supported* him *on that decision."*

Bwhahaha. Dad's dry humor broke the tension and put the goal-setting party back on track.

But Mom? She remained stiff and aloof, tight-lipped. If she had something to say, she couldn't find the words.

From back off the road, several houses still danced with Christmas lights, and Haley allowed a moment of sentiment.

She loved her hometown, for all of its busybodies and small-town mind-set. It'd been a great place to grow up. After years in the military, Haley needed to find herself again, her values and integrity, the tenderness of her heart.

She'd become callous, hard. Haley gunned the gas,

pushing the bike forward down River Road, as if the motion would dislodge her sins and leave them crashing down on the road.

A stoplight flashed red up ahead, so Haley eased off the gas and squeezed the clutch, downshifting. This was a new light, bringing the town total up to four. After the goal setting, Dad brushed her up on Akron Developers, the group wanting to demolish the wedding shop.

A few years back they'd moved in southeast of town and erected high-priced homes for Nashville's elite looking for some space. And little by little they crept into Heart's Bend proper, making deals and acquiring land.

In the distance, a popping sound rocketed through the air. Someone was still celebrating the new year. Two years ago, fresh off her tour in Bagram, the slightest noise jolted her heart into overdrive.

It took her a year to steady her insides, to not jump at every sound, wondering if it was a rocket or bullet that could take her life. Meanwhile, back home, Tammy battled cancer.

The light flashed green and she started off, down First Avenue toward the old wedding shop. She needed to see it. Feel it. Confirm her New Year's decision was real. Not just another dig against Mom. She was getting too old for that stuff anymore.

Haley headed past the old storefronts. Dad was on the Reclaim Downtown committee, where they made plans to rejuvenate the old soul of Heart's Bend—the original city center.

She cruised past Ella's Diner, the light from inside

pressing against the window, beckoning her. She'd have to pop in there soon, say hi to Tina, Cole Danner's mom.

Haley spent a lot of Friday and Saturday nights at the counter drinking chocolate shakes and eating French fries with Tammy, waiting with her to get a glimpse of Cole.

But that's what best friends did for each other, right?

Haley squinted through the pockets of shadow and light as she came to a stop sign at Gardenia Park, heading for 143 First Avenue.

The avenue bent slightly to the right, and there in front of her was a tall, dark structure with large display windows hovering under the winter limbs of three large trees. Haley pulled along the front curb and cut the bike's engine. Tugging off her helmet, she studied the place with her eyes and heart wide open.

"Hey, old fort. It's just me from now on out."

A dark, sad place, if ever there was one. Had it always looked like this? Or was her perspective cleared, sharpened by worldly experiences?

As a girl, she'd thought the shop seemed alive and romantic.

But tonight the moonless night cloaked the shop with dark shadows.

Haley retrieved her phone and a thick black flashlight from a saddlebag. Tucking her phone in her pocket, she clicked on the light, waving a large, long beam over the deserted shop.

The redbrick front, with two large windows framing either side of the door, was covered with ivy. The postage-stamp yard was wild and overgrown.

But even in the dark dullness, Haley saw the beauty. Felt a glimmer of life.

Slicing her way through the weeds to the front steps, she tried to peer through the windows, but the concrete porch, no wider than the door, gave her no perspective. The railing had rusted away, so she couldn't lean on it. She made her way around back, tripping on a root or vine, something that reached out of the ground.

Stumbling, she caught herself with a hand to the brick, whispering a dark word as she trekked around the shop, weaving through fallen branches and clusters of dry, dead leaves.

Wedding shop, what happened to you?

Around back she found the porch listing to one side, pulling away from the brick.

Pulling open the porch door, which hung off its hinges, Haley stepped onto the weak, rotting floorboards. Testing each step, she made her way to the shop's door, peeking through the dirty glass.

There . . . in that small room, she and Tammy sipped from their thermoses filled with Mrs. Eason's sweet tea and played make-believe.

Haley tried the knob, wanting to sneak in like she did twenty years ago, but the old iron piece refused to yield, merely wiggling from side to side.

Next she tried the windows. But they were stuck tight.

Pressing her nose against the window to the left of the door, Haley squinted through the darkness, trying to understand if this was her future. Had she set a solid New Year's goal?

She'd not prayed much in the last decade since college. Even the devastation with Dax had not dropped her to her knees. But since the day God spoke as she crossed from New Mexico into Texas, she started lifting more and more of her words heavenward.

Lord, do I do this? Am I crazy? Just being sentimental, sticking to my little girl dream? Opening a wedding shop is silly, right? So not me.

She didn't expect an answer, really. What did it mean to hear God? She'd forgotten how. With the passage of time, all those teenage impressions of God "speaking" to her seemed made up, her imagination taking hold.

When she was fifteen, she'd adopted a mantra from a traveling evangelist. *Live for God. Everything else will fall into place.*

She'd done well by her motto until college, then lost even more of her faith in the air force. And what remained, she lost with Dax. Maybe now was the time to return. She'd chased adventure. Pursued men and what she thought was love.

Maybe now it was time to pursue God with the same abandon.

The wind trickled past, cold and dewy, with the promise of snow. Haley scanned her light over the floors, stopping on the spot where she and Tammy had lain, pinkies locked, making a promise.

She relived the moment sometimes in her dreams. Especially in Afghanistan. As if her heart longed for the innocence of childhood and the comfort of home.

"Old shop, you're my friend, aren't you?" Was it possible to feel like she belonged to a building?

"Hey, didn't you see the sign? No trespassing."

Haley was spun around by a barreling bass voice. She gripped her flashlight like a weapon. "Who's there?"

The dark figure shoved through the debris and brush hemming in the failing porch. "You know you're on city property." He cut through her flashlight beam, and Haley could see the cut of his features and the loose hair swaying about his head. "You need to get off the property."

"Cole?" She trained her beam on him.

He swung his flashlight to her face. "Haley?"

"Yeah, it's me!"

He traveled through the rest of the overgrowth and hopped onto the porch, scooping her up in a big hug. "What are you doing here? Last I saw you, at the funeral, you were raving about California life."

"Yeah, well, what do I know?"

"Tell me about it." A soft laugh accompanied his statement. "How long you in town?"

She shrugged. "Not sure. Got grad school on the horizon. If I'm going, I'll leave this week."

He put his light on her face again. "And if you're not?"

"Might hang around here." She looked around to the shop's door. "See what mischief I can get into."

"Mischief? In Heart's Bend?" His soft laugh touched a locked corridor of her heart. "Hey, remember when you pummeled me in fifth grade because I said you were pretty?"

She laughed. "Oh my gosh, what made you think of that?"

"The word *mischief*, I guess."

"Well, I'm not looking for that kind of mischief." She peeked at him. "Guess I never apologized for beating you up."

"You didn't." Cole rubbed his jaw, as if her ten-year-old's punch still stung. "But the damage is done. I was humiliated."

She laughed again, her heart a winter flower unfolding. "Sorry about that. You can blame Seth and Zack for my boxing skills. With them, I either defended myself or constantly was black-and-blue."

"I'm sure it served you well in the military. So how are you?"

"Good. You?"

"Good. Busy. Well, trying to be. Get things going after the holidays."

"I bet. D-did you have a good Christmas?" *Did you miss Tammy?*

"I did. What about you?"

"Good. You know the Morgan house . . . pretty crazy."

"I saw Seth the other day. He came into the diner. Looks like he's happy. His wife seems great."

"Abigail? She's a saint. Keeps Seth in line."

"So you're out of the military?"

"I am. Got out in October. Took a couple of months to wind down, visit friends." She held her arms wide. "Now I'm here."

"No more 'Yes ma'am, Captain Morgan'?"

She grinned, shaking her head, liking the ease of the conversation. "No more spiced rum jokes either."

Cole laughed. "That one is just too hard to pass

up. So what's next? Law school? Med school? MBA? Conquering and dividing, taking over the world?"

"Oh, see, you have me confused with the rest of the Morgan family overachievers." Haley shifted her weight, tucking her cold fingers into her jacket pockets. "I think I might just stay in town." She motioned to the shop. "Get this bad girl up and running again."

"What? This?" Cole slapped the brick wall. "The wedding shop? You're kidding."

"I'm not."

"Why? She's falling apart. About to be torn down."

"Because Tammy and I pinky swore. One day we would open up the wedding shop again."

Cole leaned against the wall. "I don't think she'd hold you to it, Haley." He ducked his head away. "You know, since she's not here."

"Maybe all the more reason why I should do it. To remember her. To keep a promise." Haley walked to the far side of the porch, staring toward Blossom Street and the lone amber streetlamp, emotion wadded up in her chest. "So what about you? What's up with Cole Danner? How are you doing?"

He shrugged. She knew that move. Something was on his mind. "I went on a date tonight."

Haley aimed her flashlight right in his eye. "Really? Someone I know?"

He shook his head, squinting, raising his hand as a shield to the beam. "No. She was a friend of a friend. Can you put that thing down?"

Haley lowered her light. "So what are you doing here?"

"Date ended abruptly when I said something that reminded her of her ex-boyfriend, who cheated on her, by the way, and boom, I was the bad guy and 'Check, please.' But not before she sang four rounds of 'All men are liars and cheaters.'"

Haley could hum a few bars of that song. "Sorry, Cole. Was this your first date since Tammy?"

"Yeah." He rapped his knuckles against the porch's wood frame. "I know I'm only thirty, but I suddenly feel too old for this. Dating. Wasn't fun in high school, so why would it be fun now? Expectations are the same yet different. People come to the table with all their gunk." He turned to her. "You don't have gunk, do you? Please don't have any gunk. 'Cause the world needs one person without gunk, and that's you, Haley."

"Don't make me the saint." Haley stepped away, feeling herself close up, wilt a little. She probably had more gunk than anyone. At least anyone on this porch.

Cole was Tammy's man, but he'd always been Haley's friend. Words flowed easily between them. In fact, once, they spent all night talking in the football stands after a particularly tough loss to their rival Memphis team. Cole, the team's kicker, missed the game-winning field goal. He needed to talk. Tammy hated football. She only went to the games for Cole.

Boy, she liked to have killed them both when she found out her boyfriend and her best friend stayed out all night, *talking*, not answering their cell phones.

"So," Haley said, patting the brick. "Do you think this old place can be restored?"

"I think it's a waste of your time. Going to be

demolished once the city sells to Akron. I've put in a bid to demolish it."

"What? No, Cole. They can't tear it down." Haley pressed her cheek against the wall. "I'm here. I won't let them hurt you."

Cole's laugh was sweet, low, full of affection. "Now you're taking me back to the old days. You and Tams . . . dreamers. How do you still have rose-colored glasses on after being in the air force? Didn't deployment burst all your bubbles?"

"I don't have any rose-colored glasses, Cole, but it's war that makes me want to reopen the shop. If we don't have love, marriage, and family, then what hope do we have? Why do we fight wars? I defended our freedoms, our way of life, down to the right of a man to propose to the woman he loves. For a woman to marry the man of her dreams." She waved her flashlight beam against the window. "Besides, I always knew this shop was my future."

"You're kidding. Not much of a future." Cole kicked the weak porch frame. "Are you sure you're not just being sentimental about Tammy? About being a kid?"

"No, yeah, maybe. But so what? I've seen a lot in the last six years, Cole, and if running this wedding shop is my destiny, what God has for me, I'd be honored. Consider myself lucky."

"Lucky? When you could go to grad school. Be one of those 'amazing Morgans' who conquer their corner of the world."

Haley stamped her foot. "This is my corner of the world. And I'm going to conquer it."

His laugh carried the sound of pity. "Good luck. But I'm telling you it's going to be demolished."

His words fell between them as Haley batted them to the porch floor. Tears swelled in her eyes. "Why not for Tammy, Cole?" Her confession was low and true. "Why not for me and our childhood dream?" She turned to him. "I miss her."

"Me too." He paused, clearing his throat.

Haley cupped her hands around her face and peered through the window again. "How do you think I should go about getting this place?"

"You're serious?" Cole tipped his head in wonder. "There's a For Sale sign. Call the Realtor. Keith Niven. You remember him? He was in your brother Will's class. He'll have ideas."

"Good ones?"

"Haley, can I be a friend? Don't get your heart set on this place. I get the sentiment, and it being a new year and all, it gets us to thinking, but Akron has deep pockets and the city wants the cash. The town council is all about the new shopping mall and renovating the old mill into lofts."

"Then why haven't they torn this place down already?"

"Because a brigade of old women who bought their wedding dresses from the shop forty, fifty, sixty years ago shows up at every town council meeting to plead for the old shop and the town council caves. But I don't think they will again. Akron is offering a lot of money. More than it's worth. The town can't afford to hold on to the building."

"How did they get it in the first place?"

"Back taxes. Figure that into your dream too."

"You're not scaring me. Cole, this place is Heart's Bend's legend. Half the families in this town have some connection to the wedding shop."

"That'd be a lot of people, Haley. We have more and more newbies and fewer and fewer oldies." He tapped his foot against a loose porch board, stooping, checking the underside, then tapping it back into place with his boot heel. "Heart's Bend needs to move on, out of the past and into the future. This place is an eyesore."

"I'm all for progress, but that doesn't mean we completely leave our history behind. Heart's Bend had a premier wedding shop for, what, ninety years? It's part of our DNA. Not to mention it's a fifty-billion-dollar business, Cole. I've done some research."

"Haley, this corner just doesn't work for business. It's been a bookstore, a record store, a computer repair center. Nothing works. Drummond Branson tried to get it turned into a visitor center, but the town council said they had enough civic buildings to maintain. They want someone to take this place off their hands."

"A visitor center? A book and record store? A computer place? No, no, no. Cole, of course those places won't work. This place is for weddings. Built to be a wedding shop. If ever a building had a calling, it's this one. Nothing will succeed in this place unless it's for weddings." Her voice rose in the darkness, butted against the cold, and fired up her passion and resolve.

Cole surrendered, taking a step back. "A building with a calling?"

"I wrote a paper on Miss Cora in sixth grade. Her

great-aunt Jane commissioned a Nashville architect to design the wedding shop. That's what this place is. Nothing else will do."

"You're passionate about this, aren't you?"

Haley peered into the window again. "More and more." She left the window to pace, to think.

"Careful, Haley. There are a lot of loose boards."

"I can do this. I mean, for crying out loud, I managed logistics teams for the United States Air Force. Stateside and in Afghanistan. I can *do* this. Open a wedding shop."

"You have a hundred grand lying around?"

She stopped short, speared on Cole's question. "A hundred grand?"

"That's what it'll take to fix this place up. Minimum."

"Whoa." Haley leaned against the wall, the breeze swirling about her, warning her of the coming cold, but the fire in her belly burning brighter. "That much?"

"Not to mention your business expenses. Website, business cards, furniture, supplies, inventory, advertising." Cole walked to the other side of the porch. "With no guarantee of success. Meanwhile, Akron Developers is hanging around city hall like a hungry dog just waiting for the council to toss them *this* bone." He kicked the wall. "They are going all out too. Besides offering above market price, they're throwing in five years of road maintenance on this side of town. But . . ." Cole came back her way.

"But what?"

"There's a stipulation in one of the town ordinances that requires them to offer the place to any good

Samaritan willing to tackle the reno, cover the taxes, and run a business."

"You're kidding. What kind of ordinance is that?"

"An old one no one's bothered to change. The wedding shop falls under some downtown code. It behooves the city to try renovating before selling. Listen, that old shop has been stuck in limbo land for so long . . ." Cole shook his head. "No one knows quite what to do with it."

"Except the women who bought their trousseaus there."

"Yeah, but they're a dying breed. And not one has stepped forward offering to make it a wedding shop again."

"So if I'm willing to take on the shop, the council would have to give it to me?"

"They have to give it weighted consideration, yes." Cole moved next to her. "Haley, do you have a hundred grand to fix up a 126-year-old building?"

"No, but I'm not going to let a little thing like money stand in my way."

"Yeah, sure, what's a little thing called money?" He slapped his thigh. "Do you really want to hang on to a kid's dream, sink a bunch of money you don't have into a place that's seen better days? Tammy would understand, trust me, if you changed your mind." He propped his hands on his waist, exhaling. "To be honest, Tammy—"

"If I died, she'd do it for me. I know she would."

Cole frowned. "Did she say that? When was the last time you two talked about this place?"

"I don't know, a few years." Maybe since the middle of their college days. "But I know her, *knew* her, and she'd have done it. She believed in the pinky promise as much as I do. I want to do this." Her confession burned within her.

"Fine, you want to open a bridal shop? I'll introduce you to Akron. They'll probably give you a deal on one of their new spaces."

Haley raised her face to the cold breeze. "I don't want to open any ole wedding shop. I want to open *the* wedding shop. Heart's Bend's wedding shop. Founded by Miss Jane Scott, then run by Miss Cora. Those women wanted to bring something regal and glamorous to the country and farm women of their day. It's my job to continue their tradition to the women of my generation."

"You're stubborn, you know that?"

"I prefer determined."

Cole walked the length of the porch and back, then stopped beside Haley, hunching up his shoulders. "Don't know about you, but I'm freezing. I think I'll head home." He swung the light over the steps. "Watch that bottom board when you leave. It's really rotted."

"Yeah, I'll go too. Getting colder by the minute."

Cole pushed open the screen door, then reached for Haley's hand, lighting the steps with the flashlight's glow. "Careful."

He held on to her. So tight. With such . . . care. A foreign sensation, for sure. And it swallowed up her hand, firing a warm sensation up her arm. Haley slipped her hand from his, shaking it in the cold, freeing herself of his touch.

What was that feeling?

"I'll just jump over." She flew from the porch over

the rotted steps to the ground. Cole followed, walking with her around front.

Haley paused at her bike, clicking off her flashlight, letting the darkness settle over her. Then caught a glimpse of Cole as he paused by his bike—which was identical to hers.

"You drive a Harley 750?"

"Yep."

She regarded him for a second, then said in time with him, "Weird."

He laughed. "This entire night is kind of weird. But in a good way. Hey, w-we should, you know, ride sometime."

"Maybe," she said. "When it warms up. I'm freezing on that thing tonight."

Familiar words. Dax taught her to ride so they could "*ride together.*" She dropped a chunk of her savings on this bike only to have it sit in the garage. Dax never wanted to ride. At least not with her.

"Tell me about it. I rode my bike to the date. Should've taken my truck."

Their conversation stalled and Haley shivered, ready to get home and warm. "Well, see you around."

"See you around."

She fired up her bike, then glanced at Cole. "You'd be married now if she'd lived."

"Yeah . . . yeah, guess so." His voice faded.

"I'm sorry. I shouldn't have brought it up."

"Talking about it is how we heal, right? Or so the infamous *they* tells us."

"Are you healing, Cole?"

"I am. I really am. What about you?"

Haley shifted into gear with a glance at the looming dark old wedding shop. Between Dax and Tammy, she had a long way to go.

"I don't know," she said, motioning to the shop. "But I think this is the place to start."

CHAPTER FIVE

CORA

"Coffee, please." Cora shuffled into the kitchen, the day's early light filling the window, making the room bright. She pulled out her chair and collapsed down with a sigh, closing her eyes for a moment to enjoy the breeze that drifted through the screen door with the scent of freshly plowed soil.

"Goodness . . . you want coffee?" Mama moved to the stove, reaching for the percolating pot with her hand wrapped in a thick dish towel. "You look wrung out. Didn't you sleep?"

"Restless is all." Cora fixed on the dark flow of coffee streaming into her cup. She didn't care for the black brew, but sleep had eluded her until the morning's early hours. When she finally drifted away, she'd awoken shortly after, her heart racing, dawn painting new-day hues on the walls of her room.

Taking her first sip, she winced. The hot bitter taste matched her memory of yesterday, of seeing Rufus. Of being mistaken.

"I can make you tea," Mama said.

"This is fine." But really, was it necessary? To drink the bitter dregs?

"Then you'd better eat. Your stomach isn't used to the grounds."

"I'm not hungry."

No matter, Mama was at the stove, filling a plate with the pancakes and sausage warming in the oven.

Before dressing and coming down to breakfast, Cora had slipped Rufus's latest letter from the top of the packet bound by a red ribbon. It was from early March. Because she'd read it so many times, she could recite each word. She just needed to *hear* his voice.

Dearest Darling Cora,

I long to see you. Business has kept me away from you, moving north, and it's tearing me apart. You mustn't think I've forgotten you. Impossible. I think of you night and day, day and night.

I'm near a phone this evening, and while the roustabouts unloaded our cargo I sought permission to use the phone. But the boathouse boss refused me access. Even after I pledged to pay the long-distance fee.

So I'm back to writing you again while we're docked on the northern Mississippi. The night is cold and quiet, making me long for your warmth. The moon is bright tonight. It comforts me to know you are seeing the same light as I.

I'll return south soon. Do not give up on me. Write me soon at the St. Louis port. I'll claim your letter within a few weeks.

Good night for now.

> All my love,
> Rufus

See, there was no reason to fret. He'd come as soon as he was able. *Take heart, Cora Beth.*

In the meantime, she merely had to endure Mama's glare as she set a loaded plate, the butter dish, and the syrup cup in front of her.

"Eat."

"You can't make me. I'm not five, Mama."

"Then don't act it."

Mama sat at her place, taking up her coffee with a soft grin—can a girl really fight her mother?

Cora took up the butter knife and prepared her pancakes, the sweet aroma coaxing her taste buds awake. Mama did make the best pancakes anywhere. Even Matilda, the cook at the Heart's Bend Diner, wanted her recipe. But Mama kept such things a secret. Her way of wielding power.

"What's in the paper today?" Cora reached for the *Tribune* by Daddy's plate.

"Cora . . . don't." Mama raised up, a bite of toast in her mouth, stretching for the paper.

But Cora slapped her hand over the newsprint, whisking it away from Mama. "Why? What's in it?" She scanned the front page, then turned inside, pausing at Hattie Lerner's "About Town" tidbits.

Nothing but a gossip column. Sheer, uncorroborated gossip.

Yesterday afternoon, the proprietress of The Wedding Shop, Miss Cora Scott, was seen running down First Avenue like her brown hair was on fire. It's unclear to this reporter why the daughter of bank president Earnest James Scott tore through town, but with Birch Good in hot pursuit, we wonder if it could be love? Or is she still waiting for her mysterious riverboat captain?

Cora gasped. "What in the world? Why-why this is downright libelous, printing my personal life in the *Tribune*. I ought to give her a piece of my mind."

"Simmer down and think about it. This is good for business."

"How in the world is my public humiliation good for business?"

"She mentioned you, the shop, your father, and the bank in one brief sentence." Mama looked up as Daddy came into the kitchen, freshly showered, handsome in his tailored suit, crisp white shirt, and dark blue tie. He smelled of Lifebuoy, talcum powder, and hair cream. "There you are, Ernie. Sit down. I'll get your breakfast."

Daddy sat down with a wink at Cora, reaching for his napkin. "The hot water felt good this morning so I lingered in the tub." He thanked Mama as she set his plate in front of him and filled his coffee. "What were you two discussing?"

"Hattie Lerner felt it necessary to spy on me and write about it." Cora slapped the paper on the table by his plate.

"I said she mentioned the shop and the bank and

both of you by name in one sentence. It's good publicity. Don't you agree, Ernest?" Mama took a cigarette from her apron pocket and stood by the open back door.

"I do like seeing our name in ink but—" He took up the paper, reading. "Why were you running down the street, Cora?"

"I was in a hurry. Late to the shop." She'd always been shy about speaking of Rufus, or of love, to her parents, especially Daddy.

"And Birch chased you?"

"He most certainly did not." He *caught* her as she was about to step in front of a car. "Once again Hattie has it wrong."

"She makes a good living getting it wrong." Daddy cut up his pancakes and slathered them with butter and syrup. "Esmé, are you outfitted for the bank dinner this Friday? We've got the bigwigs coming over from Nashville. Rogers Caldwell himself."

Cora imagined Daddy's chest puffing out another inch. He was proud of his banking accomplishments, of starting a small bank after the war and, in less than a decade, joining the Caldwell and Company network and becoming one of their top branches.

"I'm ready, Ernie." Pretty with a narrow, lean figure, Mama was always ready for a social occasion. Even in her housedress, she looked groomed and elegant. "Got my dress from the shop."

She leaned against the wall with her coffee cup in one hand, her cigarette in the other, a thin tendril of smoke drifting through the window screen's narrow netting.

"We had a lovely shipment of ready-made evening

gowns arrive this spring," Cora said. "The brides are choosing them for their trousseaus."

"Aunt Jane and her wild idea." Daddy shook his head. "Bring high fashion to middle Tennessee gals." Jane was Daddy's aunt, his father's baby sister. But she'd been like another grandmother to Cora.

"We had a customer from Birmingham yesterday. A legacy from Jane's day," Mama said. "They practically ordered the whole house, didn't they, Cora?"

"If she could've ordered more than one wedding gown I believe she would've. So her mother let her go on to evening dresses and traveling suits and lingerie."

Daddy popped up his hands. "I don't want to be hearing about a woman's unmentionables."

"Funny, that's not what you said to me the other night."

"Esmé!"

"Mama!"

She chuckled and feasted on her cigarette.

Daddy cleared his throat, fixing on his breakfast, cutting his pancakes until his knife scraped over the plate. "Oh, say, I looked at your account yesterday, Cora. You've a fine balance. I contacted Jane's attorney, asking for the rest of your trust. You're thirty now. You've met the requirements."

"But I thought you wanted me to leave it be. Let the money grow. We've plenty of money, like you say."

"I think it's wise to go ahead and bring the money into a safe place. Don't know what them Yankee bankers are up to, and I'd rather have your money in my bank where I can keep an eye on things."

"If you think it's wise . . ."

Cora did her own books so she kept a close eye on things. But Daddy knew money like most men knew boxing stats or baseball scores. She trusted him. In fact, he'd established his bank using his experience in past banking panics and crashes to build what he considered a new kind of bank. His motto was, "Heart's Bend Mutual, Your Money Is Safe with Us."

When Aunt Jane died, she left the shop and a tidy nest egg to Cora.

"So you're certain the crash from last October won't reach us down here, Ernie?" Mama said.

Daddy shook his head, mopping up syrup with a cut of his pancakes. "Not likely. Things are settling down. In fact, I'm investing. To be honest, I'm more worried about the malaria epidemic than any bank failing. Keep smart business practices, Cora, and you'll be fine. Have you given any more thought to my idea of buying a house? It's a good investment."

"Are you trying to get rid of me?"

"You know better. You're just sitting on a lot of money for a single gal. You could rent the place out, line your nest egg a bit more."

"If it's all the same to you, I'd rather wait until I move to my husband's house. Besides," Cora said, motioning between her parents, "I'm the cream between you two tough cookies and you know it." All, *ahem*, lingerie discussions aside.

"She's got you there, Ernie." Mama stamped out her cigarette in the ashtray and refilled her coffee cup. "But let's not get too far adrift. Cora, I still want to know why you were running down First Avenue yesterday. You went to get pastries and returned fifteen minutes later empty-handed, flushed, and out of breath."

"Let's not make a big to-do out of nothing, Mama."

"She sent Birch Good off to do her bidding, Ernie. Which he did, happily."

Daddy eyed Cora with one eyebrow raised. "Hmmm . . . Birch would make a fine husband. He's no dewdropper."

"Dewdropper? Now, where did you hear that word? Are you trying to be a flapper?"

"I hear things. I am a bank president, a leader in this town. I'm obliged to keep up with the times. You can't go wrong with a hard worker like Birch, daughter. The Goods have owned their farm free and clear for years. From all accounts, Birch is doing well."

Right or wrong, Daddy measured life and love in dollars and cents. Cora resigned herself to his way, his expression, finding the love in his heart through the dollar signs in his eyes. Twice he'd abandoned the family over ill-spent money and bad investments. First in the '07 panic when he put all his trust from Grandpa in TC&I.

He disappeared for three months, finally coming home when his grandpa gave him the money to straighten out his mess.

Then again in '14 when he lost money in some scheme. Once again, his grandpa bailed him out, steering him toward solid wartime investments. When the twenties rolled around he was able to start his own bank. Ten years and going strong. He'd learned his lesson.

Better have, because Grandpa wasn't around to help him out anymore.

But this business about Birch? That was *another* matter. "If he's such the duck's quack," Cora said, pulling up her own flapper lingo from her college days, "then how come no one has trapped him yet?"

"He's clever, waiting for the right gal." Daddy's goofy grin said, *"He's waiting for you."*

"Then good luck to him." Cora carried her dishes to the sink, dipped them in the cool, soapy water, and reached for the dishrag. "If you ask me he's getting a bit long in the tooth. What's he dillydallying around for? A thirty-five-year-old man with a successful farm should have a wife. And it's not like he's tomcatting around, sowing wild oats." She set the dishes in the drainer and dried her hands, then kissed Daddy's balding head on her way out. "Have a good day. Oooh, Daddy, easy on the Brilliantine."

"What? I don't know what you mean."

"Oh yes, you do, Ernie. I've told you the same thing a hundred times. I declare, some of our pillowcases will never be the same."

Cora paused at the door. "Mama, see you at the shop."

"I don't know why you don't consider Birch." The woman couldn't leave it alone. Had to shout her opinion through the house. "You said he was a bit long in the tooth, but might I point out you're not getting any younger?"

"No you may not." Cora retrieved her handbag and sweater by the front door. She knew perfectly well how old she was.

"A woman of thirty should have a husband and a baby already."

"And I will. Soon." There, she gave Mama words of hope. Cora stepped onto the porch as Liberty, the Scotts' maid, came down the drive to the back of the house. "Liberty is here, Mama. Thank you for shouting my business to the world."

"She can't hear me through the walls."

"Good morning, Liberty," Cora said, stepping onto the porch, tugging on her driving gloves.

"Morning, Miss Scott."

Cora stopped in the middle of the walk. "Liberty," she said, seeing a lightness in the young woman's step, a luminous quality to her dark, pretty expression. "Are you glowing?"

She stopped, eyes averted. "I might be."

"Do tell." Cora recognized the light of love in her eyes. She'd seen it in her brides many times.

"I done got engaged last night, Miss Cora." She raised her hand, displaying a thin gold band with a small center pearl. "Ain't it lovely? The finest thing I've ever owned. And my man got a promotion as foreman at the DuPont plant, yes he did."

"Well, congratulations." Cora drew her into an embrace. "You'll have to come by the shop, pick out a dress."

The DuPont plant along with the L&N freight system and the Cumberland River trade made Heart's Bend a middle Tennessee gem. Their little town was prospering. The Yankees could keep their collapsing economy.

"Come by your shop? Oh, Miss Cora, I don't think—"

"Well, I do think and I insist." Jim Crow be darned. "Come by on your afternoon off. I'll see what I can find for you."

"Thank you kindly, Miss Cora, but I reckon we'll be saving money for the church and a small reception."

"Nonsense. The gown will be my gift to you. You've been a good maid to the house."

"My afternoon off is Wednesdays. I work Saturdays at the plant, cleaning the offices."

"Wednesday afternoon is fine. Today, then?"

"If you're sure."

"Of course I'm sure."

Cora slipped behind the wheel of her car, rolled down the window, and fitted her key into the ignition.

When Aunt Jane died and left her with more money than she'd ever dreamed of having—which shocked Daddy as well—Cora purchased her own car. A brand-new Buick roadster for eleven hundred dollars. Daddy liked to have choked. But, oh, it was a pretty thing and very sporty. Aunt Jane would most definitely have approved.

Rufus thought the car fit her very well. He liked to drive it when he came to town, and she happily let him sport her around.

True love was all around her. Daily. At the shop. At home, despite Daddy and Mama's bickering. Now sweet Liberty had found bliss.

How long must she continue to wait? Didn't God hear her nightly pleas?

Yet, if true love brought the kind of joy that beamed

from Liberty's lovely face, then Cora would wait for
Rufus until man walked on the moon. She didn't care
if she was forty, fifty, or a hundred, that was the kind of
love she wanted.

Easing off the clutch and moving down the shaded
lane, Cora fought an image of Birch Good parading across her mind along with Daddy's, *"He's no
dewdropper."*

He was handsome enough. Fit as a fiddle with his
farm-trained muscles. He was sweet and kind, steady
as the day was long. Rock solid and . . . boring.

Cora eased to a stop at the end of the road and
dropped her head to the steering wheel. *Oh so boring.*

Every day would be the same with him. Up before
dawn to face backbreaking farm work, then to bed at
dusk, falling into an exhausted sleep. All for what? So
the elements, the pests, the market prices could devour
it all?

She imagined he'd kiss her politely in the morning, then again at night. He'd make love to her once a
week and take her to church every Sunday, after which
they'd dine at her parents'.

Maybe, for a hootenanny, he'd drive her down to
the Bluegrass Tavern on a Friday night to listen to the
band, drink a glass of sarsaparilla, and share a plate of
deep-fried chicken.

The very idea made her heart race. "Lord, please, no,
I beg of You."

A horn sounded behind her and she jerked her head
up, popping off the clutch at the same time, raising up
to see Mr. Carmichael in her rearview mirror, frowning.

Like he'd never sat at a stop sign too long. For ages, he'd stop at the end of the street to read the newspaper before going home to his six kids.

By the time Cora drove the two miles to the shop and parked in the side shade of Blossom Street, she'd affirmed her resolve. She was in love with Captain Rufus St. Claire, and if she were to have *any* adventure in life, any *passion*, she would wait an eternity for him.

CHAPTER SIX

HALEY

Tuesday morning Haley waited for Realtor Keith Niven on the shop's front walk, a messenger bag slung over her shoulder, watching the traffic pass the corner of Blossom and First.

A thick snow drifted down from a pale gray sky, but from her vantage point she could see the northeast corner of Heart's Bend, toward the shops on First Avenue, across to Gardenia Park, and down Main Street.

The day was bleak and snowy, but she was happy. Something good was about to go down.

Yesterday she spent an hour with Drummond Branson, head of the Reclaim Downtown committee and the Historical Society. He was also a respected contractor and surveyor in the area.

If anyone knew how to make her dream a reality, it was Mr. Branson. He armed her with an original drawing of the shop, tips on renovation, ideas for funding, and how to approach the town council.

There was a meeting tonight at city hall about this very corner of town.

"As for the Historical Society, we want this building preserved, so we'll give you a lot of leeway as long as you stick to the original structure." He tapped the canister containing the original architect's design. "Cole Danner would be excellent for this job. If you can get him to do it."

"What about you? Could you do it?"

"Not really my bailiwick, renovations. My work calendar is full. Doing more surveying these days than construction."

Hmmm. So that left her with Cole. She'd deal with *that* fact later. She didn't like the spark—was that the right word?—she felt between them. He was too easy to be around. Being Tammy's boyfriend and fiancé had created an easy barrier between them. But now . . .

No. She couldn't have feelings for him. She didn't come home to fall in love. What she felt for him was pure sentiment. An affection for yesteryear.

However, if he could help her get the shop going, she could manage herself around him for the renovation duration.

The best part about meeting with Drummond was his confidence that she could convince the town council to give her the building. *Give!* With no back taxes. If she promised to restore it. *And* if she ran a successful business for the first year. They'd been burned on letting other entrepreneurs in there only to have them trash the place and bug out in six months.

Drummond also said the city might pony up some renovation cash. The last of Reclaim Downtown funds he managed were designated, but the city had some set aside for historical preservation. He also gave Haley the name of a loan officer at Downtown Mutual who liked to support small businesses.

History had it that Downtown Mutual was a throwback to Miss Cora's father, Ernest Scott, who opened Heart's Bend Mutual in the twenties.

Which brought her to this moment. Pacing the sidewalk in front of the shop waiting for Keith. *Come on, man. It's cold out.*

She'd invited Cole too—based on Drummond's recommendation—but he said he wasn't sure he'd make it. *Okay, fine.* She wasn't sure she wanted to see him. Though a ping shot through her every time he came to mind.

Anyway, last night she'd done more research on the wedding business, on how to run a wedding shop, develop a business plan, and what to expect when renovating an old building.

She mocked up a budget—stabbing in the dark on that one—and listed her assets. Which included ten thousand dollars in savings and her Harley.

She'd lived large while in the air force. Spent too much money. Another aspect of her relationship with Dax. He liked to spend money.

But that was last year. *So* last year. Time to stop blaming him and own up to her foolish decisions. This was her season to start over, build a new life, and scrub the last of Dax from her memory.

A dark-tinted Mercedes pulled up along the curb.

Haley's adrenaline kicked in, like when her logistics crew had to process some top secret, classified part for a plane or tanker. *Go time.*

"Haley?" A lean, dark-haired man with lots of energy jumped the curb, slipping off his gloves, offering his bare, warm hand. "Keith Niven." He faced the redbrick structure, tucking his gloves into his pocket. "You'll be a town legend if you achieve anything with this eyesore. No one's been able to put a successful business in this place since Miss Cora closed down the shop in 1979."

"Because no one tried to open a wedding shop."

He glanced down at her with a glint of approval. "A woman with vision. I like it." He held up the keys. "Let's take a look."

Haley followed him up the walk, listening to his recitation of the shop's history. Stuff she already knew but didn't mind hearing again.

"Built in 1890 by Jane Scott, who was a real beauty, left home to be on Broadway but ended up in Paris fashion. Came home after a few years, brokenhearted, the story goes, and had an idea to bring high fashion to Heart's Bend. Her father helped her hire noted Nashville architect Hugh Cathcart Thompson, built the shop, including her own apartment on the third floor, and brought the bridal business to Heart's Bend. She passed it on to her great-niece, Cora, who ran the shop for over fifty years." Keith turned the lock and shoved the door open.

"Fifty-five years." Haley remembered the details of her sixth-grade paper, which she'd typed on the kids' computer, propping the picture she'd found when she was ten, hiding from the rain in the shop, against the desk lamp.

"Perfect. You already know more than I do. The Historical Society might have some intel, but you can bet there's some little old blue hair in town who bought her wedding trousseau here." Keith mimed sipping from a cup of tea with his pinky in the air, then stepped aside as Haley entered the foyer. "Well, what do you think?"

Haley wrinkled her nose. "What's that smell?"

She stood in the narrow foyer with Keith, pinned in by walls that hadn't been there when she was playing brides with Tammy.

"Hey, sorry I'm late." Cole cut between them, stepping into the foyer, dusting the snow from his dark brown hair, his blue eyes bright against his red-tinged cheeks.

"This was as far as we got," Haley said.

"Look at this place." Cole kicked one of the dividing walls, grabbing the edge and giving it a shake. "This is not up to code. Probably wasn't permitted."

"It's not part of the design." Haley slipped a document from her messenger bag. "Drummond Branson gave me a copy of the original plans. He said the Historical Society would give me a lot of room as long as we stick to the main structure."

Cole reached for it, studying the lines, then scanning the shop. "All of this should be open."

"Exactly." Haley cut through the doorway on her right. The walls cut off all the light coming through the front display windows. "This was the grand salon,

I think. It's the biggest room. Not sure what Miss Cora did here." She exited back into the foyer. "This is the staircase and over here"—she slipped through the doorway on the left—"is the small salon."

The smaller salon had a stained carpet covering the floor replete with a near-black pathway from the front door to the back. "This is nasty."

"Yeah, the last business in here," Keith said, "was a computer repair shop, Microfix or something, and the guy was a slob."

Cole disappeared into what looked like a butler's pantry, made some kind of racket, then reappeared. "The wall is wet. Probably a leak in the roof, which means mold."

Mold? Never good. "Do you think it will take a hundred grand to fix it up?"

"At least." Cole's flat tone said he wasn't on board with this project. "The plumbing and electricity will all have to be redone, bathrooms renovated, floors sanded and stained, not to mention what's behind the walls where we can't see. Like asbestos. Roof needs to be replaced. The windows, the light fixtures . . ." He held up his hand, running his thumb over his fingertips. *Money.*

"You know Akron Developers has offered the city a lot of money for this plot of land," Keith said. "You might be up against it on that one, Haley."

"I already told her." Cole again, sounding more enthusiastic over Akron's plan than hers. "The town's sentiment toward this place has run thin. Not many women left who got their trousseaus here. On the other hand, Akron has a good reputation in town, become a part of the community, built a park for kids with special needs on the southwest side of town. People like them."

"Though last year they tried to tear down an old wedding chapel Coach Westbrook built. Nearly ruined my reputation." Keith huffed and puffed, shifting his weight from one foot to the next. "So, Haley, what are you thinking?"

"I'm thinking Tammy stood on these steps wearing a newspaper veil." Haley jogged halfway up the stairs.

Cole shook his head, looking up at her. "You can't get through a renovation and establish a business on the fluffy clouds of sentiment."

"Do you think I'm an imbecile?" She went the rest of the way to the mezzanine. "The memories are the cherries on top. Now, what do you think needs to be done up here?"

Cole followed, repeating his laundry list of electricity, plumbing, floor sanding, adding new windows this time, pausing by the door just right of the stairs. "No telling what's in here." The knob refused to turn. "Locked."

From his pocket, his phone buzzed. He glanced at the screen, then tucked his phone away.

"You know, now that I think about it, my grandmother bought her dress from Cora in the forties. After the war," Keith said, trying the keys on the shop's key ring in the locked door. But none of them worked. "You're going to have to drill it open, Cole."

"Me? I'm just here giving an estimate."

Haley bent for a better look. "Maybe we can find the

key. I'd like to keep this doorknob. It looks old." She stood, motioning to the third-floor stairs. "Let's check out the apartment. I'd like to live in it." Haley led the way up, landing at the top level, instantly enchanted despite the stream of cold, snowy air streaming through the high, transom windows.

Cole pointed to the damaged glass. "Add another ten grand, Haley."

She turned to Keith. "Drummond said if I show up at the town council meeting, they might give it to me."

"Haley, you're crazy." Cole said.

"No, I'm not. Why does everyone think I can't know my own mind? I was sane when I went to the University of Tennessee. Sane when I majored in business. Sane—well, unless you ask my mother—when I joined the air force. Sane when I made captain. Sane when I decided to get out. And I'm sane now."

"This place is a money pit, Haley. Even if they do give you the building, you're going to have to sink a hundred and twenty grand into it."

Keith leaned against the brick wall of the alcove, arms folded, watching, amused. "You two fight like an old married couple."

"Oh no, don't even go there." Cole's heels skipped across the dull hardwood as he leaned into the torn-up bathroom and what looked to be the bedroom. White sheers swung from the window, dancing in the breeze slipping through the crack.

"We're the last two people who'd ever be a couple." Haley peeked into what might have been the kitchen.

With her imagination, she could see beyond the

barrenness, the dirt and broken windows, picturing a quaint, homey space. Even better, she could see herself here, dialing down, working with brides, putting the past behind her, and passing life as an old maid like Miss Cora.

A year or two, or a decade, without drama sounded like heaven.

"You got that right." Cole's phone beckoned again. He frowned at the screen, then tucked it away.

"Do you need to take that?" Haley said.

"No." He shook his head.

"Your biggest problem isn't money, Haley," Keith said, leaning against the brick alcove. "Or how you two protest too much over being a couple. Your problem is Akron. They make a good case for their parking lot. Other than sentiment, there's no reason to keep this shop. Akron's already sold half the lofts in the old mill they're renovating, and they haven't even started construction."

"I don't care. Heart's Bend needs this wedding shop. It's meant to be here."

"Then you best get to the town council before they side with Akron," Keith said.

"I'll be there tonight." Haley turned to Cole. "It'd help if I could say you were my contractor."

"Help? I'm not a philanthropist. I can certainly entertain a bid." Again with his buzzing phone. He didn't even bother to pull it from his pocket. He peeled away a rotten part of the wall. "Duct work looks bad. Add another ten grand."

"'Add another ten grand.' You can have that engraved

on your tombstone. Cole Danner . . . He's in heaven now, but add another ten grand."

"Hey, I'm not the one who wants to flush money down this toilet."

Why was she battling Cole? This was going nowhere. She'd learned from supervising logistics teams that a soft answer worked way better than a harsh one.

She faced him, smiling. "I'll formally ask you for a bid. Name your price."

"We'll see. If you get the place." He started down the stairs, his phone buzzing and beckoning again. "I need to run."

"Thanks for coming."

Keith leaned on the banister, peering down the stairs. "Yeah, you two would make the perfect couple."

"Stop. He was engaged to my best friend." Haley started down to the mezzanine. "Will I see you tonight?"

"Wouldn't miss it. You came back to Heart's Bend just in time. A day or two later and Akron would've had this place razed to the ground."

CHAPTER SEVEN

CORA

JUNE 1930

"Mail call! Cora, you here? Got a boatload for you today. Literally. The mail packet nearly sank from all your orders."

"What?" Cora angled over the mezzanine rail, peering down into the foyer as Morris came through the front door. "That's impossible." But there he stood with a sack of letters at his feet. Cora scurried down the steps. "Are you sure they're all for me?"

She dropped to one knee, burying her hands in the bag, gripping a stack of letters with both hands. "Wowzer, Odelia is going to faint away, I tell you. Faint away."

Morris had exaggerated, of course. There wasn't enough to sink a canoe, let alone a packet, but mercy, there were a lot of letters sent to her P.O. box.

"Where did all this come from? You got a lot of pen pals or something?"

"Last fall I scheduled an ad in *Modern Priscilla*'s April and May issue. I thought we'd try to sell some of Odelia's services. Some gals don't live near a city and need a wedding gown or a suit for the honeymoon.

Mercy! I never thought we'd have this kind of response." She shoved the letters in her right hand at Morris. "I'm not sure we can handle all of this."

"Well, goodness girl, you only advertised to nine hundred thousand women."

She laughed softly, flipping her gaze up at him. "And how do you know how many read *Modern Priscilla*?"

"I read the cover when I delivered it. What do you think? I have my own subscription?" He harrumphed, feigning offense.

"Look at these return addresses. Oregon. California. New Mexico. Louisiana. Vermont. They're from all over." Her little wedding shop had reached the nation. With one little ad.

Wait until she wrote Rufus tonight.

"Does this mean money for Odelia?" Morris knew just about everything about everyone in town. "She and Lloyd could use it. Taxes are killing them out on the farm."

"Yes, it means money, and taxes are killing us all." Cora picked up the sack to carry it upstairs, but Morris took it from her shoulder.

"Let a man do his job, now."

On the mezzanine level, Cora instructed Morris to store the bag of mail in the alcove.

"I'll get the bag from you when you're done. Don't go throwing it away." He started for the stairs, stopped short, and swerved around. "Oh, I darn near forgot. Got these for you too, Cora." He handed over letters from his pouch. "A few letters addressed to the shop, not the P.O. box."

"Thank you." Cora reached for the small stack of letters. With the wellspring of ad orders, she was feeling, well, lucky. Today she'd receive a letter from Rufus.

"All righty, I'll be off. See you at the dance over at the VFW? I believe your mama is on the planning committee."

Cora shuffled quickly through the letters, her pulse thick in her ears. "What? The dance? Oh—" Cora faced Morris, with his mop of red hair and scattering of freckles. "Of course."

She'd written Rufus about it in May, asking him to come. He pledged to make every effort. But his work had him on the Colorado for the spring. He wrote her lovely letters describing the Rocky Mountains and how he'd take her there one day. Oh, how she'd love to go. "What about you and Gena?"

"Us? No, she's expecting number six any day now." Morris scratched his head and in that moment looked much older to Cora than his thirty-five years. "I tell you, I can't hardly touch her and she don't end up with a little one growing in her belly."

"Morris!" She touched her hands to her flushed cheeks.

He angled toward Cora. "She's as amorous as they come, let me tell you." He winked and deepened her embarrassment.

"I don't think this is an altogether appropriate conversation."

Morris snapped back as if suddenly aware of his intimate confession. He marched for the stairs. "So, the dance? You'll be there? My cousin Bert is coming

over from Knoxville. Said he'd like to take a turn on
the dance floor with you."

"Your cousin Bert?" The letters burned in her hand.
One of them had to be from Rufus. She could feel it.

"The one you met at the Christmas dance. You did
the two-step with him."

"Right, Bert, I remember." A real corn shredder that
one. Cora's feet practically throbbed at the thought of
dancing with him again.

"Good. Be looking for him, now."

"You bet." When she spotted Bert, she'd duck the
other way. Not that she meant any rudeness. It's just
she'd prefer not to be in any man's arms but Rufus's.
And if it was all the same to Daddy and Mama, Morris,
Bert, and the people of Heart's Bend, she'd like to keep
it that way.

As Morris went down the stairs, Odelia came up,
stopping dead cold by the alcove. "What in tarnation is
all this?" She pointed to the small mailbag overflowing
with white envelopes.

"Orders."

"Orders!" Odelia slumped down in the chair against
the wall, pulling the bag to her. "From that little ad you
put in *Modern Pricilla*? There must be a couple hundred. How're we going to fill all of these?" Panic spiked
her voice. "I'm gonna have to hire help, Cora. You know
I'm *going* to have to hire help."

"Then hire help." Aunt Jane's money sat in the bank,
waiting to be put to good use. Even more since the lawyer released the rest of her trust into Cora's account.

She spent as little as possible. Besides salaries,

inventory, and repairs for the shop, she rarely touched the shop's money. She could afford a few hundred dollars for materials and labor.

Though lately, she'd had an itching to tuck a few dollars under the mattress. Mama kept a couple of twenties in a tin can under the back porch.

Daddy thought she was crazy, but Mama said, "You just never know."

"Cora, look at this one. Sent the money along with the order. Thirty dollars cash for a leaving suit. Trusting fool."

"Odelia, now wait." Cora reached for the clipboard and ledger on the desk. "Don't go getting them all mixed up. We won't know who ordered what and who paid."

"Ain't they ever heard of COD? Cash on delivery. How do they know we're not running a con? Cora, why in the world did you go putting an ad in a magazine?"

"Because it's good business. An alternate source of income. We're helping girls who might not otherwise have a chance at a nice dress. I think Aunt Jane would've liked it. She always believed every woman deserved a lovely wedding gown and leaving suit. No matter how poor or how remotely she lived. This ad allows us to do what we do right here in Heart's Bend for women across the country. Think of it, Odelia. You'll be sewing for . . ." Cora snagged up one of the letters. "Martha Snodgrass from Stow, Vermont."

"Like I don't have enough sewing to do round here." Odelia reached for the garment bag. "I got Miss Dunlap's evening gown right here."

From below came a sweet, lilting, "Hello? Cora?"

"Speaking of . . ." Cora rose for the stairs. The Dunlaps returned today for a final fitting. The wedding was in two weeks. Cora leaned over the mezzanine rail. "Mrs. Dunlap, Ruth, ladies, welcome. I'll be along."

The Dunlaps came with the usual crowd—grandmothers, aunts, sist-ers, cousins, and friends. But something Morris said stuck with her. "Odelia, is everything all right at home? With Lloyd?"

"Oh, law, not you too. We're fine. I wish everyone would quit pestering me." She dumped the orders back in the mail sack and disappeared into the long, narrow storeroom, shoving between the clothing racks, flipping on the light in back. "I'll work on pulling together Ruth's trousseau items. Sorry I were late."

"You'd tell me if you needed help, wouldn't you?"

"Yes. Now, leave me be. Don't keep the customer waiting."

Cora's eyes met Odelia's where a sad shadow dimmed her soul's light. "Whatever it is, Odelia, I can help."

"You can help by getting out of my workspace. Scoot. Scat."

"Have it your way, but—"

"Of course I'll have it my way."

Cora greeted the Dunlap party, her heart a swirl of Morris, Odelia, the bag of orders, and a handful of letters she had yet to inspect, one of which might be from her true love.

"Let's get settled." Cora moved the party into the main salon. "Ruthie, go on up to the mezzanine. Odelia is waiting for you."

"I can't tell you how excited I am." The young bride with the flushed pink cheeks ran up the stairs.

Mrs. Dunlap sat on the sofa with an exaggerated sigh, her posture stiff, barely glancing at the others—her youngest daughter, her two nieces, her mother, along with the groom's mother and grandmother.

"Are we ready for Ruth's big day?" Mama entered wearing a sheer lace apron over her starched and pressed blue dress, looking regal and thin, like a real Hollywood beauty. "She's going to be a beautiful bride. Would anyone care for iced tea?"

Stony silence. No one raised their hands.

"Ladies, it's a beautiful day. We're going to see Ruth in her wedding dress. Is everything all right?" Cora scanned their faces, trying to discern the source of the trouble. She paused on Mrs. Welker, the groom's mother. "Mrs. Welker?"

Light glinted off the mother-in-law-to-be's pale brown hair, a product of L'Oreal, Cora was certain.

"I'll just say it." Mrs. Welker raised her chin, brushing her hand over her skirt.

Mrs. Dunlap sighed. "Must you, Fleming?"

"Laurel, I'm sorry you have to hear it, but it's true." Mrs. Welker stood. "Recent news came to light, and we now know what I suspected all along. Ruth is not good enough for my boy." She turned to Cora. "Don't bother with a white gown for this girl. She is no virgin."

"Fleming!" Mrs. Dunlap shot from her perch so fast her hat toppled forward on her head. "How dare you?"

"I'm sorry if the truth hurts. But if you think she was sitting in her room at night saying her prayers while off at that Yankee college, then I've got a swamp to sell you down in the bayou."

"Fleming Welker, stop right there. You'll not sully my daughter's good reputation with your lies."

"Lies? You just refuse to hear the truth, Laurel."

"Mrs. Welker . . . Mama . . . W-what's going on?" Ruth hovered on the bottom step, so demure and refined in a dove-colored going-away dress with princess sleeves, belted neatly at her trim waist.

"N-nothing, sweetheart." Mrs. Dunlap moved to the stairs. "Oh my, don't you look beautiful. The suit brings out the color in your eyes."

"Now, don't lie to her, Laurel. I was telling your mother what a modern flapper you were at Wellesley."

Ruth's fine complexion flushed white. "I don't know what you mean." She glanced between her mother and future mother-in-law.

"You know precisely what I mean."

"Fleming, will you *please* be quiet?" Mrs. Dunlap said. "Ruth, darling, is that your going-away dress? It's exquisite."

"Mama, hush. Mrs. Welker, what is it you think I've done?"

Mrs. Dunlap stepped in between her daughter and her attacker, looking like a well-coiffed mother bear. "She claims you were . . . Goodness, I can hardly speak the word."

"Claims I was what?"

"Promiscuous. In college."

"And where did you hear this?" Ruth stepped around her mother, holding her chin high.

Cora grabbed Mama and shoved her toward the small salon while cheering the young bride on in her heart.

"Wait, what are you doing? I want to hear this," she whispered.

"Mama, shh." Cora tucked against the wall. "We can listen on this side."

"I have my sources," Mrs. Welker said.

"Well." Ruth's speech was slow, deliberate. "Did your source tell you your son got a young woman pregnant?"

The room gasped, quite literally. Cora sensed the air leaving the room, and for a vast moment she couldn't catch her own breath. Every woman, every nook and cranny, every beam, and every strip of hardwood exhaled.

"How dare you—"

"Doesn't feel so good, does it, Fleming?" Mrs. Dunlap's highbrow tone took control.

"Ruth Dunlap, I'll not have you denigrate my son in such a manner."

"He confessed to me after he proposed. His conscience wouldn't leave him alone."

Mama gripped Cora's hand. "I've worked in this shop for over twenty years with Jane, and you, and I never . . . simply never."

"Mama, come on." Cora grabbed her hand, trying to pull her into the pantry. "We shouldn't be eavesdropping."

"Eavesdropping? You can practically hear them from the street. We've already heard the worst. Let's see where they go from here."

Cora sighed, started to protest, but hovered against the wall with Mama, quiet as mice. She did want to see how this drama turned out.

"Mrs. Welker." Ruth's voice carried her emotion. "I might not have been the perfect Christian girl Mama raised me to be. But if you think your son is too good for me because of it, then you must think again."

"He's a young man, expected to sow his wild oats."

"Come now, Fleming. The old double standard? Don't put on Ruthie what we felt was unfair to be put on us. You never have liked Ruthie and now you're trying to come between my daughter and your son."

"I like her just fine. But . . . my Stu can do better."

Cora clapped her hand over her mouth. Such a bold confession. Tears spurred in her eyes. This was supposed to be Ruth's happiest season. A time of celebration and love, of harmony. But Mrs. Welker had brought her brand of bitter to the proceedings.

A slow bead of sweat trickled down the side of Cora's face, her back against the wall as Mama's sticky hand clung to hers.

The grandfather clock tick-tocked, tick-tocked, the only sound in the salon.

"What do you think they're doing?" Mama's low inquiry was followed by a short prayer. "Lord, help us."

Absolutely no sounds came from the grand salon. It was as if they'd all left. Another trail of sweat prickled down Cora's cheek. Mama squeezed her hand so hard it hurt.

"Get the tea and pastries." Cora freed her hand from Mama's and rounded the corner with a big inhale. "Oh,

Ruth, that dress is divine on you. Just divine. You have such exquisite tastes. The waistline shows off your figure so well."

Ruth had slouched onto the bottom step, rivulets of water cutting tracks through her lightly powdered face. "It's ruined. Everything is ruined."

"No, no, come on now, nothing is ruined." Cora sat down next to the devastated bride and wrapped her in her arms. "Family is not always easy, is it?"

"She hates me. My mother-in-law hates me."

Cora leaned to her ear. "Do you love him?"

Ruth met Cora's gaze, wiping away her tears. "Yes, very much."

"Does he love you?"

"With all his heart. He tells me every day. Twice a day even."

"Then you'll be able to face your families together. Why not let the past be just that . . . the past?"

"Here we are, here we are, ladies . . ." Mama swooped in, a tray of tea and sweets in hand, her polished southern charm beating against the tension in the salon. "Mrs. Dunlap. Mrs. Welker, girls . . . I tell you, aren't you blessed to be forming a family together? Bridesmaids, are you family or friends? Both? Oh, and a cousin. I had a cousin as a bridesmaid too."

While Mama worked her charms, Cora brought Ruth back from the edge.

"Come on, let's try on your gorgeous evening gown." Cora took Ruth's hand, leading her up to the mezzanine. "Odelia surely worked her magic for you."

She managed Ruth through the rest of the fitting,

getting a smile out of her when she modeled the dresses she bought for their Florida honeymoon. Mama served so many pastries she ran out, had to cut up Odelia's left over rock-hard cinnamon rolls. She served those with a pound of butter and a fresh pot of coffee.

"I figured if I kept their mouths full they'd leave off the arguing."

But a slight tension hovered in the grand salon, and Ruth refused to push past it. She flat out declined to model her wedding dress one last time.

"I don't want Mrs. Welker to say one hurtful word. And she will, if not from her lips then from her eyes. Did you see her frown with every dress I modeled? Mama, poor Mama, what will I ever say to her?"

"You're a grown woman, about to be married. You only need to be honest with your husband."

"He knows everything, he does. As I do about him. In college, times are different, you feel different, the old rules don't seem so important anymore."

"But aren't they?"

"More than any of us will ever know." Tears glistened in Ruth's eyes. "More than we'll ever know."

"I'll have Odelia pack up your wedding gown and load it in your car with the other things. No one has to see you wear it until you're ready."

"Do you think Stu will love it?"

"Of course he will. But he'll love the woman in the dress much, much more." Behind the room divider, Cora helped Ruth slip from her dress, then handed it over to Odelia.

When she came out in her regular clothes, carefully

setting her hat on her head, she paused in front of Cora. "I apologize again for Mrs. Welker. She wanted Stu to marry someone else. The daughter of her high school friend. She and I went to Wellesley together. I suppose that's where she heard her stories." Ruth wrung her hands together. "About me and all. Mrs. Welker thought Stu would've backed out of our marriage by now."

"Just remember Stu chose you," Cora said, walking with Ruth down the stairs. "Don't let anyone ruin your special day."

"I'll make it my mission." Ruth pressed a kiss to Cora's cheek. "Thank you for your kindness and discretion. Mama? Mrs. Welker? Y'all ready?"

When the Dunlap party had gone, Cora collapsed onto the sofa.

"Well, wasn't that something?" Mama said, collecting the china dessert plates and tea service. "I never in all my born days witnessed such a confrontation. It'll be up to the two of them to make their marriage happy." Mama turned for the pantry. "I think I'll fix a sandwich. Do you want one?"

"Yes, and for Odelia too. Thank you, Mama."

Cora closed her eyes for a moment. Poor Ruth. But if she and Stu loved each other . . .

She sat forward, blood pumping. Rufus. Surely she had a letter from him in the stack of mail on her desk.

She jogged up the stairs, flopped into her desk chair, and reached for the letters. Her hand trembled as she picked up a postcard with his name on it. Cora stared at the image of St. Louis on the front. Did he send her a postcard?

But the message was addressed *to* him rather than *from* him.

Rufus St. Claire

Heart's Bend Port
Heart's Bend, TN

Morris must have included it by mistake, thought it was a postcard to her from Rufus. Cora studied the strange, beautiful script, then turned the card over.

Rufus, darling, please telephone as soon as you dock. Most urgent. Lovingly yours, Miriam

Rufus? Darling? Lovingly yours, Miriam? The card shook in her cold, trembling fingers.

Who was Miriam? Cora read the sentence again and again, pressing down the heat of panic.

Rufus . . . darling . . .

Mama called Cora *darling* all the time. Perhaps Rufus had a sister he'd never mentioned. Or a young aunt. Rufus, as wonderful as he was, enjoyed being mysterious. Cora couldn't deny it was an aspect of his character that captivated her.

Maybe she was a cousin. Miriam sounded like a fine cousin's name. She had a cousin Miriam on Mama's side.

Lovingly yours.

Why was she lovingly his? When Cora wrote to Ernest Junior during the war, she signed her letters, "Your loving sister, Cora."

When she wrote to Rufus, she signed, "All my love, darling, forever."

A dark spark pinged around her ribs and fired into her muscles, sinking into her bones. A drain of dread deepened her shivers to a tremor.

Steady, Cora. Don't panic. Think. Be reasonable. What could a girl tell from such a cryptic note? *Nothing.* What kind of woman sends a postcard merely to ask for a telephone call?

A thought bounced through her. Oh, perhaps the wife of a mate. A very close mate. Surely such a relationship existed.

Cora exhaled, clasping the postcard to her chest. Yes, Miriam must be the wife of a friend, a shipmate, perhaps a pilot he'd sailed with in the past. Maybe even an old school chum or army buddy.

She'd nearly panicked over nothing. Daddy's preaching to always stay level-headed hadn't fallen on deaf ears as he feared. Examining the handwriting again, Cora imagined a slim, pretty woman with a worried expression.

There was no return address. No last name. The writer would remain the mysterious Miriam.

"Cora, Odelia, I made sandwiches." Mama's sweet voice wound up the stairs.

She tucked the postcard into her pocketbook. She'd carry it home with her tonight, and later, when she wrote to him, she'd mention Miriam. Surely she was no one Cora should worry herself over. Rufus was a man of his word. When she saw him face-to-face, he would reassure her with each movement of his passionate kisses.

CHAPTER EIGHT

COLE

W hat do you think? We want you in on this."
Brant Jackson, the head of Akron Developers,
passed Cole a folded piece of paper. "Be our project
manager. This salary ought to inspire you."

Cole reached for the paper. He'd left Keith and
Haley at the wedding shop to spend the last hour sitting in Akron's portable office on the southwest side of
town, listening to their pitch, reviewing the downtown
loft plans, as well as plans for the row of shops perpen-
dicular to the old downtown on Main Street and First
Avenue west of the old wedding shop.

He absorbed it all from a twenty-thousand-foot view
until he read their offer. Six figures. Plus bonus. His
heart pumped a bit faster. *Be cool, man, be cool.* "Very
generous."

"We believe you're the man for the job."

The call came out of the blue Monday afternoon.
Akron asking him to interview for a construction
manager position.

"What about my crew? Danner Construction is solid, but we're small still, growing steadily."

"We don't want Danner Construction, Cole. No offense. We want you. We have our own crews." Brant leaned forward with a knowing nod. "Got a good gig going with the unions, you know. All you have to do is manage the teams and report to me."

The other men around the table, wearing crisp button-downs and creased khakis, smiled and nodded.

Six figures was more than he'd earned in the last two years and then some.

"You have a good reputation for getting projects done on time or before. Each time you'll earn an extra bonus." Sam Bradford, the man on Brant's left, clapped his hand on the table. "It's a freaking awesome offer, Cole. What's your hesitation?"

Cole sat back, laying the paper on the table. "What about my crew?"

"Give them a good reference. They'll find work. But we have our teams in place."

"I see." But there weren't many craftsmen around like the men Cole had on his team. He'd known his main guys, Gomez, Hank, and Whiskers, since he was a kid. Friends of his dad's. Best craftsmen around. Could build, fix, repair, imagine anything. "Why can't I hire my guys?"

Brant exchanged a look with Sam. "You can. There'll be lots of side work. We have big plans for downtown Heart's Bend. She's going to be the gem of Tennessee. But the crews we have are Akron crews. They know our methods and standards."

"Then why not hire one of them to be project manager. I'm an outsider." Cole pushed away from the table, away from the swirl of doubt that reined in any excitement. He should be jumping up and down, shouting, "Yes!" But . . .

"Cole." Sam glanced around from the coffee station where he filled his stained mug. "Here's the thing. We need a lot of guns in this fight. You're our sharpshooter. The hometown boy people know and trust."

"You *do* know about my father, don't you?" The jailbird.

Brant waved him off. "Old news. We don't like to hold the sons responsible for the sins of their fathers."

"Then you're the rare exception."

He exaggerated, but it felt good to blow off steam about his old man from time to time, blame him for the jobs he didn't get. Shoot, it was a crazy mystery how he ended up in the same business as his pop in the first place. A divine sort of comedy.

"So what's the problem? Say yes!" Brant slapped his hands together as if it were a done deal, cocky confidence supporting his sporty grin.

But Cole never said yes right away. He liked to process. Think things through. But the merits of this offer were evident. Taking this job meant ease of life, no doubt. No more beating the bushes for clients. No more sleepless nights wondering how he was going to meet payroll. No more juggling bills, going without, turning down jobs because he didn't have enough resources.

This job also meant he could crawl the rest of the way out from under his father's reputation.

Cole reached for the offer still lying on the table. "You've certainly presented me with a generous offer."

"Comes with a full benefits package too. Health, dental, vision, 401k, flex vacation. If a job gets done and we're waiting to start the next one? You can take off all the time you want."

"It's almost too much to pass up." He smiled. This was starting to feel good.

"Of course it is. Come on. Say yes."

"I'd still like to think on it."

Sam and Brant exchanged glances. What were they *not* telling him? "Thing is, Cole, we need you tonight for the town council meeting."

"Me? Why?"

"Because that postage-stamp-size piece of real estate on Blossom and First is the most precious in town. At least to us." Brant angled toward Cole. "It's smack in the crossroads of all new development. Our entire First Avenue plan is kaput without it."

"We're offering the town two and a half times what it's worth," Sam said. "We can't get them to budge. There's some kind of sentimental attachment to the ugly old thing."

"You think the corner of Blossom and First is the only way to get parking?" Cole went to the town map tacked to the trailer wall. "What about here, Elm and Pike? There's nothing there but an old field. It's only a block away."

"The field is the easement for our outdoor mall. Right next to where you're pointing will be a Starbucks."

"But we have a great coffee shop in town. Java Jane's. What will happen to her?"

"She'll have to be competitive." Brant's chuckle mocked Cole's concern. "Nothing like good stiff competition."

"With a national chain?"

"Cole, take it up with the town council if you're not happy. The plans are already approved."

Now he understood why Drummond Branson bombarded half the town's inboxes with e-mails begging them to get out to the council meetings.

"Downtown shopping is where the tourism will be. They need a place to park, hop a trolley, see the sights."

"What sights?"

"We've got a dozen specialty shops all lined up. Not to mention now that we've discovered a gem of a wedding chapel, Heart's Bend has become a destination wedding stop."

Cole mused over the notion. Last year news broke that ole Coach Westbrook, a Hall of Fame football coach, had built a wedding chapel off River Road in the early fifties for his sweetheart. Only thing was it took sixty years to marry her.

"The chapel only books about four weddings a month. They aren't looking to become a cheap destination."

"That'll change when they see the demand. And the money." Sam's expression darkened with a sharp glint in his eye.

"Not everything is about money," Cole said with conviction but no authority. He could use an influx of cash right now. What with business being off for the winter.

"Not everything is about money. But money makes *everything* a whole lot better."

"There's a woman in town who wants to reopen the old wedding shop." Cole rapped his knuckle against the map. "Wouldn't that fit into your novelty shop ideas? Wouldn't it go well with the wedding chapel?"

"Sure. We'll give her a space right here. In the new mall." Brant pointed to an area northeast of the old shop. "But this?" He slapped his hand over Miss Cora's place. "Must be parking. We've gone over and over it, and there is no way we can build the lofts or the mall without that plot of land on Blossom and First. No parking, no project."

Cole regarded him for a moment, then made his way to the door. "Still, I'd like to think on it. I appreciate the offer, but when a man gets a six-figure salary and benefits tossed in front of his eyes, he needs a minute to get the stars out of the way."

Brant laughed too forced, too loud, and clapped him on the back. "Either way, come sit with us tonight. We could use you in our corner. Let the town council see we are partnering with local businessmen."

Sam filled his coffee cup again. "It's time the town took control. That old ugly building is not a town treasure. Heck, it's been empty for the better part of thirty years. It's a liability." He pointed to Cole. "You know I'm right."

"I can't say yes to your offer just yet, but if you want, I'll be there tonight."

Outside, Cole walked to his truck under a cold steel sky. *Dadgummit.* This Akron deal was stellar. It would set him up for the next few years. Maybe for life. Though it bothered him he'd have to give up his crew. But offers like this didn't come along every day. Shoot, if he was the manager he could hire whomever he wanted, right? Keep his guys working with side jobs.

He cranked the engine and backed out of the lot, setting a course for Ella's diner. Mom was always good with this sort of thing. She had a knack for seeing through the bull, for balancing integrity with business.

He shifted in his seat, adjusting the seat belt, bothered by a pinch in his chest. Must have been something he ate. Cole raised the radio volume, jamming to the new Laura Hackett Park song.

He thumped his chest with his fist. Heartburn? But no, he'd not eaten yet today. Didn't even have a cup of coffee.

Haley flashed across his mind. The pinch behind his ribs tightened. Cole brushed a bead of sweat from his forehead. Forget the dropping temperature outside. The heat of pressure was coming from the inside.

Was this concern for his crew? Shoot, those guys could find work until he could hire them on an Akron job. Always had, always would. They were the best. And he didn't care squat about that old shop. He felt no sentimental value where Tammy was concerned. She'd never talked about the place. Not that he could remember.

But he'd watched Haley, heard her heart and, dang

it, if he sided with Akron he'd be a bullet in her dream. Why she wanted to resurrect that old beast made no sense, but what right did he have to get in her way?

He wrestled with his thoughts all the way to town and as he entered Ella's and perched on his stool at the counter.

What did it matter what Haley wanted? He had to see to himself. Get his life going again. Even if it required him to stand on the other side of the aisle from his friend.

. . .

CORA

The clock on her desk pinged midnight. Twelve sweet melodic chimes. Cora rose from her desk, stretching, massaging her neck, a fragrant June breeze skipping through the open window, dallying with the curtains.

It had been a long day but a very productive one. It had taken the better part of a week, but she'd organized the orders generated by the magazine ad and created a schedule for Odelia, which, thanks to the woman's interference, took twice as long as it should have. Then she began correspondence with each customer.

Thank you for your order of a two-dress trousseau. The scheduled delivery date is October 1, 1930, COD.

> Sincerely,
> Cora Scott
> Proprietress, The Wedding Shop
> Heart's Bend, TN

On her desk were two piles, separated by those who paid cash and those who ordered COD. Cora and Odelia agreed to fulfill the cash orders first, then the CODs.

Over the summer into the fall, the orders promised to bring in fifteen thousand dollars. Odelia nearly swooned.

"That's a lot of money, sweet heaven above. Now, how in tarnation am I gonna make all them clothes? You keen on me hiring help, ain'tcha?"

"Please do. Mama's maid, Liberty, and her mama are great seamstresses."

"I got a few names in mind myself. Can I offer a better than fair wage? Ain't right to entice a woman away from her family, maybe even a second job if we ain't going to make it worth her while. And some of these gowns are mighty detailed. We ain't running no sweatshop."

"Of course." But Cora needed to hear what Odelia considered a fair wage. Once they agreed to an hourly rate versus a per-garment fee, Odelia got busy on a list of potential candidates, calling those with telephones and planning home visits for those without.

By the end of the week she hoped to have twelve women under employ with the goal of ten frocks a week.

While it was all exciting and energizing, Cora debated running any more ads. If the response kept up, she'd need a factory to meet the demand.

Well, that was her day. A long day. She should get on home. After all, the midnight hour had chimed. But she wanted to look through the mail. Unwind.

There was no letter from Rufus this week. But Cora

did hear from two of her fall brides. They sent photographs from their wedding day.

Slipping the images from the envelopes, Cora removed two clothespins from a cotton bag in her bottom desk drawer and walked to the alcove's outside wall, clipping the pictures on the rope twine she'd strung across the brick. In fact, she had several runs of twine layering over one another. All with pictures of the shop's brides. *Her* brides.

"Here you go, Myra Deshler. Welcome to my wall." Cora pinned Myra's smiling face to the twine. Didn't she look utterly beside herself, clinging to her new husband's arm? Handsome fella too. Myra waited ten years for him. Said she'd wait another ten if it meant Hammond Purdy would walk into her life.

The next photo was of young, very pretty Laura Canyon, who met Marshall Warren at a dance in Memphis and married him ten weeks later.

Love came in all sorts of sizes and packages, in the most blessed and strange ways.

Cora stepped back, admiring her brides, cherishing the journey of love these women gave her. She felt humbled to play a small part in their lives. This shop was her calling. And one day, perhaps, she would hang her own bridal picture on this wall.

"Cora?"

She whipped around at the sound of a familiar male voice. "Daddy?" She leaned over the mezzanine railing. "What are you doing here?"

"It's after midnight, darling. Your mother wouldn't

let me have one wink of shut-eye until I came down here." He raised his pant leg. "Look here, I'm wearing my pajamas underneath."

Cora laughed. "And your ugly sweater."

Daddy grabbed the worn wooly sweater tight around his lean frame. "I'll be buried in this thing."

"Not if Mama has anything to say about it." She'd tried four times in the last ten years to throw the "ugly thing" away, but Daddy saved it from the charity box every time.

"With any luck, she'll pass on before me."

"Daddy, listen to you. All for a sweater."

"You can't mess with a man's pipe, slippers, or favorite sweater. Now, come on home. I'll be falling asleep at my desk tomorrow. And you know it won't look good for the bank president to be asleep on the job."

"May it never be." Cora turned to the mezzanine. "Let me get my things and lock up. You know my car is here, don't you?"

"Ride home with me. I'll bring you in tomorrow morning. What are you doing working so late anyway?"

"Organizing the orders we got from the magazine ad." Cora snapped off the mezzanine lights, grabbed her pocketbook, and headed downstairs. "We should earn a very handsome sum by the end of the year . . . if all goes well. Odelia's working on hiring seamstresses."

"That's my girl." Daddy applauded, bowing, then joined her on the stairs, his arm about her.

This was the Daddy Cora knew and loved. Strange to think his kindness and generosity surrounded and protected a darkness deep in his soul. One that caused him to abandon the family when hard times struck. His raw, rash response to crisis that took down everyone around him.

Didn't he just love his work, though? Mama accused him of having another child—the bank. He did tend to lose himself in the bank's business.

"I'm turning out like you, Daddy." Cora settled her hat on her head. "Overly devoted to my work."

"Nothing wrong with hard work and devotion."

Daddy's abandonments and humble returns left Cora cautious about him. Careful. Never knowing if his delicate temperament, his fragile confidence might drive him away from home again. Praise be to heaven the crash last year had not touched them.

"If you like this sort of business," Daddy said. "We'll find you a better solution for order fulfillment than Odelia running around hiring help. Heaven knows, I'd never work for that woman."

"And what woman on earth would you work for?" Cora gave Daddy's arm a squeeze.

"Seems I work for your mama a good deal. 'Ernie, can you fix the oven? Ernest, I need the toilet fixed right now.'" He chuckled. "But that's the way marriage works. Look, the mill right down the street might be up for grabs. If you're interested . . ."

"Textile mill? I'm a wedding shopkeeper, not a mill owner. However, the ad was an experiment. We'll see if I keep it up. We can talk then."

Cora loved providing beautiful trousseaus for eager brides, but the *brides* were the best part of the job. What she loved most. The fellowship of women talking about love, home, and family. She'd miss the hope and excitement of the journey that blended two lives into one if she became a manufacturer.

She'd miss Odelia's ornery and grumpy countenance.

"How about we get you home?" Daddy offered Cora his arm.

She shut off the main lights with the switch by the door and, in the dark, the shop seemed to glow. Cora thought it was all the love that filled this place. Sometimes the shop felt every bit as much like her church at First Avenue Baptist.

Sometimes she wondered if the light was other-worldly. She'd seen something like that once, at a tent revival meeting. The preacher on stage prayed with such passion, and for the life of her Cora imagined she saw a glow emerging from his mouth every time he said the name Jesus.

Scared her right enough, but she couldn't take her eyes off him. She'd decided that night to follow Jesus. If He could make a man's words gold, He must be something wonderful.

But age and time had snuffed out much of her passion. It'd been too long since she experienced any light. Waiting for Rufus left her cold and dark at times, and she struggled—*yes, admit it, now*—she struggled to find the light of hope.

But he promised . . .

Cora walked alongside Daddy toward his car parked on Blossom, the day's weariness settling on her. She was glad for the ride home. And the company.

"Thanks for coming, Daddy."

He kissed her cheek, then held open the passenger door. "Of course. What's a father for if you can't count on him?"

. . .

HALEY

Room A in city hall was bright, warm, and stuffy. Haley slipped in, taking a seat three rows from the back, unzipping her jacket, tucking her gloves in the pockets.

The heat suffocated her cold skin. Riding in from the parents' place on a Harley was cold business.

She'd spent the afternoon preparing, collecting her thoughts, and practicing her town council speech with a row of childhood toys she'd found in her closet. A beat-up Barbie, a scarred Ken, two seen-better-days bears, and a one-eyed Raggedy Ann—all possessions her unsentimental mother had *not* thrown out the day Haley went to college. She claimed Haley might want them some day. Maybe, but for now, they were her attentive audience.

She'd also discovered the old photo of Miss Cora she'd found that summer afternoon while playing with Tammy. It was in a box of annual goals Haley had written over the years. Another part of Haley's past Mom held on to.

Haley glanced at her notes and the photo of Miss Cora. It made her feel as if the old proprietor were with her, cheering her on.

Making speeches was nothing new. Haley had addressed her colleagues and superiors as well as those she commanded in the air force many times. This afternoon was about getting her words right.

"... *the wedding shop is part of Heart's Bend, in ways we can't even see . . . touched all of our families . . .*"

This part of the speech required emotion, passion, for the council to hear from a woman who had vision. Passion wasn't her strong suit. She preferred a more logical and orderly approach. But she was in a fight, and unless she convinced the council, she would lose.

At seven o'clock, the room was still fairly empty. Up front, three men and two women gathered on the dais. Must be the council.

From the side door, three clipped and pressed businessmen with an air of high dollars entered, taking seats on the first row.

"I see Akron's here on time, sitting up front." Keith Niven dropped down into the seat next to Haley.

"Where is everyone else?" Haley angled around, eyeing the empty chairs.

"Who knows? People don't really care as long as they can live their lives the way they want." Keith turned to her. "I've been thinking, if you want this shop, you're going to have to speak up, fight. Be clear, concise."

"Keith, I grew up with four older brothers. I was a captain in the air force. I think I can manage this."

"But this is Akron. They have smooth words. And money. How much money do you have?"

She grimaced. "And why are you here? To cheer me on or discourage me?"

"I'm just being practical." Keith nudged her with his elbow, jerking his thumb toward the door. "Hey, an older woman. She might have been one of Miss Cora's brides."

Haley saw the woman too. In her late seventies, maybe early eighties, she could've been one of Cora's brides. She walked around to Haley's row and sat down on the end.

"Hello," she said, leaning toward Haley, her eyes clear and blue, though her wool coat was frayed at the cuffs and her gray hair thin.

"Hello."

Should she ask her if she was one of Cora's brides? How would she even know Haley was making a case for the shop? Maybe she just wanted to keep Akron from knocking it down.

"Excuse me, but are you—"

Keith knocked her with his elbow again. "Well, look who's siding with the enemy." He leaned forward, resting his arms on his knees, phone in hand, texting.

Cole.

"They aren't the enemy, Keith. I've seen the *enemy* and trust me, Akron isn't even close."

"Or they just wear a different uniform."

"Whatever." She caught Cole's eye and made a face. *What are you doing?*

He shrugged, offered her a half-hearted smile, and took a seat behind the Akron boys.

Keith's pinging phone ripped through the quiet room. He leaned toward Haley. "Cole says they offered him a job."

"Akron offered Cole a job?"

"I told you, they have money. I was blinded by them myself. Almost cost the town the wedding chapel."

"But you saw the light. The town will see the light." And Cole. He will see the light. She wanted him on her team.

"But bookoo bucks buys a lot of loyalty."

"Bookoo bucks? Stop talking about their money. You're killing my confidence."

"I'm just preparing you." Keith sat back, surrendering his point, resting his arm over the back of his chair.

Oh, Keith. He was annoying with his bling personality, but Haley admired his ability to make a casual acquaintance feel like a friend.

Little by little the chairs began to fill. Haley was surprised and happy to see her dad. She waved at him from across the way. He gave her a single nod.

Drummond Branson slipped in next to Dad, giving her a fatherly thumbs-up.

The sound of a gavel shot through her. She pressed her hand to her heart. Sudden, loud noises still made her want to run for cover while reaching for her weapon.

"That's Linus Peabody, city manager, de facto leader of the council." Keith, the town crier. "Both a rose and a thorn, if you know what I mean."

"Thank you all for coming. Looks like we have a good turnout. Thanks to Drummond Branson's e-mails." The speaker tossed a glance to Drummond with no affection in his voice or expression. "We're here to discuss Akron's proposal to divest the town of the building and land on the corner of Blossom and First. The address is 143 First

Avenue. As you know, we've been hanging on to this property, taken over when the last owner abandoned it and owed back taxes. You can read all the documentation online."

Haley listened, running her dewy palm over her jeans.

"We'll hear from Akron first, then we'll hear from any of you. Drummond, I suppose you'll want to speak."

"Not tonight, Linus. I'm here to support Haley Morgan. She wants to reestablish the wedding shop. The Historical Society is in full support."

"Well then . . ." The councilman sounded amused but looked arrogant. "I look forward to hearing from her. Brant, why don't you begin." Linus started to sit down, then addressed the room. "Just to be clear, we've already approved Akron's development of the northeast side of the town. We're in the works, all good to go. This is just the final piece. Blacky Krantz, I know you're waiting to get into one of those new loft apartments. Well, listen to Brant here, and you'll be in before you know it."

One of the men from the front row stood. "I'm Brant Jackson, CEO of Akron. We love Heart's Bend, a beautiful river city, a gem of a town, poised for growth and prosperity."

His words tapped a rat-a-tat-tat in Haley's ears. He espoused change, growth, and prosperity. The past was the past. Times change and towns have to change with them. Tourism growth would change the economic culture.

Brant was cut from the same cloth as Mom. Achieve,

achieve. Set goals. Move on, move forward, make money. Prosper.

Wasn't there something more valuable than achievement and money? Like history, tradition. People.

Haley peeked at the woman seated on the end of her row. She listened to Brant with her hands folded neatly in her lap.

Brant popped up a Keynote slide. "We're prepared to repave and landscape this entire area. There'll be a park along the side of the loft dwellings. We've offered Cole Danner, born and raised right here in Heart's Bend, the job of construction manager." Brant laughed with a fabricated CEO tone. "We're enticing him to say yes."

Cole rounded his shoulders forward. Haley resisted the urge to walk up front and pop him on the side of the head.

Don't let these blowhards use you as their token local kid.

Brant's song and dance ended when Linus brought down his gavel. "Thank you, Brant Jackson. Your five minutes are up, but I just want to remind everyone Akron has been a friend to Heart's Bend for several years now, investing in our community." Wisps of the man's thinning hair twisted above his head as if electrified with his slick schmoozing.

"Drummond, do you want the floor?" Linus said, taking his seat.

"No." Hadn't he heard what Drummond said? "I'll yield to Haley."

"All right, Haley Morgan has the floor. She's the daughter of David and Joann Morgan. Most of you know them. Longtime, respected Heart's Bendians. David, good to see you here."

"Wouldn't miss it." Dad gave Haley a nod.

Cole peeked over his shoulder, then sat forward. Haley stood, gripping her notes. She wanted to command the room like she did during one of her logistics staff meetings, but instead she felt vulnerable, weak, submitted to the will of progress.

"Hi, everyone. I'm Haley Morgan. But I guess most of you heard already. Some of you might remember Tammy Eason too. Or know her parents. We became best friends in first grade and stayed that way until she died last spring after a fierce battle with brain cancer."

The confines of the chairs were claustrophobic, so she stepped over Keith for the aisle.

"When we were ten, we discovered a way into the old wedding shop and made it our fort. We played brides, marching down the stairs in our make-believe wedding gowns. Well, Tammy mostly played the bride as she'd already determined to marry Cole Danner over there." A soft laugh rippled through the room. "I played the shopkeeper. Tammy would come down those wide, curved center stairs thinking she was queen of the world." The words came from her heart. Not her notes.

"That's how it was back in the day." The woman on the end of Haley's row had raised her voice. "You put your gown on up on the mezzanine, then descended the stairs like a beautiful debutante." She raised her chin, wafting her hand through the air.

"Were you one of Cora's brides?"

"I was, and if it wasn't for Cora, I wouldn't have had a wedding gown."

Brant Jackson was on his feet. "This is all well and good, but you can't keep a town growing on the fuel of reminiscing and sentiment. Ladies, I am for weddings." He clapped his hand to his chest. "I'm married myself with two daughters. But there are no fewer that twenty-five wedding shops in the Nashville area. Some of them not forty-five minutes from Heart's Bend. If you're so determined to have a wedding shop, open one up on the new mall. I'll give you a deal."

"Sure, and take all my profits in rent?" Haley said to a smattering of applause. And one, "Tell 'em!" Keith, of course. "Jane Scott founded a wedding shop in this small 'gem of a town,' I believe you said, Mr. Jackson, when no one ever heard of such thing. She put herself on the map without radio, television, Facebook, or Twitter, or some targeted marketing scheme. She understood women. She understood brides."

"Do you understand brides?" Mr. Jackson challenged her with his arms folded over his puffed-out chest. "Didn't you just spend the last six years in the military?"

"Excuse me, Brant, no one interrupted you." Dad was on his feet. "Let her have her say."

Thank you, Daddy. Haley walked the center aisle, her pulse hot in her veins.

"We have a wedding chapel now. Wouldn't it be great for tourists, for those seeking a destination wedding, to get their wedding attire in the same place they plan to marry? Miss Cora pioneered women in business at a time when most women worked solely in the home. She survived the Great Depression, became a leader during World War II. She was a philanthropist." Haley turned to the older woman in the chairs. "She helped women be all they could be on the finest day of their lives."

"What does this have to do with reopening a wedding shop on a prime piece of real estate?" Linus's question was driven and pointed. "Do you know how many businesses failed in that spot after Cora closed the wedding shop in 1979?"

"Of course." She moved toward the dais. "Because this shop wasn't designed for books or computers. It was designed for wedding gowns and going-away dresses, for veils and lingerie, for brides." Haley paused, searching to give words to her intuition. "I dare say that space was never intended to be a parking lot."

Brant was on his feet. "This is ridiculous."

Haley ignored him. "The shop is about escorting a woman toward love and marriage. Into the greatest time of her life."

"Of which half will find themselves in divorce." Brant just couldn't keep to himself.

"All the more reason we need to support them with a personal touch. With community and relationships." Her response fueled a fire in her bones. Haley moved closer to the dais and Brant Jackson. "The wedding shop has probably touched every family in the county. Mr. Jackson says he's about growth and business. Well, so am I." She put the room behind her as she stepped up on the dais. "Give me the shop. Let me turn it into the place it used to be. Let's stand for Heart's Bend commerce and tradition by supporting local businesses. By supporting a great Heart's Bend citizen, Miss Cora."

The room erupted with applause, a few shouts, and one whistle. When Haley turned, Dad was cheering her on.

"It's an eyesore," Linus protested with a glance at his fellow council members.

"Won't be when I'm done." She displayed a lot of confidence for not knowing what she was doing.

"Do you have the money for renovation?" The question came from the councilwoman behind the name placard Jenny Jones.

"I'll get the money."

"She's wasting your time, gentlemen and gentlewomen." Brant squeezed in next to her. "How many times have good-hearted people made the plea to keep that shop and nothing, I say *nothing,* came of it? It's *time* to let it go." He hammered his hand on the table.

"I like the idea of the shop in the new mall." This from the councilman named Art Hunter.

"Haley, why not? You can carry on Miss Cora's traditions there," Linus said.

"Exactly." Brant puffed out his chest. "We'll give you first choice on location, do the buildout for you any way you want. All on us."

"No, no, no, we already have a wedding shop. On the corner of Blossom and First." She shivered, weakening, fearing defeat. Linus and Brant made a persuasive point. She saw it on the council's faces. "Give me a chance."

"We're not here to fund your aspirations, Miss Morgan." Linus had all kinds of thoughts, didn't he?

"Really, seems you don't mind funding Brant Jackson and Akron's aspirations." Laughter and cheers peppered the room. "Don't let Akron bully you, us, into letting a piece of our history go to the almighty dollar. Give me the shop. I won't let you down."

The room exploded with shouts and opinions. Haley caught her breath, surprised by the fire building in her gut.

Linus banged his gavel, calling order. "Simmer down, simmer down. Drummond, you're standing. Do you have something to say?"

Haley faced the room, exchanging a curious glance with Cole, seeing Dad and Keith, along with Drummond, on their feet.

"I say let her have it. Give her a chance. Why not? She makes a point. Maybe the mistake was everyone trying to make something of the property other than a wedding shop."

More voices and opinions. Linus called for silence, sending Haley and Brant back to their seats.

Shaking, she moved to sit down, nodding at Dad and Drummond, slapping Keith a high five as Linus gathered his council for an impromptu discussion. Their bowed heads bobbed as Linus talked, hammering the gavel against his palm.

After a moment, the council squared up to the long glossy table. "You're prepared to restore the shop and bring it up to code?"

Ho, boy. "I am."

"Linus, you can't seriously give that money corner to a girl with no means of completing the project." Brant paced like a mad bull.

"Linus," Drummond said. "The city has money for restoration projects. Give her some of that to get her started. Need I remind the council the shop is a Hugh Cathcart Thompson design?"

The council bent together again. Drummond glanced back at her with a knowing nod.

Someone shouted, "Let her have the shop, y'all."

Linus gaveled the meeting into silence. "The council will hand down our decision by the end of the week. Haley, leave us your number. We'll give you a call."

Dad, Drummond, Keith, and a few others gathered around Haley, clapping her on the shoulder, singing her praises.

"You were brilliant." Keith, with his capped-tooth grin. "If they don't give it to you, we'll know how deep they are in Akron's pocket."

"I say this is cause for celebration." Dad drew Haley close in a side hug. "Pie at Ella's? On me. Drummond? Keith?"

"I could eat pie, sure." Haley angled around to see Cole but he was gone. "I'll meet you there."

When she stepped outside to her bike, she checked for Cole again but no sign of him. Did this shop business dredge up memories of Tammy he was trying to forget? Did he truly want the shop turned into a parking lot?

Haley rode the three blocks to Ella's against the

winter wind, going over the meeting in her mind, a quiver of anticipation in her bones.

She hated being at odds with Cole over this—he was her connection to Tammy—but more than ever she knew reopening the wedding shop was something she was born to do.

CHAPTER NINE

COLE

He sat on the end stool at Ella's counter waiting for his burger, knocking the green tinsel still swinging from the bottom of the counter with his knees.

"So how'd the meeting go?" Mom, owner-operator-chief-bottle-washer-and-hostess, dumped a couple of dirty plates in the bin under the counter, scraping a tip into her pocket—which she didn't keep, instead dividing it among the crew.

"Gives them a little bit more to carry home."

"Depends. For Akron, it went okay. For Haley, it went great. She had her stuff together."

Her passion had surprised him. Was that the right word? Surprise? Maybe convicted him. Was he supposed to be for this shop as much as she was? For the town, for their history, for the uniqueness of having a wedding shop founded in 1890? For Tammy?

The cook pushed through the kitchen door, setting Cole's plate in front of him, giving him a slap on the back. "Good to see you."

"You too, Sean."

"So have you decided, then? Go to work for Akron or stay on your own?" Mom leaned against the counter, snatching one of Cole's fries. "Man, Sean knows how to make a mean fry."

"Help yourself." Cole shoved the plate her way. He and Chris spent their teen years sitting in this very spot, doing homework, eating diner food, crawling into one of the booths to play on the Game Boys when the dinner crowd thinned out.

When Cole got his driver's license, Mom finally let them go home after school. But she called every hour. The moment she got home, she checked their homework, trolling through their backpacks to make sure they didn't "forget" to show her their papers or teacher notes.

"I don't know." He sipped his Coke and wrestled with the feeling bubbling in his gut since the meeting. "The Akron money is good, Mom."

"Remember, the love of money is what messed up your dad."

Cole grimaced. "Stealing and forgery are not the same thing as being offered a good job."

"Never said that, but you have to follow your heart too. Don't let the lure of money steer you from what you love."

Reaching for the ketchup, he shot a few squirts over his fries and on his burger. He felt like a traitor. But he didn't owe Haley anything. Or the town. Didn't owe Tammy anything. She'd moved on to a much better place and, dollars to donuts, she wasn't thinking about him, Heart's Bend, or the restoration of an antique town business.

"Well, speaking of," Mom said, "look who just walked in."

Haley with her dad, Keith Niven, and Drummond Branson. Looking like a winner too. She greeted a couple of women at a booth, Taylor and Emma, Drummond's daughters.

Then they decided to move to a larger table and packed in together.

Cole focused on his dinner, feeling like an outsider. A sensation he'd wrestled with since Dad was arrested fifteen years ago.

But he couldn't hold his gaze to his plate. When he glanced up again, Haley was looking at him. She tipped her head for him to join her outside.

Cole covered his plate with his napkin and followed her, but not before asking one of the servers to bring out two cups of hot chocolate—a peace offering, if you will. He grabbed his coat from the rack by the door.

"Hey." Haley met him at the bench out front, her thick hair falling over her shoulders, her nose tipped red from the cold. "Are we at war?"

"War? No. Haley, come on."

"I had to ask."

"Because I sat with Akron?" He joined her on the bench, the dancing red, blue, and green of the Christmas lights blinking colors over their faces.

"Keith said they offered you a job." She dug her hands into her pockets and shouldered against the biting wind.

"They did. For a lot of money."

"Bookoo money?"

"What?"

"Never mind."

"The offer was great. More than I've seen in my career so far. I could go back to sleeping at night."

"Then you should take it." She shivered when the wind cut sharp around the side of the diner. "You have to think of your future."

"My future. Is that you talking or your parents?"

"Me."

When she looked at him he remembered how much he'd always liked Haley. Might have even dated her if Tammy hadn't been between them. Haley was real and fun with an intense edge. Yet so easygoing. She was a beautiful mystery.

"You gave a pretty impassioned speech tonight."

Her smile glittered with the lights. "I surprised myself a little."

The server came out with the hot chocolate, but Haley waved him off. "I don't drink coffee."

"It's hot chocolate." Cole reached for both cups, thanked him, and handed her one.

"Oh, wow, really? Thanks." Haley hugged the cup in her hands. "Everyone is always trying to hand me coffee. I spent six years in the air force saying 'I don't drink coffee' to some of the same people over and over."

"I remembered."

She angled toward him, bumping her shoulder to his. "Thank you." Peeling off the top, she took a gentle first sip, and a silence pulled between them.

"What if they give you the shop?" he said.

"What if they don't?"

"But what if they do?"

"Then I'll make it a gem."

"With your ten grand?"

She laughed. "It's a start." Haley gazed into the shadows. "You know when you're out on your bike and you're driving through town, going the speed limit, stopping for red lights and stop signs?"

"But you want to be on the open road?" Cole sipped his hot chocolate, tending the vibe in her voice.

"Exactly. Opening up and going full throttle, leaning so far into the curves your knee almost touches the ground."

"Is the wedding shop your open road, Haley?"

"Maybe." She took a thoughtful sip of her hot chocolate. "But I feel like I've been driving through small towns with only a few fast-break moments. What I want, I think, is to hit the open road at cruising speed and settle in for a while. College was four years. The air force six, with as many moves. After my first two transfers, I got rid of almost all of my stuff. When I did arrive somewhere, I barely unpacked."

"They'll give you the shop."

She turned to him, the movement releasing a wild but tentative fragrance. "How do you know?"

"Because if they felt anything close to what I felt when you were speaking, they won't be able to say no."

She held her cup with both hands, taking another sip. "I have no idea how to run a wedding shop, but I want to do this. I can feel it in my bones."

"Bones, huh? They rarely lie."

A new Mustang pulled into the parking space in front of the bench with music pressing against the windows. The driver cut the engine and stepped out, walking around to open the door for his date.

"We were that young?" Haley said.

"Hey, come on, we're not *that* old. Please. We're just about to hit cruising speed." But sitting here now, he felt old. Like some part of life had passed him by. The part where he could've been carefree, but instead he carried the burden of being the man in the family. "Don't you want to date? Get married?"

Haley shivered. "Not really." She stared at her cup. "I see myself as that sophisticated businesswoman in town everyone respects and goes to for advice. The auntie of Heart's Bend. I'll drive a cool car even when I'm old and gray, have a house up on the hill, in the old historic district, and buy a ten-foot Christmas tree every year and load it down with presents for all the foster kids."

"So how does this great vision require you to be an old maid?"

"Because I said so. Because I think . . ." She inhaled, shaking her head, a small smile on her lips. "You . . . you start digging and tap my deepest thoughts. It's like you have some kind of superpower."

Cole chuckled. "Not really. Remember, we used to be able to talk. I could always tell you things I couldn't tell Tammy. Like when Dad was finally sentenced, six years after his arrest, I called you." The memory surfaced without his beckoning. "I just finished my sophomore year in college."

"You called me first?"

He ducked his head, picking at the top on his hot chocolate. "I guess it's okay I confess that now." He offered her his hand. "Friends?"

"Of course. Always." Their clasp held for a moment before Haley slipped her hand away, tilting her head toward the diner. "I need to get inside. They'll wonder what happened to me."

"Yeah, I left a great burger on the counter."

"Thanks for the hot chocolate."

Cole held the door for her, waved at her party, and returned to his counter stool. His plate was gone but he didn't care. He was full.

Mom came out of the kitchen. "Oh, there you are. You want your burger? I put it in the oven to keep warm."

Cole nodded. His mama was the best. Sorta like Haley. "Sure, why not."

He peered at Haley's table. She was laughing at something Taylor Gillingham, Drummond's daughter, was saying, looking like the girl he used to observe from his perch at the counter—after school or on college breaks.

He could admit to himself now that Haley had always been the girl out of reach. Not that he didn't love Tammy, he did. But he'd never even let himself consider Haley. It even felt a little like cheating to admit this to himself now.

Did Haley know? How things went with Tammy? If so, why would she be so silent? Surely Haley had something to say about how their relationship died long before cancer ended her life.

. . .

CORA

FOURTH OF JULY

By the first week of July, Cora was ready for some celebration. June had been busy at the shop what with the June brides coming for their final trousseaus.

Rufus had written her weekly through the month, which thrilled her to no end, confirming his love if not his presence, all the while promising a summer visit.

> I long to see you. I can't imagine it's been nearly a year since we were last together. I think of our kisses and how you tasted of strawberries. My favorite. As are you, Cora.

His letters strengthened her, raised her pride as she walked down First Avenue, going about her business. She was a loved woman and she defied anyone to challenge that fact. Her love could not be robbed.

And the Fourth of July was finally here. Rufus or no Rufus, today was a grand day. Daddy and Mama's annual Fourth of July celebration was gearing up on the back five acres of their homestead. Half the town would show up. She'd begged Rufus to come, but he feared his job on the Ohio would keep him away.

"Cora?" Mama came into the kitchen, fresh and pretty in her new pink afternoon dress. She had expanded her style to include puff sleeves. "Will you carry the chocolate cake? Last time I walked across the yard with something in my hands, the Saglimbenis' dog ran right in front of me, and away I went, sprawling. It's like he knew I was defenseless."

"So you'd prefer the dog send me sprawling?" Cora also wore a new dress, yellow with puff sleeves and a lace collar.

"Yes, if you must know, that's my evil plan. To ruin your beautiful dress with the shenanigans of a wild mutt." She made a wry face. "Of course not. The dog seems to mind you. But me he wants to see facedown on the ground."

Cora grinned, taking up the cake plate and following Mama out the back door. It was summer in lovely Heart's Bend. The breeze was gentle, perfumed with sun feed, growing crops, the green hills rolling along the horizon.

The Saglimbeni brothers, along with their crazy dog, set up a pony ride and roped off a section for the children to play games.

Every year Daddy hired a carnie man who brought in a shooting gallery and other games. Word in Heart's Bend was if you wanted a good Fourth of July, get out to the Scotts' place.

Councilman Patz met Cora at the food table. No doubt his laundry-basket belly was eager to be filled with chocolate cake. "Your father's a good man putting on this shindig every year. Saves the town a good bit of money. What do you have there, Cora? A chocolate layer cake?"

"Indeed I do, Mr. Patz." She set the plate on the dessert table.

"You think I might have a small sample?" Hunger echoed in the man's words.

"Of course." Cora set a slice on a chipped plate brought over from the church pantry. "Don't let anyone else see you." She covered the cake, politely shooing him away.

Then she surveyed the party. The sun rested behind the clouds, kind enough to give them a bit of shade, but the sky was blue and the breeze off the river made the temperature pleasant.

Lovely, so very lovely. *Oh, Rufus, I so wish you were here.* She was lovesick.

The lawn stretched out toward Mama's garden, then around the trees toward the river where tonight Captain Alderman of the Heart's Bend Fire Department would light up the night sky with fireworks.

"Cora, woo hoo, Cora." Odelia shuffled toward her, waving her hand in the air. She and her band of wedding shop seamstresses had exceeded everyone's expectations. Since the June bombardment of orders, the women had completed fifty of the orders.

"Slow down, Odelia. Look at you, all flushed."

"I just saw Miss Maddie Crum." Miss Crum was a bride from the spring getting married later this month, come all the way from Murfreesboro. "She's in town and wants to pick up her wedding dress if it's ready."

"What? Today? Is it ready?"

"Thank the Lord I finished it last night. She said she'd meet me there—" Odelia pressed her hand to her heart. "Oh my word, I can't draw a clean breath."

"Sit, sit, please." Cora led her to a semicircle of wooden lawn chairs. Across the way, an army of women marched four abreast toward the food table, plates and dishes in hand. No one in Heart's Bend ate any better than they did on the Fourth of July.

On the Fourth, they were all free. One people. Not rich or poor. Not black or white. Not young or old. Just Americans grateful for their independence—however limited and troubled.

"I can't believe I just ran all the way from downtown."

"You ran from downtown?" Cora said. "That's over two miles."

"Don't look so shocked. I played basketball in high school." Odelia fanned her face with her hands, her breathing growing steady. "I thought you could drive me back into town."

"Odelia, surely she doesn't need her dress today. It's a holiday."

"I know, but I promised her. It's over a two-hour drive from their place. I hate to see her have to come back because we couldn't spare a few minutes to get her dress. Consider it good customer service." Odelia made her case with sweat trickling down her cheeks.

"All right, you win." Cora caught hold of little Claire Olinski as she ran past. "Claire, get Mrs. Darnell an iced tea." She peered down at Odelia, still catching her breath, reclining in the lawn chair. "You rest. I'll *drive* to the shop to meet Miss Crum myself."

"You're a peach, Cora. I don't care what your mama says."

Cora headed for the house, smiling as Claire sloshed tea over the side of a tall glass, her pink tongue sticking out of her mouth.

Inside, Cora gathered her pocketbook, keys, and driving gloves. She shouldn't be more than twenty minutes. She'd barely miss the fun. Most folks were still arriving.

She paused in the hallway, voices billowing, pressing from behind a closed door. Daddy and Mama's room.

Suddenly the door flung open and Daddy burst into the hall with Mama trailing after. "No, Ernest, no. I just don't see the need." Mama stopped short when she saw Cora. "Cora, what is it?"

"Is everything all right?"

"Why, of course. It's the Fourth of July," Daddy said. "What do you need, sugar?"

"I'm going to the shop. Odelia promised Miss Crum she could pick up her dress."

"On a holiday?"

"They're in town and thought if the dress was ready it'd save them the trip."

"Well, invite them out," Daddy said. "Invite them out."

"I best see to our guests." Mama pressed around Daddy, smoothing her hair in place. He watched her, his wide smile not reaching his eyes.

"Daddy?" Cora said.

"Everything's good, darling." He kissed her cheek. "Get that worried look off your pretty face." He stepped through to the kitchen, whistling "God Bless America," wearing a pair of light wool knickers with knee socks, glossy brown shoes, and a vest over his short-sleeve white shirt. To mark the occasion, he wore a bright red tie.

Mama popped out from the kitchen, a platter of hardboiled eggs in her hand. "Hurry on now so you can come back for the opening prayer. Reverend Oliver from the colored church is giving the invocation this year."

"I'll be back in a jiff. I promise." Cora stepped outside, then turned back, a swirl in her middle. They were fighting again. But about what? Mama sounded worn-out.

At thirty, Cora had to admit that their fighting bothered her nearly as much as when she was a kid. A twinge of panic seeped from her thoughts into her bones and even the heat of the sun resting on her shoulders couldn't reach the chill.

It's nothing. Daddy assured her. Just a lover's quarrel. She was an adult now and surely understood marriage came with its struggles. Her parents were, after all, human.

Moving down the front walk, she saw her car was blocked in by a row of cars lining the road. "Of all things." The south lawn was designated for parking, as well as the road.

"Need a lift?"

Cora jerked around to see Birch pulling up in his wagon, hitched to his mule, Uncle Sam.

"Are you spying on me, Birch Good?" She squeezed between the cars, meeting Birch in the road, stroking Uncle Sam's soft nose. "How are you, old boy?"

"He's fit as a fiddle. I figured it was clever of me to bring him out on such an occasion as this." Birch motioned to her handbag. "You need to go somewhere? I can drive you."

"Birch, could you? Odelia made an appointment with a customer—"

"On the Fourth?"

"Yes, and let's not run through that rigmarole again." At the buckboard, she offered her hand. Birch clasped onto it, a cord of muscle twisting down his tanned arm, easing her up and onto the seat next to him. Just like that, her peace returned. Mama and Daddy would be fine. Of course. Why be blue when today was the Fourth? A happy day.

Birch chirruped to the mule. "I had to enter Uncle Sam in the buggy race this year. Have to defend our title. First place four years running."

"You and your races."

"They're fun."

"You just like to win."

"Guilty as charged."

Cora glanced sideways at him. The wind tossed his dark brown hair over his forehead, creating a contrast for the pale blueness of his eyes. His jaw was firm, like it could take a solid punch.

He'd forgone his overalls for his church trousers today, and a white oxford with pale yellow stains under the arms. If he had a wife, she'd take some bluing to that thing and straighten it out. But it was clean, and the scent of soap and aftershave wafted from his skin.

"What?" he said, catching her staring, a saucy grin popping on his full lips.

"Nothing." The steam of embarrassment straightened her around, facing forward, and concentrating on the motion of Uncle Sam. What was it about Birch that made her flush and blush? Silliness, really. He had a way about him, that's all. Half the girls in town dropped their jaws when he passed by. But did he notice? No. Not one blame time.

"Sure didn't *look* like nothing."

She pursed her lips and squared her shoulders. "Just haven't seen you in your Sunday clothes is all."

"You see me every week. In Sunday school."

"I guess I never noticed."

"Well, how-do, if that don't warm a fella's heart." Birch turned Uncle Sam onto South Broad and headed to town.

"Well, it's not like you notice me."

"Every week, Cora. Every week."

They exchanged a curt glance and she slid an inch away from him. What else was she to do with such a confession? If he had intentions for her other than friendship, she'd do well *not* to encourage him.

South Broad ended at First Avenue, which bustled with cars cruising through around the square, overflowing with teenagers and the like. Flags flew from the shops and lamp poles.

A convertible Model T eased past, a gaggle of young men and women clinging to the sides, laughing, waving, singing "My Country Tis of Thee" at the top of their lungs.

"Makes me feel old." Birch motioned to them with his chin, pulling up to the wedding shop. "Like I never got a chance to be young. Went to war when I should've been cutting up in a Model T with my friends."

"The war aged us all, Birch."

"These kids don't know. War won't ever come to them."

"We can only pray that's true."

He pulled up to the shop, hopped out, and walked around Uncle Sam to help Cora down. Another car of young ones glided past with cute Smithy Fetterman behind the wheel, slowing down to whistle at a young woman with a flouncy skirt and heeled sandals.

Here Cora stood on the side of the street with sensible shoes and a condemning heart. She'd missed her day to ride around in an open car, singing at the top of her lungs.

Has life passed me by?

"Well, hello, beautiful, I was just on my way to find you."

Cora whirled around at the sound of *his* voice, her heart booming in her chest. "Rufus!" She was in his arms, pressed against him as his vice grip raised her up and twirled her around. "I can't believe it. I can't believe it. You're here. Oh, darling, my darling . . ." She trembled against him, a freight train of sobs controlling her so she couldn't breathe.

"Shh, I'm here. I'm here. I've got you." He wrapped his arms tighter and tighter.

Cora clung to him, fearing he might vanish or that

this was just a dream and she'd wake up any moment.
"I-I can't believe . . . I cán't . . . Darling, oh my Rufus."

"There, there, why all the tears? Shh, my sweet
Cora, hush." His warm breath blew against her ear and
fanned the energy of her emotion.

She slid to the ground, her face pinned to his chest,
weeping, her fists gripping the loose sides of his blouse.
"Rufus, Rufus . . ."

"I told you I'd come."

"Yes, but, darling . . ." Her words had no power, no
real tone. She was weak from letting her soul go into
his arms. Fresh tears built behind her eyes as her heart
ached with joy and relief.

She shimmied as she cried, no awareness of anything but the block of man against which she leaned,
the scent of pipe smoke and a thick, fragrant masculine
scent that reminded her of the sea more than the river.

"Darling, are we to stand here all day?"

She nodded with a slight chortle, wiping her cheeks
with her hand. She must be a sight.

"I've been dying for a kiss," he said in her ear for her
and her alone.

Cora tried to lift her head but she couldn't move.
She was wobbly from releasing a year of tension, of all
the strength she'd mustered to hang on and believe.

"All right, we'll stand here." He gathered her to himself, kissing her cheek, resting his chin on her head. "So
I guess I don't have to ask if you're surprised to see me."

Cora sputtered a laugh, the ballast to her sobs.
"Oh, Rufus, I can't imagine a more glorious surprise."
She inhaled him, memorizing the curves of his chest

beneath her face, the rough, strong edge of his scent, the feel of his breath in her ear, and the resonating bass in his voice. "I'm so very happy to see you."

"Cora, my beautiful Cora." Rufus clung to her. "I was in St. Louis for the holiday and found it my fortune to hop a packet coming this way."

"You came? Just for me?"

"Just for you." He stepped back, cupping her face in his hands, smoothing his thumbs over her tear stains. "I've missed you."

He bent toward her. Not caring who looked on, Cora rose up on her toes, hungry, *aching* for his kiss to fill her, energize her, and burn away her sensibilities. He loved her and she'd field no doubt or discouragement from anyone, including her own heart, from here on out.

But his kiss was sweet. Tentative. Why was he spoon-feeding her milk when she was starving for the bread of his passion?

Cora gripped his shoulders, holding on, pouring her heart into his kiss. In the distance, she heard a car horn and the whistles of passersby. She didn't care. Let the town talk. She refused to let him go, kissing him as a woman in love, willing to completely give herself to him. If only he'd ask.

Then he responded, his breath a sensual rhythm as his kiss found her again and again, declaring his own hunger.

When they broke apart, she was unable to stand, let alone move toward the shop. "Darling," she whispered. "I love you so much."

Rufus rewarded her with his swashbuckling smile, tapping his forehead to hers and blessing her with another kiss. "And I you, dearest Cora." He released her but she clung to his arm. "So, now tell me." He touched the end of her nose with his finger. "What are you doing in town on the Fourth of July? I thought the Scotts had a great party on their property."

"Yes, we do. Oh, wait until you see it. Everyone is there. I came into town to meet a customer. You can blame Odelia for that. She promised Miss Crum she could pick up her dress." Cora took a step for the shop, still clinging to Rufus, when she remembered Birch. She stopped, spinning around. "Oh, darling, this is Birch Good. A friend of my father's."

But he was gone and Uncle Sam along with him. "Well, how do you like that?" She turned back to Rufus. "I'll have to pinch myself to believe you're really here." She squeezed his arm. "Are you real? My heart is all aflutter in my chest."

"This heart? Right here?" Rufus tapped his finger in the V of her dress, between her breasts, igniting a flame.

"Rufus, please. We're in public." But the sensation was intoxicating. Weakening her resistance. She wanted his kisses, his touches, and everything that came with loving a man.

"Let's go inside, then." He led her to the shop, taking the key from her hand and working the lock. "What's this you're about? You said meeting a customer?"

"She's coming by for her wedding gown any minute." Cora retrieved her keys from his hand, her whole being tingling when his fingers brushed her palm.

He kicked the door closed behind him and they were alone in the hot, stale shop, away from the curious eyes of First Avenue.

"The light switch . . . It's right over here." Cora motioned to the wall just inside the small salon. They were alone. Completely alone. She was thrilled while trembling with terror.

As she reached to snap on the light, Rufus snatched her around, pressing her against the wall. "My darling, you're so lovely." He lowered to kiss her neck.

Cora fell into him, leaning on his massive arms to stay upright. His lips, fiery and silky, burned along her collarbone.

"Rufus . . . darling . . . th-they'll . . . be . . . here." She swooned and he swept her up into his arms, his lips finding hers, each kiss more ardent than the last.

"Forgive me, but for the life of me I can't remember why I delayed seeing you for so long." He lowered her feet to the floor, his hand running gently down her side. If this was love's passion, may it never end.

"Here . . ." He pulled a glistening gold trinket from his pocket. "Ten karats. For you."

"Oh, Rufus, you shouldn't have." The chain with a heart-shaped pendant rested against her palm and her heart sank a little. Was this his proposal? Was he not offering a ring of some kind? Not every man did, but . . .

Rufus turned her around, brushed her hair aside ever so slowly with his kisses, and clasped the piece around her neck. "Let me see. Yes, very fine indeed. I saw it when I was in New York. Tiffany's."

"You were in New York! You never said."

"I had it inscribed. 'My darling Cora.' See?"

She peered into his blue eyes for a long moment. "I see all I need right now. You, Rufus. You."

He gathered her to him, letting his passionate kiss be his reply.

"Darling." Cora leaned back. "Did you get the postcard I enclosed in my letter? From a Miriam? She seemed desperate to talk to you." He'd not mentioned it in any of his letters. "Who is she?" She kept her tone soft, inquiring, far away from accusation.

"What?" His eyes searched hers. "Miriam? What are you—Oh, Miriam. Yes, the wife of a mate. She wanted to surprise him for his birthday. It was nothing."

"Nothing?"

"Come now, I want to kiss you, not talk of other women." His lips brushed hers as his arms drew tight around her.

"Yoo hoo, Miss Cora?" The front door's pealing chimes shot them apart. Rufus, gasping for air, a lock of his blond hair dashing over his brow, disappeared in the shadows of the small salon, tucking his shirttail into his trousers.

Shaking as if doused with cold river water, Cora steadied herself before coming around the small salon wall. Between the passion of her tears and the passion of Rufus's kisses, she had no idea of her appearance. She tucked her hair into place, well aware of the perspiration clotting along the collar of her dress.

"Miss Crum, do come in." Cora stood aside as the women entered, so grateful for the breeze. It barely cooled her hot skin and did nothing to quell her lover's embers.

"Miss Cora, thank you so much for meeting us." Maddie Mae Crum greeted Cora with a hug. "I'm so delighted Odelia had my dress ready. Oh, your skin is hot as blazes."

"Your cheeks are all red." Mrs. Crum gave Cora the prune face once over. "Sunburn? Take care this afternoon. Don't want that pretty skin of yours all red and blistered."

"Thank you. Of course. How kind of you, Mrs. Crum." Cora exhaled, trying not to laugh but relieved to keep her secret.

"Oh, your shop is just darling. I say that every time, don't I?" Miss Crum peeked into the small salon. Cora scooted around in front of her, blocking her view in case Rufus was sitting in the corner chair by the window. "We're so busy at the farm we can hardly get to town. This is such a treat." The Crums were middle Tennessee farmers, and Miss Crum ordered her dress through the *Modern Priscilla*. "Where are all the dresses?"

"Here, in the big salon. Just a few samples." Cora escorted Miss Crum to the grand salon, where her carefully selected gowns hung on dress forms and mannequins. "I'm sorry I have no refreshments for you, but please be seated."

"Oh no, not at all. We understand we're infringing on your time."

"I'll get your gown."

"Are these the stairs the brides come down when

they try on their dresses? I heard about it from a friend."
Miss Crum did not stay seated as Cora directed.

Cora stopped halfway up the stairs. "Y-yes, it is."

"Oh, please, do you think I could try on my dress
and come down the stairs? Mama's here . . . and you."
Miss Crum's brown eyes sparked with excitement. "It
would mean the world to me."

"Me as well." Mrs. Crum stepped forward. "I didn't
have a wedding myself, and I'm sure glad Maddie Mae
is getting her day."

Cora sighed but held on to her smile. "Then she
must make her way down the stairs in her gown. I'm
sorry it's so warm in here." She descended the stairs,
reaching for the window, tugging down the top pane.

"Never you mind. I'll crack a few windows and raise
the lights while you get Maddie Mae all duded up."
Mrs. Crum set her pocketbook in the chair by the large
display window and started off, opening windows as
Cora's heart trumpeted, *Rufus, hide.*

"Go on up, Miss Crum. I'll be along in a jiffy." Cora
peeked in the small salon. Empty. Where did he go?
She checked the pantry and the powder room. Empty.
The closet? No, he was gone. Through the mudroom,
Cora peeked out the back door. Rufus stood against a
tree, smoking his pipe, winking at her when she caught
his eye. She held up her hand. *Five minutes.* He nodded,
blowing her a kiss.

Well, in that case, four minutes.

Cora dashed up to the mezzanine, where Miss
Crum waited, and helped her out of her dress. Just
knowing Rufus was waiting fed the thick thunder of

her pulse. *Focus, Cora. Customers are the lifeblood of your business.*

But oh, Rufus was finally here.

When she had Miss Crum snapped and buttoned into her gown, Cora snatched a veil from the closet and pinned it to her head. Then raced down the stairs, put a record on the Victrola, and joined her mother in the grand salon.

"Come on down, Miss Crum."

"I think I'm going to cry." Mrs. Crum dabbed a wrinkled handkerchief under her eyes. "Look, isn't she beautiful?"

"She most certainly is."

"Are you married, Miss Cora?"

"Not yet."

"Well, look what awaits you. Maddie Mae, I declare Norbert's eyes are going to pop out of his head and roll down the altar."

Cora observed the mother and daughter scene, letting them have their moment, sure as shooting convinced that Rufus *must* propose to her tonight. Their passion, rare and beautiful, only intensified with each meeting. Surely he could delay no longer.

And when he bent to one knee and asked for her hand, she would declare "Yes!" with every fiber of her being.

CHAPTER TEN

Birch

At high noon, Birch sat on his buckboard, letting Uncle Sam graze, a heaping plate of food in his hand. Best food in the county. Made by the best cooks. Collard greens, butter beans, black-eyed peas, corn on the cob, cornbread, pickled eggs and beets. Roasted pork, beef, and chicken. Pies and cakes of every kind.

However, none of it appealed. Not even the demanding rumble of his stomach could rouse his taste buds or his desire to eat.

Instead, he chomped on the image of Cora in the arms of that big riverboat *billboard*, kissing him in broad daylight like she was some kind of nighttime floozy.

Her brazenness made him boil with anger—no, *disgust*—all the way back to the Scott homestead. So much so he plum near went straight home, foregoing the celebration, the food, the good company to sulk all alone.

But no! If she was so rude as to ignore him that-a-way,

why let it spoil his celebration? He'd been looking forward to this picnic all year.

Who was he kidding? He looked forward to seeing Cora anytime he could clap eyes on her. He wanted to side with her in the three-legged race, hear her laugh in his ear, see how the sun caught the auburn shine in her chestnut hair.

All right. Be honest. What he felt in his gut wasn't anger or disgust, but pure, sinful jealousy.

So if he went home, he'd be letting jealousy win. Letting his emotions take control, and Birch refused. If he learned anything from his pa, it was to control his emotions. Sit right down on them. Not let his heart rule his head.

If Cora preferred that river jockey, hats off to her. She'd not see Birch standing on the shore pining for her.

"Birch Good, what are you doing sitting out here all by your lonesome? Look at that, your plate is full." Janice Pettrey leaned on his knee, gazing up at him from the ground, her perfume clogging his nostrils, her blonde hair bouncing over her shoulder. "I made my famous pecan pie."

"You know how I love your pie. Just not as hungry as I thought."

"Since when is Birch Good not hungry? Wanetta Cash, can you believe Birch has not yet cleaned his plate?"

"What's a matter, Birchy, something upset your tummy?" Wanetta stretched to tickle his belly but he batted her hand away.

"I told you not to call me Birchy."

Wanetta hoisted up her skirt—showing the clip of her girdle holding on to her stocking—climbed up the wagon wheel, and plopped down on the buckboard. He glanced away, feeling his cheeks run red.

"Birch, come on, I was just having some fun with you. Janice, run round to the other side and hop up. Birch, slide my way, give her room."

"You always this bossy?"

"Now, how long you known me? Since kindie-garden? I bossed you round then too. There, Janice, limber as a cat."

Janice curled against Birch, but not because she didn't have enough room. The soft curve of her breast pressed his arm and his pulse snapped like a fire-cracker. He scooted a little closer to Wanetta, though that notion scared the what's-it out of him too.

"Who you going to sit with during the fireworks tonight?" Janice said.

"I reckon ole Uncle Sam here will need some com-forting." Birch pointed his fork at his mule. "He don't much like big noises."

"Then Janice and I will keep you company," Wanetta said.

As if he understood—and Birch believed he did—Uncle Sam raised his nose with a *hee-haw*, tossing his head, stamping his feet.

The girls laughed. "Uncle Sam, we're excited too."

Birch peeked a gander at Janice. She was nothing like Wanetta. Pretty. Sweet. Petite figure. A teacher over at the elementary school. He liked her company. They had a good talk after Sunday-night Bible study once about the preeminence of Christ. He'd never heard such a thing until she started spouting her high-brow doctrinal understanding.

He chewed on their conversation for a month, searching the Scriptures, finding it to be true. Christ was righteous, excellent, and first in all things. He didn't bow to no one. Everyone bowed to Him. Yet He went on to die for the whole world anyway.

The girls were laughing about something and Birch dug into his dinner, suddenly a might hungry now that he had the good fortune to sit with two pretty ladies.

Not that he had a lot of experience with the fairer sex. Didn't have no sisters. Worked the farm after school since he was old enough to walk behind a plow. Farming was in his blood.

The only sport he played was football because Dad let him off his chores every fall. Which Coach appreciated.

"Birch is one of the toughest offensive tackles I've ever seen."

But Birch adored the fairer sex, and maybe it was time to get on with selecting a wife.

The girls chatted and little by little drew him into the conversation, sharing town gossip, wondering who was next to jump the broom.

"I can't wait to have my turn at the wedding shop. I've been going by those front windows every Saturday since the cow jumped over the moon, just dreaming for my own day," Janice said.

"Well, what gal hasn't?" Wanetta sat up straighter, fluffing the hem of her skirt. "My aunt Pam married when I was six, and even though she had a small wedding at my grandparents' home, she bought her dress and trousseau at the wedding shop. From Miss Jane. Mama took me with her once for a fitting and that was all she wrote. My daddy was on the hook for a fancy wedding dress and a trousseau."

Birch chewed, glad his mouth was full of food. Otherwise he might just ask what they'd think of the shop if they knew Cora was making love with the riverboat captain right there in broad daylight.

"What do you think, Birch? You ever been to the wedding shop?"

"Janice, what business would Birch have at the wedding shop?" Wanetta waved her off, laughing softly.

"I've been." He cleared his throat, reaching for a cold tin of water. "Helped Cora out a time or two."

"See there, Wanetta. That's the kind of man he is."

Birch still found talking to women a strange venture. Except when he was around Cora. It was like something broke inside. He became free, remembering all kinds of jokes and stories, wanting to talk about his life. He loved to listen to her, all the while longing to be her strong man. Yet she never saw it. And he never figured a way to make her see it.

"When are you going to settle down, Birch?" Janice held no reserve and marched right over his private ground.

"When I find the right girl." *Or when she realizes I'm the right man.*

"When you find the right girl?" Wanetta touched his chin, turning his face to hers. "Look around, Farmer

Good. You got two of Heart's Bend's finest right here. Ready and willing."

"Are you saying you're in love with me?" He guffawed. "That's a good one, Wanetta."

"Fine. Maybe I'm not, but I'd like a chance to try. So would Janice."

"Wanetta, please, leave him be."

What could he say? *I've loved Cora Scott since she dunked me in the river when she was fourteen.* He'd been nineteen at the time, horsing around with her brother, EJ. Not knowing in a few years they'd be off to war.

Anyway, next thing he knew, Cora had him facedown in the current. He laughed about it now and it was his favorite memory of her. He knew her will and strength that day. Maybe that's why seeing her with the captain killed him on the inside. If Cora Scott decided for him, weren't nothing going to turn her back till she won him.

But he had to forget her. For now. "How about a piece of your famous pecan pie, Janice?"

He stood, ready to jump to the ground, when a blasting horn blew against him. He whipped around with a start, seeing a convertible Model T pull up, depositing Cora and the riverboat captain onto the Scotts' back lawn.

She stumbled out, laughing, her neat hair wild and mussed, coming free from the bobby pins. The captain caught her, his hand tight around her waist, riding high and intimate under her breast.

Birch stepped over the buckboard to the back of the wagon. "Everything all right, Cora?"

"Birch, where did you go?" Her eyes drifted from Birch to the women sitting with him. "Janice, Wanetta, what are you two doing?"

"Keeping Birch company while he eats his dinner."

"I turned to look for you, Birch, but you'd gone." Cora stepped toward them, her gaze on him, but Rufus held tight to her waist.

"Didn't seem to be needed no longer." A sour swirl launched in his belly and he wished he'd not eaten so much barbecue. "Anyway, the girls and I are going to watch the fireworks show together."

"That's right, and I'm Uncle Sam's date." Wanetta stretched forward to slap the mule's hindquarters. The old beast raised his head with a *hee-haw* and pawed the ground.

Janice's soft twitter tickled Birch and he couldn't help but join her laugh. And the joke. "She and Janice flipped for it. Janice lost. Got stuck with me."

Wanetta laughed, popping her knee, and Cora broke into a slow, confused smile. "Funny." Her gaze locked with Birch's, but he couldn't discern what she was saying behind those golden-hazel eyes.

"Nice to see you all, but Cora, darling, I'm starved." The captain lifted her off the ground and her laugh resurrected the jealousy Birch thought he'd conquered.

"He's so handsome." Janice sighed as Cora walked away with her man.

"What?" Birch sat down hard down on the buckboard. "That slimeball riverboat captain?"

"Jealous, Birch?" Wanetta said, nudging him with her elbow.

He shoved her away. "No."

"Yeah, well, I see the way you look at her every Sunday, and if you ask me, she's perfect for that *slimeball*, doing you the way she does, ignoring how you feel."

Birch peeked at his bossy friend, their eyes meeting on the plane of understanding and truth. "Well, it's hard to fight a riverboat Douglas Fairbanks."

"You can do better. Look, you have the two of us."

"Yeah," Birch said. "But one of you is dating my mule."

. . .

HALEY

JANUARY 15

Friday morning Haley got a call from Linus Peabody, asking her to meet him at the city manager's office at ten o'clock.

She headed over on her Harley, the wind cutting through her winter gear like a knife through butter. Riding the bike had always been a good way to clear her head after a fight with Dax. Or some other disappointment.

Like when she left the air force. The bike became her companion, her anchor, when she drove to visit friends in Texas, then on to Florida.

But now that she was home in Heart's Bend, in the dead of winter, the bike felt more like an albatross. A reminder of her foolishness.

"Haley, come on in." Linus opened the door before

she could knock. "Thanks for coming my way. I have several meetings I can't get out of, and I thought you'd want to hear our decision."

She inched toward his desk, waiting, her heart pulsing.

"Well, young lady, congratulations, you're the owner of 143 First Avenue." Linus dangled a set of keys from his hand. "These were the ones Keith Niven had, and be warned they're the only set."

Haley reached for the keys, smiling. "You're giving me the shop? I mean, really giving me the shop? What's the catch?"

"Yes, we're giving you the shop. Frankly, I wanted to side with Akron, but the others wanted to side with you. I got an earful from my favorite aunt about this business too. She bought her trousseau from Miss Cora and is adamant the tradition should go on for the young women of Heart's Bend if someone is willing to reopen the old place."

"I can't believe it . . ." Haley tightened her fist around the keys, pressing the hard metal into her palm. "I-I won't let you down." By the grace of God she wouldn't. "Do I have to sign something?"

She glanced at his desk, searching for papers, a deed, something.

"We're holding the deed until our requirements are met."

Ah, the catch. "Which are?"

"You know we've been burned on this space before, so we have a few conditions. We want to see renovations started within the month. We want the renovations to be completed within three months. So the clock starts ticking on the first of February. By May first, the renovations should be complete. By June fifteenth, we want the business open."

"Seems like a rather strict timeline. What's my chain of appeal if things go wrong?"

"Your appeal is to the council, but I can tell you, any tomfoolery and we'll repossess the shop with all your renovations. We're *giving* you a building, forgiving back taxes. We want to see a show of confidence from you. We're taking a chance, and for once we're going to be in control of how and when it gets done. If you fail, we take the shop back with no refund to your renovation expenses. If you succeed and stay in business for a year, you'll get the deed with our blessing."

Haley sighed, making a face. "But you're giving me a project that costs lots of money and very little time to raise the capital."

Linus relaxed against his desk and Haley thought he might have been a handsome man at one time. But he had a permanent frown between his eyes, making him appear angry. "Then I suggest you get busy. If you succeed, then you have a business for the cost of a renovation and inventory. If you don't, we will feel free and clear to sell to Akron." He arched his brow. "Akron would kill for this property."

"Metaphorically speaking."

"Of course, metaphorically speaking. We're not writing a murder-mystery here."

"What about permits and fees? Do I get a break there? What if the city jams me up about something?"

She didn't like getting jammed up. She dealt with that enough in the air force. But she'd been put on tighter timelines than this to get a job done, with way more red tape. And succeeded. The town council had met their match. Hopefully.

"The fees are nominal." He leaned toward her. "This is a more than fair offer, Miss Morgan. As for permits, standard wait time. Two to three weeks. I'd get going on those now. As I said, the clock starts ticking on the first of February."

"Thank you." Haley squeezed her fist in the air, showing her determination. "I won't let y'all down."

Somewhere beneath her jeans and leather jacket lived the remnants of Captain Haley Morgan, who ran an exemplary logistics unit in the middle of a war zone. Who barked down a colonel when he demanded a part for his private-use vehicle, refusing to let him run roughshod over regulations because he outranked her. The woman who could relocate at a moment's notice, who could literally pack up her entire life in an hour.

She wanted this shop to succeed more than going to homecoming with Brandon Lutz in eleventh grade, more than getting into the University of Tennessee, more than graduating at the top of her OCS class, more than making captain. More than Dax—who captured her heart with his first hello.

"So this is a yes?" Linus said, standing. "Because I do have a nice bonus for you." He retrieved a legal envelope from his credenza. "There was some money in the city reserve for various projects. Some of the money Drummond Branson mentioned." He handed her the envelope. "This should help you get started. But it's a loan. You have to pay back the city. Read over the paperwork, and if you want to cash that check, bring everything back signed and notarized."

Haley peeked under the envelope flap. "Twenty thousand dollars?"

"That ought to get you started."

Haley stuck out her hand. "Thank you, thank you, thank you."

"Well, all righty then." Stiff and formal, he endured her enthusiastic handshake.

"I'll bring the papers back later. Y'all won't regret this, Mr. Peabody."

"Make sure we don't."

Outside in the cold, she tossed her head back in a silent scream, stamping and giggling. *Thank You, Jesus, thank You, Jesus.*

In the midst of her joy, she heard the tick-tock of the council's timeline. She dug her phone from her pocket and dialed Cole.

"I got the shop."

"What?"

"Did I stutter? I got the shop. The town gave it to me."

"Gave? Wow, okay. What did they say?"

"Linus gave me a boatload of conditions." Haley outlined the town council's stipulations, ending with, "But they gave me twenty grand to get started."

"Nice, but barely a spit in the bucket, Haley. You need about another eighty, if not more."

"Hey, dark cloud, don't rain on my sunshine.

Twenty grand ought to be enough to get me started, right? I'm going over to Downtown Mutual to see if I can get a loan."

"Congratulations."

"So, you in with me? I need a contractor." She heard the clink of dishes in the background and the collective murmur of diner voices.

"Haley, I know what you're going to say and—"

"Then don't say it. Are you at Ella's? Don't leave. I'm on my way. Let me plead my case."

She snapped on her helmet and tucked the check with the paperwork inside her saddlebag. Cole could huff and puff all he wanted, but he was going to help her. Surely the ping vibrating through her when he was around would fade once she got used to him. It was inspired by nothing more than a girlish infatuation with the way his blue eyes seemed to glow when he looked at her. See? What a dreamer. But he had to help her. If he didn't do it for Haley, maybe he'd do it for Tammy. In her memory and honor. Their mutual love for her had to count for something.

Besides all of that, he was the only one she trusted to do the job.

The waitress Jasmine met her at the door, her hair half blue and half pink.

"Hey, Jasmine, I'm looking for Cole."

"He's at the counter. Where he always sits."

Haley dropped onto the stool next to him. "Hey."

"I'm not changing my mind. Let me eat my breakfast in peace." He jammed his fork into a big plate of lettuce and salad trimmings.

"You're eating salad for breakfast? Are you on a diet?"

"Needing some greens and trying to cut back some. With Chris and Cap home for Christmas, all we ate was pizza and cookies."

"Haley, well, how-do. My counter just got a might prettier." Tina came in from the kitchen, setting an ice cream float in front of Cole. "What can I get you, darling?"

She nodded at Cole's ice cream float. "This is how you cut back?"

"I said I ate too much pizza and cookies. Didn't say anything about ice cream."

"You tell him, girl," Tina said. "I'm just glad to get some lettuce and tomato in him."

"The town council gave Haley the old wedding shop, Mom." Cole rammed a forkful of lettuce into his mouth.

"Good for you! Is Cole going to be your contractor? He's good at his job. Really good."

"So I hear. But seems he has other plans." Haley snatched one of his tomatoes and he slid the plate over to her, reaching for his float. "Will you be my contractor?"

"Not if I go to work for Akron."

Tina backed away, grabbed the coffeepots, and headed out to the floor.

"Will you help me, please? This is an unbelievable opportunity. Dream of a lifetime. If you won't do it for me, do it for Tammy."

He held up his hand. "Just stop." He swiveled around, facing her. "I wasn't going to say anything, Haley, but

I don't think Tammy wanted to open the old wedding shop. She never even talked about it."

"That's not true. She talked about it. With me." Well, sometimes. Not so much once they got to college. Even less when Haley joined the air force, but it had been, always was, their plan. "We pinky promised."

"Pinky promised?" Cole made a face. "I don't even know what that means." He gripped his root beer float without taking a drink. "Look, I don't mean to hurt your feelings, but there's no currency here between you, me, Tammy, and this wedding shop. I'm sorry, Haley."

"Just because she never said anything to you doesn't mean she changed her mind. Maybe she thought it was for later in our lives. All I know is we promised each other we were going to open the shop. She died, but that—" She hated the burn of tears. Always had. Especially in front of boys.

Cole slipped his hand over hers. "Yeah, she died. So why do you feel so obligated? Even marriage vows end at 'death do we part.'"

His hand was firm and warm. She wanted to pull away but found his touch inspired the same sensation as the night at the shop. "Because . . ." She swallowed, gently pulling her hand free. "I have to keep our promise, Cole. I can't explain it, but the shop . . . I've always felt an odd connection to that place. Like we belonged together."

He released her, turning around, facing forward. "The job with Akron means I don't have to worry about money anymore, Haley."

"How are you going to sleep when I fail because you

didn't help me? When the corner of First and Blossom is an ugly parking lot?"

Cole drank from his float glass, then stirred the ice cream in with the soda. "I can give you some names of excellent contractors. Gomez Sanchez for one. I can't take my guys with me to Akron, so they'll be free to work for you."

"But I don't know what I'm doing. And I don't know them. You I know and trust." The ping she felt for him earlier, and the warmth of his touch, was beginning to fade.

"I'm taking the Akron job." He peered over at her, his blue gaze unapologetic.

"Fine, but can you meet me this afternoon? Let me know *in detail* what I need to do? Not a verbal list, but a written one with dollar amounts. Bring this Gomez character around and let me meet him."

"I can do that." Cole took out his phone. "Calling Gomez now."

Haley slipped off the stool and leaned toward him. "But I still want you."

CHAPTER ELEVEN

CORA

S he walked through the trees on the back acres of the homestead to think, kicking fallen leaves out of her way.

Back at the house, Mama and the aunts were in the kitchen, laughing, cutting up cakes and pies for dessert, brewing coffee.

The men, gathered on the front porch, sipping port and puffing on cigars, debated college football and whether the Vanderbilt Commodores would defeat the Maryland Terps this weekend.

In the side yard, the younger boys actually played the sport, tossing the football about, shouting, "Touchdown!"

Breaking into a clearing, Cora lifted her face to the gray sky, breathing in the fine molecules of the cool, crisp breeze. Down the embankment, the Cumberland sauntered along a lazy current around the bend and Cora faced the west, longing for him.

It'd been almost five months since he surprised her for the Fourth. Since she tasted the passion of his kisses. Since she heard the huskiness in his voice. Since she felt his arms about her.

She quick-like brushed her tears from her cheeks as anger brewed beneath her breast with a mixture of disappointment and longing. She was back to clinching, willing herself to hang on, believing, waiting.

He promised to see her again, and sooner or later Rufus kept his promises. But how long could she go on, a mature woman of thirty, only seeing the man she loved twice a year?

Back at the house, the rooms overflowed with friends and family, cozy around Mama's large table.

It'd been a good day, hearing the sound of familiar voices and laughter. Cora's heart brimmed with the love of family. All the while aching for the love of her man. She wanted Rufus St. Claire at their table today. She'd invited him. He said he'd try.

Cora dealt with her disappointment honorably enough. Even fielded Aunt Dinah's frank, nosy questions about her marriage plans.

"Wait too long and all you're gonna get is the old men and the formerly unmarriageable. But they look pretty good up next to a life of spinsterhood."

"Mercy sakes, Dinah, leave the girl be." Mama never held back with Daddy's sister. "You're just jealous Jane picked her as her successor instead of you."

Bravo, Mama. Thank you. Of course, Mama broached no such restrictions for herself when it came to her opinions on Cora's life.

It was after Dinah's daughter, Cora's cousin Irma, announced she was expecting that Cora had to escape.

Irma was all of twenty-two. Married to a solid, hard-working boy named Rob and already starting a family.

Cora had fallen in love with a man who had a mistress. The river. So she made her way down the path to confront the other lover. To see what power she had that kept her man away.

Closing her eyes, she envisioned Rufus, her thoughts rereading the details of his letters.

I'm heading down the Arkansas, darling. I wish you could be with me.

You should see the Mississippi, my sweets. She's powerful and wild. Puts me in mind of you.

I'll see you as soon as I can. Know that you're always on my mind.

Wild? She? Cora loved seeing herself through Rufus's eyes. She tried to understand him, tried to see the world from his pilot house. Lately when she couldn't sleep, she looked beyond the curtains of her longings and made up her mind.

She would run away with him the next time he docked at Heart's Bend. She'd miss the shop. And the brides who entrusted her with so much. But it was time to consummate their love.

Rufus pledged to marry her over and over when he was here for the Fourth—for three glorious days. She was going to hold him to it.

He'd nearly convinced her to surrender her virtue on the salon davenport the night before his departure. So filled with passion, Cora could barely think, let alone find her moral center. Rufus owned her heart and soul.

"Cora!" She swerved to see Mama marching through

the high grass. "I thought I'd find you out here." The scent of a menthol cigarette floated toward her.

"The kitchen was warm. Crowded." The breeze pushed the ends of Cora's curled hair over her eyes. She gently brushed them aside. Rufus liked when her hair fell into her eyes. Said it made her mysterious.

"We're ready for dessert." Mama settled beside Cora, her free hand in her dress pocket, her cheeks already turning red from the sharp cut of the wind. "Liberty is serving. Darn if that girl isn't so generous. Coming over this afternoon to help and clean up."

"She can use the extra pay."

Liberty married her man in August and was already expecting her first child. She glowed, her dark eyes bright, her skin a creamy milk chocolate. Cora envied her. For all the restrictions the coloreds faced in the law, Liberty was free to love the man she wanted. Jim Crow could do nothing to her heart, could do nothing to change who she was on the inside, who she was when she was alone with her Jake.

That's what she wanted with Rufus. To love freely. Cora might be able to walk around town, go wherever she willed, but a man captaining a riverboat held her bound. Restricted her ability to love. He baited her, then left her on the hook. She was *not* free to go where she wished. Because she wished to be with him.

Mama took a long drag from her cigarette. Cora batted away a cloud of smoke though she didn't mind the scent of menthol. It reminded her of Pop and Granny and rainy afternoons in the parlor playing checkers, singing songs, reading books.

"You know what Reverend Clinton says about smoking, Mama." The good reverend was a guest at Daddy and Mama's table today. Along with his wife and two sons.

"Why do you think I came out here? Wasn't in the mood for a sermon."

"Everything all right?" Mama tended to smoke more when she was tense. While Cora heard no more closed-door arguments between her parents, they seemed to be fighting without words. Stiff and stilted conversation. Saying only what was necessary.

"If not, it will be."

"Daddy doesn't seem to be the same since Caldwell and Company closed." The big bank chain out of Nashville, who drew Daddy's hometown bank into their network, shut down two weeks ago, taking several banks down with them. The newspaper speculated more would follow.

"He's been brooding. Tells me everything is fine, we're fine, that yes, he had to close the bank for a few weeks but he'll reopen by the first of the year. But I've seen him like this before, and let me tell you, he's not fine. We're not fine."

Mama sighed, dropping her cigarette to the ground, crushing it with the toe of her brown Happy Delux oxfords.

"I can't remember too much, but he seemed rather silent and brooding during the '07 and '14 panic."

"Exactly. I'm scared for him, Cora. No matter how hard I try to coax it out of him, he seems stuck in whatever ails him. All the while telling me there's nothing to worry over." Mama took another cigarette from her pocket along with Daddy's silver American Legion lighter. The smell of menthol kicked against the scent of rain. "So, what are you doing out here, Cora?"

"I told you the house was warm. Felt crowded."

"Was it the business with Irma and Rob?"

"I'm very excited for them. We need more babies around here."

"It'd be good for you to do your part."

"It's Thanksgiving, Mama. Be thankful."

"Fair enough. Birch stopped by. On his way home from the Melsons. Your daddy talked him into staying for dessert. He's asking after you."

"I couldn't eat another bite." Cora patted her belly, fighting a wash of tears. "I ate too many of your good yeast rolls."

Mama angled forward for a good look at her face. "Mercy, Cora, don't tell me. You're out here brooding about Rufus. Land sakes, you are your father's daughter."

"If you don't want to know, then don't ask."

"For the life of me I can't understand why you pine for him. He writes you fancy lies only intending to keep you on his string. Please tell me you didn't go to bed with him."

"Mama!"

"Well, you're a grown woman of thirty. I'm not naive."

"No." An honest *no* for once. "But I will marry him. I will."

"When? Cora Beth, it's been over four years. He's been promising to come back and marry you ever since you met. So why doesn't he? Shoot fire, he was out here to the farm in July. He could've asked your daddy for your hand."

"He wants to make sure he's ready. He's building his business. He wants a nice house for me and our children. He's almost saved enough." Cora glanced at Mama. "In St. Louis."

"St. Louis? You are seriously considering leaving the shop? Jane's rolling over in her grave." Mama cackled. "What will Dinah say?"

"Jane would want me to fall in love, be happy. She regretted never marrying. She didn't talk much about it but I know she did. And who cares what Dinah says? I thought you and Odelia could run the shop. I'll come back from time to time to check on things."

Mama scowled, clicking the fingernails of her cigarette hand. "I've no desire for an outside job. Your daddy's worked hard to give us a good name and allow me to work in the community as I saw fit. I only work for you out of courtesy, as a supportive mother. But I tell you again, I doubt this Rufus's sincerity."

"You've made that clear."

"But if you trust him, then I guess I'm beholden to trust him too." Mama puffed on her cigarette, scenting the wind with its smoke. "I raised you right. But, Cora, promise me this. You won't wait another year. Please. Most of your friends are married with children. Getting on with their lives."

"Do they own a wedding shop? Run a business?"

"Most of them wouldn't dare choose a career over a home and children. What's a better business than wife and mom? Haven't you heard, the hand that rocks the cradle rules the world?"

"Yes, it's all fine and noble, but if you don't mind I'd like to be in the business of marriage with the man I love. You were head over heels with Daddy when you married him."

"It's your life, Cora." Mama stamped out her cigarette in the same spot as the first one. "It's not what I want for you, but it's your life."

"Mama, can't you be proud of me? For at least being faithful to my heart? What about the business? We're doing splendidly. We made a lot of money this fall on mail orders. Even after I pulled the magazine ad. Women found back issues and sent in their orders. We're employing twenty women. Bit Jenkins earned enough to buy the family a radio."

"It does make me proud to see what you're doing. How the shop employs women in town. How the shop helps brides during their most glorious time."

"Is it still glorious, Mama? Being married after thirty-four years?"

"Marriage is work, Cora, I'm not going to lie. It's glorious some days and not so much on others." Mama faced the strong breeze and raked her hair away from her face. "But it's a worthy endeavor. I'd hate to see you miss out on such happiness after you have helped so many. Jane didn't marry because she got her heart broken. She never let a man in. If you're not careful, you'll end up exactly like her."

Cora faced the river and the bend in the Cumberland where she first saw Rufus's *Wayfarer* five years ago.

She had no idea the dashing captain would personally deliver goods to her shop. She had no idea he'd own her heart.

"No I won't, Mama. I won't. Rufus is a man of his word."

"I have to ask, what about poor Birch, huh? He's just not appealing to you?"

"The first time I saw Rufus it was summer. His skin was so brown from working in the sun. His hair golden to almost white. And his eyes, like endless blue skies. He walked through the shop's back door, big as you please . . ."

"I remember that day but not the golden god you describe."

Cora sighed. "Then perhaps it wasn't for you to see. Birch never made me feel the way Rufus does."

"Hello there." Birch emerged from the trees, his slacks neatly creased, the cuff of his shirt sleeves rolled up, revealing the power of his forearms. "I wondered where you women had escaped to."

His gaze met Cora's and she turned away.

"Did Liberty serve the pie?" Mama said, patting her pocket, a habit she developed to make sure her cigarettes were both safe and hidden.

"She did. I had a slice of pumpkin *and* pecan."

"You are always welcome at our table, Birch. Cora, I'm going in. Don't stay out here too long. The air has a powerful chill."

"I think I'll go with you." Cora turned to follow Mama, but Birch reached for her arm.

"Could I have a moment?"

"You two take your time."

"How are you?" Birch released his grip.

"I'm well. But I can't believe you came out here to ask me how I am."

"It seemed more polite than starting with, 'What is going on with you?'"

"What's going on with . . . Nothing. Whatever do you mean?"

"Well, maybe it's my imagination, but it seems you're avoiding me. Ever since the summer, since the Fourth of July party when your river man showed up out of nowhere, you hardly speak to me. You pass by me in church like I'm a leper."

"A leper? Birch, I never took you for exaggerations." She folded her arms, building up her defense. "You pass me, if truth be told. I seem to recall you keeping the company of Janice and Wanetta last Fourth. You were quite busy with the two of them. Ever since, you've given *me* the wide leper's berth."

"Pshaw, you make something out of nothing. At least they wanted to sit with me and ole Uncle Sam. I'd rather have been with you. But you had your riverboat captain."

She trembled from the snap in the breeze, from the truth rising in this conversation. "I can't be who you want me to be, Birch. I can't."

"How do you know?" He stepped forward, reaching for her, wrapping her in his arms. "You've never given me a chance."

"Don't." She pressed against his chest, trying to twist free.

"I think you're wasting your life on a man who doesn't care."

"You have no right, Birch. The best you've ever done is scowl at him." The scent of a wood fire rode on the wind and it made Cora homesick for her youth, when Ernest Junior was alive and they'd run through the woods, building forts, playing make-believe, going home in the evening to a warm, cozy supper.

Even when Daddy disappeared in '07 and '14, Mama made sure their home was solid and safe.

"Because I don't trust him."

"So I'm a fool? I don't know a bad man when I meet him?"

"You're no one's fool, Cora. I'm just saying—"

"That I love the wrong man? I should love you instead?" No more beating around the bush. She tossed back the covers of innuendo that had blanketed their relationship for years.

"Yes." He pressed his fingers into her back, drawing her closer. "Love me." He was her shield, in that moment, against the cold. "I love you. I've always loved you. Don't you know? Can't you see?"

She refused with a shake of her head, freeing herself from his arms. "Don't you see? Y-you can't love me, Birch. You can't."

"Why not?"

"Because I don't love you and I can't pretend. I don't want to hurt you."

"I can manage my own heart, Cora."

"Do you hear yourself? You can choose but I can't? Birch, he loves me, and if he has plans, goals that cause me to wait, then wait I will. So see, you cannot wait for me. I don't love you in that way. Him, I love him. He's the one for me." She gripped the collar of his shirt. *Hear me.* "I've given him my heart and my word."

"You're a smart, wonderful woman, Cora. But you've let your heart become a slave to a river man's charms."

"Then let me never be free." Did she mean it? She wanted to have in her heart what she saw on Liberty's face.

"Cora, Birch, come. It's Esmé." Cousin Porky from Knox County popped out from the trees. "She's collapsed."

"What? Mama . . ." Cora darted down the path toward the house. "Did you call the doctor?"

Birch ran alongside her, shoving aside low-swinging branches and overgrown bushes. "What happened, Porky?"

"It came out over dessert. Ernest finally told Esmé what's going on. He's lost everything, Cora. The bank, the house, the land, everything."

She stopped running, crashing into a cold wall of dread. "Porky, you heard wrong. He's reopening the bank before the new year. This was just a bump, a hiccup. He can't have lost everything. That makes no sense. How could he have *lost* everything?" She wanted to run to the house, but her feet refused to leave their safe, very safe spot between the woods and the river.

"The Caldwell collapse devastated the south, Cora," Porky said with a glance at Birch. "We've only seen the beginning. If he says he's lost everything, he means he lost *everything*."

. . .

HALEY

"Well?" Cole and Gomez conferred on the steps, talking contractorese.

Cole held up his finger. "One sec."

Sigh. But, oh, this was her place. *Hers*.

"You're smiling," Cole said.

"I know. I can't help it. I love it here. It feels so good. Clean and bright."

"Clean? You've seen this place, the bathrooms? The third floor?"

Yeah, she'd seen the mess. Toured it all afternoon with Cole and Gomez. There was a lot of work *and* cleaning to be done. One part of her was knotted around eighty plus thousand dollars she needed to get this place up and running. The other part of her was wild with excitement.

But it wasn't the externals that captured her. It was the aura, the feel of the place. All the hope and love stories hidden within the walls.

"Haley, Gomez will go with you to file the permits.

He's got the information you need to get it done right without hiccups."

"You think we could get the third floor done first so I can move in?" Even if she had to camp out, use lanterns and candles, microwave box dinners at Java Jane's, she was ready to be on her own.

"We can, but if you have a tight timeline, I'd get the shop part renovated first. You can pass inspection without the third floor being complete." He called Haley over to sit with him on the steps. "Let's go over this." He turned his iPad for Haley to see. "Electric and plumbing all need to be redone. We don't know what's behind the walls, but I'm hoping no asbestos. The foundation seems good, but we'll know more after the inspection. Gomez has a guy who can get out here right away. We need to sand and refinish the floors, including the stairs. All the walls need to be repaired in some fashion and painted. I'd go with white or gray paint with a dark wood floor."

"I have a style in mind. Hollywood regency."

"Hollywood regency. Never heard of it."

"It's perfect for this place." She tapped the iPad. "What else?"

"The roof needs to be redone. Get ready to empty your wallet on that one. The windows need to be replaced. We can put in new, thick-pane windows except in the front where I'd recommend restoring the lead-pane windows. That'll make the Historical Society happy."

"And keep the shop's charm."

"Yes, and keep the shop's charm." His leg tapped

hers as he shifted his position, and Haley braced against the ping his presence inspired. She'd have to battle this one. Not let him get the best of her. Romance was not even a speck on the horizon for her. "The front elevation needs to be cleaned up and landscaped, and the back porch is falling off. I suggest we knock it down."

"No, I want to keep it."

He sighed. "It's not part of the original design."

"But I want to keep it."

Cole peeked over at Gomez. "The lady wants it." He tapped on his screen. "Rebuild back porch. Kitchen on third floor. New powder room and bathroom." With each word the reno budget multiplied. "Not sure what you want to do for inventory, but you'll need furniture. Display cases and whatever else a bridal shop needs. Cash register, etcetera. I ballparked that number, trying to keep this thing around eighty grand."

"I know. I know. I'm looking into it." She found some 1890s display cases online, but they were out of this world on price. She'd do better to find pieces that needed refurbishing. But that only added to her timeline and renovation budget.

She figured she needed another ten grand to get started, but she was still researching gowns and veils and other trousseau items.

"And, oh, up here." Cole jogged up to the mezzanine, Gomez and Haley following. "You'll remember this door is locked. We can't find the key so we don't know what's behind it."

"Right. Keith thought we'd have to drill it open."

Cole squatted down to inspect the lock. "The knob looks original. You sure you want to drill through it?" He looked back at Gomez. "You think you can get in here without breaking the kit?"

The man bent for a better look. "Bean Wells is the best locksmith around. I'll get him to look at it."

"Okay with you?" Cole glanced up at Haley. "Add another hundred to the budget, but you said you wanted to try to preserve it."

"What's another hundred to the hundred grand I don't have?"

Gomez stepped back as Haley bent next to Cole, inspecting the lock. When she looked at him, their eyes were level, peering beyond the surface. The edge of his breath breezed past her face with the fragrance of mint. Haley stood. These *moments* had to stop.

"Hey," she said. "What about the MicroFixIt guy? Would he have the key?"

"If he does, the key is long gone with him. He's not even around here anymore." Cole rose up, tapping notes on his iPad, then trying the door again. "I can't believe no one's tried to get in here before."

"Maybe it's reserved only for people who want to make it a wedding shop."

"Ha!" Cole glanced back at her with a wink, making her stomach go into a free fall.

"Cole?" A deep voice billowed up from the main floor.

He made a face, exchanged a look with Gomez, then looked over the railing. "Brant Jackson, what's up?"

Haley watched as Cole descended the stairs,

meeting the man from Akron by the front door with a low, terse exchange. She couldn't hear much. Just "You can't blame me—"

"Don't need you . . ."

"What about—"

Brant said a final word and walked out, leaving Cole standing in the shop's small foyer, hands on his belt, lowering his head.

Haley descended the steps. "What'd he want?"

"Nothing."

She bent to see his face. "Sure doesn't look like nothing."

"He fired me."

"Fired you? Had he even hired you?"

"He said if I wasn't going to be any help in getting this corner of Heart's Bend for his parking lot, then he'd find someone else." Cole glanced back into the shop.

"Hey, Brant Jackson, get a life. This is *one* little shop!"

Cole laughed, slipping his arm around her waist, pulling her away from the open front door. "Shh, he'll hear you." He reached around, shutting the door with his foot.

"From outside? Who cares?" Haley waited for him to release her, but instead he held on. "Hey, I'm sorry." She glanced up at him, turning slightly out of his arms, freeing herself. "I know how much you wanted that job."

"Yeah, well, you win some and you lose some."

"Then I have to ask. Cole, will you be my contractor?"

He regarded her for a second, then stuck out his hand. "Under one condition."

Haley popped her hand into his. "Anything."

"You don't mention Tammy anymore."

Haley hesitated, searching his face for a hint of why. But she only saw a determined resolve. "All right. Deal."

CHAPTER TWELVE

CORA

Cora awoke to a clap of thunder and a flash of lightning. The noise roused her from a hard, dreamless sleep. All her nights were dreamless since the bank failed. Since Daddy left.

Her heart beat a restless staccato as she kicked off the covers and moved to the window, opening the sash.

"Thundersnow," she whispered, leaning out the window, inhaling the cold and clean snow.

Swirling, falling, drifting, downward, downward. Raising her palm, she tried to capture one, two, or three frozen crystals. But they melted in the warmth of her hand.

"God, please melt our troubles."

Those simple words were her first real prayer since Daddy left two weeks before Christmas. He told Mama he was going out for pipe tobacco—she hollered for him to bring her a pack of cigarettes—and never returned.

He was man enough to send a Christmas card telling them not to worry, that he was all right.

However, Mama was not. She walked around in a daze, muttering to herself.

"Your father runs off when the times squeeze him, but he'll be back. He always comes back. And look, we're still in the house. Everything will be fine."

She decorated for the holidays, putting up a Christmas tree so big the tip bent against the highest point of the ceiling.

Together Cora and Mama trimmed the tree, including three strings of those newfangled electric lights. Mama kept up appearances, shopping, volunteering with her charities, and teaching Sunday school.

She filled the house with the aroma of cakes, pies, and cookies. Cora guessed she gained a pound or two just breathing the sugary sweet air.

Mama held a Christmas Tea for the shop seamstresses who churned out 321 wedding gowns, going-away dresses, and evening gowns, along with an assortment of veils and other sundries.

On Christmas Day they slept in, though Cora wondered if Mama slept at all. She'd taken to sitting up in the dark kitchen, smoking.

They opened presents and ate pancakes, eggs, bacon, and hot chocolate for breakfast. Then Mama set about preparing a feast for friends and family. Cora, Aunt Dinah, Cousin Porky, the lot of them tried to tell her she didn't need to go to all the trouble this year, but Mama fired back with a fury.

"Oh yes I do. Now, do you want turkey or ham?"

Two days before New Year's, a stranger knocked on the door. He wore a dark suit and tie, his fedora low over his forehead. Mama made a fuss, inviting him in for tea and freshly baked pumpkin bread. She was so sure he had good news on Daddy. On this whole *silly* financial debacle.

The man obliged her, but after one sip of his tea, he delivered his purpose without any sort of preamble. "Your home was used as collateral on several loans. I'm afraid you're going to have to pay the balance due or find yourself in foreclosure."

The light Mama had been stoking in her soul with an unwavering belief that Daddy would return home any day snuffed out as the man's words still lingered in the air.

Her countenance became stony and cold.

And now, as the thundersnow fell over Heart's Bend, Cora and Mama lived on the third floor of the shop. In a quarter of the space they'd once had. But having lost everything but their clothes, beds, and Mama's dining room table, the apartment was a godsend.

"Cora, what are you doing?" Mama's voice sounded from the other side of the small bedroom. "You'll freeze us to death."

"Looking at the snow. It's beautiful." Another crack of lightning shed a ghostly light across the surface of the trees, haloing the minuscule drops floating in the air.

Mama's hand slipped over her shoulder. "Yes, it's beautiful. But it's also cold." She slammed the window shut. "Now, get back in bed." She padded across the cold floor to her bed.

Gone was Mama's softness, her humor, her gentility. Nothing remained but hard edges and judgment.

Cora showed her compassion. Would she have fared any better if she lost her husband, her home, her prize-winning garden, her reputation?

Mama saw her possessions sold at auction to the highest bidder. Cora feared she'd lose her mind that day. While the feds had foreclosed on dozens of families in the area, Mama was not comforted to be in their company.

"Mama?" Cora returned to her bed, tucking her feet under the cool sheets.

"What?"

"Don't you wonder if he's okay?"

"No. He's a coward. Like no other. What kind of man abandons his family over money three times?"

"Money is how Daddy measures his success."

"What about me? And you? Don't we count? Not to mention all the people in this town he's hurt because of his banking practices."

"Mama, Caldwell's failing has taken down a hundred and twenty banks."

"Why did he have to join with them? We were doing fine before. Now look—"

Another flash of lightning ricocheted off the snow and against the polished pane, casting a stark light on Mama's drawn expression.

"Fool me once, shame on you. Fool me twice, shame on me. Fool me three times? Shame on us all."

"What will you do when he comes back?"

"Go to sleep, Cora."

"He'll come back, you know."

"Well, let's hope he doesn't." Mama sat up. "I might shoot him."

"No you won't."

"How can you be so calm? It'd help me if you'd get a little mad. He lost your aunt Jane's money too. If you had deposited the last of the magazine ad money, you'd have lost that too."

"Not all of Aunt Jane's money. I had some cash in the shop."

Looking back, she marveled at her intuition to sock money away in the shop. Then she realized her loss. Cora tried to be mad at Daddy, but she mostly felt compassion. She missed him.

"Promise me, Cora, if you ever see him again, you will not give him one dime. Not one dime." Mama fluffed her pillow. Cora could see the long lines of her face in the flashes of light. "Look at us, living in this tiny apartment like a couple of immigrant women just off the boat."

"Be kind, Mama."

"I am kind. Bless those women and their courage, but our ancestors came over a hundred and seventy years ago. They worked hard to make Tennessee a great state and create a legacy for their children. For us."

"Daddy didn't know the banks would fail. We should be grateful we have the shop."

"Don't defend him, Cora."

She slid farther down under her covers. She wasn't defending him. But she sure wasn't going to let bitterness take hold. Its ravishes showed on Mama's face.

"The apartment isn't so bad," she said.

But Mama declared her broom closet at the house was bigger. However, Aunt Jane brought her exquisite taste to the shop's design, keeping it up-to-date, even installing a new bathroom and kitchen the year before she died. The living and bedroom space was actually quite roomy.

Birch made a room divider from old lumber to give Mama and Cora some privacy for dressing. He also helped them move. Mama's dining room set would not fit, so she told Birch to cart the whole caboodle over to Liberty and Jake's.

Their modest place on the edge of town now sported a Chippendale dining room set with a Hepplewhite china cabinet. Mama also threw in her everyday dishes and crystal for Liberty and Daddy's prize humidor for Jake.

"Mama?"

"Hmmm?"

"You'll get your house back, I promise."

"I say we get a better house, huh? What do you think about that, darling?"

"Lovely. When Daddy comes home, we'll get a new, bigger, better house."

"We don't need him. Let's sell more dresses and we'll do it on our own."

Cora turned on her side, watching the dance of snow in the strikes of lightning.

The wedding shop saved them. Gave them a home and a job to fix on. Cora was grateful. Yet, as she faced a new life in the new year, she wondered if this was all God had for her.

Of course, she loved the shop. Loved employing twenty women to work the magazine orders. Odelia urged her to place another ad in *Modern Priscilla*.

But she also faced another birthday without Rufus securely in her life. She'd written to him about Daddy, and his letters returned with words of comfort and support.

The idea of another year without being his wife settled over her with a deep, cold loneliness. There weren't enough blankets to warm it away.

CHAPTER THIRTEEN

HALEY

When she wanted something from her parents, she hovered. Haley couldn't remember exactly when this habit started, but for most of her life it had worked, more or less.

The parents were big readers. Instead of watching the eighty-ninth season of *Survivor* or *CSI Dubuque*, they actually read books. Dad read naval novels; Mom, medical journals, how-tos, and memoirs.

"What is it, Haley?" Mom didn't even bother to look up.

She'd been leaning against the wall of their den, tucking her hands in her jeans pockets, commenting every once in a while how much she loved the plush leather reading chairs.

"I need to talk to you." She bolted in, sitting on the edge of the matching leather sofa, the tip of her boots disturbing the golden angle of Dad's reading lamp.

Mom removed her reading glasses and closed her book, keeping her place with her thumb. "Is this about the shop?"

"Yes. Look, I know y'all—"

Dad held up his finger. "Hold on, Hal, let me finish this paragraph." He could never stop reading in the middle of a sentence. "Okay, now, what is it?" He set his book on the end table and leaned forward, arms on his thighs, his focus on Haley.

"I need money."

"I knew it." Mom slapped the wide wooden arm of her chair. "What did I tell you, David? There's no way Haley can renovate that shop without help."

"Did you talk to the bank?" Dad said.

Haley nodded. "This afternoon. They are happy for me to have the shop. They are not happy to give me a loan. I have no collateral." She glanced from one parent to the next. "You two could cosign for me."

"Nope, we did that with Aaron and we'll never do it again." Mom lived by the rules she set. Dad claimed it was her way of feeling secure. She was fifteen when her father died, and it was the rules and the boundaries her mother set that helped her feel safe.

"I'm not Aaron." Oldest brother Aaron asked the folks to cosign on a sprawling place in north Atlanta five or so years ago. But his wife wanted a bigger house, and after that Haley only knew about some kerfuffle over money and being upside down and defaulting. Brother Seth said the tension was pretty thick for over a year. Haley missed the fun by being in Afghanistan and California. "I have twenty thousand from the city as well as some of my own money. Ten grand. I've earmarked that to get the business going. Website, advertising, inventory, blah, blah."

Haley leaned forward. "Cole Danner's going to be my foreman."

"Cole?" Mom said. "How can you trust him after what his father did?"

"Joann, come on." Daddy's rebuke was subtle but unmistakable. "Cole's a good contractor. A good man."

"I agree. Don't blame him for what his dad did, Mom. Look at his mother, Tina. She's running Ella's like a well-oiled machine."

"Then maybe ask her for a loan."

"Right. 'Hey, Tina, my wealthy parents can't see their way to give me a loan so they sent me to ask you.'" Sarcasm rarely worked on Mom, but Haley employed it anyway. "You know I'll pay you back."

"How much do you need?" Daddy, the engineer of the family, always asked for the details and facts.

"Eighty grand."

"Eighty grand!" Mom fired out of her chair. "David, don't even think about it. No."

"Why not?" Haley stood, arms wide. "Look at this place. You have a beautiful home, nice cars, a pool, a maid and lawn crew, a country club membership. You go to Hawaii or Europe every other year. You're successful people. I know you have money in the bank. I'm your daughter. Why can't I have a loan? *Loan*. I'm not asking for a freebie."

The three of them stood in a triangle of silence. Cold, stone silence. Daddy jiggled the change in his pocket while studying his old, worn slippers. Mom stared at the loaded built-in bookshelves, her hands resting on the back of her hips.

"Okay, well, thanks." Haley started for the door. Weirdness from the parents wasn't unusual. They were kind and thoughtful, loving, but lived by an unusual set of ideals. Dad said it went back to Mom's teen years, but Haley figured Mom got it naturally, born in her genes. She paused at the door. "Is this about grad school?"

"No." Daddy's clipped response raised more questions.

"Then what?"

"Joann, you want to field this?"

Haley waited, her pulse deep and steady in her ears. "Mom, is something wrong? Is it your practice? Are you sick or something?"

"I'm not sick. And it's not my practice."

"But you just don't want to help your only daughter with the shop." Haley stated it plain, leaving no room for doubt, pulling her "only daughter" card. Desperate times called for desperate measures.

Mom faced her. "I do not want you opening the old wedding shop. Let them raze it to the ground and put up the stupid parking lot. Akron wants to bring a lot of business to Heart's Bend, Haley. That wedding shop is only going to service a small portion of the population. You'll employ, what, one or two people? Akron will employ hundreds."

"You're more concerned about Heart's Bend's economy than your daughter's personal venture?"

"Of course not. But I *am* concerned that a wedding shop doesn't make sense. This is not 1890 or 1930 when women dress up to go into town to buy a slab of beef or a pair of stockings. Brides order online today. They go to Atlanta or New York for gowns. No one buys a trousseau anymore. How are you going to make it work? Huh, tell me?"

"I'll make it work. I have a plan. The wedding market is a billion-dollar industry." Haley glanced back and forth between her parents. Something was up. Mom's opposition wasn't about Haley. Or the shop. "Are you two in with Akron?"

"No, we're not in business with Akron," Daddy said.

"But you agree the corner of Blossom and First needs to be a big parking lot? Makes no sense. Daddy, you're on the Downtown Restoration committee. You supported me at the town council meeting. Mom, you used to be on the board of the Historical Society."

"Joann, tell her."

"Tell me what?"

"There's nothing to tell." Mom disappeared from the room, leaving Haley surfing a wave of confusion.

"Daddy, help me out here."

"Hal, I'll support you any way I can, but that's my wife who just left the room and I have to be on her side. Can you understand?"

"Why is there a side, Dad? I'm not *against* her."

"I know. I know. But she's got something on her heart that bothers her and this shop just pokes at it." Dad gave her a gentle shoulder squeeze. "Buck up. She'll tell you when she's ready. I've been telling her it's time."

"Tell me what? What does the wedding shop have to do with Mom?"

"That's her story." Daddy leaned to see down the hall. "Sometimes the things that hurt us don't make sense, but they hurt all the same. Your mom is a stellar woman. A rock. Raised you kids while starting her career, then her clinic." Dad wagged his finger in the air. "But she's got a pain deep in her craw she doesn't talk about. It shadows her decisions sometimes."

"I'm only asking for a loan, Daddy. Me, your daughter."

"I know, kiddo, and I'd give it to you in a heartbeat if this thing didn't touch a deep chord with your mother."

"Then tell me. What is it?"

"It's not for me to say." Daddy kissed her forehead. "As for your shop, I remember a young woman of faith in this house who took her brothers' teasing without so much as batting an eye when she came home from a church camp with Tammy saying she'd met Jesus. Trust in your prayers and your God. If it's meant to be, the money will come."

Haley leaned against the doorframe. For a man who didn't see the need for God or faith in his life, who only attended church on Christmas and Easter, Daddy spoke an awful lot of truth.

"To be honest, Daddy, I'm not sure where my faith got off to the last few years."

"Then hunt it down. Bring it back. And don't let it go."

CHAPTER FOURTEEN

CORA

JULY 1931

The Wedding Shop Providing for
Brides Faced with Hard Times

By Hattie Lerner

Brides from all over Heart's Bend and Cheatum County are swarming The Wedding Shop this summer as Cora Scott, owner and operator, extends a helping hand to those unable to afford a wedding gown or trousseau.

How does she do it? this reporter asked.

"We take donations," Scott said. "If any woman has a dress she no longer wears, or a wedding gown not intended for a daughter or niece, consider donating it to our shop. We remake them for brides in need. We sincerely want every bride to feel special and beautiful on her big day."

Scott went on to say she and her assistant, Mrs. Odelia Darnell, and her mother, Mrs. Esmé Scott, wife of former banker Ernest Scott, will serve any bride who comes to them, cash in hand or not.

. . .

She just had to mention Ernie, didn't she?" Mama moved from hovering over Cora's shoulder, reading out loud even though Cora was perfectly capable of reading the article on her own.

She was beginning to understand more and more why grown children needed their own homes. Or apartments.

"When she wrote about me running down First like a mad woman, you said it was good for business."

"What do I know?"

In the third-floor alcove, Mama fried eggs on the stove, slamming the cast iron against the burners.

"Really, it just gets my insides. She knows how humiliated I am, we are—"

"Leave it be, Mama. Aren't we doing well?"

Mama had turned the apartment into a lovely home, finding beautiful secondhand pieces of furniture and a rather rich-looking chandelier from an abandoned home near Nashville.

"I suppose we are." Mama joined Cora at the table, diving into her breakfast.

Cora set the paper aside. "Shall we say grace?"

Mama raised her gaze as she bit into her toast. "Grace? Thanking the Lord for taking everything away from us?"

"Yes." Cora reached for her mother's hand, but she withdrew, curling her hand against her plate. Mercy, when did they switch roles? Cora was the mama and Mama was the errant child. "Weren't you the one who taught me 'The Lord giveth and the Lord taketh away'? Look at all we have despite the bank's closing."

"Say your prayers, then. Be quick about it. I hate cold eggs."

Cora could endure Daddy leaving and Mama growing bitter. But she refused to leave her faith. What other hope did she have if not in the Almighty?

When Cora said amen, Mama squeezed her hand. "You keep believing for us both, won't you?"

These weak moments were rare, but occasionally Mama cracked and Cora saw the goo of her wounded soul.

"Always, Mama."

By the kindness of Birch, Mama planted a garden at his farm, though this first year it wasn't near the size she plowed up at the homestead. Nevertheless, the crops she planted were yielding well. She also started raising chickens, half for fryers and the other half for eggs.

To preserve gas, Mama rode her bike six miles six days a week to care for her garden and feed the chickens. On Sundays, Birch threw the chicken scratch to give her a day off. Cora slipped off to church while Mama slept in.

Daddy had been gone seven months now. And his last letter was four months ago. Even Rufus wrote more frequently. He even visited in March for three days. It was heavenly. What fun they had taking walks down by the river and going to the pictures.

His latest letter rested under Cora's pillow. She read it nightly as she fell asleep.

My darling Cora, I think of you so much my mind hurts. But what lovely thoughts . . .

"Cora." Odelia marched into the apartment without knocking. "Avril Kreyling is out on the front steps. Says she wants to talk to you." Odelia held up a tin of something delicious smelling. "I brought in my cinnamon rolls."

"Good. I was needing a new paperweight," Mama said, stabbing at her eggs.

"You're one to talk, Esmé. I've tasted your pecan pie."

Odelia sat down, joining them at the small table that had once been on the front porch of the old house, reached for a knife, and opened her tin of rolls. "I tried to get Avril up here but she was glued to the front steps."

"Well, what does she want?" Cora set aside her napkin. Avril was a bride of Aunt Jane's back in 1919 or 1920. A friend of Cora's from high school and a mama of three little ones.

"Could hardly get a word out of her. Esmé, these cinnamon rolls are fluffy as a feather. Look at this." She dropped one onto Mama's plate.

"Odelia, careful, you'll crack my good china."

"I'm going to check on Avril. You two . . ." Cora motioned between Mama and Odelia. "Behave yourselves. If I find bloodshed when I come back up, I'm not calling the doc."

Their laughter followed her down the steps and across the mezzanine.

In the foyer, Cora unlocked the door, swinging it wide, letting in a flood of July light.

"Avril?" She stepped out, joining the woman on the

stoop. The early morning was crisp and beautiful, the brightness soaking the breeze-laden trees. "Are you all right?"

Avril cast her a sideways glance, her arms folded over her knees, her lean hands gripping her elbows.

She was thin, and a small section of her sleeve had ripped away from her housedress. Faded stains dotted her once white apron, and her toe nearly peeked out of the scuffed toe of her brown shoes.

"We had big plans, Billy and me. Oh boy, we were going to take on the world."

"I remember. The two of you were really going places."

"He was so handsome. Charming. Swept me off my feet." Avril peered at Cora, her eyes sad pools of mud in a dry, sunken earth. "Do you remember, Cora? All the girls wanted to go with him, but he chose me. Me, Avril Falk."

"I do remember. He was everything you say. But none of the girls stood a chance. He was head over heels for you."

"But now look at me." She rubbed at a stain on her hand, pulling her skin tight. "I'm old before my time. I'm only thirty, but I have lines and wrinkles on my face. I move like a fifty-year-old." She pressed her hand against her unkempt, dry hair. "Ain't been to the beauty parlor in two years. None of my clothes fit." She pulled at the loose waist of her dress.

"Avril, where's Billy?"

"Gone. Took all the money and nearly all our food. Everything I put up last summer." She retrieved a note from her pocket and handed it to Cora. "He left this."

Cora hesitated, her hand trembling, the buried sensation of when Daddy left rising to her skin. "I know how you feel, Avril, but he'll be back."

"I know you know. That's one of the reasons I'm here."

Cora glanced at Billy's elongated, even handwriting, smooth, nothing like what she imagined for a farmer.

I can't take it. I'm sorry, Avril. I'm sorry.

"He can't take it. Well, what am I supposed to do? Tell me that, Billy boy?" Avril brushed her weathered hand against her wet cheeks, then reached for the note as Cora handed it back, her fingernails broken and dirty. "You're sorry but you take all the money. Take precious jars of food, vegetables, and fruit that were supposed to feed our family. I got three kids at home, Cora, and no money. Who does he think is going to feed them?"

"Avril, what drove him away?" Cora kept busy with the shop but knew banks foreclosed on homes, businesses, and farms weekly.

"The bank took our land but said if Billy agreed to farm it, they'd pay him. Slave wages, I tell you. Pennies on the dollar for backbreaking work." She steadied herself with a tight grip on Cora's arm, her thin, pale fingers trembling. "I thought he'd come home . . . I thought he'd come home."

"How long's he been gone?"

"Spring. First of. I tried to go ahead with the planting, but even with the eight-year-old helping me, I can't get it done. My dear Willie thinks he's got to be the man now. You should see him, getting up before the rooster crows, hitching up the plow to old Brutus, doing the chores, then coming in and making coffee while I tend the littler ones. My eight-year-old son, doin' a man's work 'cause his daddy can't take it." Avril balled her hands into fists, shaking, shimmying, clenching her jaw. "It ain't right, Cora. It ain't right. He should be in school, learning, running round, playing baseball."

"You're right. He should. Hard times are no respecter of age."

Avril tapped her thumb to her chest. "But I am. I know what it's like to lose your childhood to work. My mama worked in a factory when she was ten years old, down in Birmingham." Avril held up her hand, with the first two fingers bent. "Lost two fingers and they put her back on the line the next day. My daddy sent me to the factory when I was ten. Without my mama knowing."

"Avril, really. I never heard this before."

A smile of remembrance tugged on her lips. "She marched into that place, dragged me off the line, and gave the owner a string of words that'd peel paint from a wall. That night my folks had a blow out. Mama said if he ever sent me to the factory again, she'd kill him. Six months later he got a job at the feed plant up here and we moved to Heart's Bend. Life was good after that. I got to be a normal girl. Met Billy. Got hitched. I never imagined I'd be faced with seeing my children go hungry, Cora. Never in all my born days."

Cora slipped her arm around Avril's shoulders but she remained stiff and unmoved. "Would you like to come in for some coffee? Mama will make you some eggs. Odelia brought in her cinnamon rolls."

Avril shook her head. "Am I so hard up as to eat Odelia's rolls?" A slight laugh gurgled in her chest. "Daddy broke his tooth on one during a potluck dinner a few years back. Dern things are like rocks."

"Well, Mama makes a mean batch of scrambled eggs. We have toast and coffee too."

Avril sobered. "I can't eat eggs when the children had dry toast for breakfast." She glanced back at her. "How long has your daddy been gone?"

Cora withdrew her hand, folding her arms about her waist and leaning forward, eyes fixed toward the Cumberland and the port where Rufus would return one day soon. "Seven months."

"Does he write or call?"

"He used to write but it's been awhile."

"A bank president and a farmer . . . who'd have thought? Men who went to war yet neither one cut out for hard times."

"Billy loves you, Avril. He'll return. Daddy left twice before. Came back both times."

"Oh, Cora, what times do we live in? Men abandoning their families with not two nickels to rub together. Banks closing. Crops failing. Drought." A fresh wash of tears struck her cheek. "I been holding in my tears 'cause there ain't nothing worse than a crying mama. Can't even cry into my pillow at night because I'm afraid they might hear me."

"Avril, let me give you some of our stores. Mama has a decent garden out at the Good farm."

Her soft smile was small. "I can still taste her blue-berry pie at the county fair. She always did have a lovely garden, your mama."

"Then you must take home some of her preserves."

"I didn't come here looking for a handout, Cora. Or seeking pity."

"Then why did you come? How can I help you?"

"I just . . ." Her lower lip quivered, erasing her words. She breathed in, then out, batting away her tears. "I just wanted to remember the happiest time of my life, save for my kids being born. Wanted to go to a place where all my dreams were possible. When I was young and beau-tiful, and so in love with Billy. Your shop, Cora, your wedding shop was about the happiest I've ever been." Avril leaned forward, wiping her nose on the edge of her apron. "The war was over, our boys were home, and finally, Billy and I could start our life. I loved every moment I spent in this shop. Every moment planning my wedding. There was so much joy. I laughed and laughed." Her voice faded to melancholy as she added, "I can't remember the last time I laughed."

From the street, a motor rumbled pulling up to the shop. The driver cut the engine and a lithe young woman with shining hair falling about her face in Greta Garbo waves stepped out. She was followed by two equally lithe and well-dressed women—perhaps the mother and grandmother—and two young women.

"I 'spect I need to be heading out." Avril pushed up from the stoop. "I left the kids playing in the yard." Her blank gaze rested on the blue horizon. "Do you think it will rain today? We could sure use some rain."

"Hello." The woman, who looked like the mother, called, waving. "We're the Kirkpatricks. My daughter just became engaged. We heard this is the wedding shop from which to buy her trousseau."

"You heard right." Avril stood, punctuating her hearty endorsement. "This is the best wedding shop, bar none, in these parts and beyond."

"Nice to meet you. Do come in." Cora introduced herself with one hand clapped on Avril's arm. "Let me say good-bye to my friend and I'll be right with you. There's a lovely divan to your right." She turned to Avril. "Wait here."

Scurrying around the side of the shop, Cora ducked into the mudroom, tapped her heel against a loose board, lifted it free, and knelt down, fishing for the can tucked under the floor against the wall.

Got it. Prying away the lid, she counted out twenty dollars. Her reserves were dwindling, but she could not send Avril home empty-handed.

Five hundred dollars was all she had left in this can. But she had two more hidden. She took out another forty, folding them into her palm, and headed around the outside of the shop to find Avril across the way, heading through Gardenia Park.

"Avril!" Cora paused for a slow-moving Lincoln, then darted across the street. "Wait."

When the women met on the edge of the thin and brown grass, Cora pressed the money into her hand.

"I knew you were going to do something like this." Avril pressed the money back. "I can't take your money. I can't be beholden. When would I pay you back?"

"It's a gift. You don't need to pay me back."

"I can't."

"Avril Kreyling, if you let your children go hungry on account of your pride, I'll never forgive you. You'll never forgive yourself. Take it or I'll go shopping and show up with groceries. At least this way, you have the dignity of doing your own marketing."

"Then let me earn it. I can't just take it. Can I clean the shop? Take in your laundry?"

Cora exhaled. With mail orders down this spring, Odelia and only four other women handled the sewing. Mama did the laundry but hated it. She missed Liberty to no end.

"You can take in our washing."

Avril's smile put a light in her rising tears. "Thank you . . . thank you."

"Come around Friday to pick it up. If we like the arrangement, we can keep it up for as long as you need. But this"—Cora pressed the money into her hand—"is a gift."

Avril broke, dropping her forehead to Cora's chest, gripping her arms, sobbing. "I knew this old shop was the place to come. I did. You've saved me, Cora Scott. Saved me."

CHAPTER FIFTEEN

BIRCH

He pulled his wagon along Blossom Lane, hopped down, and gave Uncle Sam a smooth pat on the rump. "Be right back, boy."

He jumped the curb and made his way under the oak tree to the back of the wedding shop. "Cora!"

He waited with one eye on the back door. He was right proud of Cora and Esmé, but it didn't look like Ernest Scott was coming home any time soon. The man had plum lost his mind skipping out like he did just before Christmas. Did he know his women were living on the third floor of the shop? In that tiny space? In this heat?

Couldn't be a hotter summer. He was worried for his crops. Every morning he woke asking the good Father for rain. "I can do the plowing and planting, Lord, but only You can make my fields grow."

"Cora!" He stopped at the back door, rapping his knuckles against the screen. "It's eight o'clock, woman. You best be up."

Sadly, he'd not seen much of Cora this summer. Passed her in church, but she kept to herself. Any ill he had toward her over that riverboat captain, he set aside. Love hoped in all things.

He saw Esmé every day when she came out to the farm to tend her garden. She had his tomatoes and cucumbers beat by a country mile.

He used stored rainwater to keep the garden growing, but his cornfields needed the clouds to cry.

If the drought continued, how would the Scott women eat this winter? He'd decided already to give them a side of beef from the cow he'd butcher this fall. And have mercy if Esmé didn't have enough chickens to frustrate the roosters and keep them busy.

In fact, he was just a might jealous. He'd like to have a hen to chase after. Well, he was working on her. If she'd just stop clucking for the captain and look at him.

"Cora Scott!" He knocked harder this time.

The back door flew open. "Birch Good, land sakes, what in the world are you doing out here yelling like an uncouth for everyone to hear?" She appeared rushed, mussed, and beautiful with her chestnut hair flying about her face, her eyes snapping.

"What are you worried about?" Birch yanked off his hat and beat it against his overalls, scooping his hands through his mass of curls, twisting and knotting every which way. "All the shops are closed until nine, at least."

"The Everlys live right next to us. Above their shop. And they have a new baby. Now, what do you want?"

"Come on, I want to show you something." He set

his cap back on his head and snatched her hand, dragging her off the narrow back stoop.

"Let go of me. I can't be dragged out in public like this. I'm barefoot, my hair is a mess, and I've no lipstick. Do you want to get me banned from the Women's League?"

"Ain't no one gonna ban you. Besides, don't pretend to me you like the Women's League. Bunch of snooty old hags." They arrived at the wagon and Birch slapped the side. "What do you think?"

Cora peered over the tailgate. "Lumber. You drag me from my back door to get excited about a bunch of sawed trees?" She faced him, hand on her lean hip. "Times are hard, Birch, but not that hard."

"I'm building you a porch. Off the back of the shop." He held up his hands toward the house, making a box by touching his thumbs together. "You and your mama can have dinner out there all summer, into the fall. Give you a break from the hot third floor. I know you're roasting up there. I can run some electric wires, too, so you can have a lamp for some cozy reading."

Birch glanced back at her, dropping his gaze and clearing his throat when he saw her misty golden eyes. It made his heart burn to see a gal cry. Made his arms itch to hold her.

"Thank you." She wrapped him in a hug.

He slowly brought his arms around her. "I thought you'd like a bit of space for yourselves. Make this shop more of a home. Your mama loved her porch back at the homestead."

Cora laughed through her tears, stepping out of his

embrace, brushing her cheek dry. "We did go at each other last night." She reached over the wagon's gate and patted the smooth golden boards. "You beautiful, beautiful lumber."

"You okay for me to get started?"

"Please. The sooner, the better. Did you have breakfast?"

"Just a cup of coffee."

"Eggs and toast coming up." Cora hurried toward the house, her skirt swinging over her slender calves and bare feet. Dang if Birch's heart didn't burst into flames. Drawing in a deep breath, he lowered the wagon's gate, trying to clear his head of that image, but his stubborn soul refused. He loved every image he'd stored of Cora Scott. He'd be blazes if this one wasn't one to savor.

Just as he reached in for the first set of boards, her fragrance filled his senses as she hooked her arms about his shoulders and kissed his cheek.

"Thank you again, Birch."

He righted himself, turning to her, gathering her into his arms, stepping into her, weakened by her long, narrow form leaning against him. "You know I'd do anything for you. I love you." He touched the heart-shaped pendant at the base of her neck. "Why do you wear that thing? He's only buying your affection."

"Birch . . ."

He let her go, though her presence increased his desire to make her his. It didn't matter his love was unrequited. It only mattered that he loved her.

When she ridded herself of that dastardly riverboat

captain, he'd be there for her. She'd see Birch was made for her. Look how easily their bodies fitted together.

"I'd better see to your eggs." She backed toward the shop. "Thank you again. Mama will be thrilled."

"Wade Fry is coming to help. We'll be done by end of the day."

"Really? How wonderful. Rufus comes next month and we can dine on my porch."

Birch stepped back, the colors of the day fading from brilliant to gray. "Rufus, you say?"

"Yes, finally he has a spare moment to spend with me. He's been on every river but the Cumberland this spring and summer."

"Not sure I like building you a porch to spend time with another man." Unable to glance her way, the sting of the moment quelled his excitement.

"I've always been honest with you."

"True, you have . . ."

"Shall I make eggs? Or are you changing your mind? Because if you're building this porch with strings attached . . ."

"Ain't no strings or conditions." He was no reneger.

Birch raised the first set of boards to his shoulder.

Over time he'd come to suspect her riverboat captain was a philanderer. From the rumors and whispers, he guessed half the town knew it too. So hows come Cora didn't?

Where was *Rufus* when Cora and Esmé had no place to live? Where was *Rufus* when Esmé needed a plot of land for her garden? Where was he when they wanted wood for the apartment fireplace last winter?

Cora disappeared inside and he could hear the echo of her voice. "Mama, eggs and toast for Birch. He's building us a porch."

He sighed, fighting the heaviness in his heart as he walked back to the wagon. One of these days he'd talk himself into forgetting her and moving on.

He hoisted another load to his shoulder and carted it to the back of the shop, dropping it to the ground with a clatter. Pausing, he raised his gaze to the blue sky peeking through the shading elm.

Yep, one of these days he was going to move on from Cora. However, today was not that day.

. . .

HALEY

Heart's Bend allowed for interior demolition if requests for renovation permits were on file, so Monday Cole and his team got things going. Light flooded into the shop the moment they busted down the added walls.

The hardwood under the nasty carpet was dull and thirsty but in great shape. "That's a win," Cole said.

Over the weekend Haley worked on her business plan, grateful she could consign gowns from designers. Now to get one or two that she liked to go into business with her. She had no credit or history in this business, so . . .

What she needed was a mentor. Someone to show her the ropes. She Googled around and discovered a shop in Birmingham called Malone & Co. Apparently the owner, Charlotte Rose, found her wedding dress in a trunk and it'd been worn by three other women throughout history. Intrigued, Haley searched until she came across an article in the Birmingham newspaper.

The dress, made and first worn in 1912, found its way to two other brides before Charlotte in 2012. One in 1939 and another in 1968.

The gown fit all four women without needing to be altered or changed. Like some sort of magic dress. The sisterhood of the traveling wedding gown.

Haley's pulse raced as she read the account. She had to meet Charlotte Rose.

Standing over Cole, she announced her plans. "I put a call into a wedding shop owner in Birmingham. I'm going to see if she'll meet with me."

Cole looked around from where he was pulling carpet nails from the small salon floor. "Birmingham? Don't they have wedding shops in Nashville?"

"There's something special about this shop owner. I liked what I read about her."

He handed her an extra hammer. "Here, start pulling out nails. Man, whoever kicked this carpet did not know what they were doing."

Haley dropped to the floor, getting to work.

"How's it going with the money?"

"Do desperate prayers count?"

"In my book, yes," Cole said. "What about your folks?"

"Dad would but Mom refuses. She hates this place and I can't get a reason out of her." Haley recounted her conversation with her parents, raising more questions in her heart.

What did Mom have against the wedding shop? And why wouldn't she tell Haley?

Cole stopped pulling nails. "Are you sure you want to start down this road if you have no money? What about the bank?"

"They said no."

"Haley—"

"Cole, I'm not giving up. If I have to open the shop with only half of it done—"

"You won't pass inspection."

"I'll find the money. Shoot, I found a rare part for a tank in the middle of the desert. I think I can find a few measly dollars to redo this place."

"You think eighty thousand is a few measly dollars?"

"Remember the story where the prophet Elisha prayed for the widow and her bottle of oil never ran out? She had money to pay her debt."

"Do you have a bottle of expensive oil to sell? Stock in Exxon?"

"No, but I'm talking to the same God Elisha talked to, and He has a whole lot of money."

"You're really doing this on faith?"

Haley sat down against the wall. "I don't have any other option, Cole. Ever have that feeling in your gut that says 'this is the right thing to do,' but it makes no sense?"

He lightly tapped his hammer against the floor-board at an imaginary nail. "I do. Rather, I knew when something wasn't right even though it made no sense."

"Did you act on it?"

He jutted out his chin. "I did. Hardest thing I'd ever done."

"Really? Even with your dad—"

"Knock, knock. Hello?"

Haley exchanged a glance with Cole, rising up to find an older woman entering the foyer, leaning on her cane. Behind her, on the stoop, sat a distressed leather suitcase.

"Can I help you?"

"Are you Haley?"

"I am. Please come in." Haley offered her a steadying hand, helping her to the old metal chair Cole set down for her, then closing the door.

"It's cold out there," she said with a shiver. "I read about you in the paper. About the city giving you this shop. I had to come see for myself."

The woman had an aura about her, a timeless quality, and Haley ached to hear what she had to say.

Cole bounded up to the mezzanine, returning with another old metal chair from the third floor, setting it down for Haley. He took a seat on the stairs as the woman glanced around the dusty shop.

"None worse for the wear, I see. The shop's bones are still here. Strong bones."

Haley leaned toward her. "Did you get your wedding trousseau at this shop?"

"Indeed I did." She nodded, a dreamy quality in her voice. "Back in the day, the large room there was called the grand salon." The woman pointed ahead of her, then behind. "That there was the small salon."

"That's what I've been calling them," Haley said, smiling at the woman, feeling the smallest ping of confirmation. Her sixth-grade research was coming to bear.

The woman sighed, resting her hands on her lap. "This is good. So very good. You're the one to be here. You're the one."

"I'm the one? W-what do you mean?"

"Let's see, the brides would come down the stairs wearing their beautiful wedding gown for their mothers and grandmothers to see, and all the women kinfolk and friends." The woman pointed to the stairs, moving on with her story. "Everyone would ooh and aah. It was such a *thrilling* moment."

Haley peeked up the stairs toward the mezzanine, envisioning bride after bride in her wedding gown descending the stairs. "It must have been beautiful." She faced the woman. "How can I help you, Mrs.—"

"Peabody. Lillian Peabody." She motioned to the door. "My daughter-in-law left a suitcase on the porch. Young man, can you get it?"

Cole jumped up, easily lifting the vintage case and setting it at Mrs. Peabody's feet. He made a face at Haley.

What's this about?

I don't know.

"Peabody? Are you any relation to Linus Peabody?"

"He's my nephew. Now, don't let him go giving you a hard time." Mrs. Peabody motioned for Cole to unlock her bag. "My mother married in 1934. Her folks lost everything when the banks failed. She had a job as a teacher, but turned over most of her salary to support the family. When harder times hit, the women teachers lost their positions so the men could stay on, supporting their families. Anyway, when my father proposed, my mother had it in her head to have a church wedding. Well, her daddy couldn't afford a church wedding with a proper wedding dress, flowers, and cake. My grandmother insisted my mother put aside her foolishness, put on her Sunday dress, and get married by the preacher in the farmhouse parlor."

"Something tells me she refused," Haley said.

"So you knew my mother, then?" Mrs. Peabody laughed softly, giving Haley a slow wink. "'My Sunday dress?' says my mother. 'I wear that rag every week. Everyone's seen me in it a hundred times. I'm not getting married in a faded blue print dress.'"

"I don't blame her."

"My father offered to buy her a dress, but my grandfather wouldn't hear of it. Even though he was barely feeding the family, he was a proud man. So my mother set about figuring a way to get her a wedding dress."

"So she came here? To the shop?"

"You're a bright girl. Don't let this one go, young man."

"Oh, we're not—"

"We're friends. We're just friends."

"Friends make the best lovers. Now, where was I?"

Haley bit back her laugh. Racy Mrs. Peabody!

Mrs. Peabody tapped the box with her cane. "The dress my mother wore is inside. And I'm returning it."

"Returning it?" Haley resisted the urge to glance at Cole every time Mrs. Peabody amused her. "I don't understand. Why would you return it?"

"My mother never could come up with the money to buy a dress. She scrimped and saved for a few months, but Daddy wasn't willing to put off their wedding much longer. So my grandmother went to Miss Cora asking her to *lend* Mama a wedding gown." Mrs. Peabody gazed off into the distance. "Mama never returned it. I think there was some ill will between the two of them, Miss Cora and Mama."

"Maybe Miss Cora gave it to her," Cole said.

"No, it was a loan. I remember hearing my grandmother talk of it. When I was a girl, if the family had a wedding to attend, Granny would say, 'Janice, did you *ever* return that gown to Cora?' And Mama always answered with a curt, 'No.' When I got married I asked her about the dress . . . Worst thing I ever said to my mother. Shew wee. So I bought a new gown. Right here in this shop. Daddy insisted, but Mama never came around with me when I tried it on. Said she trusted me."

"Sounds like she and Miss Cora had a falling out."

"If they did, she never spoke of it. Right before she died, we were going through her things, and don't you know? I found her dress. The one Miss Cora loaned her. 'Mama, your dress! I thought it was lost.'" Mrs. Peabody captured Haley with her storytelling. "Mama's eyes watered, and she shook her head. 'I did Cora wrong. I should've returned her dress. I stole it from her.'" Mrs. Peabody tapped the suitcase with her cane. "I made up my mind that if the shop ever opened again, I'd bring the dress back around, leave it here for another bride. Maybe she'd have some happy memories with it."

Haley raised the lid to find a beautiful dress with a V-neckline and a high pleated collar in the back nestled in a lining of gold satin. The skirt was plain but long. Haley raised it from the case.

"Mrs. Peabody, it's beautiful."

"It's a bit yellow and needs a good cleaning, but I think the gals today like older clothes. Vintage, I think they call it."

"Vintage is all the rage."

Under the dress was a tarnished silver tiara with a small row of sparkling jewels.

"Mrs. Peabody, you don't have to return this. Cora's been dead a long time. The shop's been closed for over thirty years." But Haley could see the older woman's pride in her eyes. She could feel it. "I don't have any money to pay for it right now anyway."

"I didn't come to get money from you, Haley." Mrs. Peabody reached in her pocketbook and passed Haley a white envelope. "It's not much, but that should cover the interest on the price of a gown. In 1934, a dress like Mama's cost a whopping three hundred dollars. Can you imagine?"

Haley immediately offered the envelope back. "Mrs. Peabody, I can't take your money. Especially if you're returning the gown. It wasn't even my shop when your mother was here. And it didn't belong to anyone in my family or in any of my friends' families. I'm not even related to the Scotts."

"Then consider it for the shop." The woman shoved

the envelope toward Haley. "Consider my money as an investment. I'm giving back the dress Mama stole, and I want to make it right."

Haley peeked in the envelope. "Five thousand dollars. Mrs. Peabody, really, I can't take this."

"Please, darling. My Gilbert did all right. I don't know your plans for the place, but it looks to need some work. Are you rich? Don't you need some money?" Mrs. Peabody tapped her hand to her heart. "I felt right here that I was to bring you the dress and this money. Like I said, Gil did all right. We put a good bit by. On behalf of my mother, the Peabody and Cook family debt is settled."

Haley peered back at Cole, a wash of tears in her eyes. *What do I do?* If this happened on her watch in the air force, she'd know what to do. Follow regulations. But now she was out in life on her own, figuring the regulations out as she went.

"I found these and thought you'd like them." She reached into her bag again, retrieving two photographs, passing them to Haley. "I had sons, and their wives are more interested in their own mothers' wedding gowns than mine." The old bride, a shop alumnus, tapped the picture on the right over two photographs. "This is me in my dress. Miss Cora helped me pick it out in 1955."

A much younger version of Mrs. Peabody stared back at Haley from the world of black and white. Her dark hair was piled high on her head, showing her slender neck. The off-the-shoulder bodice was made of lace and sat atop a wide tulle skirt.

"Mrs. Peabody, what a beauty."

"Me or the dress? I tell you, the dress stole the show."

"Where is your dress now?"

"Gil and I moved a good bit in our younger years, and somewhere along the way it was lost. Breaks my heart to think of it. I'd bring it here if I still had it."

"I'd love to hear more about Miss Cora." Haley handed the pictures to Cole, who stored them in the suitcase with the gown. "From people who actually knew her."

"Well, plenty of folks in town knew her. She was something. A handsome woman. Tall, thin-boned. Not especially pretty on the outside but a beauty in her heart."

"Did you know her parents? Or her husband?"

"Saw her mama around town and her husband, heard stories—you know how townsfolk do—about her being in love with a riverboat captain. Quite the tale. How she and her mother lived up top the shop in the thirties after all the banks closed."

"Here? They lived here?"

Mrs. Peabody squinted at a muted memory. "My memory ain't what it used to be, but seems I heard her father done like *my* father-in-law when hard times hit—bugged out on the family. Mr. Scott ran a bank, which was caught up with a chain that closed. They lost everything. The whole town was affected when Heart's Bend Mutual closed."

"Did he ever return?" This part of Cora's story was new to Haley.

"Not to my recollection. Now, my father-in-law wised up and skedaddled on back home." She laughed, pressing her slender, age-formed fingers to her lips. "My husband was born nine months later. No, now wait. I think Mr. Scott died during the Depression years. Least that's what Mrs. Scott said. But there were whispers. Something about a divorce. No one ever saw Mr. Scott again, but he's got a headstone in the church-yard. We didn't see much of the Scotts. Just in church now and then."

The front door opened and a regal-looking blonde in a dress with heels peeked in. "You ready?"

"Haley, my daughter-in-law, Beatriz. Beatriz, this is Haley. She's bringing back the wedding shop." Mrs. Peabody moved toward her daughter-in-law with the aid of her cane. "Haley, it was a pleasure."

"No, Mrs. Peabody, the pleasure was all mine. Please come again." Haley aided the woman to the door, then tried to give the check to the daughter-in-law. "She gave me money but—"

"Then you should take it. We've not seen her this excited about something in a long time. I think Linus let you have the shop just to make her happy." Beatriz folded her hand over Haley's. "Take it. Keep it. Use it to open the shop. I don't understand, but the old place means a lot to her."

Haley closed the door behind her surprise guest, a swirl in her chest, the push-pull of opposing emotions. With the check from Mrs. Peabody, Haley understood opening this shop was no longer her idea. It was about more than fulfilling a childhood pledge.

God was in this. And He'd made Himself known.

"Well, there's your first bottle of oil, Haley." Cole

reached for the check, then handed it back to Haley. "That gut sense you have just might be right. And . . ." He picked up the pictures. "I have an idea for these."

"I'm shaking." Haley sat next to him, absorbing what happened in her heart, in her thoughts, through her skin.

"Over pictures? I was just going to frame them. Make a pictorial history. I bet we'll find more. Maybe if we can get that locked room opened."

"Goofball. I mean over this money."

He bumped her with his shoulder, grinning, locking up the suitcase, setting it beside the staircase. "Yeah, I know. Pretty amazing."

"I said I'd have faith for it and wham, some lady walks in and gives me five thousand dollars. Who does that?"

"Who knows? But I've always heard when you're doing God's will, all kinds of crazy things can happen."

"Is that it, Cole? Am I doing God's will?" Haley reached for his shoulder, turning him to face her. "When I think of my past, I feel like the least likely candidate to be blessed by God."

"You and every other sinner in the world." Cole regarded her for a moment, a slow smile tipping his lips, his shoulder slightly touching hers. "Want to pull more nails out of the floor?" He offered his hammer.

She laughed, reaching for the well-used tool. "You really know how to show a girl a good time."

He grinned. "Thanks. I like to think it's my superpower."

CHAPTER SIXTEEN

COLE

A fresh snow whitened Heart's Bend Wednesday morning as Cole and Gomez, along with Haley and the crew, finished cleaning up the shop from the demo. Now all they had to do was wait for the permits.

He'd run into political red tape for permits before, and he hoped this project wouldn't fall between the cracks at the Department of Codes & Building Safety.

Was it too good to be true that the council gave Haley the shop so easily while Akron barked on their heels?

He'd keep an eye out. In the meantime, he called on a couple of the bids he put in before Christmas. But everyone said, "We're holding."

Yeah, the winter was slow but this was ridiculous. No one wanted to pull the trigger on new projects?

Standing on the front steps of the shop, he stared toward the freshly plowed streets. He had a whole day ahead with nothing to do.

Cole waited for the rise of anxiety, the shiver of panic,

but instead, a warm it's-gonna-be-all-right wrapped him up.

The shop door closed behind him and Haley came out, zipping up her jacket, taking her gloves from her pocket. "I hate waiting."

"I'm president of that club." He roped his arm around her shoulders, purely in a brotherly fashion, and gave her a squeeze. But touching her made his heart hammer in his chest. "Want to be my vice president?"

"I don't know. How much work is involved?"

"Ah, not much. A little worry here, a little worry there, a sleepless night or two."

Haley laughed and he peeked sideways at her. She'd always fascinated him, the pretty little sister of his friend Seth. The baby girl in a family of boys. She grew up rough and tumble but she looked like a china doll. Petite, but with wide eyes and full lips cast in her delicate features.

"What?"

He'd stared too long. Cole shook his head, stepping off the porch. "Nothing."

"Do I have something on my face? You looked like I might have something on my face." She followed him, wiping her hands under her eyes, across her cheeks, and down to her chin.

"No, your face is fine." *Beautiful.*

Cole made a beeline for his truck. What was this sensation? Wanting to stare at her, touch her, think about her. For crying out loud, she was Tammy's best friend.

Tammy's not here.

At the truck he pulled his keys from his pocket, an idea rising. "Hopefully we'll get the permits next week."

"We better. It's already the middle of January and the town council's clock starts ticking in a couple of weeks."

"If they take too much longer we can ask for an extension."

"We can, but I get the feeling Linus Peabody won't budge. Not with Akron willing to pay so much for the land."

"So what are you up to the rest of the day?" Cole said, his idea solidifying.

"I have no idea. I wanted to head down to Birmingham to see Charlotte Rose, but she's out of town. I've been working on design ideas for the shop. I want to capture some feel of yesteryear. How the world might have looked in Miss Cora's day. Give it that twenties and thirties feel."

"Hollywood regency?"

"Right. You remembered."

"So, you want to go shopping? I know some antique malls . . ."

She shook her head. "Not until I have the money. It will only depress me if I find something I can't buy."

"Credit card?"

"No can do." She glanced away, down the avenue, shaking her head. Cole knew that move. One born of regret. Of wishing for wiser times. "I'm using my own money to get the website going, buying inventory. The furniture I want might have to wait. Cole?"

"Haley?"

"Am I crazy for wanting to do this?"

Cole leaned against the passenger side door of his truck. "Why would anyone be crazy for pursuing a dream?"

"Because it's a dumb dream? I know you don't want me to mention Tammy, but—"

"It's okay."

She leveled her gaze at him. "She never really mentioned the shop to you?"

"No, she didn't. But—"

"But what? If she changed her mind I look all the more foolish."

"Maybe you look brave. And devoted." He searched for a word to match the feeling in his chest. "How many people would pursue something like this out of devotion to a friend? To a pinky promise?"

Haley tugged on her gloves. "When I got out of the air force I was pretty lost, banged up from a relationship. Tammy had just died . . ." The wind pushed her hair back from her face. "So I sold everything, hopped on my bike, and drove across the southwest, trying to clear my head and heart."

She paused and he waited, resisting the urge to fill the space with some trite comment.

"I'd just crossed the Texas line on my way to visit friends when I heard 'Go home' rattle across my mind. I knew it was God, but I resisted at first. Because going home meant living with the parents. At least in the beginning."

"What changed your mind?"

Her laugh was low with resolve. "My heart knew it

was right. And I actually didn't know what else to do. It's getting cold." She smiled at Cole, walking backward toward her bike. "Check you later?"

Cole walked with her, working up the nerve to deploy his idea. "What are you doing today?"

Ever since she'd whispered, "*But I want you,*" in his ear that morning at the diner, a small flame ignited in his soul, catching him off guard. But it was waking up desires he'd buried long before Tammy died. It was making him *want* her.

Don't get mixed up over pleasure and business. She wanted a contractor, not a boyfriend.

"Research, I guess. Call around about inventory. Which I hate because I'm not really sure what I'm doing yet. I sound stupid to the designers."

"So how about doing something fun?"

She regarded him with a narrow gaze. "Define fun."

He laughed. "Oh no, you have to trust me on this. Are you game or not?"

Seeing her inner debate in her expression, he was pretty sure she'd say yes. If memory served, she wasn't one to back down from a challenge.

"Game. Let's go." She shook her head, making her way toward her Harley. "You hit my Achilles heel."

"My place. Follow me. I live down River Road."

At the house, she parked her bike in the shade of his detached garage. Removing her helmet, she followed him as he opened the bay doors and scanned the property.

"I love this place. Wasn't this the old Good farm?"

"Yep. A distant cousin inherited the place, second

cousin once removed or something, and he parceled up the land and sold it. However, he wanted the house and six acres to stay together." Cole grinned back at her. "I was in the right place at the right time. He gave me a great deal."

"Wow, that's weird." She followed him into the garage. "I'm getting the wedding shop and you have the Good farm. Spooky." She paused, hands on her hips. "So what are we doing here? Please don't tell me we're going to clean your garage."

"Spooky?" He made a face. "What's spooky about me getting the farm and you the shop? And yes, ta-da, we're going to clean out my garage." He swept his arm toward an immaculate, pristine space.

"Ha! If I'd had men like you in my unit . . . *Sigh*. It would've been glorious." She stood in the doorway, her slight frame haloed in the midmorning sunlight glinting off the snow.

She was gorgeous. He'd not allowed himself to see how much so before now. Nor since fifth grade when she socked him.

But as Tammy's BFF and little sister of his friend Seth, Haley had always been off-limits. Until now.

"Yeah, it's spooky. You bought the Good farm. Now I'm buying the wedding shop." She laced her fingers together, demonstrating some kind of point. "Those two places are intertwined. Birch and Miss Cora. Me and . . . you . . ." Her voice trailed off and she diverted her attention to his workbench. "Seriously, you're a freak, Danner. This place is spotless. Every tool is in place."

"Makes them easier to find." Birch Good and Miss Cora? He'd forgotten they had a story. It wasn't anything to pay attention to, was it? He heard bits from the second cousin when he signed the final papers but . . .

His heart ran hot under his churning thoughts, sensing some kind of cosmic connection neither one of them planned. Glancing toward Haley, he didn't know how to form his feeling into words, so he shook the sensation to the ground and moved to the storage closets.

Unlocking the doors, he reached inside and tossed Haley a flak jacket and a pair of goggles. "Heads up."

She caught the bundled gear with one hand. "What's this?"

"Paintball." Cole handed her a Tiberius T9.

"Paintball?"

She stared at the gear, her expression sober, and for a moment he wondered if he'd treaded over a wartime memory she wanted to forget.

"Look, Haley, I'm sorry. I wasn't thinking . . . I don't know how Bagram went for you . . . ."

She glanced up. "Sorry?" Her grin waxed his heart. "Dude, let's do this."

Shoving her way into his storage closet, she chose her own gear—an old fleece of Cole's and a pair of his brother's camo pants—which were too big for her small frame, but she hitched them up by tying scarves to her thighs.

Then she inspected the guns. "I want to make sure you're giving me the best one. Not some piece of garbage where the paintballs get jammed."

"Would I do that to you?"

"Yes."

He laughed. She was right. He would. But not today. Not when he wanted a fair fight. When he wanted to just be with her. And laugh. He really needed to laugh.

When they'd geared up, Haley headed out, leading the way with the Tiberius anchored on her hip. For the baby in the family, she was bossy. "Let's go, Danner. I'm going to paint you like a Rembrandt."

Yeah, this was going to be a fun. "We'll see about that, Morgan."

On the edge of the drive, Haley paused to tie a bandana over her head, then added a worn wool hat. "Ready?"

"I gotta tell you, Haley, you're scaring me a bit."

"Be afraid, Cole." She cocked her gun. "Very afraid."

In that moment, his heart cracked open a little bit more. *What if . . .* Cole cauterized the notion, unwilling to entertain any possible answer. So why entertain the question?

He grabbed the University of Tennessee flag and headed toward the stand of trees, detailing the boundaries and the rules.

"The game is capture the flag." He raised the flag.

"I know the game, Cole."

"Just reminding you of the rules. Besides, you've been to real war since we last played and I want to make sure you know *my* rules."

"Whatever. Go on." She jogged ahead of him, turning, running backward. "I'm ready to play."

"I'll set this in the center of the stand of trees, in the mini woods, not more than a couple hundred yards square. Once I do, give me ten Mississippis to get to my base and start the game. The goal is to capture the flag and return to your base without getting shot. We'll go three rounds. Winner take all." He held up two scarves. "Red or blue?"

"Blue."

He tossed Haley the scarf. "Pick your home base and tie this to the tree. If you get painted trying to capture the flag, you're dead for five seconds, giving the other team time to take the flag and run. You have to count the Mississippis out loud when you're dead. If you shoot and miss, it's another five seconds."

Cole heard the pop of the gun and felt the sting of a close-range shot against his arm.

"You're dead. Start counting."

He made a face. "That shot doesn't count."

She walked on. "What's the prize when I win?"

"Bragging rights. And the game hasn't started yet."

"But you're holding the flag." She paused, anchoring her gun on her hip, pointing the muzzle skyward.

"Yes, so I can set it up on the field of play."

"But you didn't say anything about a *field of play*." Before he could blink, she fired again, painting a green splash on his leg. "That's two. I think I'm going to need more than bragging rights. Maybe dinner. Or free labor for the shop. Ooh, can I keep this gun?"

"No, you can't keep the gun." Cole leaned over her, staring her down, trying not to laugh. "My toys, my rules. Right now all you're doing is wasting shots."

"I'm only going to need three."

"You have to hit me three *separate* times, with the

flag *in my hand*, to win. If I get it to my base without getting painted, that's ten seconds of dead time for *you*."

"Won't happen."

"Yeah, well, we'll see." Cole started off, trotting backward, taunting her, loving the liberty swelling in his soul. He'd not felt this free since before Tammy died. Since before she called off the wedding.

They'd arrived at the trees, the flag flapping in the breeze over Cole's head.

"I'm going to plant the flag and set up my base. No cheating, Morgan." He grinned. "At least not in the first five minutes."

"I don't have to cheat."

"So you say, so you say."

"Hey, there are a lot of disadvantages to being the baby girl in a family of four boys, but being the best at paintball isn't one of them." She peeled off, racing toward her tree, running under the lowest limbs. She was compact, a cannonball, a lightning strike. "You best get going, Danner. I'm itching to shoot you."

Cole watched her run up a tree trunk, leaping to catch onto the bottom limb, then bounce back to the ground and disappear among the dense trees. He was in trouble. Big trouble.

In more ways than one.

CHAPTER SEVENTEEN

HALEY

I warned you." Haley breathed in the cold, crisp, beautiful air, her gun anchored on her hip, watching Cole limp toward her, his Tennessee flag all but dragging on the ground.

"That you were going to cheat like crazy."

"Cheater? If that's how you have to guard your pride . . ."

"Give me *something*, please. I was humiliated." Cole stopped beside her, out of breath. "But between you and me, well played, Morgan, well played."

"Next time I'll let you win." She laughed, turned for the house, and two steps in Cole tripped her up with the tip of the flagpole, sending her face-first into the snow. Haley scrambled up, protesting. "Oh, I see how it is."

He feigned shock. "What? I don't know what you're talking about."

Dropping her gun, Haley inhaled a cold, deep breath and ran at him with a rebel yell, hitting him so quick he had no reaction time. Tackling him to the ground, she scooped snow into his face, on his head, and around the back of his neck.

He tried to fight back but was laughing so hard he just laid there and took it. Haley rolled into the soft snow next to him and stared at the brilliant blue day, breathing deep.

"Thanks, Cole."

He sat up, brushing the snow from his neck and face. "For what?" He motioned to her torso. "You have no paint on you whatsoever. Please don't tell anyone about this. I'll never be able to show my face in town again."

She sat up. "I already posted on Facebook, Tumblr, and Twitter."

He smashed a wad of snow in her face. "Ha-ha, I win. I win." He tossed his head back and beat his chest.

Haley hit him square in his open mouth with a ball of snow. He sputtered, laughing, coughing, shaking the cold crystals, then regarded her for a moment.

"I had fun."

"Yeah, me too." She tried to hold his gaze, tried to see beyond his "just-a-guy-having-fun-with-a-friend" demeanor. Was it her imagination or did they have *moments* here and there? "Th-thanks for today. I needed this. Been a long time since I laughed."

"Me too." He angled forward to see her face. "Tammy's death took the joy out of life for a while."

"I should've been there more for her. But I was so wrapped up in my life-sucking relationship."

"She understood, Haley. Besides, everything happened so fast. She was so worn-out and weak . . ."

"When I made it to the hospital the week before she died, I cried in the hall at how emaciated she was. But her eyes, you know, I could still see my Tammy in her eyes."

"She had an inner fire to the end."

Haley looked back at him. "Can I ask you something?"

"Sure, but I don't promise to answer."

"Do you see your dad? Ever?" Haley was at the community pool the day the FBI arrested his dad for fraud. She was there when his mom frantically demanded they let him go, declaring to everyone the feds were railroading her husband.

Cole shook his head. "He's out, lives in Nashville, but our paths don't cross."

"What about your brothers or your mom?"

"Not sure about Mom. I think Chris and Cap do, but I don't ask." Cole patted down the snow on his right, then shoved the crystals at nothing.

"Know what I've learned over the years, Cole? Good people make bad mistakes."

"If they're good people, then why do they make bad mistakes?"

Haley had been asking herself that for the last year. "I wish I knew. But isn't your dad repentant?"

"Sure, once the feds got hold of him. He turned over and showed his belly. But he still bilked people out of their money." Cole shoved up from the snowy ground. "I have forgiven him, Haley. After Tammy died, I got back to church and realized if God required my life from me, I'd not be ready to face Him. I didn't want to go into heaven with unforgiveness toward Dad. Not when God had forgiven me. But that doesn't mean I want to see him or have a relationship."

"It's easy to walk out forgiveness from a distance."

"I'm required to forgive, not have a relationship." He jammed the flagpole against the ground. "What about you? Have your forgiven the person who wronged you?"

"Only a thousand times." Haley fought to stay in a place of letting go, forgiving, not reliving the past. "My first Sunday back in church, I slipped in the back, and this sweet woman was preaching. She said the most profound thing I've ever heard in the most gentle voice. 'The problem,' she said, 'is most people talk as if we will demand an account from God one day. But the harsh reality is God will demand an account from us. He will owe us nothing but justice.' Scared the what's-it out of me."

Haley edged around the rest of the truth. How her life with Dax took her soul places she never, ever wanted to go.

"I remember you were pretty much a Jesus freak in high school," Cole said.

"Well, remove Jesus and you have just a freak." Once she decided on a direction, she gave herself to it. No going back.

Cole laughed low. "What? I can't see it. Little, blonde, beautiful Haley Morgan a freak? Like how? You dyed your hair black and wore a nose ring?"

"Child's play. Externals. Symbolism over substance. I gave myself to my freakishness." She shivered, the body heat she'd generated during the game was dissipating, and the cold settled in her bones. She shoved up from the ground. "I think I'll go. I'm getting cold."

"As long as we're asking questions . . ." Cole pushed himself up with the help of the flagpole. "How come you never ask me about it . . . you know, Tammy and me?"

Haley squinted up at him through the shifting sunlight. "Ask about what? How much you loved each other?"

Cole regarded her. "She never told you, did she?"

"Told me what?"

Cole hesitated with a sigh. Then, "Haley, we broke up. Called off the wedding."

"No." She tented her eyes with her hand, trying to see his expression. If he was joking, he showed poor taste. "You broke up? A call-off-the-wedding breakup?"

"It all happened so fast. We broke up the November before last, right before Thanksgiving. So we kept it quiet. Didn't want to ruin the holidays. Though I thought she told you. She quietly canceled things and we figured we'd tell everyone in January. But a week later she was diagnosed with cancer, and we were in a swirl of surgeries and treatments."

Haley stared off over the white snow-covered field. "She never said a word."

"I'd have called you if I'd known." Cole crunched a wad of snow in his bare hand. "The cancer took over everything."

Haley glanced over at him. "Why? Why'd you break up?"

"She said she wasn't ready. Wanted to go to law school."

"Do you have to be single to go to law school?"

"Apparently she thought so. Getting close to the marriage she realized she'd never gone on the adventure you went on. Said she'd determined at eight she was going to marry me and now at twenty-eight, that seemed foolish. Did she really want to marry *me* or her childhood idea?"

"I keep asking myself that about the shop," Haley said. "Do you know why she didn't tell me? I-I can't believe she didn't talk to me about this. Of course, I was filling her ear with my woes."

Was she so consumed with her fears and mistakes over Dax, how she felt betrayed, how she wept over the choice she had made that she didn't *hear* Tammy?

"She didn't feel good, Haley. I'd wondered if that's why she called things off at first. She'd been fighting blazing headaches and all kinds of stuff for months."

"It hurts to know how much she suffered in silence." Haley brushed a cold tear from under her eyes. "So that's probably how she felt about the wedding shop? Just a childhood fantasy?"

Maybe this whole wedding shop ordeal was a farce. She was only pining for something long gone—the innocence and hope of her youth.

"I don't know. Just that she never said a word to me about it."

"And she never said a word to me about walking away from the only boy she ever loved? It doesn't make sense."

"Looking back, I see how the onset of the cancer changed her. After the diagnosis, she really changed," Cole said. "Guess I can say it now, but things had been strained between us. Got worse after we got engaged and the closer we got to the wedding. I thought it was just stress, but she was pulling away. Meanwhile, I kept waking up with dread, realizing I didn't love her the way a man should love the woman he's about to marry."

"But you'd been together forever. How could you not have known?" She was one to talk. How her emotions had fooled her. She stuck with Dax far too long. She had no gavel to bring down in judgment here. "Why did you propose, then?"

He shook his head, tossing another snowball into the icy wind. Overhead, thick gray clouds rolled in from the northwest. "I never officially proposed."

"What? Then how were you getting married?"

"I don't know . . . We were talking about our relationship, the future, and the next thing I knew her parents were involved—you know how her dad can be—and they were pulling out calendars and setting a date. I left the house in a daze."

"But said nothing. You went along with it."

"Haley." His voice spiked as he faced her. "I thought it was right. Tammy was beautiful, smart, talented, a good woman. Why wouldn't I want to marry her? Whatever hesitation I had seemed stupid. I refused to let my fears and wounds hold me back. We'd dated off and on since high school . . . Well, you know. You were there. If Tammy and I weren't meant to be together, why'd we keep coming back to each other? So I went along with it."

"Wow. I don't know what to say . . ." Haley started for the house, stopped, then spun around to Cole. "This makes me angry. I'm sorry, it does. Tammy was my best friend. I can live with the fact she wasn't interested in the wedding shop, but breaking up with you? Being diagnosed with cancer? I wasn't there for her. In any of it. Only at the end."

She was so blinded and stupid with Dax. The world could've spun off its axis for all she knew or cared.

"Being sick changed her, Haley," Cole said. "As for the shop, I don't know that she wouldn't have come around to the idea eventually. Five, ten years from now. "

Haley started away, her boots slipping over the solid snow, warm tears stunning her cold heart. Was she just chasing a sentiment? A faux childhood dream? Haley paused outside the garage doors, a reservoir of tears leaking to the surface, zapping her strength.

"It's just . . . I don't know . . . What's the point . . ." Haley fell against him, pushed by the power of her sobs.

"Shh, shh, it's okay, Haley." Cole wrapped her tight, his strong arms holding in the heat of her tears. "It's going to be okay."

The broken pieces of her heart spilled out—her sorrow over Tammy, over Dax—and soaked Cole's chest.

She molded into him, slipping her arms around his back, finding his steady heartbeat a calming reassurance. But when he drew her closer with an intimate, "Haley . . ." She pressed out of his arms, backing up, brushing her hand over her wet cheeks.

"I should go . . . I can't . . ." The wind muscled up, slapping against her with an ice refrain. "Not again."

Cole reached for her but she stepped out of his grasp. "What are you talking about? What 'not again'?"

"Cole . . ." She shook her head, shivering from the

cold, from her emotions, making her way into the garage. "I need to go."

"Haley," he said. "Come inside. Warm up. Have some hot chocolate. We can talk more. Tell me what's going on."

"I really need to go." Being in his arms, being with him, felt like a place she'd wanted to be for a long time. But he wasn't hers. Never had been. More concerning was she'd barely washed the stench of Dax from her soul. Romance was the last thing Haley Morgan wanted or needed.

Inside the garage, she dropped her gun and gear on Cole's workbench, slipping from his fleece and his brother's camo pants. On her way out, she paused for one last thing. "Tammy *really* never spoke of the shop?"

"She didn't." Cole held her arm with a light touch. "However, you should follow your heart, Haley. Forget what Tammy would or wouldn't have done. Go for what you want. If she were alive today, you know that's what she'd tell you."

Haley raised her gaze to his, finding there all kinds of unspoken sentiment. "Do I? Because after today, I'm not sure."

. . .

CORA

August 1931

August came with a rainless heat. Dust rose from the ground, thirsty for a taste of heaven. In the evening, the crickets' dirge saturated the stale air and Cora imagined their song begged God for relief.

Sitting on the back porch Birch built, she cooled herself with a Main Street Baptist Church fan. She'd heard tell of a newfangled device that cooled a home in the summer, an air conditioner. One day when things turned around in this town, Cora thought she'd find out how to install one of those contraptions in the shop.

The summer brides were sticky with sweat by the time they descended the stairs—even with the ceiling fans whirring.

"I'm having second thoughts," Mama said, coming to the porch with two glasses of iced tea. "I'm not sure I should leave you. Or my garden." She handed Cora a glass as she sat in the adjacent rocker.

"Mama, it's been discussed and decided. You're to go to New York. Besides, Aunt Marian went out of her way to find you a position in the secretarial pool. You can't sully her reputation by changing your mind."

"People change their minds all the time. You're just trying to get rid of me."

"Yes. You came up with this idea to move to New York and, frankly, I think it's a good one. I'm helping you stick to it." Cora reached across the little table for Mama's arm. "But I'm going to miss you."

"I'll miss you too, darling. But oh, won't it be good to earn a salary? My own money. I don't believe I've ever had my own money. First it was my daddy's, then my husband's. What times we live in."

Right after Birch built the back porch and Cora started using it as a living space, setting meals on the table, sitting out in the evening reading, something changed in Mama. She started batting around ideas of moving on with her life.

So she wrote to her sister in New York, who was married to a prominent insurance man, and asked about a job. Marian approached her husband's boss about an opening in the secretarial pool and, well, Mama was booked on the noon bus tomorrow.

"What are you going to do with your first paycheck?" Cora said, keeping Mama's thoughts forward-thinking.

Mama sipped her tea, her face creased with concern. "I thought I'd send some to you. I'll be living with Marian and George, so I won't need much."

"Keep your money, Mama. I have plenty."

"You have plenty to run a business, but you need to hold on to that, Cora. Who knows how long this Depression and drought will last? Or what it will take to recover? Who knew any of this would ever happen? Besides, why can't I help out? You've been taking care of me since your da—well, since everything."

"You've helped me more than you'll ever know. The best hostess this shop could ever have, all as a volunteer."

Mama waved her off. "We're family."

"Why don't you go shopping with your first paycheck?" Cora said. "Buy a new dress or two.

"Well, I would like to update my wardrobe. Most likely I'll be out of date with New York fashions."

Cora more than heard Mama's sigh. She felt it. Less than a year ago she was a bank president's wife, a pillar in Heart's Bend society. Now she lived on the third floor of her daughter's shop. Tomorrow she'd leave town on a bus, alone, to a strange city, taking on a job she'd barely been trained to do in high school over thirty years ago. To be nameless and faceless in a secretarial pool.

"Mama." Cora squeezed her arm. "I know this is not what you expected of your life—"

"I expected to be entertaining my grandchildren, having large Sunday dinners with you and EJ. I planned to work my garden and tend to your father, being the good wife of a prominent man. It was a good plan, Cora. And for a long while, it worked like a charm. Now look at me." She rubbed her thumb against the top of her hand. "A charity case. Leaving town in shame." She glanced back at Cora. "Leaving you to face it all alone."

"Lots of men have left their families. Remember Avril?" Word whispered through town of more and more men leaving, the desperate times forcing them into unthinkable actions.

"Yes, well, a lot of men did *not* leave their families too. They faced the difficulties like real men."

"Daddy is a real man, Mama." She couldn't help but defend him. Her heart always hoped. "As for me, I won't be alone. I have Odelia. My friends. Rufus."

"Rufus. Well, I have warmed to him some, but, Cora, be careful. Please. He reminds me too much of your daddy. So handsome and charming, but saying one thing and doing another." Mama faced away. "I'd like to know what sins I committed to bring this ruin down on me."

"You know better."

"Do I?"

"So the Jesus you taught in Sunday school to half of Heart's Bend citizens is not the God you believe in? Not the One who is good and kind, whose love and faithfulness never ends or fails?"

"How can you be so pious? Look at our plight."

"What plight? I have a roof over my head and food on the table. Clothes to wear. We lost our house and our land, but so what? We still have each other and our health. You may have lost hope in Daddy, but I have not."

Mama shook her head. "He wrote, Cora, the day Birch built the porch."

"What? You didn't tell me." Cora bent forward to see Mama's face as she brushed her trembling hand over her wet cheeks.

"He's not coming back, Cora. He's too ashamed."

So that's what caused her to change. "Tell him that's too bad." Cora moved in front of Mama, taking hold of her shoulders. "Tell him to come home anyway. Everyone is dealing with some sort of shame and failure. Where is he, anyway?"

"In Georgia, or Florida. He can't decide." Mama broke forward with a sob, burying her head in her hands. "He's gone. The man I knew and loved since I was sixteen is gone. Even if he came back, he'd not be the same. Not this time. How could I ever trust him?"

Cora slipped her arms around Mama's shoulders, holding her while she wept, her own tears blocked behind a barricade of anger.

Mama lifted her head, pulling a handkerchief from her pocket to dry her eyes and blow her nose.

"I shouldn't burden my girl with my troubles." She whirled around with a fixed smile pressed on her lips. "I'm the mother, the one who should bear the family burdens."

"No one can bear burdens alone." Cora slipped back into her chair. "W-what did Daddy say in his letter?"

"He feels he's done me a great injustice, and he cannot bear to see my disappointment."

"But it was all about money . . . things . . . Things we can do without. Yet we can't do without him."

Mama pressed her hand to Cora's arm. "You said it yourself. Daddy can't separate his role as a provider from his role as a bank president, as a money man. If he can't be and *do* those things, then he can't be who he needs to be . . . for you and me." She brushed her handkerchief under her nose. "Listen to me making a defense for him."

She disappeared into the house, and the sound of the closing door resonated through Cora as the final note in a long song.

Life had changed, was changing, and very possibly would never be the same. The only constants in her life were the shop and Rufus. She refused to give up her own hope of a happy ending.

"Cora?" A tender voice called from the edge of the porch.

"Millie?" Cora shoved open the screen door, inviting the woman in. "Millie Kuehn? How are you? I've not seen you in a good long while."

Millie Kuehn, another shop alum, a few years older than Cora, stepped tentatively onto the porch.

"How long's it been? Ten years?" Cora said, offering her mama's rocker.

"Twelve." She clicked her fingernails together, a vacant, haunting shadow in her eyes. "I still remember it like it was yesterday, though." Her eyes welled up, a reflection of these hard times.

"Please sit, Millie," Cora led her to the chair. "What's on your mind?"

"I can't complain." She sat gently, folding her hands in her lap, setting the rocker in motion. "We ain't got no troubles no one else has, though Charles is still angry about the bank's closing and losing all our savings." She swiped a bit of perspiration from her brow. "Don't help, this heat . . . He's afraid we're going to lose the corn crop."

"Reverend Clinton is calling for a meeting to pray for rain. I'm planning on going."

"Well, if'n God cared, I suppose He'd be the one to ask for rain," Millie said.

How did Cora find herself the arbitrator of faith this morning? She'd certainly had her doubts. But that's why she fought to believe, why she held on to Rufus. To be faithful to the end.

"My girl Annie just turned ten and she found my wedding dress. Begged me to try it on." Millie's watery laugh joined the song of the birds slipping through the screen. "She swam in it. She's such a little bit of a thing, but she said, 'Mama, I'm going to wear this someday.' I said, 'Annie, I'd be honored, but don't you want your day at the wedding shop? Walk down those grand stairs, all dolled up and beautiful in your own gown, us women gazing up at you, fawning over you?'" Millie inhaled, pressing her hands over her heart. "I never wanted to lose the feeling I had when I came down the stairs, so hopeful, so full of love. Then, when I walked down the aisle to Charles, I just knew everything was going to be grand and lovely." Her fingers fluttered against her lace collar. "But I can't . . . I can't feel it . . . It's fading, Cora. Time is so cruel that-a-way."

"But we have our memories plus the faith in times ahead. Think of your Annie walking down the stairs in your gown, Millie. What a grand day that will be. We can alter the dress for her any way she needs." In a small town like Heart's Bend, there were few debutantes. The community didn't have much room for social stratospheres. Getting married was a girl's debut. "I remember how lovely you looked. Aunt Jane and I declared you had the best trousseau that year."

"Did I?" Her smile wavered. "I lost it all, except my gown, in the fire our first year." Millie absently rubbed the pink scar along the side of her arm. "I think I mourned that leaving suit more than losing half the house."

"We can make Annie a nice suit. Or order one from New York. And get a nice mother's gown for you. You'll see. It'll be right again, Millie. Things for brides changed so much after the war. A girl has so many options. Used to be all bridal fashion came from Europe, but these days New York is all the rage. More affordable. By the time Annie gets married, who knows what a working family will be able to afford."

"Well, she ain't getting nothing if times don't change."

"She's only ten, Millie." Cora's voice buoyed with hope.

"If Charles has his way she won't marry until she's an old maid of thirty." Millie sucked in a sharp breath. "Oh, Cora, I'm sorry. I didn't mean—"

"Better to be unmarried at thirty, waiting for the right man, than married at twenty to the wrong one."

"Truer words were never spoken. I was blessed. Married me a good one." Millie tipped her head back, resting it on the top of the rocker, and closed her eyes. "I just wanted to be someplace happy. Take a load off my mind. I remember the tea your aunt served, sitting in the big salon with my mother and grandmother, my sisters, and my cousin, excited, so very excited. It was the best day, simply the best."

"Would you care for some iced tea now?"

"Wouldn't that be lovely?" Sitting back, rocking slightly to and fro, Millie drifted away, her eyelids fluttering with sleep.

Cora shoved out of her chair and tiptoed inside. Mama met her in the mudroom wearing her hat and gloves, an envelope in her hand. "I was just coming to find you. I'm off to run errands before my bus trip. And this came for you by special messenger."

Cora glanced at the plain white envelope with nothing written on the outside. "Millie Kuehn is on the porch."

"What does she want?" Mama moved aside the lace sheer at the window.

"Same thing as Avril Kreyling and the others who've stopped by. To remember happy times."

"We all cling to what good we can." Mama stepped into the small salon. "Also, Gwen Parker was just here. She got engaged and wanted to set an appointment. She's been saving her money since she was eight to get her dress here. I set her up for Monday."

"All right. Thank you." The unspoken words shouted between them. Mama wouldn't be here Monday.

After Mama left to do her errands, Cora slipped the envelope into her pocket while she fixed Millie a glass of tea. But when she stepped outside, the woman was gone, her chair still rocking from her exit.

"God bless you, Millie." Cora set down the tea and retrieved her letter. Her pulse ignited when she discovered it was from Rufus, with yesterday's date.

My dearest, I'm in port tomorrow evening. Dinner? 7:00? I'm in such need of your company. I miss you.
Yours, Rufus

Cora crushed the note to her chest, then sniffed the plain white paper, breathing in his scent. See, God looked after His own. One just needed to be patient. Steadfast.

True love always triumphed.

CHAPTER EIGHTEEN

COLE

Monday morning Cole pulled into Java Jane's for a quick cup of coffee before heading off to Heart's Bend Inn. Thank goodness they called with a job, wanting some rooms renovated. This was an answer to prayer, no denying it.

Since his paintball game and confession in the snow with Haley last week, he'd not seen much of her. There was an unspoken need for space. To wrestle with the truth. Wrestle with things still unsaid. Wrestle with feelings that wouldn't let go.

The way she cried against him sank into his heart and mind. Something, *someone* hurt her. Beyond the secrets Tammy kept from her. Darned if he didn't want to be there for her. He spent Friday and Saturday making calls, seeing what kind of deals he could get for the remodel, getting set up and ready to go once the permits were released.

So far, his effort yielded nothing, but he was hopeful.

Inside Java Jane's, the barista called to him. "Morning, Cole. The usual?"

"Hey, Alice Sue. Yes, the usual please." Regular coffee with a dash of cream. Cole dropped a five on the counter as he glanced around. Looked like the usual nine a.m. crowd.

"Oh, almost forgot, someone is waiting for you in the corner." Alice Sue reached for the five as she slid over his large coffee.

"Who?" He glanced to the corners of the shop. Heat rose under his skin when he spotted his dad at a far table. "Keep the change."

"Thanks, Cole. Have a good one."

Taking a deep breath, he thought about just walking out, but the man had seen him, nodded, hoisting his coffee cup in salute. Stepping around the tables, Cole made his way over. When was the last time he'd seen his father? Chris's graduation from high school? Right before he was sentenced for six years.

Dad stood as he approached. "Morning, Cole."

"What are you doing here?" Cole's gaze scraped over his father's thin cheeks and gray hair in need of a cut. A shell of the man he was while Cole was a kid. He was a powerful mover and shaker fifteen years ago, his construction business reaching through middle Tennessee. Akron wasn't even a speck on the map.

But he exchanged it for an all-expenses-paid trip to the state pen for ten-to-twenty. He got a reduced sentence for turning over evidence and good behavior.

"I came to see you."

"You working?" Cole remained standing, so Dad slid back from the table, rising to his full six two, meeting his son's gaze.

"Got a job up in Nashville. On a crew taking care of city property. It's mindless. But keeps me busy."

"Then what are you doing here?" Cole motioned to the clock on the wall. "Shouldn't you be working?"

"Working on a later crew today. Thought I'd run down and see you."

"Got an apartment?"

"Little one. Hole in the wall." Dad sipped his coffee. "How's your mother?"

"Fantastic. Running Ella's like a champ." Bragging on Mom felt good, like he was stabbing Dad with the reality of his stupidity. He'd never find another woman like Mom and, hey, she made a good life for herself without him. "Cap is at Vanderbilt. Chris, at Georgetown, about to get his MBA."

"Yeah, I know. I saw Cap and Chris before Christmas."

Cole hesitated over his coffee. So his brothers did see Dad.

"How's business for you?" Dad said after a second. "Things going well? Read in the paper the council gave that old wedding shop to Haley Morgan. That Dave and Joann's girl?"

"Yeah, she's bringing back the old wedding shop."

"You working with her on it?"

"Maybe."

"The bones of that place are solid. I did some minor fix-ups on it before Miss Cora shut her down in the late seventies. I was eighteen. On my first construction crew with Jim Bartholomew. That man taught me everything I know."

"Except not to commit fraud."

Dad turned his stir stick over and over with his fingers. "I guess I deserved that one."

"I need to get going, Dad. Did you come down here just to say hi?" Cole backed toward the door, waiting, unsure what answer his heart longed to hear.

Dad hesitated, shifting his focus to his coffee, then the large pane window facing Main Street. "I was wondering about the Stratocaster. Chris told me you have the guitar boxed up in a glass case, hanging on your wall."

"Chris talks too much."

"That may be, but it seems we shared that guitar, Cole, and when times were good, I could afford to hold on to such a luxury. But times aren't so good, and yes, I know, it was all my doing. If you're not playing it, I thought you might consider selling it."

"Money, everything with you is about money."

"Well, when you're in need, yes, everything is about money. I've served my time. I'm working, making my own way, but I could use a car, Cole. You could sell that thing for the price of two brand-new cars."

"So I sell it and give you the money?"

"I figure we split it. I know what it's like to get up a business. I'm sure you could use some cash about now."

"I'm not selling the Stratocaster."

"Just to spite me? Because I'm in need. It's a valid possession of mine."

Cole stepped into him. "And mine. You may not care about me or the family, but I do. Like it or not, that guitar was the last good memory I have of you, and it's not for sale."

"The guitar isn't the memory, but the time we had finding it, playing it, fixing it up."

"I've got to go." Cole headed for the door, his heart blazing. He had some nerve, his dad. But just as he pushed outside, he caught Brant Jackson and Linus Peabody head-to-head in another corner of the shop. What were they cooking up? The image cooled his jets over Dad.

At his truck, he slammed the door, anchoring his coffee in the cup holder, firing up the engine. Sell the rare Fender Stratocaster? He'd rather don a wedding dress and parade down the shop's grand staircase into a sea of smiling old ladies. If he ever sold it, he'd give the money to Mom or his brothers, or some other deserving soul.

Nevertheless, the scene of Linus and Brant disturbed Cole almost as much as his dad's request. The city manager, the de facto head of the town council, looking all too cozy with the enemy of the wedding shop.

Backing out of the parking lot, Cole aimed for city hall to check on the permits, a *grr* in his gut, declaring war on anything that got in his way.

CHAPTER NINETEEN

CORA

In the dim candlelight, Cora waited on the back porch, absently running Rufus's gold heart pendant along the chain around her neck as music from the radio propped against the windowsill filled the porch. Sophie Tucker sang, "To me it's clear, he'll appear . . . the man I love."

But just where was the man she loved? Rufus was an hour late. Cora jumped up, reached inside, and snapped off the radio. She scurried up two flights of stairs to check on dinner, the heat from the stove making the third floor unbearable—even though she'd turned the oven off an hour ago. Overhead the fans whirled, trying to draw in some cooler air through the open windows.

Tonight she might just drag her mattress downstairs and sleep on the porch.

Opening the oven door, Cora assessed the roast to be surviving, praise be. She sat in the chair by the dining table, still set with a place for her and Mama.

Oh, law, if Mama were here, she'd have a few words to say.

Cora was glad she was alone, away from Mama's judging eyes. But she sure could use Mama's famous gravy recipe to save her drying-out meat. Daddy used to say she could slather it on leather and have the folks banging the table for more.

But Mama was on a bus bound for New York.

Cora peeked out the third-floor window to Blossom Street. Five after eight. What could be keeping him? Every ticking minute sat like stone in her belly.

Back down to the shop, she adjusted the gown she'd put in the window this afternoon, moving the shoes forward more so they caught the edge of the streetlight.

This gown was one of her favorites. Odelia pieced it together from three different patterns. The long sleeves of lace would be perfect for any season save for the dead of summer.

She'd have it sold by the end of the week.

At the front door, she leaned to see if Rufus might be coming from across the way, through Gardenia Park. But his large shadow did not darken any street corner.

Back on the porch, the breeze pushed through the screen, setting the tapered candle flames dancing. Cora bent to blow them out but changed her mind. What if Rufus showed and her romantic evening was nothing more than darkness serenaded by cicadas?

She sat at the table, adjusting the silverware, making sure everything was just right. But impatient adrenaline lifted her from her seat. She walked to the curb on Blossom.

"Rufus?" She raised her voice ever so slightly. "Are you here?"

But her only answer was the *ka-boom* of a car engine backfiring.

On the corner of First Avenue, gazing west toward the port, an eerie chill crept over her skin. Downtown was dark. Quiet. Several of the streetlamps had burned out.

Wrapping her arms about her waist, Cora hurried back to the porch. Inside the shop, she sat in the small salon where she had the luxury of a second phone.

"Operator? The port house, please."

Cora pressed her thumb to her lips as she waited, listening to the phone ring with no answer. She hung up. Something was wrong. She knew it. Trouble brewed in her gut.

Running up to the third floor, the skirt of her dress ruffling, swinging about her legs, the thick heels of her Sunday Mary Janes resounding with a determination, Cora gathered her hat and gloves, purse, and keys.

In her car, her trembling hands gripped the wheel, her mind blank, her heart thudding. She had no idea what she'd find at the port, but she had to try.

She knew the *Wayfarer* docked earlier this afternoon. She saw Rufus's roustabouts down the street at the diner.

Lord, please let me lay eyes on him.

She would kiss him first, then give him a piece of her mind for being tardy, scaring her half to death. A packet sank at the head of the Greasy Creek shoals not too long ago.

At the port, she parked along the street, then traveled the walkway and the length of the quay to the boathouse, where a man in a blue cap and graying beard greeted her.

"I'm looking for Rufus St. Claire."

"He ain't here. Pulled away around six o'clock."

"What? No, he couldn't have. I saw his roustabouts in town this afternoon. He's the captain of the *Wayfarer*."

"I know who he is, and I tell you Captain St. Claire pulled away around six. Saw it with my own eyes. He came in, used my phone, collected some mail, muttered something not polite to repeat to a lady, then gathered his boys and headed downriver. He was a bit agitated."

"Did he leave any messages? Perhaps for Miss Cora Scott?"

"Nope, but I stepped away for a moment." The man disappeared into a back room and Cora heard the thumping of boxes. He reappeared with a white envelope in hand. She breathed relief, reaching for her letter. *Thank goodness.*

The man held his hand close to his chest. "Hold on now, this ain't for you. It's for the captain. Guess it got left behind. I'll put it in his box for the next time."

"Please, may I see?" Cora sighed, softening her posture. "I was supposed to meet him this evening and I'm worried."

The old man hesitated, then handed it over. "Guess it don't hurt to look. But don't open it or it'll be my job."

Dread fired up Cora's worry. The handwriting was familiar, reminding her of the handwriting on the postcard two springs ago. And the name was the same. The top left corner read "Miriam." This time with a return address. Which Cora memorized before she handed back the letter. "Thank you."

"Do you have a message for the captain should he return?"

"No, no, I don't." Cora pressed through the door into the night, the breeze off the river thick and dewy, scented with summer.

Rufus, you're breaking my heart.

"You Cora?"

She jerked around with a start to find a man leaning against the boathouse, the scent of a pipe tinging the fragrance of the river.

"I don't have any money, if you're wondering." She held up her pocketbook. It was empty save for her car keys. Which she'd hate to lose, but rather her car than her money.

"You looking for the captain? St. Claire?"

She stepped toward the man with eager intent. "I am. Do you know where I might find him? Or when he'll be back?"

"You're the one, ain'tcha?"

"Whatever do you mean, 'You're the one'?"

"The one who's in love with him? Living in town? It's a fabled story on the river that some gal on the Cumberland has been waiting for him for five years. She ain't figured him out yet."

"I have no idea what you're talking about." But she did, didn't she? "Figured out what, exactly?"

The man puffed on his pipe and stared toward the

river. "I ain't aiming to be the one that breaks your heart."

A hunger for truth trumped her fears as she moved closer to the stranger. "Tell me what you know. Please."

He tapped his pipe against the wall of the boathouse. "Sure you want to know? Like I said, I ain't aiming to be the one that breaks your heart."

"How can you if you don't even know me?"

He laughed. "I suppose you got a point there." He gave her the squinty-eye, then sighed. "I hate to see what appears to be a good woman being used by a man like Rufus. Word is the captain's got him several women along the river. Except you're actually in love with him. The others figured him out and use him as much as he uses them."

"That's not true." But on her words, the inner tremors started, shaking her from the inside out. "He's asked me to marry him."

The man's laugh floated over her, a dark, decadent sound. "You own the wedding shop? Is that right? I work on the *Rowena* over yonder." He tipped his head to the packet docked and sleeping. "Been to Heart's Bend dozens of times. A man hears things. Trouble is, I can't figure out how's come you ain't wised up yet."

Because she believed. Because she hoped. Because she loved him. Because . . .

Cora rose up in defense. "He's building his business, saving his money. Then we'll marry." Though she didn't know why she defended their plans to this man. Maybe she just needed to hear them spoken out loud for her own sake.

"Building his business? Miss, he's one of the richest men on the river. His father owns two different river boat companies."

He flicked a lighter and touched the flame to the barrel of the pipe. In the small yellow boathouse light, Cora saw a jagged scar creeping across his cheek.

"As a captain his reputation is legend. I've seen him maneuver waters that give me nightmares, and I been on the river since I was a boy. As a Romeo, his reputation is equally legend. Miss, he's not in love with you. Nor is he going to marry you. Word along the dock is he left tonight because his wife is having his baby tonight up in St. Louis."

His wife? "You're lying." But the man's words pressed her until Cora thought she'd collapse.

"I'm just telling you the word on the river. But the captain is crafty. Can't get hide nor hair of truth out of him. Even when he's stone drunk."

"He doesn't drink. He swore to me."

"He swore, did he?" The man puffed on his pipe, his voice low and conciliatory. "I sure hate to see a pretty broad like you get hornswoggled by a man like St. Claire, but he's got the charm, all right. The magic touch."

She wanted to walk away, stop listening to his lies, but her feet refused to move. Because she knew, didn't she? Truth laced his throaty, raspy tale.

"Th-thank you, Mr.—"

"Daughtry. Everyone calls me Daughtry."

Cora headed up to the street to her parked car, barely registering the shrill call of sirens splitting the night air.

Several men scuffled from the boathouse. "Fire!" One jumped behind an old truck's wheel while several others hopped into the bed. They clung to the sides as the driver peeled out, smoke bursting from the tailpipe.

In sympathetic harmony, the wind moaned over the still river, stirring up the current. The siren sounded again, its eerie song sending gooseflesh over Cora's arms.

A coursing pain shot through her, the wail echoing in her heart's deepest chamber. *Rufus! Rufus!*

The siren wound up again, revving the air with its warning. More men ran out of the darkness through the streetlights, then disappeared again.

Gazing in the direction they ran, Cora saw the dark smoke curling against the twilight sky.

She arrived at her car just as Joe McPherson pulled up in his pickup, leaning out the window. "Thank goodness you're safe."

"Of course, why wouldn't I be?"

"Because, Cora, your shop is on fire."

. . .

BIRCH

He jolted awake, the alarm of the rooster driving through him, setting his heart to beating. He must have dozed off. Last thing he remembered was cooling Cora's face with a damp cloth, then sitting down in the corner chair to rest. Just for a moment . . .

Now the reddish-gold hue of an August morning

inched around the drawn blinds. The lamp next to Cora's bed flickered, the wick thirsty for more oil.

Birch pushed out of the chair and gathered the wash-bowl and pitcher as he headed down to his kitchen. He needed coffee. And to see about breakfast. He'd let Cora sleep until he came back up with a tray for her. Hopefully she'd be hungry.

Then they could settle where she might live while the shop got repaired. *If* the shop got repaired. From what he saw last night, it would take a hay bale of money to make it right again.

He paused at the sink, resting his hands on the porcelain edge, and gazed out the window toward the horizon, pink and gold with the dawn.

His neighbor Wade came by to feed the stock, but Birch needed to weed the garden and mend the leather harnesses. Birch appreciated Wade; his kindness gave him room to tend to the woman he loved.

Last night liked to scare him to death. Hearing the fire siren was one thing. But racing toward town to fulfill his volunteer duties only to discover it was the wedding shop under the weight of the smoke nearly tripped him to the ground.

He arrived just as Cora ran into the burning build-ing to get her "things." Birch took off after her even though Chief Hayes stopped him.

"It's too dangerous."

"So you're going to leave her in there by herself?" He broke free and charged after her, finding her on the mezzanine floor, fainted on the other side of a fallen, burning beam.

Birch leaned against the sink, staring out of the window, his heart pulsing at the memory of seeing her collapsed amid the flames. He'd nearly lost her. The only woman he'd ever loved. And by gum, he wasn't going to waste another minute standing back and watching, wishing she were part of his life.

She'd been a-muttering in her sleep. Something about Rufus, calling out to him. But that scalawag wasn't even in town.

Birch yanked the loaf of bread from the wooden box and slapped the skillet on the stove, greasing the cast iron with a scoop of lard. He whipped up some eggs and milk and dipped in the bread.

He got the coffee to percolating, and a kettle of hot water for Cora's tea. She never cared much for coffee.

From the china cabinet in the dining room, he gently reached in for two cups and saucers of Mama's good Lennox set. It was a wedding present from her aunt when she married Daddy. Boy, did she treasure it with all her heart.

Setting the china on a tray along with butter and syrup and Mama's polished silverware, Birch tended to the frying toast, letting it get good and crispy.

He poured a cup of coffee for himself, then fixed Cora a cup of tea with sugar and cream and carried the tray up to the guest room, the stairs creaking with each step.

"How bad is it?" Cora said, sitting up as he came in. She looked tired but pretty, so very pretty with her thick tresses wild around her face.

Birch left the door open, swallowing the lump in

his throat, setting the tray on the bed next to Cora. "The porch is gone, and the whole back of the shop is pretty charred. The pantry is pretty burned up. Place smells like smoke and, of course, there's water damage."

"My money, my deposits . . . tins of money . . . under the mudroom floor . . ."

Birch nodded to the table under the window. "I found the money tins. Brought them back with me."

"Thank you." She exhaled, sitting back, covering her face with her hands. "Do I want to ask about the inventory? I'm such a fool. Such a fool."

"Don't say that, Cora."

"But I am, and the whole town knows it."

"I reckon no one is saying you're a fool. Especially since you nearly bought it when you collapsed in the smoke." He offered her the cup of tea. "Why in tarnation did you run into a burning building?"

"My ledgers, two days' worth of deposits. I've *just* started banking at the new bank on High Avenue. Downtown Mutual. Oh, Birch, tell me, how is my inventory?"

"Well, if you mean what you stored in that locked room, probably fine. The stuff in the window might have smoke damage, but the fire embers didn't get that far. The flames got put out before it spread across the mezzanine. Your ledgers and all should be fine. I'll run in today, look for your deposit."

"Thank the Lord." She sipped her tea, her golden-brown eyes brimming. "Was it the candles? That caused the fire?"

"If they did, they melted in the blaze. Were they on the back porch?"

"Yes." The word caught in her throat. "I left them burning when I went to find Rufus."

"The wind was mighty strong last night."

She tilted her gaze toward the ceiling, tears slipping down her cheeks. "The only thing I have in this world is the shop and I nearly destroyed it. For what? A man who was supposed to love me? Supposed to marry me? But couldn't even keep his date for dinner."

"What happened?" Birch set a slice of fried bread on a plate, spread it with butter and syrup, and passed it to Cora. She took it, but she didn't seem to recognize what she was doing.

"He was late, so I went down to the dock only to find out he'd gone. Some sort of emergency. But, Birch . . ." Cora fixed her gaze on him. "I saw him, through the smoke, coming to rescue me." She shifted around, plumping pillows behind her back. "Yes, now I remember. I saw his blue coat. Rufus came in and rescued me. Didn't he? Tell me, was he there? Where is he?"

"Rufus didn't rescue you, Cora." Birch shook his head. "That was me. I rescued you."

"You?" She pressed her hand to her forehead. "You were the man with the buttons, like the captain jacket?"

"The chief made me throw on bunker gear. Said he wasn't going to lose two of us in the fire."

"So it was you?"

Birch motioned to her plate. "Breakfast ought to make you feel right again. Eat." He sipped his coffee, the delicate china felt foreign in his big rough hands.

She took a small bite. "When I was little, the dark always frightened me," she began, not so much to Birch but to the room. Perhaps to herself. "I'd crawl into bed with Daddy and Mama, and Daddy would tell me I was only afraid of the dark because I couldn't see. Then he'd light a match and with that one little flame I could see the whole room." She dabbed her cheek with her fingers, a soft laugh on her lips. "He'd let the match burn down to his fingers before blowing it out, but he'd usually burn himself. He'd toss the match away, swearing, and Mama would scold him. 'Ernie, please, your language.' Then he left when I was seven. I was really scared. But Mama was strong. Ernest Junior tried to be the man even though he was only ten. They'd remind me that the only thing we can't see in the dark is the light. But if we light a lamp or a match, or look at the moon, then we *can* see. I wanted to *see* Daddy so badly. Then after a few months, he came home. And the whole house was filled with his light."

Birch eased back down into the corner chair, listening, barely breathing, wanting her to go on.

"He left again in the panic of '14. Returned again on a bright fall day. Everything was right again. Then EJ went off to war. Only to die. Those were *dark* days."

"Yes, they were."

She glanced over at him as if realizing he was there. "Of course . . . you were there. In the war, in the darkness." She glanced at the plate in her lap. "This looks good, Birch."

He was happy to see her cut up a bite and chew, nodding her approval.

"Can I ask you something?"

She peered at him, waiting.

"What is it about Rufus that holds you, Cora? Why do you wait for him?"

She set down her fork and knife. "Because I . . . I guess . . . I guess I want to believe him. If I hold on to hope, then he can't abandon me. Not like Daddy. Not like EJ."

"EJ didn't abandon you. He was killed."

"But he's not here, is he? Nor is Daddy. I just can't believe one more man would abandon me, Birch." She fingered the pendant about her throat. The one that Rufus gave her that glorious Fourth of July. Why? To prove his affection. What did that Daughtry fellow know? "Not one more man. I'll shrivel up and die if it's true."

He scooted to the side of the bed. "But I'm here, Cora. Right here with you. I won't abandon you. I'd never abandon you."

"Sweet Birch," she said, smoothing her hand along his cheek. "You are always there for me, Birch."

"Then marry me." The words flowed with the force of his heart. He'd meant to propose in a sweet, kind way, holding hands, giving her his mother's ring, but he could not let this moment escape.

"Marry you?" She pulled her hand back.

"Yes, marry me." He jumped up, ran down the hall to his bedroom, and fished Mama's ring from the velvet box in his sock drawer. When he returned to Cora, he knelt beside her, holding up the box. "I love you. I'll always be here for you."

"Oh, Birch." Her fingers trembled as she pressed them to her mouth.

"No, not 'Oh, Birch.' Say, 'Yes, Birch, I'll marry you.' I've waited for you, Cora. Waited through the war, waited while you mourned EJ, waited while you mourned your aunt Jane, waited while you took over the shop. I ignored my dad when he said to go on and court you. I thought you needed time. Well, it backfired. Rufus came along, and I've watched you pine for that bumpkin ever since. If he loves you, why ain't he married you?"

Cora sighed, setting her plate back on the tray, tears glistening in her eyes. "To be honest, I don't know. He was supposed to come for dinner last night. He didn't show so I went down to the dock. I was told he'd left. Something about St. Louis and a baby. Some man named Daughtry told me he was married."

Birch sat back with a sigh, cradling the ring box in his palm. "I'd heard things but never knew for sure. Rumors."

"The man went on to say I was the only woman who'd not figured him out. And he's not building his business like he keeps telling me. He's one of the richest men on the river."

"So he's been lying to you?"

"Birch . . ." Her cheeks flushed a bright red, and for a moment, she shook off the burden of the fire. "Will you go with me to St. Louis, Birch?"

"Why on earth do you want to go to St. Louis? To see him? Cora, you have a shop to rebuild. Don't waste time and money chasing that cad."

"I have money, Birch. Believe it or not. I can rebuild

the shop. Daddy made me get insurance when I first took over. But what I want is the truth. Please, drive with me to St. Louis. I have an address. I think it might be where he lives."

"Cora, you sat here reminiscing about the darkness, and now you're asking me to go with you straight into it?"

"Because I need to find the light. I'm tired of being in this . . . darkness. Yes, that's what it is. A darkness and I can't see. What is the truth? Otherwise, I think I'll keep foolishly hoping." She'd cupped her hand against his arm, her voice firm, her gaze bold. "I waited my whole life for a man like Rufus. One who would sweep me off my feet. Just when I thought I was too old for such romantic ideas, he walked into the shop and straight into my heart. He had this twinkle in his eye, the kind one is born with, as if one of heaven's stars thought he was so lovely it swooped down to live in his gaze. I could barely breathe. He smiled at me and I thought I'd swoon right then and there."

Birch pulled away, tucked the ring box in his pocket, and hovered by the door. "Now you know how I feel about you."

"I'm sorry, Birch, but I must be honest."

"If you value honesty so much, then why do you put up with lies from him?"

"Love, I guess. Birch, will you go with me? Do I even have a right to ask you? I'd ask one of my friends, but most of them are married with families to tend. Daddy's gone . . . Mama."

"Cora, rest." He moved back to the bed, gently

pressing her against the pillows, removing her plate. "You're still wrung out from last night. The doc said you took in a good bit of smoke. You need to take it easy."

"But will you? Please."

"You're a grown woman, ain't you? Go by yourself when you're all recovered." He didn't want to witness that brute with his hands, and lips, on Cora.

"Birch, I can't do it alone. One look at him, one sweet word of explanation, and I'm afraid I'll get all confused and confounded. Believe whatever lies he tells me. I don't trust my heart to discover the truth. I'm asking you. Be my light."

He yanked up the tray and started for the door. "Only time I can go is on a Sunday. I can't leave on a weekday to go gallivanting. But I'm not going with you until you're recovered."

"Thank you, Birch, thank you."

"What if he's not there, Cora? Or worse, what if there is a wife and baby?"

"Then I'll know it, won't I? I can close the door on Rufus St. Claire and go on with my life."

Then perhaps she'd say yes to him. Become Mrs. Good. "All right, but you think long and hard about this, Cora. You'll be busting into another woman's life, telling her the man she loves ain't true."

"Doesn't she deserve to know?"

"What for? You seemed to enjoy being in the *dark* all this time."

"That's rather unfair. All I wanted was to believe." Her lip quivered. "I loved him. I suppose I still do."

He sighed. Darn if she didn't just wiggle into his

heart even further. "I'll go with you. In the meantime, you be thinking about where you want to live while the shop is being rebuilt."

Her smile was just about all the reward he needed.

"I'll go by Tony Nance's place later," he said. "See about getting a crew to clean up the shop and start putting it back together."

"You really are too good to me."

"What would be the point in telling you I love you if I didn't show you?" He collected his cup and saucer and put them on the tray. "You eat your breakfast now." He motioned to Cora's plate on the nightstand. "I got some chores to attend. There's clean towels in the bathroom down the hall. If you need me, just ring that bell." Cora reached for the cowbell on the nightstand, gave it a clang. Birch grinned. "I'll come running."

Jogging down the stairs, he set the tray by the sink and snatched up the rest of the fried toast, dunking it into his coffee. She was in his house. He was taking care of her. If that didn't win her heart for marriage, what would?

Grabbing his hat off the hook by the back door, he walked out of the house whistling a tune, into the dew of the dawn, into the day's welcoming light.

. . .

HALEY

FEBRUARY 4

There couldn't have been a better day to ride the Harley down I-65 to Birmingham. The first Thursday in

February, yielding a perfect, beautiful, clear, cold day. Mom suggested she take Dad's truck since he drove his new BMW to work, but Haley wanted the freedom of the Harley.

A month after applying for the wedding shop renovation permits, she needed a day on the road to think, clear her head, connect with God.

But before hitting the road, Haley pulled up to the shop. She'd left her notebook with all her plans on the mezzanine.

Up the stairs two at a time, energy surged through her. It happened every time she entered the shop. Since Cole and Gomez had knocked down the walls, a light filled the salons. Haley gazed down from the mezzanine. A glow emanated from the shop beyond the light falling through the windows. As if the old place was relieved someone loved it again.

She patted the banister. "Don't worry. I'm doing all I can." She'd returned to her knees again and again, asking God to help her find the money and resources she needed.

She had an appointment with a bank in Nashville next week.

Back down the stairs, she hit the foyer when the front door swung open. Dax's tall broadform filled the doorway.

Haley stumbled backward, her heels tripping over the bottom step. "W-what are you doing here?"

"Looking for you." Dax inched inside, a faux humble expression on the high cut of his cheeks.

"Out. Right now." She fired toward him, shoving his

six-foot-three frame out the door. His presence tainted her shop, its beauty and innocence. "Get out."

Dax stepped back, her force against him like a fly hitting a tree. "Calm down, Haley. Geez."

"Don't tell me what to do." She pressed the old lock push button and pulled the door closed behind her, locking it, then clutched her notebook to her chest. "How'd you know I was here?"

"I didn't. But I remembered you said something about an old wedding shop downtown. I saw your bike out front when I drove past." He grinned like he'd discovered gold at the end of a rainbow.

"Good-bye then." Haley started down the walk, toward her bike and the dark car parked behind it, a shiver in her bones deeper than the cold.

This was *so* Dax. Just showing up. Trying to inch back into her life. Win her over with his big fat lying eyes and corny grin that used to make her knees weak. That still carved a pit in her stomach, if she were honest.

"I've missed you." Dax leaned his muscled frame against his car, his feet buried in the black snow lining the curb. "I wanted to see if we could—"

"We? There's no we. No us." She'd punch him in the arm if he'd feel any of it beneath his coat and wad of California beach muscles. "What about 'I never want to see you again' left room for doubt?"

"You were mad."

"Of course I was mad. Dax, you *are* married." She balled her fist, ready to swing. Oh, she wanted to swing, hit his perfect nose with her fist. "And you drew me into your web of lies and deceit. I can't blame you because I willingly, stupidly went along!"

"Then you'll be glad to know that the situation has been rectified."

"Rectified? Your marriage and children have been *rectified*. Do you even hear yourself?"

"I'm getting divorced."

Haley laughed. "Sure, like the ten thousand other times you said that? All the times I begged you to leave her?" She'd lost a piece of her soul when she hooked up with the ox watching her with a smirk and steel-blue eyes. "Do what you want, Dax, but count me out. There is not now nor ever will be a *we*, as in you and me."

Once she heard "home" was the next direction in her life, she hoped, prayed, believed that returning to Heart's Bend—and now opening this shop—would restore some of what she'd surrendered to this man.

Her innocence. Her dignity. Self-respect. Her hope and zest for life.

Now he stood before her threatening it all.

"So this is it? The wedding shop?" He moved up the front walk again, inspecting the storefront, the pillars by the display window, the ratty landscaping.

"Dax," Haley said, checking the time on her phone. "I have to go. I have an appointment."

He peered back at her. "I can help you with this place. I told you I would. Whatever you want, darling."

Darling? The word on his lips filled her being with a sour taste. "No thanks."

"Really? Come on, I know you don't have any money."

"Thanks to you."

Dax ran a chain of gyms and hawked a series of workout videos that was getting him some acclaim. Haley's credit card and savings helped bankroll his first exercise video.

"You know I owe you. You helped me. Now it's my turn to help you." He cocked a sporty grin, wiggling his eyebrows. "Last year was a very good year for DM Enterprises."

And have his nasty tentacles touching her life, her precious shop? No way. If not for herself, then for the love of Miss Cora.

"Dax, you came a long way for nothing. And I really do have to go."

"Actually, I have a meeting in Nashville." He walked toward her. "A couple of country music artists got in shape with my videos. We're talking partnership, music to go with a new series of videos." He waited for her to respond, to be impressed. "Will you meet me for dinner tonight?"

"No." She turned for her bike, sliding her notebook into the saddlebag. "Have a good meeting and a good life."

"Come on, babe, why're you doing me this way?" He came around her bike, reaching for her.

"Dax—" As she twisted free, Cole pulled alongside, powering down the passenger window.

"Haley, are you ready? For the *thing*."

Right, the *thing*. "Yes, I'm on my way. Am I late? So sorry." At her bike, she pounded on her helmet and revved the engine. All the while Cole waited, his expression like the idling rumble of the truck's engine.

But wait. She had to make one thing clear. Hopping off her bike, Haley walked back to Dax, who stood beside his car.

"When I get back, don't be here. Don't even be in this town."

CHAPTER TWENTY

CORA

OCTOBER 1931

I believe I feel rather ill." She parked along the curb of the central west end of St. Louis, near Forest Park. Had her car not been a luxury purchase a few years ago she feared someone might come along and ask her to "park round back."

What a fine, *fine* neighborhood.

Beside her, in the passenger seat, Birch, with his fedora riding low over his brow, accentuating the fine angles of his face, whistled low. "Did you know about this?"

"Not a clue," she said low, more to herself.

"I guess if he is one of the richest men on the river, this shouldn't be a surprise."

The green lawn was thick and carefully maintained. Most of the lawns in Heart's Bend were brown due to the heat and lack of rain.

Pulling the emergency brake, Cora left the engine to idle, twisting her hands around the firm steering wheel, staring toward the grand front door centered between a row of windows.

The only sound between her and Birch was their individual breathing. After a moment, Birch shifted around, running his hand down his Sunday trousers, his tan, muscled arm peeking from behind the rolled-up sleeve of a well-worn, well-washed dress shirt. His dark tie hung loose about his neck, the top collar button open. Perspiration beads dotted his forehead and a single trickle of sweat eased down beside his ear.

"Birch." Cora stretched her hand to his knee. "Thank you."

He peered at her, but only for a moment. "Anything for you. You know that."

It'd been almost two months since the shop burned. Cora moved in with Odelia while Tony Nance put together a crew to repair the place.

The fact that Odelia and Cora didn't kill each other was a testament of God's good grace. She'd recovered from the smoke inhalation but still battled headaches and evening fatigue.

Cora dug up her insurance policy and sent a telegram to the main office in New York. They sent an inspector who determined the fire was not arson and authorized funds for the repairs.

Daddy had his many flaws, but his insistence that she purchase insurance saved the shop in these hard times.

But none of her good fortune flowed toward her relationship with Rufus. Here she sat in St. Louis, looking for answers.

"When I was a kid," Birch said, "my dad drove up to see the sights of the World's Fair. He wanted me to ride along, but Mama thought it'd be too overwhelming for a nine-year-old. Years later Dad said he regretted letting her have her way on that one."

"Daddy and Mama went too. Left me and EJ with Aunt Jane."

"If I ever have a kid, I'm taking him to the World's Fair. Dad said it was a sight to see and brought me a coin from the Louisiana Purchase Exposition. I still have it."

"Really? Mama and Daddy brought us a book on the Louisiana Purchase Exposition. And I still have it." She sighed. "Thank goodness. I can't imagine the loss if the whole shop had gone up in flames."

Her momentary sadness solidified into anger. The same emotional melting and freezing she experienced all weekend. Because of her foolish devotion to Rufus, she'd almost lost everything—her business, pictures, furniture, dishes, treasured memories like the book from the fair. Her future.

"We should get your book and my coin together." He meant to be lighthearted, but Cora felt the deeper intention of his comment. And by the way he cleared his throat and stared away, he felt it too.

They'd not addressed his proposal since that day at his house. Nor on the drive up. Instead, they chatted about farming, the weather, who in the community was most impacted by the collapse of the banks. How the shop repairs were coming. The fall harvest and coming fair.

Cora brought him up-to-date on Mama since she telephoned last night.

"I still haven't told her about the fire. I just couldn't.

Birch, you should've heard the happiness, and relief, in her voice. She laughed heartily when she told me about going to the theater with my aunt and uncle and getting lost during intermission. It was a melodious sound I could not crush with news of a fire. If I told her, she'd be on the next bus home. I just can't do it to her."

Birch agreed. Cora was handling everything well. No need to drag Esmé back.

"Well, we've stalled long enough for them to look out the window and see us." Birch folded the map and tucked it neatly into the glove box. "Do you want to turn round? You don't have to go in there."

"But we drove all this way."

"So?"

"Do you think he lied, Birch? Really? Why should I trust some Daughtry fella when Rufus is the man I know, love, and trust?"

"Don't ask me. Go inside and find out."

She snatched up her Ingber beaded bag from where it sat on the seat and popped it open, took out her gloves, and slipped them on with determination. But with each move, her nerves stirred, arousing her adrenaline and making her weak.

"Stop." Birch placed his hands over hers. "I'm not going in there if you're a nervous wreck. You'll just appear to be begging and, I'm sorry, you're better than that. Cora, I don't understand why you can't see yourself as you truly are—strong, independent, kind, a fine, *fine* Christian woman."

"I see myself as I am. A rather tall, skinny, plain, foolish woman who needs a lot more Christ in her life."

Birch stirred in his seat, hands clasped over his knees. "Well, if you're determined to say everything negative I won't try to change your mind with truth."

"Birch, can we just get through this? Then you can scold me."

"Let's go." He huffed and puffed, tugging at his tie. "I don't promise not to punch his lights out."

"Don't be ridiculous. Have you seen him? He's got arms like Gene Tunney."

Birch frowned. "And have you seen my arms?" Yes, as a matter of fact she had. "I'm plenty strong, Cora."

"Precisely. So no fighting." Cora yanked on her door handle and there she froze. "I'm all tingly and afraid."

"Because you'll find out the truth."

"You think you know me so well, don't you?"

"Don't I?" He brushed back his loose, dark bangs, his pale blue eyes fixed on her. "Been knowing you since we were kids. Since y'all came out to Granny's farm for picnics and such." He laughed, deep and rich, pressing his fisted hand to his lips. "Remember the time we went swimming in the pond and a big ole water snake surfaced and swam alongside us?" He slapped his knee as his laugh filled the car. "I swear you walked on water getting away from it."

"Goodness, I was twelve. And hush up. You're laughing as hard now as you did then."

"It's still the funniest thing I've ever seen. Should be in a picture show."

"You're not helping."

"Laughter always helps." He popped open his car door and walked around to her side. "Come on." He opened her door, offering his hand. "If you want, I'll wait out here. Might run to the drugstore for something cold to drink."

"What?" Cora hesitated, then gave him her hand. As she rose from the car, his warm hand steadied her. Calmed her cold nerves. "You're going to send me in there by myself? I'd have thought more of you, Birch Good." She clung to his hand.

"If you ask me, you ought to walk in there like Gunga Din, give him what for and then some."

"Gunga Din, huh? All right." She stepped forward, but her weak limbs betrayed her. She stumbled against the car.

Birch slipped his hand about her waist. "Dang, long ride up here must have made your legs fall asleep."

Her gaze met his. "In case I forget to say it later, you're sweet, Birch. Thank you for being here."

They walked up the three short steps to the glossy black wrought iron fence surrounding the three-story redbrick home. At the gate, Birch lifted the latch as Cora started the long walk to the front door. Once or twice, Birch touched her back ever so gently. *I'm here.*

She rang the bell. On the other side, footsteps hammered against what sounded like a marble floor. Then the door opened to reveal a young colored woman in a maid's uniform, and Cora ached to see her darling Liberty.

"May I help you?"

"Y-yes. I'm looking for Miriam." Her heart beat with each syllable.

"Who may I say is calling?"

"Miss Cora Scott."

"It is Sunday afternoon. She spends time with her family. I'll have to see if she can receive you." The maid pushed the storm door open. "Wait in the foyer."

"Th-thank you." Cora leaned into Birch. "I think I'm going to be ill, Birch. I declare I do." Cora drew a deep breath. Steady now, steady. Glancing about the vast foyer, indeed whoever lived here had money. The marble floor and damask curtains were merely surface indicators.

Low, murmuring voices came from the other side of the wall. "Well, here, take Rufie. Change his diaper."

In the next breath, a slender, very beautiful woman with pearls around her neck and rich auburn hair framing her delicate face approached, her belly round with life. "I'm Miriam St. Claire. Can I help you?"

Birch's thick arm came about Cora's waist.

"Sorry to barge in on you unannounced. I-I'm Cora Scott." She offered her hand, a routine, mechanical move, because she certainly had no idea what she'd say next. She'd told herself Miriam was a sister, a cousin, a girl Rufus cared nothing about, really. But she was his wife. With child!

"Birch Good." He shook Miriam's hand. "Pleased to make your acquaintance."

"Florence said you needed to speak with me?" She rested one hand on her belly, glancing between Cora and Birch.

"W-when is your baby due?"

She smiled, relaxing. "One month." She pressed her hand to her forehead. "Almost thought I lost him, or

her, two months ago. Praise be . . . Well now, how can
I help you?"

Could she just turn tail and run? Miriam grew more
stunning by the moment. And when she smiled Cora
knew then she'd been tricked, lied to, by Rufus. Who
would want *her*, with her plain brown hair and sharp
features, when this Clara Bow–like darling waited at
home? Bearing him children, no less.

"Darling, I heard the door. Who's here?"

Rufus. She'd know his voice anywhere.

Cora dug her fingers into Birch's arm as Rufus
descended the stairs, wearing dark trousers and a
smoking jacket, his wild mane combed and in place.

"A Miss Cora Scott, darling."

He stopped, the color draining from his high
cheeks. A dark, wicked bolt licked through his eyes and
fear bloomed in Cora's middle. She'd never feared him.
Until now.

He walked toward her with calculated, stealth
movements. A lion protecting his pride. She'd invaded
his lair and he'd not tolerate it.

Birch tightened his grip. She couldn't stop shaking.
How magnificent he looked. So powerful and handsome. And truly terrifying.

"Miss Scott," he said, his tone, his eyes, his expression directing her. *Do not say a word.* "Miriam, is this
a friend of yours from the Women's League?" His gaze
locked with hers and she could feel the draw, the pull,
the intent to control.

"No, darling. She just came to the door asking to
see me."

"I'm Birch Good." He stepped forward, offering his hand to Rufus, but the man ignored him, drilling his gaze deeper into Cora's.

"If you're looking for a charity donation, we've given our allotment for this month." He wooed her into lying.

"Darling, we have the clothes for the charity barrel." Miriam gave Cora the once-over. "We mustn't forget people have fallen on hard times. Let me send Florence to box them up." She squeezed her husband's arm, dazzling him with her perfect smile.

"No," Cora blurted, finding her courage, her Gunga Din. "We don't need charity. We've not c-come here for a handout."

"Oh, my mistake." Miriam turned back to the foyer. Surely she felt the tension. "Well then, how can I help? Florence said you needed to speak to me. What is it?"

"Darling," Rufus said. "I am parched. Can you get me a glass of tea? The sweet kind I like. With a few ice cubes."

"Yes, I'll just ring for Florence." She moved to the front corner, to the damask pull hidden among the draperies. "Shall we sit? I'll have Florence bring us all some iced tea. Have you had iced tea before, Cora? Rufus brought the recipe back to us from somewhere deep in the south. How lucky he is to travel, see the country."

"Yes, I've had iced tea."

"Miriam," Rufus said, his voice smooth, sweet. "Please, can you supervise Florence? She didn't get the concoction correct the last time. The tea was entirely too sweet."

"I'm not sure that's possible," Birch said, his awkward chuckle increasing the tension.

Miriam consented with a nod and a dark glance at Rufus, before disappearing down the shadowed corridor. Rufus stepped into Cora the moment she was out of sight, swearing through gritted teeth.

"What are you doing here?"

Birch shoved him back. "Ease up there, Captain."

"My shop burned. Caught fire."

"So you came here? Why on earth . . ." He peered out the window by the door. "You drove five hours to tell me your shop burned?"

"It burned because of you." Cora jabbed his chest with her finger. "Because you missed dinner and I went to look for you. The wind blew the candles over."

His laugh inspired taut, aching chills. "Don't blame me for your carelessness."

"Hold on, St. Claire." Birch shoved him back. "She was concerned for you."

"Not my problem."

"Yes, it is your problem." Cora crashed into him, pushing him backward. "You lying pig. You're married." Words flew from her lips on the wings of hurt. "How could you? How could you?"

Birch reached from behind, pulling her back, pinning her arms at her side. "Don't give him the satisfaction, Cora. If Miriam sees she'll blame you and defend her husband."

"Do you think I care?" She jerked free. "You have a wife. With a child and one on the way."

"How did you find me?"

"'How did you find me?' That's what you ask? Not, 'I'm sorry I hurt you, Cora. I'm sorry I lied to you, Cora.'" She swung at him, blinded by her tears, hitting nothing but air.

"You have to go." Rufus shoved her toward the door, his focus on Birch. "I don't care who you are, but if you care for her, get her out of here."

He talked over her, through her, as if she mattered not. And Birch was aiding him.

No! Cora broke free, smashing Rufus's foot with her heel. "I'll not be put off." Giving Rufus her own dark glint, she ran down the corridor, emerging into a grand kitchen with an electric stove and refrigerator. "Miriam?"

A hand grabbed hold of her hair, jerking her back. "Shut up, you little witch."

"Let her go, St. Claire." Birch's voice boomed through the kitchen as his body slammed against Rufus.

"Get off of me."

Cora screamed, sinking to the ground as the men tussled, Rufus maintaining a fistful of her hair.

"Unhand her."

Cora heard the pop of one man's fist against another man's jaw. Reaching up, she dug her fingernails into Rufus's hand. "Stop it . . . Let me go."

"What in the world . . ." Miriam said. "Rufus, unhand her. What has gotten into you?"

Rufus released Cora, shoving her to the hardwood. Pushing up from the floor to lean on Birch, she saw Rufus rubbing his jaw.

"Nothing," he said, facing his wife. "These two are swindlers."

Miriam adjusted the baby boy riding on her hip. "Miss Scott, why have you disrupted my home on a quiet Sunday afternoon?"

Overhead the ceiling fans peacefully hummed and whirred, stirring the hot air.

"He's my fiancé," Cora said, hearing the mistake in her declaration. "Well, practically. He's promised to propose to me when—"

"This is outrageous. Miriam, darling. Why are you listening to her?"

Birch stepped up, staring down the liar. "St. Claire, let her speak."

"How could he make such promises?" Miriam's fake cackle trembled. "He's married to me."

"I didn't know. I didn't know. He told me as soon as he made his fortune and he could support me in the manner I deserved, he'd marry me."

"Darling," Rufus cooed to his wife. "She's lying."

Cora recoiled, her blinders peeled back, hearing, sensing the snake oil in his voice.

"She's not lying, Mrs. St. Claire," Birch said.

Miriam shoved her hand against her husband with a harsh glance. "Hush up, Rufus. I'd like to hear her out. Are you his lover?"

Cora hung her head. "No." Not that she hadn't almost succumbed on many occasions. "But I love him."

"And where do you live, Miss Scott?"

"Heart's Bend, Tennessee. I learned about you when a postcard you sent to Rufus came to my wedding shop."

"Miriam, darling, why are you listening to her? She's a liar."

"St. Claire, I'm warning you!" Birch inched a step in front of Cora toward Rufus. "Let her speak."

"Are you a liar, Miss Scott? What has my husband done to you that you'd drive up from, what is it, Heart's Bend, to tell such fantastic tales on him?"

"He was supposed to meet me for dinner two months ago. When he didn't arrive, I went looking for him. I left candles burning and my wedding shop caught fire."

"See, she's an imbecile. Why would I even be seen with the likes of her? She's plain. Unimaginative."

The words whipped her soul, cutting, and blood oozed from her heart. "A man at the dock told me he had many women. Only I was the foolish one who'd not figured him out yet. He told me Rufus was one of the richest men on the river. So I came to see for myself."

"Rufus? Is this true?" The hem of Miriam's fine dress shimmied, revealing what her steel composure tried to hide. "Did you promise to marry Miss Scott? Do you have other women?"

"Miriam, I command you to stop engaging this woman in her lies. How can I lower myself to even consider your question?"

"Mrs. St. Claire, I received a postcard you sent to your husband. It came to my shop in Heart's Bend. I inquired about you. He told me you were the wife of a mate." The color drained from Miriam's delicate features. Her now-pale cheeks made her large, round green eyes seem otherworldly. Cora grabbed Birch's arm. "Let's go."

"Are you sure?" Birch said, pulling her back. "Have you said all you're going to say, because you'll never get this chance again."

She drew a deep breath, aching to look at Rufus one more time but seeing nothing but Miriam's expression. With her own heart on the verge of flying apart, she wasn't sure she could find the proper words anyway.

What did it matter that she had loved Rufus with every fiber of her being? That she'd waited for him? Dreamt of their wedding day and their honeymoon when she'd give herself to him completely? That she'd endured the scorn of her mother, her friends to defend him? That she trusted him?

He was married.

If she said more, Cora sensed she'd lose a part of herself she'd never get back. Besides, she'd only wound Miriam, who was as much a victim of Rufus's lies and betrayal as anyone. For what? Her own comeuppance?

And what of the sweet child with the ruddy cheeks and puppy dog eyes? Or the one in the womb? They deserved to have their father—no matter how wretched a man.

"I'm sorry I disturbed your afternoon, Mrs. St. Claire. I'll be going now and you won't hear from me ever again."

"But is it true?" She reached for Cora's arm. "I must know. Has he, did he, promise to marry you?" She dug in her fingers. "I can leave him. He used my father's money to build his life on the river."

"I heard it was his father's money."

"No, it was *my* father's." She turned to Rufus. "Have you been telling people it was your father's money?"

"I can't believe you're siding with this . . . this . . . harlot."

"Miriam," Cora said. "If you leave, it will be your decision. Not because of me."

"But it's true? He spoke to you of marriage?"

What answer could she give? Miriam St. Claire was more the victim than Cora would ever be. "Yes, he did."

Miriam shrank back, hand over her mouth, cradled her son closer, and hurried down a side hall, out of the kitchen and away from the truth.

"Now look what you've done," Rufus growled in her face.

"No, look what *you've* done."

Head raised, heels singing an exit dirge against the marble, Cora marched out of the house, holding herself together until she was out the front door, through the gate, and down the walk.

Beyond her, somewhere against the blue sky, birds sang their song as the wind pushed through the changing October trees.

In the car, she slammed her door and tried to ram her key into the ignition, but she trembled so she couldn't control her movements.

"Here, here, let me." Birch took the jangling keys from her and slipped one into the ignition. "I can drive if you want."

"No." Her voice sank into her chest, though she tried to hold her head high. "I-I can drive."

"You did it, Gunga Din."

"Did I? Really? I may have just busted up that child's home because I had to feel justified."

"Don't you dare, Cora Scott. Don't you dare take on Rufus St. Claire's sins." Birch reclined against the passenger door. "He wrongs a woman and somehow she feels guilty for confronting him about it? For hurting his wife, who, if you asked me, needed to know the truth."

"But the children don't have to be hurt by it. If she leaves him . . ."

"She won't. Trust me."

"How do you know? She's got money. She doesn't need him."

"She won't leave him because he's the father of her children. Because her daddy's money will keep him in line. Because he's rugged and good-looking, and as long as he treats her like a queen when he's in town, she'll forget all about his tomcatting around when he's away. It's a perfect life for her. The scandal of divorce would crush her more than what you just did in there. But she needed to know. And you?" He rested his hand on her shoulder. "You needed to close the door on him. Cora, you're free of him now. You're free."

"Am I? Really?"

Cranking the motor, she brushed a stream of tears from her cheeks with the back of her hand.

"The fact remains, Birch, I loved him. Still do. I wanted to make a life with him." Cora shifted into gear, but couldn't release the clutch and drive.

Crashing her head against the steering wheel, shaking so hard each inhale filled her lungs with pain. Sobs gathered in her chest, and when she exhaled she collapsed into Birch's waiting arms.

"Oh, Birch, oh, Birch . . ."

He held her, catching her tears with the hook of his finger. "You are more than you believe, Cora. So much more. You'll see, darling, everything will be right as rain. That's it, let it all out. Everything will be right as rain."

. . .

HALEY

Malone & Co. was a gorgeous shop. Haley loved the vibe, and Charlotte, immediately. Beyond striking, she was confident with a kind aura that helped Haley wash away the last of her confrontation with Dax.

It'd taken the two-and-a-half-hour chilly ride down I-65 and a lot of prayer to dislodge that man from her emotions.

He had nerve on top of nerve.

But now that she was in Charlotte's good graces, Haley righted her thoughts and emotions.

She'd reviewed Haley's business plan, giving her a thumbs-up, reminding her to budget for part-time help and shop upkeep. She gave her ideas on how to work with local businesses, enlisting their support. Ways to barter for advertising, get sponsorships.

She advised her on how to order her gowns, what

items to buy outright, what items to buy on consign-
ment. She gave insight on everything from how to steer
brides to the right gown to bookkeeping to what Haley
could expect to make in her first five years.

"Tennessee's wedding business is over one billion."
Charlotte arched one brow. "You shouldn't have trouble
getting a piece of that. Do you have an opening date?"

"Sort of. The town gave me the building, but I have
to have it renovated by May first with the doors open in
June. Only trouble is, I don't have all the money I need
and the construction permits are held up with red tape.
The town gave me twenty thousand, which I have to pay
back, but it's not enough. But then this older woman
came by with her *mother's* wedding dress." Recalling
the story buzzed a spark of life through Haley. "Said
Miss Cora lent the gown to her but her mother never
returned it. She gave me the dress *and* five thousand
dollars. Called it interest."

Charlotte regarded her. "Sounds like people believe
in what you're doing."

"I guess. I just have to keep believing." The image
and sound of Dax offering to help flashed across her
mind. No, no, no. Letting him in would destroy her
and the shop.

Charlotte gave her a tour of her place, then moved
toward the stairs, wide and grand, much like the ones
in her own shop, motioning for Haley to follow.

"I love that the former bride brought her mother's
gown to you. Very sweet, but consider if you want to
be both vintage and modern. Do you have the space to
do both?"

"Actually, I do. There's a small and large salon. Could one be for vintage, one for modern?"

"I like it. It's unique. Gives you a niche."

Charlotte detailed how she spent years building relationships with designers in New York, Paris, and Milan. How her business was built on one-of-a-kind, expensive dresses.

"I have a flair for it. My assistant, Dixie, calls me the wedding dress whisperer. But your demographic is different, your gifts and talents . . . so do what feels right for you. The vintage with modern seems really interesting to me. I'd just advise you not to go the discount or warehouse sort of route. It takes the fun out of it."

Haley agreed. "The shop was run by the founder, Jane Scott, until the mid 1920s. Then her great-niece operated the shop until the late seventies. From what I can tell, the stories I've heard, they were all about community, the bride, and her family."

"Community is key. If that's the history of this shop, then build on it."

At the top of the steps, Charlotte flipped on a bank of lights. "This is our grand salon."

Haley drew in a deep breath. The recessed lights spilled down the wall, glowing, twinkling, moving her into another dimension.

"I put all the brides up on the pedestal, dim the lights, turn on the stardust," Charlotte said.

With the flip of another switch, the salon transformed into a fairy wonderland.

"This takes my breath away." Haley walked through

the twinkling, swirling lights. "This is beautiful. How did you do it?"

"Have your contractor guy call my contractor guy because I have no idea. These lights were his genius."

"It's incredible."

"But here's the best part." Charlotte moved another lever on the wall and the velvet voice of Michael Bublé sang over them. "Stardust melodies . . ."

"You're killing me. Bublé?"

"He usually seals the deal."

Haley scribbled on her notepad. "Unbelievable, unbelievable. You got *me* wanting to get married." Oops.

"You don't want to get married?" Charlotte's question was wrapped in surprise and a touch of sadness.

Haley lowered her notepad with a sigh, glancing around at Charlotte. She'd not purged as much of her Dax bitterness from her heart as she'd hoped. "No, not really. I'd rather be on *this* side of the wedding business."

Charlotte squeezed her arm. "Don't give up on love, Haley. After all, you're in the business of love. You're going to have all kinds of brides come through your shop, and some of them will challenge you, make you want to tell them the wedding is about the marriage, not the most expensive gown or the reception hall. You have to believe in the institution they are entering. You have to remind them about the beauty of love and marriage. I tell you, your lack of experience is nothing compared to your lack of faith in marriage."

Haley dropped down on the suede chair, her heart racing, tears stinging to the surface. "I want to believe, I do."

Charlotte eased down next to her. "What happened to steal your hope?"

"A really wrong decision. In fact, that wrong decision showed up in Heart's Bend this morning. Go figure. But even so, Charlotte, I always saw myself as the bridesmaid instead of the bride, you know? I grew up with brothers so I was a tomboy. Dressed like a boy until junior high. I wanted to be girlie but no one in my family was girlie . . ."

"You don't have to be girlie to be a woman or a bride."

Haley peered at her, nodding, grinning. "True, true."

Charlotte brushed her hand over Haley's shoulder. "I didn't believe in love either until I met Tim. I never knew my father, and my mother was killed when I was twelve. A friend of hers, cranky Gert, raised me."

"I read about the gown you found in a trunk."

"I didn't find it, Haley. It found me. I went to Red Mountain to think, not sure I was ready to marry Tim, when I got caught in a bidding for this ugly old trunk. A thousand dollars. It was crazy. But the auctioneer was so persuasive, and he zeroed in on me."

"So you bought the trunk? Did he know what was in it?"

"I think he did. He was more than an auctioneer, Haley. He was a divine interruption."

"I could use a divine interruption." Haley laughed, but her words were true.

"We never know how or when God will break into our lives, but we have to believe He is always working for our good. I found the dress, and it sent me on an amazing journey of discovering who I really was." Charlotte's story waxed sentimental. "I met two of the other women who wore the dress after my great-grandmother. I learned how the dress was divinely passed from bride to bride. How the dress fit each one who tried it on even though none of us are the same size."

"I wonder if women in my town will bring their dresses around and, I don't know, one day a distant relative will happen upon it."

"Quite possible. My dress had a divine journey assigned to it. Those of us who wore it were healed in some way. It never needed to be altered or fixed up. Though it was designed in 1912, it never looked outdated. Mary Grace and Hilary look like modern brides in their pictures. The old preacher who married Tim and me was Mary Grace's husband. He said, 'This dress is like the gospel—never wears out, always on time, always in style, never needs to be altered.' The dress wasn't about me marrying Tim so much as me realizing God loved me."

"Where is it now?"

"In my home, boxed up. Stored away."

"Hmmm," Haley said.

"Hmmm?" Charlotte echoed, peering at Haley through misty eyes. "What do you mean?"

"I don't know . . ." Haley glanced down, trying to find meaning to her verbal musing. "I guess if the dress has some kind of divine journey, who's to say it should be boxed up and stored away? Maybe you should wonder who the next bride might be."

When she peeked over at Charlotte, her complexion had paled. Haley wished back her observation. "Hey, don't listen to me. What do I know? I'm full of crazy ideas."

"No, no . . ." Charlotte paced away. "It's just . . . I always thought the dress belonged to me. That it finally made its way home. I never knew my great-grandmother or grandmother. The dress became like family."

"You're right, of course. You hold on to it for your daughters. It's something you should pass on. I think I'm seeing that with the stories the old brides in Heart's Bend are telling me. They want their gowns, their experiences to be passed on. Like the sisterhood of the wedding shop."

"Right, exactly. For me, it was the sisterhood of the wedding dress."

The conversation stalled. Mom always warned Haley not to speak every thought. One of these days she'd learn.

"Haley, have you ever tried on a wedding dress?" Charlotte leaned to see her face.

"What? No, no, I mean, I'm not a bride."

"But if you're going to sell to brides, you should know what it feels like to slip on that silky white gown." Charlotte urged her to her feet.

"No, I can't. No, why, why would I do that?"

Haley resisted. Charlotte was no match for big brothers, drill sergeants, or bucking privates. "I don't mean to be rude, but I'm not trying on a dress."

"Haley—" Charlotte shoved aside a glossy, dark wood barn door, revealing a river of white gowns. "You have to do this."

"But I don't want to do this."

Charlotte glanced over at her. "Because . . . ?" The shop proprietor smiled. "Come on, it might ease whatever ails your heart about marriage."

"Nothing ails my heart about marriage. I'm just not sure it's for me."

"Really? Then what's the harm in trying on a dress?" She motioned to the row of white satin gowns. "Do you see one you like? When I opened the shop I tried on every dress."

Charlotte removed a gown from the rack. "This is a local designer. Heidi Elnora. It's simple but beautiful, off the shoulder with an A-line skirt. It looks like you, Haley."

"Me? No, I'm a fatigues and jeans girl."

"Maybe you used to be, but . . ." Charlotte deposited Haley with the dress in a triangular room with muted canned lights and a lamp in the peak of the ceiling. The deep purple carpet was plush under her feet. "Get into as much as you can, then I'll come help with the buttons."

Charlotte shut the door and Haley was alone. She breathed out, avoiding her reflection in the mirror.

Lord, how did she get in this mess? She wanted to help brides, not be one. She'd forfeited her right to a happy ending because of the damage she'd done between Dax and his wife.

"How's it going in there?" Charlotte's voice slipped through the narrow door.

"Okay." Sorta.

The dressing room door opened and in came

Charlotte with a veil and a fascinator. "What do you think, this two-layer, shoulder-length blusher veil or the birdcage? You're so petite I think the birdcage . . . Haley, you're not changed."

She sank down on the cushioned bench, the burden of seeing Dax, of remembering the life she'd lived with him surfacing again, so fresh and raw.

"Ever wish you'd lived some part of your life differently?"

Charlotte set the veils on the bench with the shoes and sat on the floor by Haley's feet. "Sure. Is that what's bothering you? I realize we just met, but I'm here if you want to talk."

"Are you a woman of faith, Charlotte?" Haley turned her gaze to the dress hanging on the wall.

"I am."

Haley crumpled back with a sigh. "I met Jesus when I was fourteen. I was really passionate all through high school. Only one in my family who went to church, but I believed, you know?"

"I do."

"When I went to college I walked away some, got into some partying, but nothing too wild. Then came the air force and at the most I drank too much, maybe hooked up with a guy for the night." She peered at Charlotte. "But that wasn't me. I didn't want to be that girl."

"So asking you to wear the dress brings all that into focus?" Charlotte said.

"When I was in California, I met a man who swept me off my feet."

"And?"

"He was married. I didn't know at first, was mad as a hornet when I found out. But I didn't end it, Charlotte. I believed he loved me and would leave her. I urged him to walk away from his vows and commitment."

"So *that* disqualifies you from wearing a wedding gown?"

Haley stood. "Doesn't it? Doesn't a white dress mean something? Or isn't it supposed to? I fought to break up a marriage, Charlotte. Who does that? I told him to leave his wife and kids. I wanted him for myself at the cost of someone else's heart and happiness."

The unburdening freed her.

"You can't let your past define you, or your future, Haley. What you *did* isn't who you are now or who you'll become. Isn't that the point of the cross, of forgiveness? Being washed *white* as snow." She took the dress from the hook. "This gown is actually called Snow White."

Haley collapsed against the wall, eyes brimming. "I can't. I'm *no* Snow White."

"Haley, take it from me, you can't punish yourself into righteousness. If God's forgiven you, why can't you forgive yourself?"

"I have forgiven myself." Until she remembered the depths to which she sank.

"Really? Then why are you disqualifying yourself when God says you're qualified?" Charlotte walked to the door. "Now, put on the dress and shoes, choose the veil you like, and come out. I'll fix the buttons and you, my new friend, are going to have your moment on the pedestal with the lights and stardust."

"Charlotte, look, I appreciate—"

"Get to it." Charlotte's bark was reminiscent of Haley's drill sergeant when she was in basic. The door slammed behind Charlotte, punctuating her command.

So the owner of Malone & Co. didn't hold back any punches. What Haley wanted more than anything was to put Dax *behind* her. His surprise visit stirred her regret, her disdain for herself, and the life she'd lived with him. Would she ever be rid of the shame?

With a sigh of resolve, Haley wrenched off her boots, jeans, and blouse, and carefully stepped into the dress, the silk running against her legs, cooling the heat of her struggle.

The bodice slipped over her hips and sat at her waist. She worked her arms through the short lace sleeves.

Gathering the skirt with shaking hands, she wiggled her feet into the shoes. Twenties-style Mary Janes. She grabbed the birdcage fascinator and emerged into the salon, all the while avoiding her reflection in the mirror. She couldn't look . . . just couldn't.

What would she see looking back at her? Would the Snow White gown mock her?

"Haley . . . Oh my." Charlotte approached, wonder in her eyes, her hand pressed to her chest. "You are *stunning.*"

"Please, my hair's a mess and my makeup is all runny from the drive down."

"Stop, no more telling me what's wrong with you. Or that I'm wrong." Charlotte turned Haley toward the mirror. "See?"

Raising her gaze ever so slightly, Haley caught

a glimpse of the dress. But stopped at her shoulders. She'd seen a picture of Dax's wife in her wedding dress and that was the last straw for Haley.

"Step up on the pedestal. I'm going to turn on the lights and music."

Haley hesitated. "Charlotte, there's no need—"

"Oh, but there is."

"Isn't it enough I tried on the dress? I get it. It feels amazing. The rich silk against my skin . . ."

Charlotte adjusted the lights and a sparkling glow dropped on Haley. When she looked up, she saw her entire reflection in the mirrors. The gown was beautiful. And she was . . .

Stringed music entered the atmosphere and her heart began to quake, shaking her body, shifting her stones. Then the tears took over.

"I can't . . . I can't." She turned to flee, but Charlotte was in the way, blocking her escape.

"Haley, I'm no prophet, but this is not about a wedding dress. This is about seeing yourself as He sees you." She turned her around, walking her to the pedestal. "White as snow."

A male voice began to sing softly. But it wasn't Bublé this time. "What can wash away my sins, nothing but the blood of Jesus."

Gritting her teeth and gripping her fists, Haley battled her tears, fought the anger burning from deep within.

"I-I wrecked a family, a marriage. And for a year I didn't care. I wanted my man."

"Forgive yourself, Haley. If the Lord has, then how dare you hold on to your offense?"

"Wrecking a marriage . . . It is unforgivable." She raised her fist. "How could I? How could I? I knew better. I *know* better." Haley shook so, she barely stood.

Charlotte gently touched her arm. "Let it go or it will taint everything you do in life, Haley. Everything."

Who was this woman she barely knew lobbing truths into her soul?

Haley stumbled off the pedestal, collapsing against Charlotte, then sinking to the floor, staining the lace and silk of the Snow White wedding dress with her tears of shame, regret, and forgiveness.

Blindsided by the moment, by a woman she barely knew, this was God's coming in like a flood, overwhelming her by His Spirit. And she was undone by the simple act of putting on a garment she did not deserve to wear.

CHAPTER TWENTY-ONE

CORA

MARCH 1932

A glorious day. Truly glorious. Spring's promise pushed back the dreary chill of winter and Cora felt like celebrating.

She'd spent a grand five dollars on an ad in the *Tennessean* and $1.35 on an ad in the Heart's Bend *Tribune* announcing The Wedding Shop's reopening after a cruel fire.

Hattie Lerner did a quick write-up in the *Tribune*'s society section with a sweet headline:

> **The Wedding Shop Reopens
> for Brides Everywhere.**

Thank you, Hattie.

Cora folded the paper, tucking it under her arm, content with her ads, content with getting back to work. Moving forward and forgetting the last eight months.

Other than Daddy losing her childhood home and leaving the family, getting over Rufus had been the most trying time of her life. She despised her naïveté.

Worse, the embarrassment of weeping on Birch's shoulder, then of confessing the truth to Odelia and, finally, to Mama, who graciously refrained to only two, "I told you. I told you," during the initial dialogue.

Well, it was all done now. Over. A thing of the past.

Leaving the newspaper in the pantry, breathing in the scent of new lumber and paint that sweetened the shop . . . it made the shop feel new again. Revitalized.

Cora hurried up to the mezzanine, grateful ruined things could be restored, and pulled the key from her skirt pocket, unlocking the storage door.

A drop of joy spilled on her heart. While the new part of the shop was being painted, Cora had the storage room spruced up. The fresh pink wall was contrasted by a row of white wedding gowns. At the end of the room, on the far wall, a window captured the outside in. The room was fresh, bright, airy, and full of everything Cora loved.

She'd splurged, yes she did, ordering all sorts of new things from New York—gowns, veils and gloves, shoes. She paid Odelia and her seamstresses an extra three dollars each for going-away dresses and wedding-night apparel.

If she couldn't be a bride, she'd be the best bride's *maid* anywhere. Let the brides commence shopping.

Cora walked the length of the room, inspecting each milky-white gown. And weren't the going-away dresses such bold colors this season? Reds, blues, and purples.

At the window, she paused to look out, then with a burst of energy shouted against the glass, "I'm back and going to win the day."

Whirling around, ready to work, Cora gathered two mannequin heads and the box of veils, taking a quick survey of the room. What else would she need? She'd come back for the shoes. She had a lovely idea to display them along the staircase—a pair on each step.

The fire, as shocking as it was, turned out to be a blessing. The purging flames awoke her to her foolishness, *purged* her really, from the evils of Rufus St. Claire.

Her first Sunday in church after the fire, Cora begged God's forgiveness, begged for His balm on her sorrow. While she sensed His touch, there were dark waves throughout her day when a memory surfaced, or a longing, and she'd break down.

How could she have been so blind? Could she ever trust her heart again?

At the display case in the small salon, Cora fashioned the veils on the mannequin heads, then opened the front door, allowing the morning breeze to sweep away the stale air of the night. To clear her mind of cobwebs of shame.

She raised the window sash and saw Odelia walking down the street. "Did you pick up the pastries?" she called.

"Right here." Odelia raised two large boxes over her head.

"Cora, please, stop yelling like a heathen."

She turned to see Mama gliding down the stairs, so lithe and sophisticated in her New York Saks Fifth Avenue dress, her hair the color of the morning sun and permanent waved.

She returned home when Odelia wrote her about the fire. Cora had planned to leave the tale for another time, when things were right again. But Odelia thought different. And Mama thanked her for it.

"If Daddy could see you now, Mama."

She smiled, raising her cigarette to her lips. "I sent him a photograph of me right after I had my hair done, wearing this dress."

"Has he written?" Cora asked. She'd not heard from Daddy since Christmas

Mama's smile faded. "No, but it's to be expected." Smoke from her cigarette swirled around her hair. Despite her thin, exotic appearance, Mama could not keep her despair from reflecting in her eyes.

"Pastries are in the pantry." Odelia came from the back, tying on her work apron. "I heard at the Women's Club that quite a number of the town's younger women want to come out, take a look. They have no hope of affording a wedding trousseau, but they'd like to dream."

"This danged Depression can't last forever," Mama said. "President Hoover must do something to help."

"The president can't make it rain, Mama. Nor does he care about brides in Heart's Bend, Tennessee, but we do. We can help them afford some sort of trousseau." Cora's rejuvenated mission welled within her. "We'll find a way."

"Yes, and if you're not careful you'll run out of money before it's all over. You can't keep giving stuff away," Mama said, disappearing into the new pantry, her favorite place in this whole shop. So she said.

Now that she'd worked a real job for a few months in a big city, she was more of an expert on everything than before. And not timid at all about sharing her opinion.

"The usual, Cora?" Odelia said, heading up to the mezzanine.

"Yes, dresses from New York on the mannequins. And let's bring down the entire inventory for the new built-in racks in the grand salon." Another idea from the reconstruction. Cora installed dress racks in the grand salon. She and Odelia wouldn't have to put it all away at night. "On the dress forms, put your favorite pattern dresses. Oh, I saw an ad in *Vogue* last fall with shoes positioned on the staircase. It looked marvelous. Let's do something similar, shall we?"

"We shall." Odelia hustled up the stairs. "I think someone is in love."

"In love?" Mama came from the pantry with a cup of coffee and a fresh cigarette. "Who's in love?"

"Cora."

"What on earth? I am *not* in love."

"You're mighty chipper lately. Especially when Birch Good comes around."

Mama sipped her coffee, peering at Cora over the rim. "I agree. I declare you officially Rufus-free. Thank goodness."

"Fine and dandy, but that does not mean I'm in love with Birch." Good grief. Two crazy old ladies . . . That's what she was dealing with here.

Sure, Cora liked Birch. Very, very much. She adored him, really. He'd been a lifesaver the past eight months, but love? No, no, no.

He was a farmer. He lived by the will of the sun and the rain. The land was his master. She wanted no such life.

She was about to head up to help Odelia when a young man dressed in a messenger uniform appeared at the door. "I'm looking for Mrs. Scott."

Mama stepped in from the small salon. "I'm Mrs. Scott."

"I've a registered mail for you, ma'am."

Mama anchored her cigarette between her lips, handed Cora her coffee, and signed for her letter. Cora dug a quarter from her pocket for a tip.

"Mama, what is it?"

Standing in the sun-filled foyer, Mama scanned the letter. "It's from your father."

"Daddy? What does he say?" Cora set Mama's coffee on the small planter between the windows and tried to read over her shoulder.

"H-he wants a divorce."

"A divorce?" Cora snatched the letter. "He can't mean it. He can't."

He had written over Christmas saying he was well, thinking of them, but couldn't bring himself to face the shame of Heart's Bend and all he'd done to their friends.

But divorce. Had he lost his mind? It was scandalous.

Yet there before Cora's eyes, in black and white, was a writ of divorce.

"He can't do this, Mama. The courts won't let him. He deserted *us*, not the other way around."

Mama's hand trembled as she drew a long puff from

her cigarette. "If he wants a divorce, then why would I stand in his way? He's left me, *us*, three times, Cora."

"He'll come home again."

"Cora, darling, you're so hopeful. But not this time. It's been well over a year." Mama turned for the stairs. "Now, how can I help Odelia? Shall I arrange the shoes?"

"Mama, how can you be so blasé? This doesn't bother you? It's one thing for Daddy to leave, but another to divorce you."

Mama sighed. "If you must know, he wrote to me already asking if I wanted to divorce him. I said I would not put my good name through the courts that way, but if he wanted to divorce me I'd not stand in his way. Now, let's get to the grand reopening of The Wedding Shop." She turned to call up the stairs. "Odelia, don't forget the long satin gloves. Those are so lovely."

Mama started up the stairs and Cora chased after her. "Mama, how are you not sad? How can you be all right with this?"

At the top of the stairs, Mama pulled another cigarette from her pocket. Cora snatched it from her fingers.

"Not around the dresses."

Mama sighed. "Cora, I've thought a lot about this and I want to move on. Is that all right with you? Plenty of women get divorced. I'll be more than fine." She punched the air with her fist. "I'm a feisty one."

"Plenty of women? Who, Mama? Who do you know in this town who's gotten divorced?" Cora couldn't think of anyone. "And who cares about other women. You've loved Daddy since you were sixteen. Married him at eighteen. How can you be all right with this?"

Mary Denton got divorced, but her husband went to jail for fraud. The Andersons got divorced a few years back, but she was a drunk. Other than that . . .

"Cora, leave it." Mama patted her shoulder. "I want to be happy today."

"But are you happy, Mama?" Cora touched her arm. If losing Rufus hurt like the dickens, how must Mama feel losing her husband of more than thirty-six years?

"You make me happy. This shop makes me happy. Cora, don't fret over me. Now, let's get those shoes lined up on the stairs."

The grand reopening started slow but ended with the shop full of women young and old celebrating the shop's return. Cora had three appointments on the books for next week and fully expected more.

When she closed the shop and shut off the lights at seven, Mama and Odelia met her in the foyer with a glass of tea. Mama hoisted her glass. "To our success!"

"To a good day," Odelia said. "Well done, Cora. I'm happy things are getting back to normal round here."

Mama sputtered a laugh, choking on her tea, pressing her fingers to her lips, shaking her head, listening to Odelia go on to complain her "dogs were barking" and she was heading on home.

Cora and Mama ate a light supper in the apartment, enjoying their new stove and refrigerator, keeping the conversation light and away from the matter of the divorce.

When they finished, Cora stood, clearing away the dishes. "I'll clean up, Mama. You go rest."

"Thank you, darling. I do feel rather worn-out today. But we had a good one, didn't we?"

"We did."

As she set the dishes in the sink, a wild sob contorted her forward. "Daddy . . ."

He wasn't coming back. Her family was no more. Cora muffled her soft cry with the dish towel, resting against the wall. Mama must not see or hear.

She collected herself enough to put away the corned beef, then snuck downstairs to the back porch.

Along the dark horizon, the final glow of the sunset hung on but offered no warmth. Cora drew her sweater around her, the night chilly, winter not ready to let go.

"Care for some company?" Birch peered through the screen on the far side of the porch.

"Please, please, come in." She stood as he entered, removing his hat, kissing her on the cheek. "What are you doing here?"

"Came to see how the reopen went." Birch took the chair next to hers, setting his hat on his knee. "Nice night."

"Beautiful."

"So, you had a good day?"

"The reopening was a success. I'm very pleased. How was your day?"

"Started the plowing with the new tractor. Uncle Sam's glad he can rest in the barn."

"He's been a good ole mule, Uncle Sam."

"A partner, really. Where would we be without him?"

She peeked at Birch. He was a handsome man with his hair smoothed back and the spring sun coloring his cheeks a pale red. "Daddy served Mama divorce papers."

"Cora, no . . ." He leaned forward, arms on his legs, slapping his hat between his hands. "I'm so sorry. How's Esmé?"

"She says fine. Apparently Daddy had already written to her about it." Cora glanced at her hands folded in her lap. "Makes me wonder if there is such a thing as true love."

"Right here, darling. Look right at me." He reached for her hand, pulling her to her feet, smoothing his hand around her waist. His breath was sweet and hot on her skin. "I love you, truly. If you marry me, I'll not leave you. Divorce won't be an option."

Cora weakened in his embrace. "Oh, Birch, you are so good to me." She pressed her hand to his cheek. "Handsome and fine."

"Then marry me, Cora. Marry me."

"I want to say yes, I do. But—"

"But what? There's nothing stopping you but your own fears. Is it Rufus? Do you still love him?"

"No, it's not Rufus. I-I just don't know if I want to live on a farm, Birch. I'm a town girl, a shop owner."

"I'm not asking you to give that up." Birch touched her chin with the edge of his finger. "I've been asking you to marry me since the fire. But I've been waiting for, well, since I can remember. Won't you be my wife?"

"Birch . . ." She walked toward the screen, gazing toward the park. The town was dark at this late hour. Almost nine o'clock. The streets were quiet, deserted. But the roads to Cora's heart were clogged, stuffed with the ambient noise of her past, of the impending divorce. "I'm not sure I feel for you as a girl ought when she gets married. Besides, I can't leave Mama right now. Not with Daddy divorcing her."

He caught her in his arms again. "I can love us enough for the both of us. And we can be there for your mama together. She can move out to the farm. I'll give her a big plot of land for her gardens."

"She won't want to live with us if we're just married."

"Then she can mind the shop. Live on the third floor. Come out to the farm whenever she wants. I'll still give her all the ground she wants to work her gardens. We'll have Sunday dinners together. Play checkers by the fire, listen to the radio." He released her but stood by her, gazing toward the park. "Truth is, Wade and I've been talking about building a little one-room place on the other side of the cornfield. She could live there. Even have her own driveway."

"She doesn't drive."

"We could teach her."

Cora laughed. "Do you hate your fellow Heart's Bendians? Mama would be a terror behind the wheel." She smoothed her hand over his chest and down his arm. "What did we do to deserve you, Birch Good?"

"Love has a way of fortifying a man's heart. And I love you, Cora."

She pressed her hand to his chest. "I just don't know . . ."

He raised her gaze to his, the porch light falling between them. "Just say yes. What's to not know? Cora, I've given you room, like you asked, when you was hurting from Rufus. Then when the shop was under construction after the fire. But time's marching on and I'm weary of standing still."

"Did I ask you to stand still for me?"

"Yes, by not telling me out and out, 'No, I won't marry you, Birch.'"

"Did I know Mama would be going through a hard time?" She folded her arms and lowered her voice. "A divorce. Think of the scandal."

"I hate to remind you, Cora, but your mama's been going through a hard time and scandal for over a year. You know I would never stand in the way of you being there for her. I'll come alongside, help, do all I can. Aren't two better than one? You led me to believe, given time, you'd consider me. It's been months. I need an answer."

"Are you giving me an ultimatum?"

"I've been patient, Cora."

She walked back to her rocker, sitting down hard, the light from the lamp cutting a swath through the growing night. "How do I know I'm not making another foolish decision? That I'm not inclined to marry you just because another man broke my heart?"

"If you want an honest answer, you'd be a fool *not* to marry me. Times are hard. Men all over these parts are losing their farms. Not me. My farm's not mortgaged. I ain't in any debt. I got some money set aside, not in the bank, mind you, but I have a good bit put back. I got a cellar full of canned vegetables and fruit. The house don't have electricity or plumbing, but I'll get a generator if you marry me. We've always been real warm in winter and cool in the summer what with the elms standing so tall. Well, you know, you been to my house a hundred times. You can make it your own, Cora. New paint, new wallpaper. The stove is from before the war, but I'll buy you a new one. And a refrigerator. Like the ones here in the shop. How'd you like that?"

"Birch, you want me to say yes? How will that play out, hmmm? Me running upstairs to say to my mama, 'Sorry Daddy's divorcing you but I'm a-marrying Birch!'"

"Fair enough, fair enough. I'll give you time to tell her," he said, reaching for her again, pulling her out of the chair and into him, the scent of God's green earth on his skin. His eyes, like the summer sky, searched hers. "Say yes and it'll be our secret until you feel right to tell Esmé. I just want to hear you say you'll marry me. I'll give you a man's loving, Cora. Trust me."

She quivered at his intimate confession. "Give me time, Birch. Let me tell Mama, and then I'll say yes."

He released her. "All right. How long do you think it will take?"

"A month? I-I don't know. I can't put a time limit on Mama's pain."

"But you can on your deliberations. If you don't want to marry me, just say so. Otherwise, you're doing me like Rufus did you. Fooling with my affections. Keeping me around for your own needs."

"I am not. Birch Good, how dare you!"

"But I'm not far off, am I? Cora . . ." His tone wooed her as his lips brushed her neck with a feathery touch.

"Birch—"

"I love you. I *want* you. Don't you have any of the same feelings for me?"

"Some, yes, but oh, stop, you're confusing me."

"I'm not confusing you. You're just resisting. I have no doubt we will be the best of lovers." Birch took another step into her, weakening her resolve with passionate shivers, finding no desire to escape. *Mercy . . . Birch.* He'd never shown her this side before. He raised her hand to his chest. "My heart's a-beating."

So was hers. "Birch, no, behave yourself." She shoved him aside, gasping, steadying her own rapid pulse.

But he turned her to him, his lips finding hers without pretense, without expectation. Just giving her everything in his heart. She held her stiff arms against his chest as his hand tightened around her back, but after a moment, when his kiss deepened, she let go, wrapping her arms about him, surrendering to the power of his persuasion.

Birch, Birch. She gasped for air when he broke away, stepping back, setting his hat on his wild, dark hair. The sensation of fire running under her skin made her want to reach for him again.

"Just so you know . . ." His voice broke with a laugh. "There's plenty more where that came from, Cora." He pushed through the screen door and off the porch. "When you make up your mind, come find me. I hope you say yes."

Cora pressed her face against the screen, watching him go, her pulse still ablaze, her heart exploding. He'd awakened a passion in her, a strange, fiery kind that even Rufus did not ignite. Instead of feeling alone and empty, she felt full and loved.

She sank into her chair, clinging to the arms, her *yes* lingering on the tip of her tongue. He was a good man. A kind man. God-fearing. Was it possible? Could it be?

She was in love with Birch Good?

CHAPTER TWENTY-TWO

HALEY

She sat on the stairs, phone pressed to her ear, fingers pressed to her forehead. "I understand. Thank you. Okay . . . I will." She hung up, dropping the phone beside her on the step.

The city hall was confused about the status of her permits and it was the second week of February.

Glancing toward the ceiling, Haley made an appeal to heaven for help, for favor. Since that day in Charlotte's shop, she'd found a bit of freedom, her confidence in the God of her youth returning.

Prayer came more quickly. Not vacant words to a God she wasn't sure listened, but hope-filled words to a God who would never forsake her.

Last week she went to church for the first time since before Dax. Looking back, she could see he was just the end of a long, slow slide away from everything she believed in. She let life obliterate her truth and values.

Well, back to the shop. Nothing was going on with the renovation because the permits were lost in red tape.

But yesterday she joined the Downtown Business Owners Association. Afterward she met with Emma Branson and Taylor Gillingham at Ella's about the wedding chapel on River Road to see if they could partner up. Taylor's husband was in advertising and Haley hoped he could offer some help. Pro bono.

"I'm the mother of his child. He'll do what I ask," Taylor informed her with a sneaky laugh.

Haley had also written out a plan to involve local businesses on her opening day, which was tentatively scheduled for June 15. If she could get enough inventory. Turns out renovations were cake compared to getting the inventory she wanted.

Using Charlotte's contacts, she'd called a few designers in New York and one in Atlanta to see about consigning inventory for an opening-day trunk show, but they all but laughed at her. Polite silk-and-tulle laughter, of course.

"We're booked this season. Maybe next May. Call us in the fall to set it up."

Haley closed her eyes, tipping her head toward the ceiling, trying to listen with her spirit. What should she do?

"Lord, if this shop is not what I'm supposed to do, make it clear. If You don't want it, I don't want it."

Haley relished in a peaceful repose, not thinking of anything, half listening to what God might say, half drifting to sleep, when the shop door eased open.

An older woman with tender lines marking her face stepped inside, her fur-lined coat buttoned to her chin.

"Are you Haley?"

"I am. Can I help you?"

She gripped her gloved hands at her waist. "I'm Mrs. Elliot. Lenora Elliot."

"Welcome to The Wedding Shop. Well, what I hope will be The Wedding Shop."

"I've been here before."

"You bought your dress here? From Cora?"

"Indeed I did. Sixty years ago. Walked down those wide stairs." She moved to the base of the steps without faltering, her countenance strong, her gaze fixed toward the mezzanine. "My mother and mother-in-law sat right over here along with my sisters and best friend." She pointed to the large salon. "It was spring-time, but winter's chill was still in the air. The shop was so cozy and warm with wedding talk, hot tea, and music. We all cried when I descended the stairs. I wore a white dress with a full tea-length skirt and a sweet-heart neckline, and a simple veil, but wasn't I princess for the day? A southern Jackie O. Miss Cora suggested the most lovely suit for my going-away outfit. We couldn't afford both so she gave me what had to be a very generous discount."

"I hear she did that a lot with her customers."

"A finer woman never lived. She threw in some lovely jewelry too. Of course it wasn't anything expensive, costume stuff, but I'd have had nothing otherwise. She made me the beautiful bride I always wanted to be."

"Do you live in Heart's Bend, Mrs. Elliot?"

"I did the first year of marriage, but then I moved to Los Angeles with my husband. We raised our family there. Bean died a week ago." Her hazel eyes misted. "He wanted to come home to be buried."

"I'm sorry for your loss."

"I loved that man for sixty-five years. Sixty of them married. We had four children—two boys, two girls. I wanted to bring my girls here for their trousseaus, you know, pay Miss Cora back for her kindness to me, but she'd closed the shop by the time they married." The woman's eyes glistened as she raised her gaze to Haley. "Of course, they were modern California girls who had their own ideas of what to wear for their wedding. Couldn't interest them in my fifties-style gown. Now my granddaughters are clamoring for it. Calling it 'classic vintage.'" Mrs. Elliot reached for Haley, pressing a piece of paper into her palm. "I heard someone was reopening the shop and I just want to say good luck with your plans. God bless you."

"Thank you." Haley glanced down to find a folded check. "Mrs. Elliot, please, I can't take your money."

"You can and you will." She raised her chin, pointing a long manicured finger at Haley. "I want to bring my granddaughters here in a few years." She paused at the door. "Such a lovely, splendid place with so many brides as its heritage."

"But you don't even know me." She offered back the check. "How can you trust me with your money?"

Mrs. Elliot closed her hand over Haley's. "The moment I heard someone was opening the shop, my heart leapt in my chest. I knew I was to help. Just knew it. Bring this place back to life, let it be the darling of Heart's Bend again."

"Thank you. I won't let you down." Haley slipped the check into her pocket.

Mrs. Elliot toured the shop one more time, describing the old grandfather clock, the wide gold divan, the plush chairs, the china tea service, the light and aura of the shop. Then she made her way to the front door. "I hope to see you soon with my granddaughters."

Haley drew her into a gentle hug. "I would love that, Mrs. Elliot. And thank you again. It means everything to me."

Alone in the shop, Haley retrieved the check from her pocket. She dropped against the banister as she read the amount.

Ten thousand dollars. *Ten.* Thousand. Dollars.

She couldn't. Just couldn't take this amount of money. "Mrs. Elliot." Haley called to her from the front door, then raced to the curb, but Mrs. Elliot had already gone.

Back inside, she sat on the steps and glanced at the check. Great. No address. Just her name.

Well, okay. Then she'd take it. She didn't feel worthy of this generosity, but as she waved the check toward heaven, gratitude spilled into her soul. "Thank you."

"Haley?" Cole stepped inside, joining her on the bottom step. "I was just at city hall to check on the permits."

She glanced up at him. "You don't have to do that. I'm calling them every day."

"I thought I'd add my muscle." He sat forward, arms resting on his legs.

"Really?" She squeezed his arm. "Do you have any to spare?"

"Ha-ha, such a funny girl." He slipped from his jacket and popped his bicep, letting it strain against his shirtsleeve. "I can spare a few inches."

"I'll take all the help I can get."

He rubbed his hands together, slipping back into his jacket. The shop was cold with no heat running. "Not doing anything is driving me crazy. Did I tell you I saw Brant Jackson in Linus Peabody's office? And I saw them together at Java Jane's, scheming. If those two are in cahoots . . ."

"Cole, look." Haley handed him the check. "Another of Cora's brides stopped by. She gave me this. I'm halfway to our reno budget."

He snatched the check from her hand. "She walked in and handed you ten thousand dollars?"

"She reminisced first, *then* she handed me ten thousand dollars."

Cole's grin slipped wide. "Haley, *someone* is watching out for you. I don't want you to doubt ever again."

"Not someone." Haley took the check, tucking it into her pocket, a smile burning in her gut. "*God* is watching out for me."

"All right, God is watching out for you." Cole stood, shoving his hands into his jeans pockets. Jeans that fit all too nicely. Had he always been so good-looking? Hard to tell since she was always looking at him through Tammy's lens.

"Why do you think God would want a 126-year-old shop reopened in Heart's Bend? Or for me to do it?"

He glanced back at her and the intensity in his gaze made her heart stutter. "Good question."

"Other than playing here as a kid, I don't have any connection to the place. But I loved it."

"Maybe that's all it takes," Cole said. "To just love a place. Isn't that the gospel, 'For God so loved us'?"

"But is it about the place or the people who will come here? The brides?"

"I think you're on to something." He crouched down in front of her, his blue eyes searching hers. "I-I was . . ." He stopped, clearing the catch from his voice. "Would you like to come to the house tonight, eat pizza, watch a movie?"

Her skin flamed with the intimacy of his voice, of his question. "Are you asking me on a date?"

He grinned, glancing down, brushing at something imaginary on the floor. "Yeah, I think I am."

"Wow, okay, well . . ." But he'd been Tammy's, even though in the end they had broken their engagement. Haley was nothing like her. "Cole, I'm not Tammy."

"I know."

"You realize you're asking out Haley Morgan."

"Pretty sure I do." His blue gaze watched her for a long moment. "Is it too weird?"

"No, I'm just surprised."

He laughed and dropped down to the floor, resting his forearms on his raised knees. "I've known you twenty-some odd years, but I'm not sure I ever got to know *you*. Tammy or one of your brothers was always around. Except for that night we stayed up talking."

"Yea . . ."

"I like the woman I'm getting to know."

"Cole, you should know there's a Haley you don't

know. One who made some pretty dark choices in her life."

"Like that guy? Dax Mills? The one from the other day?"

"Yes. You recognized him? Is that why you stopped?" Dax would be thrilled to know someone recognized him on the street. At one point, Haley thought it was his only true goal in life.

"I recognized him. Used to work out to one of his videos. But I stopped at the shop because you looked upset."

"You saw I was upset from the street?"

He shrugged. "Is that a crime? So how do you know Dax?"

No, not at all. "We were in a relationship."

"Ah." Cole thought for a moment. "Isn't he married?"

He was getting the picture without Haley coloring in all the numbers. "Do you still want to have pizza with me?"

"Yeah, I do. I'm no saint, Haley. Are things over between you two?"

"For me, yes. But he seems to think he can drop in on my life anytime he wants, tell me what to do."

"All right, then pizza and a movie at my place. Six?"

"You sure?"

He regarded her for a long blue moment. "I'm sure, but if you're not—"

"I'm game. Hey, if it creeps us both out, then we call it a fun experiment."

"Deal." He stuck out his hand. When Haley slipped her hand into his, the same sensation washed over her as the first night they talked. On the shop porch. Gentle, warm, her cares falling from her shoulders.

"But, Cole, you should know, I'm not looking for a relationship." As soon as the words left her mouth, she wished them back. Her confession was presumptuous. Rude. And cast a shadow on Cole's otherwise light countenance.

"It's pizza and a movie, Haley." He started for the door. "Not a marriage proposal."

"Right." Was he mad? "Six o'clock?"

He paused at the door, his smile wide, forgiving. And she felt its energy all the way to her toes. "Don't be late."

CHAPTER TWENTY-THREE

HALEY

Her keys. She just needed to find her keys and she'd be off. Ten till six. She might be a few minutes late to Cole's, but she'd called Charlotte this afternoon for more advice on how to break in with designers and they ended up talking about life, love, and God.

Having met her once and talked to her on the phone twice, Haley made a heart connection with Charlotte. She admired her. Already called her friend.

In the light of Cole, Charlotte, and Mrs. Elliot's ten-thousand-dollar check, Haley felt a breeze blowing through the dark tunnel that was Dax. She neared the end. Saw the light.

Downstairs, she found her keys on the kitchen island. At the refrigerator, Mom took out a bottle of water.

"Where are you headed?" she said. "Your dad and I were thinking of going out to dinner. There's a new vegetarian place on the east side of town."

"Since when have I ever indicated I liked vegetarian?" Haley laughed. "I'm eating pizza."

"By yourself?"

"If you must know, with Cole."

"Is that wise?" Mom took a short swig of her water. "I know he's working with you on the *shop* . . ." There was definite 'tude when she said *shop*. "But if you hang out too much—"

"What, Mom? We might like each other? Maybe make out? Have a few laughs?"

"Fall in love."

"I'm not going to fall in love with him, but so what if I did? He's a really great guy."

"Look, I don't know what happened between you and Dax, but I know it tore you apart." Mom used her intuition to shine her light behind Haley's closed doors. "Between your breakup, Tammy's death, reopening this crazy wedding *shop*, I think you're trying to capture something that's been lost. There's a danger of transferring affection to Cole, thinking it's love when it's not."

"Mom, I'm fully aware of my breakup with Dax, of losing my best friend. And yes, opening the shop is very sentimental for me. And frustrating. But I'm not trying to capture anything. I'm trying to build something. A business. Cole is a friend. That's all."

"If you're sure."

"I'm sure. I already told him I didn't want a relationship."

"No one ever accused you of not being honest." Mom's soft laugh cracked open Haley's heart a wee bit to her. She was a perfectionist, an overachiever, and often more like a drill sergeant than a mom, but she loved her family.

"I'm sorry, Mom."

She popped wide eyes at Haley. "For what?"

"Judging you."

"Judging me?" Mom swigged from her water bottle, keeping her gaze on Haley.

"Yeah, thinking you didn't really love us, that your career and success were more important."

"Is that how I appeared to you?" Mom held steady, never one to back down from a confrontation or hard truth.

"Pretty much. Didn't think you had much use for a girl either. You preferred the boys."

"Haley, my goodness, the reason we had five kids was because I refused to give up on having a girl."

"So I was just something to achieve?"

Mom came around the island, reaching for Haley, but hesitated and lowered her hand. "I wanted a daughter. My relationship with my mother was always so special. We were very close."

"But from my chair, you never wanted a relationship with me other than parent-child. You took good care of me, Mom. Not denying that, but I was a would-be boy until junior high. I never got the impression you wanted a daughter."

"Wow, well, then I apologize." Mom's eyes swam with her confession. "I wanted a daughter, though I never considered if I'd be a good mother of one."

Haley regarded her, then laughed softly. "No one ever said you'd get a good daughter either."

"You are a great daughter. I'm very proud of you."

Mom pressed her hand over her heart. "I'm sorry if you felt unwanted or unloved. That was never, ever in my heart."

Haley jiggled her keys. Time ticked away and Cole was waiting. "All things work together for good. I'm not sure I'd ever have found God without the little hurts I carried."

"Hurts? Oh, Haley—"

"Mom, it's fine. I'm good, really."

Mom gently took hold of Haley's arm. "I love you. Please know how much. You were wanted. If anyone should feel unwanted, it's Seth. When the ultrasound told us it was a boy, I was ready to send him back."

"Don't tell him. Abigail would have a field day psychoanalyzing that. Seth adores you. He's a true mama's boy."

"I know. And I can't imagine life without him. Or you."

The sentiment hung between them. These spontaneous words were more than they'd shared in a long time. Probably since Haley was in high school and broken-hearted over Brandon Lutz—who went to homecoming with Misty Stone instead of her. Mom was a trooper during that dastardly teen drama.

"So . . ." Mom drew a deep breath, twirling her water bottle between her hands. "H-how's the *shop*?"

Haley grinned. She was trying. "Um, good. I think. We still don't have our permits. It's been six weeks." Haley glanced at the stove clock. She was officially late.

"What about money?"

"I'm getting there. Believe it or not, a woman came in today and gave me a check for ten grand."

Mom's eyes popped wide. "You're kidding."

"She was one of Miss Cora's brides. Said the shop was important to her and she was glad someone was reopening it. Mrs. Peabody, Linus Peabody's aunt, gave me money too."

Mom took a swig of water. "You know Linus was the one who spearheaded Akron coming to Heart's Bend."

"Cole mentioned it. Do you think Linus might be behind the delayed permits?"

"Would not surprise me."

"Okay, I might talk to Cole about it tonight." Haley started for the door. "Thanks, Mom, for asking about the shop. I know you're against it."

"I have no affection for it, but . . ." She exhaled. "I'm not against you."

"Then can I ask what you have against the wedding shop?"

She hesitated, such a rare thing from Dr. Morgan, who was sharp and quick. "You're jiggling your keys. You must be late."

"Cole can wait."

Mom headed out of the kitchen. "You best get going. Your father will be here soon, ready to eat. Have a good time."

"Are you ever going to tell me?" Haley said.

"I don't know," she said without turning around. "There are times when I'm not really sure I know myself."

. . .

Cole greeted Haley at the front door in his bare feet, his Tennessee Volunteers T-shirt clinging to his shoulders and swinging loose about his waist.

"You're on chopping duty."

"Oooh, didn't you get the memo?" Haley said. "I don't do chopping. Or mixing. Or sautéing or cooking in general." She set her backpack down by the front door, removing her gloves, still a bit chilled from the ride out. But still feeling the warmth of the honest moment with Mom.

"Well, today you're on chopping duty. Kick off your shoes. Make yourself at home."

"If you want me to make myself at home, I'm not chopping anything." She wiggled out of her boots and followed him to the kitchen where he'd set out veggies and a cutting board on the quartz counter.

"This is your station." He passed her a large knife and turned back to his pizza dough with a glance at her. "You look good."

"Thank you." She fluffed her hair free of the biker-helmet mash.

Her gaze met his. He was smiling, watching her, a dancing light in his eyes. She reached for the knife, her pulse thumping a little faster.

Keep it simple, easy breezy.

"So, what do I do here?" She sat on the stool, noticing the guitar in a glass case stuck to the wall over the dining table. "Hey, is that the guitar you used to play when we were but wild-eyed teens?"

He laughed. "Yeah, that's the Fender Stratocaster."

"I remember Tammy telling me about it. Said it was worth some ridiculous amount of money."

"Dad bought it for us at an estate auction. It's worth way more than he paid. I don't think the auctioneer knew what he had."

"Why'd you put it in a glass case? Don't you want to play it?"

"Hey, sister," Cole said, motioning to the pile of veggies in front of Haley. "Get to chopping."

Nice avoid. Haley considered pressing, but where the senior Danner was concerned Cole had little to share.

Haley stared at the knife and the pepper, tomato, and onion waiting to be sliced and diced. "Do you think Linus is holding up our permits?"

"There's a good chance. But he's smart enough to keep his fingerprints off any shenanigans." Cole worked the pizza dough from a large bowl, dumping it onto the floured countertop.

"Should we do something? I mean, if he's holding up the works, then he can't expect me to have the shop renovated by the end of April."

"Sure he can. He's making up the rules as we go along."

"Then I'm going to see him tomorrow."

"I can stop by in the morning." Cole peeked at her. "Check on it for you."

"Thanks, but I'll go."

"Are you sure? I know folks in the permit office, I know Linus—"

"I don't need to be rescued, Cole."

"Never said you did."

Haley sighed. *Lower your defenses, girl.* "I should do it, don't you think? This is my fight."

He sighed with a soft nod. "Yeah, sure. Just, you know, let me know if you need anything."

"I need some pizza. That's what I need." Haley set down the knife, watching Cole for a sec. Did he seem disappointed? He'd already done so much for her that she figured she should take on some battles for herself. It's not like she needed him in the fray with her. If she was going to be a businesswoman in Heart's Bend, she needed to learn the system. "S-so how'd you learn to make pizza?"

"My grandmother was Italian. She taught us boys to cook."

"We had a cook when I was growing up. Remember her? Hilda."

"I do." Cole made a face. "She wasn't that good."

"You're telling me. I swear she served boiled bark and roasted pine cones one time. Mom loved it. Did you know there's a new vegetarian restaurant in town? The parents are trying it out tonight." Haley shivered.

"Ever wonder how you came from them?"

"Almost daily when I was a kid. Dad I understood, but Mom? The only two women in a house of men and we could not have been more opposite. But Mom and I had a good chat about that tonight." Haley rested her chin in her hand. "It was good."

"Yeah?" Cole glanced at her, working the dough, then stretching it out on one of three pizza stones. "Hey, you're not chopping."

"I told you, I don't chop."

He shook flour from his hands and walked around the island, standing behind Haley. "Take the knife . . ." He cupped his right hand around hers, taking up the utensil. His hand was soft with flour, warm, covering hers. A buzzing pulse shivered up her arm.

"Take the pepper." Cole set the vegetable on the chopping block, molded his left hand over Haley's, and aimed the knife at the deep green skin. The scent of his skin, of his shirt, awakened cautious desires. "Curl your fingers back so you don't cut them off. Good."

He surrounded her. With his body, with his voice, with the gentle motion of chopping a pepper. His breath grazed the side of her cheek and, at one point, she felt lost in his presence.

But when she glanced up at him, he was focused on chopping. "See?" he said, looking at her as she looked at him.

"Y-yes, I see." But nothing about cutting peppers. She saw the cut of his jaw with the end-of-day beard, the sweet bow of his lips, the endless blue meadows in his eyes, and the steadiness of his countenance.

"Haley—"

"Cole." His nearness robbed her breath. "I-I'm not looking for—"

He stepped back. "For what? A relationship?" Returning to his pizza station, he gave her his back and finished spreading out the dough on a pizza stone. "You like veggie pizza? With pepperoni?"

"I like everything but olives and anchovies." Didn't she sound the fool. Assigning her feelings to him.

He grinned over his shoulder. "Me too."

But the light had gone out of him. Haley reached for the onion, cutting away the skin, doing her best not to cut off her thumb. "Dax was married when I met him, but I didn't know it."

He regarded her for a long second. "You don't have to tell me, Haley."

"But I do. I want to. He charmed the pants right off of me. Literally."

"Haley—"

"I was head over heels. Wanted to marry him so bad. From almost the moment I met him. He was amazing. I'd never met anyone like him. When he started to pursue me, I was queen of the world. This gorgeous man wants me?"

"You're very beautiful, Haley."

She drove the knife through the onion, letting his compliment pass. Because she felt it. Because it carried more punch than she imagined.

"Not like the women fawning over Dax. He was the type of man who dated amazon-like bikini models with rivers of gorgeous hair and perfect boobs. Now Tammy, she would've been his type. But not me, not a short, petite air force captain."

"What happened?" Cole took out a knife and reached for the pepper, but his attention was leveled on her.

"When I found out he was married, it killed me."

"Did you leave him?"

"No, I asked him to leave his wife. I'm not proud of it."

She waited. For the look. For the sad sigh. The

shake of his head. She deserved it. Every ounce of his judgment.

Instead, Cole shifted his attention from chopping and gazed at her with kindness. "I take it he didn't leave his wife."

"He promised he would. For six months. Then I found out he had children and, man, it was like crashing into a mountain going a hundred miles an hour. What was I mixed up in? But I strung along for another six months." Haley slipped from the stool and peered out the French doors leading to the patio and garage breezeway. "Home wrecker, that's what I turned out to be. Captain home wrecker."

"He played a part, Haley."

"That doesn't excuse me. The fact that I played a part at all makes me ill."

"What made you leave him?"

"Tammy's death. I'd left him three months before but had relapse moments. Then when she died, heaven invaded earth for me. For two months I had nightmares about facing God's judgment seat in my present condition. I'd wake up drenched in sweat, shaking. I knew my life was not right. One afternoon I met Dax at a park to tell him it was over, over, over. In the middle of arguing about us, his wife called. One of his kids got hurt skateboarding. The look on his face . . . Dax loved his kids. I told him to never call me again. He needed to be with his family. I got out of the air force and came home."

When she turned around, Cole stood behind her. "I'm glad you came home." He brushed her bangs aside, sending a battalion of fiery tingles through her.

Her eyes welled up. "Don't, Cole. We can't . . . I can't . . ."

She'd thought weeping with Charlotte had cleansed her shameful palate, but Cole, with his kind acceptance and tender expression, raised the raw, real, deep-down Haley.

She wasn't good enough for a man like Cole. She wasn't. Since she couldn't speak, she stood there shaking as Cole pulled her to him, wrapping her against his chest.

Haley leaned without responding, a rebel sob rolling through her chest. She broke with a wail, clinging to Cole with her fists full of his shirt.

"It's okay, Haley." Cole rocked her side to side, shaking loose every clinging thought of shame and fear. "Let it go." He cradled her, his cheek on her head. "Let it go."

CHAPTER TWENTY-FOUR

CHARLOTTE

The clock across the room flashed 3:01. Charlotte sat up, the room dark and still, but an undeniable stirring in her bones.

"What is it?" she whispered, a prayer to the One who heard from on high.

She'd experienced His nudging in the night many times, a call to prayer, a call to worship. She didn't mind His three a.m. beckoning. Not when she used to jolt awake in the wee hours gripped with fear or anxiety.

She wasn't that girl anymore. She'd found the Love that drove away all fear. Propping a pillow behind her back, she leaned against the headboard and closed her eyes, her husband, Tim, sleeping beside her, his breathing soft and peaceful.

She prayed in the Spirit for a while, letting her soul open to His whispers.

Her thoughts drifted backward to her day, to her work at the shop, the brides she assisted and the— Charlotte sat forward, eyes open.

Him. She thought she saw *him* today, the purple man. She didn't know what else to call him. He appeared out of nowhere four years ago and spoke into her life, setting her spirit on fire.

She'd concluded he was an angel of some sort. Perhaps the Lord Himself, if she could be so bold. One Sunday at church she heard stories of those who saw *beyond* this world's veil. Those who saw the Lord. Charlotte just never imagined she'd be one of them.

The purple man appeared in her life when she wrestled with marrying Tim. He'd been the auctioneer up on Red Mountain that day, drawing her in to bidding on an ugly, battered trunk that contained the wedding dress.

She had no idea that ugly, battered trunk contained a hundred-year-old wedding dress and her heritage.

The purple man showed up at her shop. When she needed nudging. When she needed confidence.

"Babe, you awake?" Her husband's hand pressed against her back.

"Yes, thinking, praying." Charlotte dropped down into his arms. "Did I wake you?"

"I thought I heard you praying."

"Tim, I think I saw the purple man today."

"Think?"

She smiled against his chest. "Okay, I did see the purple man."

"At the shop?"

"Yes, outside, on the sidewalk, looking in, like he was waiting." Charlotte quivered. "I think he wanted me to come out to him, but I was with a customer."

Just remembering, she felt the blue intensity of his gaze, the yearning for her to come out to him. But she'd been too busy.

Charlotte sat up, restless. Bothered.

"You missed him?"

"By the time I finished, he was gone." Charlotte rolled out of bed, thinking, staring toward the window. "I've not seen him since we got married. He surprised me."

"What do you think he wanted?"

"I have no idea." Charlotte paced out of their room, down the hall to her office where she flipped on the lights.

The dress? Did he want the dress?

"Char?" Tim followed. "What are you doing?"

"Where did we put the dress?"

They'd moved into the two-story home Tim designed for them last year. The angst of moving came with the joy of discovering she was pregnant. Charlotte was ready to fill their home with baby Rose. But she miscarried a few weeks later.

"Your wedding dress?" Tim said, walking around her to the closet. "I put it in here . . . unless you took it to the shop." He slid the barn-style door to one side.

After her wedding, Charlotte had stored the dress her great-grandmother wore for her wedding in 1912. She was the lovely Emily Ludlow, a Birmingham socialite and philanthropist.

But when she found the gown in the trunk, the dress had taken a hundred-year journey of its own, being worn by two other women who had no connection to her other than their faith in the One who authored their lives.

Then at last, as if by accident, the dress came home to Charlotte.

"Here it is." Tim reached in the back for a box—which sat atop the old battered trunk where Charlotte had discovered the gown.

He set the box on her desk. "Are you sure you want to open it? You seemed so convinced you needed to preserve it."

Charlotte nodded, Tim's observation breathing life into the Spirit's earlier stirring. "That's just it, Tim. I wasn't supposed to box it up and put it away, zip, bam, it had served *my* purpose. What about God's purpose?"

He dug through the desk drawers for a pair of scissors. "I thought you wanted it for our kids."

"I did . . . I do . . . but I'm not so sure *He* wants it *just* for our kids." Her beating heart painted a clearer picture.

"It's not yours to keep or protect, is it?" Tim sliced the packing tape with the edge of the scissors.

"I thought it was my heritage, from my grandmother. Finally I had something of the family's. But, Tim, what a miracle it came to me at all. This dress isn't mine. It's God's. That's why the purple man stood out there today." Charlotte buzzed to life with revelation. "To tell me it's time to give it away. Only I was too busy to be with him. To hear him. Five minutes, that's all it would have taken. Five minutes. Instead, I stayed with my customer and forgot about him until it was too late."

"Well, the Lord is talking to you now." Tim stepped back, walking around Charlotte to put the scissors away. "The box is open."

Raising the lid brought a level of joy only seeing the dress could bring. Like reliving every special day in her life over and over.

The notion of giving the dress away sat on her like a mantle. But to whom?

Charlotte removed the gown from its linen bag, the silky bodice smooth against her arm, the train collecting at her feet like windswept snow. The bodice and sleeves absorbed the light so the gown glowed.

"You think it's for one of your customers?" Tim hauled a dress form from the back of the closet and set it in the corner. "Did you have a special bride in the shop today? If the man appeared today, maybe that's a clue."

"I don't know. I mean, I meet so many brides, but the dress has never come to mind before. Not even today when I saw him." Charlotte slipped the gown over the dress form. "I don't know . . ."

She stood back, observing, thinking, praying. Only one person came to mind. "A few weeks ago I helped a new shop owner from Heart's Bend. I think I told you about her. I made her try on a dress and—"

"The Lord touched her. Something about her past."

Charlotte glanced at her husband. "Haley. The dress goes to Haley." She spoke at first in faith, but once the words were in the air, they brought life to her soul. "Yes, Haley."

"Are you sure?" Tim yawned, scratching his head, the thrill of the chase fading.

"I am. I really am. I mean, I'll give it a few days, but yeah, Tim, Haley is the next bride for the wedding dress." The thick chills down her arm punctuated her declaration.

"Then give her a call. When is she getting married?"

"That's just it. She's not. Said she doesn't want to get married. She'll be the bride's *maid*, so to speak, but never the bride. She had a really devastating breakup."

"Sounds like the perfect time to tell her God's got something grand for her." Tim kissed her cheek. "I'm going back to bed."

"I'm going to stay in here and pray." Charlotte dragged one of the chairs over to the dress and sat down, peaceful, ready to meditate. *Dress, where is your new home?*

Tim paused at the door. "And if we have a daughter one day?"

"Then the Lord will have to send it back to her. If it is hers to wear."

When she was alone, Charlotte sat for a long while in the quiet, in the glow of the dress. The gold threads from a hundred years ago still held. This gown's journey and existence were a miracle.

It had never been altered, yet it fit every one of the brides who wore it. Though it was designed a hundred years ago, it looked as if it could be on the cover of a bride's magazine today.

A blend of vintage and modern. The gown was timeless.

Charlotte's confidence grew. Haley Morgan was the next bride to own the wedding dress.

CHAPTER TWENTY-FIVE

CORA

THANKSGIVING 1932

You ought to accept Birch today." Mama sat with her hands folded in her lap, her passenger window rolled halfway down, the delectable aroma of her good fried chicken, lima beans, and fresh baked bread filling Cora's car. "If he'll still have you."

"Your brave act is not fooling me." Cora took the bend in Mason Road toward the Good farm, a patch of blue trying to break through the overcast gray. "You don't want to live in the shop alone, Mama."

"You're the one being fooled, Cora. You think you're denying Birch for me, but you're hiding. Afraid. You think he's your last chance at happiness, but what if he turns out like your daddy or Rufus." Mama raised her chin a little higher. "And if I were you, I'd have thrown that piece of junk around your neck into the river. Don't stand for nothing good. It's an insult to Birch if you accept him."

"It's a fine piece. Real gold. Just because Rufus was a bad egg doesn't mean the necklace is . . ." Cora pressed her fingers against the gold heart. She'd not taken it off since he gave it to her, kissing her in such a way she turned into ice cream on a hot summer day. "I don't think Birch will be like Daddy or Rufus. I just had to consider if I wanted to be a farmer's wife." She'd thought about it all spring, summer, and into the fall, even though he had assured her she did not need to give up her shop.

Despite her emotional wrestling, she couldn't get away from the truth. Birch was a stellar man and he loved her. And that scared her the most. Something felt wrong to be so humbly loved by one man. In his light, she could see Rufus hadn't loved her at all.

"At least a farmer's wife eats."

"After she works all day in the dirt."

"You work all day, just in a different dirt. And Birch won't make you leave the shop. He already said so. He knows how important it is to you, to Heart's Bend." Mama pulled a cigarette from her pocket. She wore a new fashion—culottes. Some sort of skirt-like pants swinging loose about her hips and legs. Her hair was a new blinding shade of blonde, and she'd plucked her eyebrows so she could draw on a pair like Joan Crawford's.

"When the divorce is final I think I'll head on back to New York. It'll be spring by then. I'd like to know you're married and settled before I go."

"You can move in with me and Birch."

She looked askance at Cora. "So you've decided then."

She nodded. "But I thought I'd tell him first."

Mama blew a long stream of smoke out the car

window. "It's time to move on, Cora. For both of us. I'm happy for you."

But she was nervous. "I've not seen him since the Labor Day parade." Where he bought her an ice cream and walked her around town, talking, holding her hand. In Gardenia Park he asked again if she'd decided.

"I've given you all spring and summer, Cora. Surely you know your answer by now."

Her answer, *"Mama's still so fragile,"* seemed acceptable to him.

"He'll be happy to finally have your answer," Mama said. "I just hope you are worth the wait."

"Mama!"

Meanwhile, the wedding business was slow. The drought across the south caused more farm failures than the bank closings, and brides were choosing to wed in Sunday dresses or refashioning their mothers' gowns into their own.

Cora kept a close watch on her money, however, mindful that every time she withdrew money she was not compromising all Aunt Jane worked so hard to build.

"I hear Birch invited half the town to his Thanksgiving feast this year." Mama sighed, shaking her head. "I sure do miss our big parties at the homestead."

Hard to believe it'd been two years since Daddy informed them the bank was closing and he'd lost everything.

"When I marry Birch, you can play hostess again. You are far better at it than I am."

"I'll be in New York."

"You'll only have to turn around and come back for your first grandchild." Cora spoke what she believed was right, what she wanted to be true. But the words felt foreign, as if they weren't truly for her.

Loving a man like Rufus took the wind from her heart. Might loving a man like Birch restore her?

"We'll see then." Yet the corner of Mama's lips tugged into a smile.

All spring and summer, Mama had managed her grief and the dramatic changes in her life by driving out to Birch's farm, daily tending her gardens, which produced blue-ribbon winners at the county fair.

Cora slowed the car, taking the long drive down to the Good farmhouse. Yes, this *would* be a good place to build the rest of her life. She parked in the open field, the last in a long line of cars.

Mama scanned the horizon and the meadow. "Look at all the folks. Now, this is what you call a real Thanksgiving feast. Just think, you'll be the mistress of this place very soon." She reached into the backseat for her tin of chicken, slipping her arm through the bread basket handle.

"One thing at a time, Mama." She pictured Birch swinging her up in his arms with a shout, whirling her around, shouting to the guests, "I'm engaged!"

As they walked along the dusty, gravely drive toward the gathered crowd, Cora scanned the sea of faces for Birch.

When they arrived at the food tables, Mama was immediately surrounded by a group of women fascinated and aghast by her attire, fear mixed with envy in their shrill voices.

"I could never."

"Dean would not let me out of the house!"

"Well, I think you look darling."

"Good for you, taking charge of your own life, Esmé."

Cora greeted friends, smiling, all the while scanning the faces for Birch.

"Cora, dear, how are you?" Reverend Clinton's wife squeezed her shoulders in a light hug. "We're so very sorry about your daddy."

"Yes, well, it can't be helped." Cora fixed a shallow smile. Was the reverend's wife talking about the divorce? Mama claimed she'd told no one. "So Mama told you?"

"Yes, of course. Such a tragedy for you and Esmé. You have our prayers. We are here for you."

"Th-thank you. Prayers certainly make a difference."

Odd. Very odd. Cora grabbed Mama as she walked past. "Mama, why was Rosalee Clinton consoling me about Daddy? Please don't say you told them about the divorce." She didn't want to think about divorce on her engagement day.

"No, I didn't mention the divorce." Mama pinched her lips together with a sigh. "But I might have told a small white lie."

"Oh, law, what did you tell them?" Cora squeezed Mama's arm, shoving her off to one side. "There is no such thing as a small white lie. I know because my mother told me. When she washed my mouth out with soap for fibbing."

"Well, everyone kept asking about him." Mama twisted her hands together, staring over the pasture where the boys and men played football. Cora's heartbeat quickened when she finally spotted Birch. "It seemed a good idea at the time. What did you want me to say? The truth? A divorce means shame and humiliation, whispers and shunning. It means I lose my place on the Women's League board. I might want to marry again. I'm only fifty-four."

"I can't even imagine what you said." Cora folded her arms, waiting. "Go on, what did you tell them?"

"I might have told a few people . . ." She dipped her head as she lowered her voice. "That he, well, died."

Cora gasped, stepping back. "That's a big, bold *black* lie. Mama, how could you?"

She jerked her arm from Cora's grasp. "I did it to save us."

"Us? You mean yourself. You're moving back to New York, so why do you care? Now you're leaving me with this lie."

"I'm doing you a favor, girl." Mama stepped forward with bravado. "I do this because you're my daughter. Because you're about to get married. You think I want Ernie's cowardice and selfishness following you into your marriage? Making a mockery of our family because he can't come home and face the world he created? Be a man? Now folks actually have *sympathy* for us, and for him too, I might add. I'd rather face his fake death than the scandal of divorce."

"Then where's the funeral? The fresh burial in the family plot?"

"I said he died in Florida and was buried there. Folks are too kind to ask any more questions."

"Buried in Florida. Not in the Scott section of the Heart's Bend Memorial Gardens? Where three generations of Scotts and your son are buried? You're telling me folks are buying that?"

"Oh, for crying out loud, Cora, what's with the semantics? He's not really dead, you know. Go find Birch. Tell him yes. Think about your life, your future. That's what I'm doing."

"You are a rascal through and through, Mama. What do you think the *kind* townsfolk will do when they find out he's alive?"

"Praise be!" Mama raised her hands in shocked surprise. "A miracle. Ernie Scott come back from the dead."

"Oh my gosh, Mama, you are going to answer for this one day."

But when she raised her gaze to Cora's, her lips quivered and her eyes swam with tears. "Don't be angry with me, but Ernie's fake death was the best out for us all. You know I'm right."

Cora clung to her mother, the stately, kind woman who raised her to love God and love others, who was trying her darndest to save face among the people she'd known her whole life, to walk among them with some shred of dignity.

"I love you, Mama."

"Love you too, honey-darling." Mama gave her a hard squeeze, then stepped out of Cora's embrace, tipping her head to the field. "Go get your man."

Her skin flushed warm. "I'm nervous."

"Come on now, you ain't getting any younger."

"That's the kind of pep talk every girl likes to hear." Cora smoothed her hand over the skirt of the new dress she'd waited to wear until today.

"You look beautiful." Mama touched the end of Cora's chin. "The dress brings out the honey flecks in your eyes. Now, go show those young girls how a mature, wise, beautiful woman handles her man. Come on, where's that pretty smile of yours? Ah, there it is. That's my girl." Mama raised her hand, waving to Janice Pettrey. "Look at Janice, young and in love with that boy Ricky Cantwell. Now, *you* go get with Birch."

Nervous! Cora was so very nervous as she started across the field, walking into the wind, the sun rising to its noon perch, casting a light along her path. This *was* her moment. Their moment.

Raising her hand over her eyes, she spotted Birch running through the field, his shirt tossed off, the ball tucked against his ribs, laughing, his tanned arms taut with muscle.

His hair gleamed as his bangs bounced over his forehead. He looked like one of the boys chasing him. At thirty-seven, he even looked as fit and energetic as Orie Westbrook, a former Rock Mill High football star, who'd only graduated a few years ago. He was married now to Vera, with a little baby. Jimmy.

Orie tackled Birch, dropping him hard to the ground. He popped up laughing, tossing the ball to Fred Clemson, who seemed to be acting as referee.

Daddy loved football so Cora listened to the radio broadcasts with him. When she agreed to listen to the first nationally broadcasted Rose Bowl game in 1927, a game between Daddy's beloved Alabama and a California school, Stanford, his eyes misted a little.

Cora approached the fan section, greeting everyone, cooing over baby Jimmy, waiting for Birch to notice her. He looked so *vibrant* and happy. His grand smile nearly tipped her heart over. How had she not seen him like this before? Seems now that she'd made her decision to marry him, her heart woke up to love.

After a touchdown, the teams ran for the water bucket. Cora waved at Birch, hoping he'd come over her way. But he seemed caught up with his team.

"You want some water, Cora?" Vera said. "I'll walk over with you."

"How do you like being a mother?" She was young, not more than nineteen. At thirty-two, Cora felt ancient next to her.

"It's a lot of work." She looked at Jimmy, who munched on a teething ring. "He's a sweet boy but I—"

Vera's voice faded in Cora's ears as a scene up ahead captured her attention. Twenty yards away, beautiful Janice Pettrey ran toward Birch, leaving *that boy* Ricky behind, and launched into his arms. Birch caught her up and swung her around, his face buried in her neck. Her excited scream-laugh pierced the air. Pierced Cora.

She stopped walking. Birch? What was happening?

"Cora?" Vera said, looking back at her. "You coming?"

"Yes, yes, of course." Cora forced her feet to comply though the vision of Janice in Birch's arms burned into her soul.

Had he not proposed to her? She was *his* girl. But

Cora couldn't keep her eyes from the intimate exchange in front of her. Birch and Janice.

Setting Janice on her feet, Birch bent toward her, his lips touching hers, kissing her as if he'd done it a thousand times, wrapping her tight against him as her arms looped around his neck.

No, no . . . What was going on? Panic, fear consumed Cora. The scene before her obliterated every hopeful emotion. In an instant she was back in Rufus's kitchen, staring at his wife, her pregnant belly, and their little boy, hearing him deny his claims of love.

What was it he called her? An imbecile. Plain and unimaginative.

At the water bucket, Birch slapped Orie on the back, laughing, then incidentally glanced her way. When their eyes locked, his brightness went behind a cloud.

"Cora!" He made his way to her. "I didn't know you were coming."

She shook her head, unable to speak, tears starting to blind her view. Fool me once, fool me twice . . . How could she fall for the wrong man again?

Birch caught her up in a big hug. "You're here and I'm glad."

She pushed out of his arms and narrowed her gaze, quivering as she tipped her head toward Janice. *Come on, Gunga Din. Rise up.* "What's going on?"

Birch lowered his head, running his hand over the back of his neck, kicking the tall grass with his shoe. "We've been seeing each other, Cora."

"'Seeing each other.' W-what does that mean? You

proposed marriage to me." Her words boomeranged between her ribs, cutting, hurting.

"You never gave me an answer. I waited eight months for you to say yes. Even after your mama found out I proposed and encouraged you to accept me, you never did."

"I was trying to be sure."

"No, Cora, you were trying to find a way out."

"I don't want a way out. I want to marry you."

"I finally took your silence as a no, Cora." Birch peeked over his shoulder to where Janice laughed and talked with the others. Though she kept a constant eye on Birch.

"So you just took up with Janice Pettrey?"

"We started talking at her brother's birthday party. One you were invited to, I believe. We've always had a good rapport and that night hit it off. Been getting closer since Labor Day."

Birch stood adjacent to Cora, putting their bodies at odd, cold postures. She'd hoped to run into his arms with her answer. Instead she ran straight into a slammed door.

"You told me to let you know when I was ready. Well, I'm ready."

"That was way back in the spring. I gave you a month, then five more. On Labor Day you still weren't ready. You never made one step my way. Not one, Cora. How was I to know you'd come traipsing in here Thanksgiving Day jealous of Janice? Did you come to tell me something? 'Cause I've not heard hide nor hair out of you. So I moved on. I'd have waited another year for you if you'd have made one step, *one* step my way, Cora. But you didn't."

"With Janice?" She gestured toward the young teacher, the cool whip of the November breeze in her hair. "You moved on with a girl ten years your junior? Well, w-why didn't you tell me?"

"Don't be putting this on me, Cora. I put my heart on the line for you and all I got was 'Go with me to see Rufus,' and 'Mama's hurting.' I understood. I did. Still do. But I finally realized that's your life, not mine. I can't stop living because you can't make up your mind. By the way, did you know she's telling folks your father died?"

"Yes. She wanted to save the shame of divorce. Birch—" Cora pressed her fingers to her forehead, the tension between her eyes starting to twist. "I realize I made you wait and I'm sorry. But I also know I'm ready. I'll marry you. I'm here to say yes. Yes. Birch, yes!" She smiled, stepping toward him. "I'll marry you."

He exhaled a rare rude word, shaking his head, gazing off into the distance. "But it's too late, Cora. I can't marry you."

"W-what do you mean? I-I don't understand." She'd leapt and there was no net. *Dear Lord . . .*

"I'm with Janice." He refused to look at Cora. "We have a lot of laughs. Get along well. She's ready to get married and have a family."

"So am I." She pressed her hand to his side. "Birch, I'm here." *Accept me.*

"Do you love me, Cora? Because Janice does. She's eager. She wants to be a farmer's wife and raise a bunch of babies. Do you want any of those things?"

She couldn't answer. Just stood there trembling like a fading fall leaf.

"Cora? Do you?"

"Yes, and I'm willing—"

"Willing?" Birch shook his head, peering at the gang by the water bucket. "At one time I thought that'd be enough. If you were *willing* to love me. But not now. Not since I met Janice." He shifted a step away from her. "I free you from my proposal, Cora. I withdraw my sentiments."

"No, no, Birch, I don't want to be free."

"But you don't love me, do you?"

Say it. Say you love him. Cora inhaled, long and deep, batting down a wave of tears, staring overhead, wishing the stupid sun would do its job and burn away the gray clouds.

"As I thought. Look, I was coming to see you next week, but I might as well tell you now." Birch shifted another step away. "I'm proposing to Janice and I wanted you to know. It don't seem like I should tell you first, but given our situation and all, it's only right."

Cora shook, careening toward a dark edge while standing stock-still, staring at the horizon. "Do you love her?"

"We get on well. She's energetic and pretty, handy with cooking and cleaning, sewing and like I said, ready for a family."

"You didn't answer me." Cora moved toward him. "Do you love her?"

"Cora—" His expression sobered as he stared at her. "Janice and I talked already. We want to get married

soon as we can in the new year. It's my slow time around
the farm, so we'll have time to get to know one another."

"So it's all settled then." She drew a response from
somewhere in her being. "I wish you all the best."

She'd waited for Rufus while Birch had waited for
her, and now she was without either. Seemed love didn't
find its way easily to her. But she couldn't blame Birch.
He had waited. This was all her doing.

"Thank you. I do appreciate it."

She peered at him. "I wanted to love you."

"Did you?" He brushed a gleam of perspiration from
his brow. "After Labor Day I realized you weren't ever
going to say yes. All you ever wanted from me was
more time. Janice told me she loved me after our first
date. She was so infectious she was hard to resist. She
felt about me the way I think you felt about Rufus. I
didn't realize how thirsty I'd become waiting for you.
Love's a powerful force, Cora. A strong, strong pull. It's
darn intoxicating when someone loves you."

She stared at her hands as she twisted them together,
a tear splashing down on her thumb. "Then you love
her back with all you have, Birch Good."

"You were going to marry me even though you
didn't love me?"

She raised her chin. "Aren't you the one who just
said when someone loves you, it's a powerful force?"
Say it. Say you love him.

"But just not strong enough for you and me, Cora.
My love never turned your head. Janice's love has
turned mine."

"Are you happy?"

He nodded. "I believe so."

"Would you have been happy with me if I'd said yes in March?"

"Why ask the question when the answer don't matter?"

She pressed her hand against his arm. "I'm sorry, Birch. The best of everything to you and Janice."

"Thank you." His hand slipped under hers as she pulled away. "And, uh, Cora, she's right excited about coming to the shop. Show her kindness, if not for my sake, for hers. Her folks don't have much money. Lost it all when the banks closed. She's been giving them her teacher salary to make ends meet. But I'd like her to have her wedding happiness, her day at the shop."

"Of course. She'll be most welcome."

Cora made her way toward the dinner tables, her heart tumbling between confusion and tears, as the sun cracked through the cirrus clouds, dropping gold light on the Thanksgiving feast, on Cora, and another year of her life.

CHAPTER TWENTY-SIX

COLE

FEBRUARY 22

He walked into Linus's office without knocking, telling his protesting admin he'd only need a minute.

Ever since his date with Haley, she lived in his thoughts. He'd loved discovering who she was all on his own. Loved seeing her weak, vulnerable side. Loved that she was so passionate about the old wedding shop.

His heart quickened at the idea of pursuing her. But he had to take it slow. Or she'd spook and he might not get another chance.

"Linus, where're our permits?" Cole leaned over Linus's desk, causing the man to rock back in his chair.

"Linus, I tried to stop him."

He raised his hand for peace. "It's okay, Sandy. Why don't you bring us some coffee?"

"None for me, thanks." Cole straightened up, giving Sandy a conciliatory smile.

"So, Cole, what seems to be the trouble?" Linus stood, trying to meet him eye to eye. But he was too small.

"I want the permits to do the work on the wedding shop."

Linus made a face. "You know I don't have anything to do with permitting. That's Alastair's department. Go down the hall. Last door on the right. Think a man in your business would know that, Cole."

Cole chuckled, shaking his head. The man was good, no doubt. "He checks with you on everything. You're his boss. He's your lackey."

"I don't like what you're implying, Cole."

"I don't like that the city council gave Haley the building, imposed a deadline for the renovation, then held up all the permits. Know anything about that, oh friend of Brant Jackson?"

"You best not come in here accusing me of anything underhanded."

Cole sighed. "Linus, just give us the permits. She filed the first of January. We're into the third week of February. That's unheard of in this town. Even with your brand of red tape."

"What can I say? We're a growing town." He was a snake. A smiling rat-snake. No offense to the official rat-snake. Or snakes or rats.

"I'm not leaving here without those permits. So let's just get down to it. What do you want?"

Linus sat, facing his computer, his balding head glinting in the sterile overhead light. How did he get into power in the first place?

"You know what I want," he said.

"Excuse me? How would I know what you want?"

Linus looked up at him for a long, pointed moment. "Think about it. You *know* what I want."

"No, I don't . . ." Cole stepped back with a force of realization. "You want the . . . No, Linus. No. What kind of crazy, nut job . . . How can you do this to Haley? She's not tied to me, or the Stratocaster. Really, this is how you run your office?"

"The Stratocaster sure would be a nice piece to add to my music collection."

Cole headed for the door. "You're not getting that guitar." Then back to Linus's desk with a pointed, "That's extortion."

Linus rocked back in his chair, poking out his lower lip, begging for a good punch. "Oh, I think it's more like motivation, don't you?"

"I should go to the DA's office."

"And report what? We argued over permits? Over which I have no control?"

Cole laughed. This was unreal. "Linus, do you even have the kind of money it takes to buy that guitar?"

Linus stood. "I could cut you a check for fifty grand this afternoon."

"Fifty grand? Oh no, that's way too low. Sixty. No, seventy grand." Cole paced, patting his middle. "I feel an increase coming on."

Linus bolted around his desk, hand extended. "Deal. Seventy thousand."

Cole stepped back, hand in the air. "Never said I was really offering."

"Cole, I'm saying 'deal.' You bring that guitar." He moved back to his desk, yanked open the middle drawer, and took out a folder. He flashed it open, revealing the wedding shop's permits. "And these are yours."

"You lying son of a—"

"Don't go unchristian on me, now. You had to figure sometimes this is the way business got done around here. After all, your daddy gave eight years of his life for getting caught."

"Yet here you are stupid enough to still do it."

"I ain't undercutting suppliers and greasing palms. I've never taken a dime from Brant Jackson. There's no law in holding up building permits. No law against striking a bargain with a guy about a guitar."

"Except when you hold up permits to get the guitar." Cole paced the office, hands on his belt. "I can't believe you. I always had my suspicions."

"I don't care what you believe, Cole. I saw my chance to gain a little leverage on something I wanted, so I took it."

"This is Haley's shop, not mine, you imbecile. Why are you punishing her because of me?"

"Like I said, I saw some leverage." Linus perched on the edge of his desk. "Seems to me she must be pretty special for you to be even considering selling me that guitar."

"I'm *not* considering selling you that guitar."

"Have a nice day." Linus stuffed the permits back in his desk drawer and slammed it shut.

"You won't get away with this." Cole stormed out. "How do you work with him, Sandy?"

"He pays me well."

"He's a criminal."

"He's not so bad. Just a tad shady."

Outside, the sunshine felt miles away from his cold soul and that heated exchange with Linus. Yeah, sure, Heart's Bend had a bit of the you-scratch-my-back-I'll-scratch-yours politics, but Linus was wanting a scratch from the wrong guy.

He slammed the door to his truck as he slipped inside, fired up the engine. For all he knew, that rat-snake could be holding up Cole's bids for city work.

Circling the town center, he whipped in at Ella's, his chest taut with turmoil. Mom came out of the kitchen as Cole schlepped over to his well-worn stool. She set a cup in front of him and filled it with coffee.

"What's bugging you?"

Cole reached for the cream and dumped in a couple of mini-cups. "This stupid town."

"This stupid town took good care of us when your daddy left. So be kind. What's going on?"

"Linus."

"Oh?" Mom propped her elbow on the counter, leaning toward Cole.

"He's holding up the permits on the wedding shop because he wants the Stratocaster."

She stood back and shrugged. "So?" Then waved toward the door. "Mert, how are you?"

"So? You're saying I should sell it?"

"What are you going to do with it? Leave it hanging on the wall, in a glass case? You don't play it. Why not make it work for you?"

"Dad and I bought the guitar together. *We* played it."

Mom sighed and angled toward him, propping her elbows on the counter. "And holding on to it isn't going to bring back the man you want him to be. He's not the father you knew or wanted or still want. But he's willing to be a father as things are now."

Cole raised his coffee mug. "You have customers."

"I'm right and you know it."

"Mert's waving you over."

"Jasmine can get her." Mom gently lowered his hand, peering into his eyes with her mom radar. "That guitar is not a relationship with your dad. You want a relationship with him, then drive to Nashville once a month for a bite of pie or something. Why are you holding on to that guitar? I think it'd be freeing to let it go. And that last shred of bitterness you have with it." Mom moved around the counter. "Sell it. Help out Haley, who, by the way, I like *very* much."

"I should report Linus to the DA's office."

"You could, but it's your word against his. You'll lose more time in the court process. Haley needs that shop open by June sometime or she loses it. The town loses it and we get an ugly parking lot."

Cole bore a hard gaze into his mother, sipping his coffee. She was right about that but not about the guitar. Was she? Did he really want the guitar? Or just the idea of the guitar?

He'd not played it in years. In an instant, he traveled through his memories, through the happy days with Dad, then through the dark. Seeing Dad arrested at the city pool, watching him walk away with an FBI escort, then sinking beneath the water. The nights he sat on his bed in the dark, playing the Fender, turning up the amp as loud as he could to dull his pain.

But the guitar was more of a wedge between them than a tether. It was his old Gibson he played to connect to God, to truth and light.

Last, he pictured Dad at Java Jane's, asking him to sell the guitar to help him out. Cole sighed. Man, Haley and this wedding shop business were invading places he'd not explored in a long time.

Glancing across the diner, he nodded to his mom and reached for his cell phone. Dialing Linus, he said seven words. "Seventy thousand. Take it or leave it."

"Deal."

"And, Linus, you pull this crap again, I'm going to the authorities. I mean it." He dropped a couple of dollars on the counter for his coffee and headed out the door, pausing by his mom, leaning toward her ear.

"What's his number? Dad's."

She glanced up, smiling, taking her phone from her pocket. "This is good, Cole. Really good."

"We'll see." He searched her contacts for Wilson Danner. Then drawing a deep breath, he dialed his dad.

. . .

HALEY

She'd gone to city hall every day looking for her permits. The staff knew her by name. Yesterday they offered her a slice of pie Harriet brought in for Bill's birthday.

But construction permits? No, those were never ready.

Today hope buoyed in her spirit. Two more wedding shop alums popped into the shop this week, depositing memories and cash in Haley's hand.

Mrs. Reinhold and Mrs. Patterson. Both gave sizable contributions. She was almost up to fifty thousand. Miraculously. God's generosity humbled her healing heart.

Inside city hall, she passed through security, whispering a "Please, Lord" on her way to the Department of Codes & Building Safety office.

When she pressed through the door, the clerk, Darlene, jumped up, smiling, waving a folder. "Look what I have for you, Haley."

. . .

CORA

DECEMBER 4, 1932

"I declare, I was so taken by surprise when he proposed I about fell over." Feminine giggles filled the shop as Cora came in through the back door, a box of pastries in hand.

"You are simply glowing." Mama's voice came from the grand salon buoyant and lively. "We will do everything we can to make your day as beautiful as you are. Now, have a seat on the sofa and Cora will be right with you. Can I get y'all some hot tea? A little snack to nibble on? Can you believe Christmas is right around the corner?"

The voices chorused, "Yes, oh yes."

Mama's heels clicked on the hardwood as she made her way through the shop. Cora leaned against the pantry shelves. Janice Pettrey. It had to be. Who else could it be?

Most men wait for Christmas to propose. But not Birch.

"We've got customers early this morning," Mama said, reaching for the cups and saucers.

"I heard." Cora broke the string on the pastry box. "Can you handle the day without me?"

"No, I cannot. Odelia's not in and you two are the only ones who know how to really dress the brides. You're simply marvelous about it. I am the hostess." Mama leaned back to see Cora's face. "What's the matter with you?"

"I just don't feel good."

"Well, push through. Is it your monthly? You can lie down when they're gone." She set out the teacups. "I have to go upstairs to boil the water for the tea." Mama grabbed Cora by the shoulders. "Go see to your customers. Chin up. Smile. That's my girl. A little more sincere."

"Mama, I can't . . . I just can't."

"Sure you can. We're Scott women. Cut from the Scotland high country. Now, get out there."

Mama had been through her heartbreak and was out on the other side. Surely Cora could ride the rapids of her own heartache with as much courage and dignity.

Yet she felt so wounded and weak, as if she couldn't hold up her head or draw a deep breath.

"Go on now. They're waiting," Mama said.

Around the wall of the small salon Cora braced to see a smiling and glowing Janice, though her knees wobbled with each step. Anxiety burned in her belly.

"Good morning, ladies. Welcome to The Wedding Shop."

An older woman with a rich-looking coat stood. "We are thrilled to be here. We've heard so many good things from the Dunlaps. I'm Pasty Connery, and this is my daughter, the newly engaged Miranda, and her sisters . . ."

Cora scanned the faces on the sofa as the woman made introductions. It was the beautiful Connery women. Not Janice Pettrey at all. She wobbled with relief.

"The Dunlaps, of course, wonderful family. How is Ruth?"

"Expecting her first child." The younger women smiled with a blush on their cheeks.

"Well, Miranda." Cora turned to the bride. "Congratulations." The lovely brunette with long waves about her shoulders held up her left hand where a diamond brought a new light into the room.

"Isn't that stunning?"

"Very." Cora had seen only a few diamond engagement rings since they were not popular with folks. Or in these hard times, *possible*.

"It belonged to his grandmother. Wylie had it put in a new setting for me." The bride clutched her hand to her chest. "I'm never taking it off."

"As you never should. Shall we look at dresses?" Cora escorted Miranda and her mother through the shop, showing them all their options, then escorting them upstairs to explain Odelia's services.

But Miranda was a decisive woman and knew what she wanted. She selected a premade gown with lace sleeves and bodice, which buttoned up the front to a neat square collar. The skirt was full and long, made of satin and tulle.

"I want to be the most beautiful woman in the room," Miranda said to Cora as she stepped behind the divider to change.

"No doubt you will be."

Miranda giggled. "I'm so nervous already. Were you nervous when you got married?"

Cora handed her the gown around the edge. "I-I've never been married."

The girl's wide brown eyes appeared over the top of the divider. "Oh, really. I just assumed."

"Quite all right. Let me know when you need help. You can fasten this gown in the front, but the sleeves are a bit tricky. I'm stepping in the storeroom to find a veil."

"I want a long one. My cousin tried a shorter one and I just didn't care for it. Seemed like something was missing. Oh, please, can you help me with the sleeves?"

Cora backed up to step behind the divider, helping the slender young woman into the gown that would take her on the adventure of a lifetime. "How old are you, Miranda?"

"Twenty. I met Wylie at my cousin's debutante ball.

He was the brother of her escort." She looked up at Cora. "I fell for him the moment I saw him."

"Then you are blessed." She settled the shoulders in place and stepped back. "There. You can finish up. I'll be right back."

"I-is there a reason you never married?" Miranda's question chased Cora to the edge of the stairs.

She wavered, pressed back a bullet of emotion. "Just hasn't happened for me."

"I hope it does soon. Love is so thrilling."

Yes, wasn't it, though? It was also terribly painful. At the bottom of the stairs, Cora addressed the waiting women, who sat on the edge of the sofa and chairs, sipping the tea and nibbling pastries Mama had served.

"She's picked a beautiful gown. She'll be down in a moment." Behind the display case, Cora selected the longest veil she had in stock. Smoothing it over her arm, she showed the others, who ooh'd their approval, then started back up the steps.

The shop's back door slammed, rattling the entire place. Mama stood, glancing around. "What in the world?"

"Cora Scott! Where are you?" A booming voice followed by heavy footsteps bounced against the hardwood, reverberating against the wall and in Cora's chest. "I need to talk to you—now."

Birch appeared around the wall of the small salon, gazing up to the mezzanine, his blue eyes wild and snapping, his dark hair combed but refusing to stay in place.

"Birch, I have customers." Cora came down a few

steps. "Keep your voice down. Mrs. Connery, I do apologize. I don't know what this is about. Mama?" She motioned for her to come up and take the veil, give it to Miranda.

"Don't anyone move. Esmé, stop right there." Birch held up his hands. "I've got something to say and I'm going to say it right now."

"There's no need for rudeness, young man." Mrs. Connery, God bless her.

"Cora, I'd moved on with my life." He started up the steps slowly, his cheeks flushed a deep red. "I waited and waited for you. Fourteen years all told. And finally, I just gave up."

"Is this necessary? I know all of this. Have you come to rub my face in it before these fine customers?"

Miranda stood at the top of the stairs, her soft features contorted with confusion. "What's going on?"

"Begging your pardon, young lady, but I got a piece to say and I'm saying it. Cora, I found me a gal. A good one. She was pretty, fun, and she loved me." Birch patted his chest. "She loved *me*. Wanted to marry me."

"Then marry her. Go on with your plans. I'm not stopping you."

Birch took another step up, moving close to Cora. "Yes, yes you are. Because you finally said yes. Finally, after months and months, *years*, of waiting, listening to all your excuses, you waltz onto my farm one fine afternoon and announce pretty as you please that *you are ready.* 'I'll marry you, Birch.' On Thanksgiving, to boot."

"This is ridiculous." Cora turned back for the mezzanine. "Go on home, Birch. I've got work to do."

But Birch ran interference, stopping her on the staircase. "I made my peace with it. You and I were going different ways. But dang it if I couldn't get you out of my head. I tried. Spent more time with Janice than ever. Got out Mama's ring. Tried to propose to her three times. Gall darn if I could do it. Why? Because I'm in love with you, Cora Scott. I'm so lost in love I can't even find my way out."

The women serenaded his confession with a collective gasp.

"Birch . . . I don't . . . So what are you saying?"

"I'm saying . . ." He dropped to one knee, right there on the stairs, and pulled a box from his jacket pocket. "Cora Scott, will you marry me? Gal, don't you even say no, 'cause my heart will explode in my chest. I'll die right here. I'm not wasting another moment without you in my life, as my wife." He popped open the ring box revealing a glistening sapphire stone in a gold setting. "Please, marry me."

Cora dropped the veil so it floated down the stairs like a carefree cloud and sank to the stairs, her heart drumming in her ears, her gaze boring into his. "Really? Oh really? I love you, Birch Good. Yes, yes! I'll marry you, of course." Her hand trembled as he slid the ring on her finger. Above and below her, the women approved with whispered gasps and a soft, "How beautiful."

She fell against him, burying her face against his neck, watering his warm skin with tears of joy. Finally.

Birch stood, drawing Cora to her feet, snatching her up in a grand hug to the raucous cheers of the women, holding her so tight she couldn't draw a long breath.

When he touched his lips to hers, her entire body was filled with air and light and love.

When Birch broke the kiss, he pressed his forehead to hers. "Is this real?"

"Yes, very, very real." Hands against his neck, she kissed him, giving him her all—her heart, her word, her pledge.

"Y'all ladies carry on," Birch said, starting down the steps. "I've got work to do myself. But what do you know? I'm getting *married*."

Cora ran down the steps to kiss him one last time, his lips warm and wanting, her heart pressed against his. This was the love she'd been waiting for all her life. Right here in her arms.

CHAPTER TWENTY-SEVEN

HALEY

L ong day. Haley pulled up to her parents' home, parking Dad's truck under the oak tree, crawling from behind the wheel like an old lady.

Man, construction was backbreaking work. Once she tacked the permits in the front window with pride, she joined Cole's crew, showing up to work before they did and being the last one to leave.

While the permits came through, the change in her deadline did not. The shop needed to pass inspection by May 1.

Through the back door, she kicked off her work boots in the mudroom, dropping her dusty coat on a hook.

The house was quiet and warm, a soft glow coming from the den.

"I'm home." Haley reached into the kitchen cabinet for a bowl. Then in the pantry for a box of cereal.

Mom didn't allow cereal in the house when Haley was a kid, but she managed to squeak it past her as an adult.

"Haley?" Mom appeared around the kitchen doorway,

a glass of wine and her readers in hand. "How was your day?"

"Busy." She retrieved the milk from the fridge, but her arms were so tired she could barely hold up the carton.

"Will you meet your deadline?"

"Busting our backs to try. I think we will. The electric and plumbing are done. Cole thinks the third-floor apartment will be finished by Monday." Haley glanced back at Mom. "I'll move in when it's ready."

Mom came to the island counter as Haley took a seat and dove into her cereal. "We've enjoyed having you around."

Haley peeked at her mother. Since their heart-to-heart, the air between them had changed. Words of affection flowed a little easier. "Thanks for letting me crash."

A slight smile tipped Mom's lips. "I never realized how driven you were before."

"Because I got lost in the shuffle."

Mom frowned. "Well, now you're standing out."

Haley scooped a large spoonful of cereal and checked her phone. She was waiting to hear from a designer. Charlotte put her in touch with a European designer, Melinda House, who'd opened up a shop in New York. They'd promised to send whatever they had in stock. But that was two weeks ago and so far, nothing. Haley understood these things took time, but time was closing in on her.

"I have something for you." Mom ducked out of the room.

Haley slipped from her chair. What this late-night

dinner needed was toast. She checked the pantry. No bread. Darn anti-wheat people.

Mom reappeared with a white envelope and a key. "Here."

Haley turned as Mom set the envelope and key on the island counter. "What's this?"

"Well, in the envelope is money. I-I want to help with the shop." She sighed, rubbing her fingers over her forehead. "There's more to the story, but for now just take the money. And the key."

"Mom, are you sure?" Haley drew her into a tight hug, love rising in her heart for her secretly tender-hearted mother. "Thank you. But what's the key for?"

"It goes to the locked storage room in the shop."

Haley regarded her for a moment. "W-where did you get it?"

"Well, um, Cora gave it to me."

"Cora? Miss Cora. The wedding shop owner. You knew her?"

"I did, but not well."

"What? W-why did she give you the key?"

"Because"—Mom averted her gaze, her lower lip quivering—"Cora was my sister."

. . .

CORA

JANUARY 1935
She stood along the bank of the Cumberland just down the way from the old homestead. From where she grew

up playing with EJ, from where she heard the news Daddy lost the bank, from where Birch proposed the first time, telling her he loved her.

A thick gray fog hung over the winter day as Cora faced the waters, remembering how she stared along the bend in the river, aching for a sign of Rufus St. Claire.

Today was her second anniversary with Birch. She never knew she could love a man so much. Or be so loved. And how closely she had almost missed this life she now built with her husband.

They were hoping for children soon.

Last year she'd burned Rufus's letters. Not that Birch ever mentioned the man, but when she told him she'd dumped them in the trash drum and set them aflame, the look on his face was worth a thousand words. He loved her ardently that night.

But still, every now and then, Rufus walked across her heart, stirring old whispers and old longings. Lately, more than before, and it brought her to her knees.

Remove every trace of him, Lord.

Then, during Wednesday-night services, the pendant came to mind. She'd taken it off after Birch proposed, but kept it in a box in the back of her sock drawer. This morning she retrieved it and drove down to the river.

Cora peered down at her hand, the gold locket Rufus had given her laying against her leather glove. The wind cut along the bank, slapping the hem of her dress about her legs.

She'd hung on to this as what? A memento? A treasure? When all it stood for was lies and pain.

"Good-bye forever, Rufus. You can't interrupt my life ever again."

Flinging the jeweled piece toward the river, she watched it soar and then float down, twisting and turning in the wind, tapping the water, then quickly disappearing beneath the river's swift current.

CHAPTER TWENTY-EIGHT

COLE

He dropped his keys on the table just inside the door and reached down to unlace his boots. Passing the fireplace, he paused, deciding, then stooped before the grate, tossing in a few logs and lighting a flame.

The fragrance of phosphorous and the crackling of burning logs drifted through the house as Cole made his way to the kitchen, trying not to look at the holes on the wall above the dining table.

He'd patch them tomorrow and cover them with paint, but somehow the whole house felt vacant without that guitar. As if he'd given away the last of his childhood.

But he'd put the money to good use. A sound investment. He was almost grateful for Linus's evil manipulation.

He yanked open the fridge, his stomach rumbling, his limbs quivering from lack of sustenance and the ebb of his adrenaline.

He was tired, putting in twelve-hour days to get the

shop done for Haley. But being around her every day was worth it.

Spying a plate covered with tin foil, Cole found dinner. Leftover pizza. What else? He set it on a paper plate and tossed it into the microwave.

Waiting for the pizza to warm, he faced the wall where the Stratocaster once hung. When he'd called Dad to tell him the news, he broke down, and it was all Cole could do to get off the phone before his own heart collapsed with emotion. Worse than your mom crying was hearing the sobs of your father.

"Thank you, son, thank you. This means the world to me."

Cole grinned, remembering Dad's "that-a-boy" when he told him what Linus paid for the guitar.

"Good going, son."

Son. He was his father's son. If God could overlook his sins, why couldn't Cole overlook his father's? Dad's brokenness humbled Cole, and in recent days he found it a bit easier to let go of the past.

He gave Dad half the money. Deposited his half in the bank, grateful to have a backup for himself, for the wedding shop, and maybe someday soon, a nice engagement ring.

The microwave beeped. Cole retrieved his plate and a bottle of water and walked to his chair. Should be a good basketball game on tonight.

He was surfing channels when a booming knock rattled his door.

"Cole! Open up. Cole!"

"Haley?" He opened the door, stepping aside to let her in. "What's going on?"

She breezed in, her bold fragrance matched by her bold countenance. "Better yet, what's *not* going on?" Her smile owned the room. *You're no match, flickering fire.*

Cole's fingers ached to touch her, pull her to him, smooth her hair away from her face and—

"I have the key to the storage room." Haley marched into the kitchen, a force of energy, whipping a key out of her pocket. "My mother had the key." She slapped it on the kitchen island, then glanced at the wall, frowning. "Hey, where's your guitar? The one in the case?"

"I sold it." He set his pizza and water down, stretching for the key. "Your mom had this? Where'd she get it?"

"You sold your guitar? Why? You loved that thing."

He waved her off. "Haley, how did your mom get the key?"

She angled his way. "Ready for your blue eyes to be blown out of your head? Miss Cora was Mom's sister."

"Look." He pointed to the floor. "My blue eyes, on the floor. How is your mom Cora's sister?"

"According to Mom's Facebook post version—she's very brief with her news reports—her father, my grandfather, married a war widow in 1946 and a year later my mom comes along. Cora was from his first marriage, and she was the same age as my grandma. Can you imagine?" She made a face. "Anyway, Grandpa was in his sixties when Mom was born. Cora was like forty-seven years older. Old enough to be her grandmother."

Cole shook his head, leading her into the kitchen, dropping a slice of pizza onto a paper plate for her. "You read about stuff like this, but wow . . . Were they close? Is that why your mom was against the shop?"

"She won't tell me the rest of the story, but, Cole, she gave me the key and a check for ten grand. Said she wanted to support me. Not the shop so much, but me."

He roped his arm about her shoulders. She tucked nicely under his side. "We almost have the money we need to finish up. By the way, I got the electrician and plumber bills. They didn't charge us labor. Just for materials."

"You're kidding."

"Never say God is not a God of miracles."

"I never said that."

"I didn't say you did."

"You just said, 'Never say God is not a God of miracles.'"

"It's a figure of speech." Cole kissed the top of her head. Their eyes met and she stepped away from him. But he reached for her hand. "Haley—"

"Cole, what are you doing?"

"I-I . . ." The microwave beeped, calling a time-out as he struggled to speak his heart. His blood moved through his veins like the spring river.

Haley moved to the other side of the island, point-ing. "The microwave—"

"I heard."

Retrieving her pizza and setting it in front of her,

Cole scanned her face with a quick gaze and reached for a napkin from the holder on the lazy Susan. "It's two-day-old pizza."

That's his great line? The age of his pizza? Behind his ribs his heart pounded out his desire. His lips buzzed, eager to taste hers.

"G-good pizza," Haley said, swallowing a hot bite, dabbing her lips with the napkin.

Silence. Not the good kind that came from sweet, easy company but the kind that came from his awkward, clumsy stupidity.

Cole walked around into the living room for his cold, waiting slice of pizza. He took a big bite but his appetite had waned.

From her end of the island, Haley worked on her pizza, gazing up at him. "If you kiss me, it could get complicated." She dropped her focus back to her plate. "I'm still not looking for a relationship."

Cole shoved his pizza plate forward and propped against the counter. "Kiss you? What? Is that what you think I was going to—"

She laughed, pressing her fist to her lips and a mouthful of pizza. He reached for the fridge, getting her a bottle of water.

"Okay, yes, I was going to kiss you."

After a long swig, Haley smiled and patted her hand on top of his, sobering. "You . . . you were the cutest boy in class since I could remember. Smart. Sweet. Grew up to be a man's man, you know, despite all that happened with your dad." Her blue eyes met his. "But you were Tammy's. Always Tammy's."

Cole captured her hand and drew her to him, touching his forehead to hers. "Tammy's not here."

"I know, but—" Haley tapped her heart. "She's here. Besides, I'm not ready . . ."

"Haley, I'm not Dax."

She pulled away. "I know, and if anyone has a chance, it's you, Cole. I just need time . . . to adjust. To heal. Forgive myself. For being fooled. I just want to make sure my head is on straight and my heart is really rooted in what God thinks of me, not some man."

He nodded, liking the feel of her subtle yield. "Fair enough, fair enough." Spying his pizza, he went for another bite. "When Tammy and I broke up, I wondered the same thing for a while. How could I have let it get this far? Mom could tell something was bothering me about the wedding, and she said if I was getting cold feet, then I should remember I was committed, and commitment could go the distance when love failed. And love went the distance when the commitment was tested. Add God to the mix and there's the cord of three that can't be broken. Even if we'd married, I think we would've made it. It would've been work, but we'd have done okay."

"Doesn't sound very romantic, does it?"

He laughed low, to himself. "You sound like Tammy in the end. 'You didn't even really propose,' she said."

"So how is what you feel for me, if you feel anything, different than with Tammy? That's my struggle, Cole. Can I trust you? Myself? How do I know what I feel for you, that is, if I feel anything for you, is not the same blind love I felt for Dax? I don't want to ever be controlled and manipulated by a human being again."

"You're not Tammy. I'm not Dax. That's a huge start. Please don't lump me in with that muscle-bound womanizer."

She tried to smile but her eyes filled with sorrow. "Haley . . ." He reached for her, drawing her around the island to him. "You make my heart beat faster. You crowd my thoughts. When I'm not with you, I *want* to be with you. When you walk into the shop, my whole body smiles. Every day is a good day when you're in it. I want to talk to you, listen to you, hear what's going on in your life. I pray for you. I want the shop to work because it would make *you* happy."

"What you just said"—tears dripped from the corner of her eyes—"is by definition love. D-do you *love* me?"

He stood back with an exhale. "Kind of awkward to confess it like this, but yeah, I think I do."

CHAPTER TWENTY-NINE

CORA

OCTOBER 1950

Thank you all for coming, Grace, Ray." Cora walked Grace Kirby to the wedding shop's front door, through the thin white light dropping through the window.

Birch stood on the front steps with Grace's husband, Ray. Cora joined Birch, slipping her arm through his, leaning against his still farmer-lean frame.

She'd lost him for a few years during the second war. Orie Westbrook and his son Jimmy kept the farm going along with one of Birch's cousins. When he came home, she wept in his arms. "Never leave me again."

"I'm home now, darling. I'm home."

She thought perhaps their reunion would produce a child. Even at forty-six, she ached for a baby. But it was not to be. Instead, Mama began a long battle with cancer.

"We're just so sorry about your mama." Grace drew Cora into a bouncy bosom embrace. "We are going to miss her. She was the light of our lives, wasn't she?"

"She was a light for sure."

This morning Cora and Birch laid Mama to rest in Heart's Bend Memorial Gardens. And in her honor, temporarily turned the wedding shop into a place of grieving, where folks from all over came to remember Esmé Scott and all she'd done for the community. For the brides of the wedding shop.

"I was a nervous bride." Grace paused on the stoop, smiling. "Remember that, Ray? What with my mama dying so young. But Esmé took me aside and told me everything was going to be all right. Cora, you helped me put together the most perfect trousseau." She glanced at the shop. "I have such fond memories of being here those few times. I still think of Odelia's sweet rolls." She nudged Cora. "More like sweet *rocks*."

"Grace, it's getting late." Ray started down the shop's walk. "Leave them be."

"Good-bye, Cora. You're in our prayers." Grace kissed Cora's cheek, then Birch's. She was a bride from Aunt Jane's era, but even so, after a while, time ran together and Grace was just plain *family*. All the brides, sooner or later, formed one beautiful image in Cora's heart, representing all the women who came through the shop.

"Hold yer horses, Ray." Grace faced Cora. "You and your mama were pillars during the Depression, then during the war. I know my Mary Jane will never forget your kindness to her when she was getting married and Ray lost his job."

"We were honored to serve."

"Grace, I'm starting the car and if you're not in it by

the time I shift into Drive, I'm leaving without you."
Ray stepped down off the curb.

Birch's low chuckle rumbled in his chest.

Grace made a face, flipping her hand at Cora. "He
don't scare me. If I weren't there to butter his toast the
big oaf would starve." She winked. "Got him right where
I want him." Nevertheless, Grace hurried down the
walk as Ray gunned the big engine of his Oldsmobile.
"Call if you need anything, Cora, anything at all."

"Thank you, Grace. Will do."

Back inside, Cora exhaled, collapsing on the grand
salon sofa as Birch shut the shop door, then joined her,
pulling her into his arms. And so the day was over.

"How are you?" He kissed her forehead. In the
eighteen years they'd been married, he'd proven to be
everything he said he'd be and more.

He was what Cora dreamed for in a husband. Kind.
Patient. Faithful. Devoted and loyal. And to her won-
drous surprise, passionate. He was a farmer by day and
Romeo by night.

Cutesy or romantic would never be used to describe
Birch Good. Cora could count on one hand how many
times he'd given her flowers. But he was attentive and
caring, in tune with her heart.

"I've been thinking." He slipped his hand into hers.
"Why don't we go on vacation? We've been talking
about it since we got married. California or Florida."

Cora sat up. "Really, Birch? Do you think we could?"

"Why not?" He kissed her with a grin on his lips and
a spark in his eye. "Orie can watch the farm for me. Not
much to do in January."

"I could just close the shop."

The battle with Mama's cancer had been so intense that Birch and Cora had merely existed the last year and a half. Cora spent more nights up with Mama than in her bed with her husband.

His hand drifted slowly down her check to the base of her neck. "You're more beautiful today than when I married you."

"Stop. I'm a fright. Exhausted and, mercy, I haven't seen the inside of the beauty parlor since Mama's last bout."

Birch raised her chin, lowering his lips to hers. "You don't have regrets, do you? Marrying me?"

Cora reared back. "Birch Good, how could you ever?" She brushed the back of her hand along the high lines of his cheek bones. "Don't you know by now I couldn't breathe without you? Why do you ask?"

"'Cause . . . walking your mama through dying and not having any children of our own makes me wonder if—"

"Shh, no doubts. I'd be alone now it if wasn't for you."

"Some man would've come along. Trust me."

"I don't want some man. I want you."

"You have me, Cora. I'm yours."

She collapsed against his chest, her heart brimming. That was the most they'd declared to one another in a good long while. Perhaps since their wedding night. Cora slipped her hand over his firm chest. He was fifty-four now, but as youthful as the day they married.

Four years ago, Cora went through a few changes, actually put on some weight and added curves to her stick figure. She was thrilled, but Mama started right away with the warnings.

"It'll get ahold of you, Cora," she'd said, urging Cora toward coffee and cigarettes to keep her trim.

But the doc suspected it was the cigarettes that tore up Mama's lungs. Besides, Birch liked her soft curves, and he was the only one she wanted to please.

"Did you hear from your father?" Birch smoothed his hand over Cora's hair, pulling it away from her face.

"I didn't write him. I don't know where he is."

She stood, glancing about the room. "I'd best clean up before I'm too tired. I have to open the shop tomorrow."

"Cora, why not leave it? Take a few days to grieve."

She smiled at her husband. "Working will help me grieve. But you . . ." She bent to poke him in the chest. "I want to hear all about this vacation."

Cora gathered empty cups and glasses on a serving tray. The food table in the small salon had been picked clean, but there was enough ham and potato salad to last them for days.

"I'll call a travel agent this week." Birch began folding chairs and stacking them against the wall. "It was good to see the Millers back for the funeral."

"I can't believe they drove all the way from Texas. And did you see Clark and Darcy Hath? I'd not seen them since high school."

"He did well in oil. Makes me wish—"

"Nothing, Birch. You wish nothing." With the tray in hand, Cora headed for the pantry, but paused by her husband. "I'd have no other life."

In the pantry she set the dishes by the sink. Birch fixed a sink in the counter a few years back, along with electricity, so Mama could percolate coffee and tea for the customers without running up two flights of stairs.

Cora glanced out the window, the color of fall skirting across the thinning green lawn. *Oh, Mama . . .* Sorrow mixed with relief swirled through her. *What'll I do without you?*

She was as spunky as she ever was right to the end. Wearing blonde wigs and red lipstick. But so weak. Clinging to Cora's hand as she read her the newspaper. Hattie Lerner was still writing the About Town column.

"Am I ready to see Jesus, Cora?"

"Do you believe, Mama? Have you forgiven Daddy?"

"Yes, yes, I believe. I do forgive your daddy."

Cora reached around for a chair, facing the window, her thoughts tripping back to when she was young, when Mama was cooking up good smells in the kitchen, when Daddy came traipsing in to breakfast with his strong cologne and slicked hair. To when Cora ran through the fall leaves, laughing, with EJ.

Not even fifty and she'd lost them all. So she let the tears come.

Birch's hands smoothed over her shoulders. "Why don't we lock up and head home? I'll swing by Ella's Diner for takeout? Hmmm?"

Cora wiped her cheeks. "We have tons of leftovers."

"They can keep. How about one of those newfangled pizza pies? We can see what's on the television tonight."

"We don't get any channels at the farmhouse."

Birch chuckled. "Well, one, but the picture is all fuzzy. We'll turn on the radio." He gently helped her to her feet. "I'll come in with you in the morning to help clean up."

"Just let me put the leftovers in the ice box."

As they cleaned up the last, Cora took one last sweep around the shop. Tomorrow it needed to look like a unique bridal boutique, not a funeral parlor.

A dark shadow hit the floor from the front doorway.

"Cora?" An older gentleman stepped inside, a beautiful little girl about three years old, in a lacy dress, white socks, and very shiny black Mary Janes, clinging to his hand. Her dark hair had been pin curled, then brushed out, curving around her pretty, heart-shaped face. Her blue eyes peered intensely at Cora, taking in everything around her.

"Can I help you?"

"Is that how you greet your ole daddy?"

She drew a deep inhale and regarded him for a mere moment, seeing through his thinning gray hair and lined features. "Daddy?"

"Yes, it's Daddy." He nodded, stepping forward like he might hug her, then stepped back. Slick tears glistened in his tired eyes. "I'm so sorry about your mother."

Cora gripped her hands together, holding on to decorum. Otherwise she was a leaf in a summer storm. "What are you doing here?" She'd given up on being mad at him. His annual Christmas cards signed, "Love, Dad," let her know he was alive and well. But nothing more.

He was, perhaps as Mama intended, dead to them.

"I heard about Esmé. I wanted to pay my respects."

"Then go to Memorial Gardens. She's buried next to EJ."

"Thank you. I-I will. Cora . . ." He cleared his throat. "I suppose it's too late to say I'm sorry."

"For Mama it is, yes." Cora folded her arms, resenting his intrusion on her grieving, in her life. He was nothing more than a robber.

"And you?"

"Daddy, I've made my peace with you. Let's not stir stuff up."

"Cora, you 'bout ready?" Birch entered, his steps slowing as he came alongside Cora. "Ernie."

"Birch." A slow grin lit Daddy's face and he jutted forward to shake his hand, dragging the little girl along with him. "Well, I'll be. You finally roped her."

"Actually, Daddy, I roped him."

"H-how long y'all been married? Kids?"

"Eighteen years," Cora said.

"No children." Birch slipped his arms about her waist. "We enjoy each other's company."

Daddy nodded, then took a slow look at the girl by his side. "This is . . . well . . ." Daddy knelt next to her, drawing her close, stirring a pang of longing in Cora. "Someone really special. Cora, I was hoping you might watch her for me while I go visit the grave. She's a bit young to go. And I've some things to say to your mama."

"You know she's not really there. If you want to say them to the air, take a walk across the park."

He lowered his head at her sharp intonation. But she didn't wish it back.

"Will you watch her for me? Her mother is at the inn. She didn't want to come."

"Then take her back to the inn. Who is her mother, anyway, and why do you have her daughter?"

"I-I . . ." Daddy rose up, clearing his voice, looking around the shop, looking everywhere but at Cora. "I remarried."

Birch's fingers dug into Cora's waist, holding her steady and upright. "You remarried?"

Cora glanced between the little girl, who still watched her with baby doll blue eyes, and Daddy.

"I did. Lydia was a war widow. We met in Nashville. At the USO. I was playing banjo with a bluegrass group. Well, anyway, we're . . . we're coming back here to live, Cora. We want to raise Joann here in Heart's Bend. Small town, you see."

Cora's mouth was arid, and any words she longed to say evaporated. She fell into Birch, shaking her head. "No, no . . ."

Most of the war widows Cora knew were half her age, in their twenties. A few women in their thirties. Even fewer in their forties. Widowed by officers caught in battle.

What war widow wanted her worn-out, coward of a father? Since their friends and Mama's side of the family thought Daddy was dead, no one talked about him. No one asked, "What's Ernie up to these days?" No one speculated or announced, "I heard from Ernie. He remarried, you know."

The news found no place to rest in her mind.

"Cora." Daddy ushered the little girl forward. "I know it's a lot to take in. But . . . this is your little sister, Joann."

· · ·

HALEY

When Haley and Cole stepped into the shop's locked storeroom, they were swept into another time. Into yesteryear. The 1930s, '40s, and '50s.

Cole moved the flashlight's beam over the floor and walls, searching for a light switch, the white orb spotlighting ancient mannequins and dress forms, a clothes rack of wedding gowns, linen and wool suits, a row of dusty Mary Janes and tattered, ripped veils.

They'd left his commitment of love drifting in the air above them in his kitchen. When he suggested they use the key to inspect the storeroom, Haley all but ran for the door.

He unnerved her. Crossed all of her boundaries. Worse. She kind of liked it. *Not yet, Lord. Not yet.*

"A time capsule," she whispered, unable to move.

Cole propped the door open with a large box, then tugged on the string swinging from a bare lightbulb in the center of the ceiling.

The wood-grain walls went from floor to ceiling, trimmed with white crown molding and wide baseboards.

On Haley's left, old-time racks on wheels held the

gowns and dresses, the suits. On her right, the wall consisted of built-in shelves holding the shoe, hat, and glove boxes.

Inching farther inside were two display cases, one empty, one housing tinted and tarnished costume jewelry.

Then along the back wall, pinned to weak and rotting twine, was the greatest treasure of all. Photograph after photograph.

"There must be hundreds of them." Haley bent forward, examining each one.

Cole shoved a box of photographs toward Haley as he moved his flashlight over the black-and-white images, over the faded color photographs, over the Polaroids. "Why would she leave this stuff? How did a previous tenant not bust the door down?"

Haley pressed her hand to her middle, a distant but longed-for rise of joy engaging her senses. "Because, Cole, this place was always meant to be *the* wedding shop."

Cole examined the ceiling down the seam of the built-ins to the floor. "These are solid. Just need to be cleaned up. There won't be a lot of work in here. Do you want to keep this room?" He ran the light over the outer wall. "We could knock this down, open up to the mezzanine."

"No, no . . ." Haley turned slowly, breathing in the fragrance of cedar and time gone by, of lavender, Chanel No. 5, old wood, and leather. "This room is a forever room. When I'm gone, the next owner will see that Cora's been here, that I've been here." Haley spied a photograph of Cora on the shelf under the window. "She wanted us to remember her. To know she'd been here, done her time with humanity. Served her brides."

Haley studied the image. Cora in her wedding dress with a handsome man in a suit, his dark hair slicked back, his smile so . . . *happy*. Genuine.

Cole regarded her for a second. "Good-looking couple."

"Must be when she married Birch Good." Haley turned the photograph over, removing the back to check for a date. "I'm still wrestling with the notion she's my *aunt*." Haley whipped around to face Cole. "She's my aunt. Do you think . . . Is that why I've loved this place so much?"

He grinned, a twitch on his lips, like he wanted to kiss her. Maybe she wouldn't mind. "God works in mysterious ways."

She made a face. "That's your answer? Platitudes?" She laughed, snapping the back off the picture. An envelope fell to her feet.

"It's a good platitude. And true." He stooped for the letter. "Says 'Joann' on the front."

"It's to Mom." Haley set the picture and frame on the built-in work desk. "Should I open it?" She pulled out her phone with a glance at Cole. "I'll call Mom."

But Mom was with a patient, and despite all rights to privacy, Haley couldn't resist. She slipped the flap open, retrieving a handwritten letter on linen stationery.

"May 1980. Her handwriting is perfect. Beautiful."

"What's it say?" Cole didn't hover but gave her room, leaning against the workbench.

Haley sank to the floor, sitting cross-legged, and read aloud.

Dear Joann,

You are on my mind. My little sister. The one I never got to know. Sentiment grabs hold of me these days, in my later years. I've just turned eighty, closed the shop, and am on the farm with my Birch.

I spoke with your mother in the market recently. She informed me of your medical achievements and that you had your first child, a son. How very wonderful for you.

Dad would be proud. To be honest, I am proud. After EJ died I never anticipated another sibling, much less a sister forty-seven years my junior. When I met you that day in the shop, my heart still grieved Mama's death. Perhaps in some ways, grieved my own barrenness. Birch and I'd just been speaking of it when you came in with Daddy.

You could've been my child. My grandchild. But you were my sister. Are my sister.

I've watched you grow up from afar. A fact I mourn in my latter years. I want to apologize for our confrontation in Ella's the afternoon you informed me Daddy was dying.

You see, Mama and I considered him dead for almost thirty years by the time you brought me the news. I just didn't have it in my heart to grieve again. I'd grieved, Joann. I'd said good-bye to the daddy I knew when my parents divorced in 1932.

But I wish now I'd come to his side to say a true

good-bye, to let him know I'd forgiven him. I am so sorry if my actions hurt you in any way.

I'd entertained thoughts of perhaps leaving the shop to you, but as your medical endeavors are yielding good fruit, running a shop for brides may not be your cup of tea.

I've thought about this letter over and over for years. Wondering if and when and how I might speak to you of my life, of who I am. While you may not give a wit now, there may come a time when you do. If not you, then your children.

I have the advantage of eighty years to know the ideals I had when I was twenty, thirty, forty, or fifty are not the ones I cling to today. Age has gentled my heart. What seemed so gosh darn important when I was younger seems frivolous now.

The wedding shop was my life until I married at thirty-two. Even after, the shop was a large part of my day. But Birch became my life. Joann, if you've found a good man, cling to him. There is nothing more soothing, comforting, enjoyable in life than living out your years with a man you love. And one who loves you.

There's a verse in Proverbs that speaks to me. "There are three things which are too wonderful for me, four which I do not understand. The way of an eagle in the sky, the way of a serpent on a rock, the way of a ship in the middle of the sea, and the way of a man with a maid."

The way of a man with a maid. Doesn't that just pull you into wonder? I've come to learn of this glorious way and indeed it is a mystery, but such a wonderful one! Am I not waxing sentimental? Goodness.

I was in love with the wrong man for too many years. A rugged and charming riverboat captain who swept me off my feet and out of my sound mind. He consumed me until I learned he was married with children of his own.

Haley gasped, shooting a wide glance at Cole. "Oh my gosh, she had a Dax in her life." She ran her hand down her arm. "Look, chills."

"But she found her way to the right man."

"I guess so."

Birch had always been in my life, a friend to our brother, EJ.

"*Our* brother. Mom had a brother. He died in World War One. Think of it, Cole. We are all connected so much more than we know."

"Cora's clearly drawing your mom into the family. Making *that* connection real."

He was there for me during my foolishness, sticking by me and with me, much more than I deserved. When I finally came to my senses, I almost lost him to Janice Pettrey. But praise be to the God of love, Birch came back to me.

I was just so scared, Joann, of my error with Rufus. If I'd been so fooled once, how could I be sure I'd not be fooled again even though my heart, mind, eyes, and ears knew Birch Good was a worthy, honorable, good man?

My hesitation almost cost me the love of my life.

Haley's voice trailed off. She peeked up at Cole. "Cora almost lost the love of her life."

He dropped down next to her, brushing aside her bangs, the light touch of his fingertips over her forehead inspiring a new set of chills. "If Birch can wait, I can wait."

She raised her gaze to his deep blues. "I-I don't know if you're the love of my life, Cole."

"Neither did she. But she gave him a chance. She gave herself a chance."

"So I shouldn't be afraid? I should trust the good man sitting before me?"

"I think that's what she's saying. Maybe you don't feel the passion for me, yet, that you felt for Dax—"

"Dax wasn't passion. Dax was sickness. After we . . . well . . . When we were together, I felt lost and empty, hungry for something he never gave me. He took. Stole." She sighed. "Sex-without-commitment hype is bull."

"I wouldn't know." He winked when she looked at him, her face burning red.

"Good for you."

He leaned to read over her shoulder. "Come on, read the rest of Cora's wisdom."

I suspect you're upset about the inheritance Daddy left me. But when his bank closed, I lost a good deal of

Aunt Jane's money. I think he wanted to make up for that, Joann. For all his faults, Daddy could be a man of honor.

I never needed the money. I put it in the safe. The combination is 24–82–16. Use it for yourself. For my nephew. Or any other children you may have. Oh, how lovely to write I've a nephew!

I'm renting at the shop for now, but upon my death, it will go up for sale unless you come forward. I hope you do.

Aunt Jane built a wedding shop for the women of Heart's Bend, our daughters and granddaughters. But I can't carry on. My old bones tire too easily. I failed Aunt Jane in that I've left no heir for the shop.

Edwina Park is using it as an everyday dress shop, so we shall see. I said to her, "Where's the imagination in that, Edie? Carry on with the brides." But she wants to reach more women. Oh, she doesn't know what she's missing.

Another thing I've learned in life is that control is in the hands of the Almighty. It will go well for me to trust Him. As it will for you.

I'll close with my sincere desire for you to have a good and prosperous life, my sister. We may not have known each other in this life, but perhaps in the next.

All my love,
Cora Beth Scott Good

Haley clutched the letter to her heart, sending a river of emotion roaring through her. Cole cradled her head on his shoulder.

"Kind of all makes sense now, doesn't it?"

She nodded, wiping her tears. "Aunt Jane to Aunt Cora to me." The giant reality of how life, how the Lord, worked all together for good crushed her fears. "What seemed so random now seems right, divine, like everything, even Dax, led me to this moment."

Her face was so close to Cole's when she peered up at him. She swallowed the pulse of her heart beat. Would she be ready for him? Soon? "I won't make you wait forever."

"Good." He swept his hand around the back of her neck, kissing her forehead. "My heart's about to burst." He searched her eyes, slowly lowering his lips to hers . . .

"Boss!" Below them a door slammed. Gomez's voice vibrated through the floor. "You in here?"

Cole cleared his throat, laughing low. "Up here." He stood, glancing down at Haley. "I'm not going to let our first kiss be rushed with G coming up the stairs." He stood in the doorway, calling out, "In the storeroom. We found the key."

Gomez's dark broad form appeared in the doorway. "No fooling. Look at this place. What is all this?"

"A time capsule. Inventory from Cora's day." Haley jumped up. "We have a letter."

Cole reached for it. "And a safe. Cora said she left money in a safe."

"Safe? We didn't find no safe during the demo." Gomez wrinkled his expression, leaning to inspect the shelves of shoes. "My daughter's into this old stuff."

Cole paced along the wall. "The safe must be in here."

Gomez started searching opposite Cole, tapping the floor boards with his heel, grinning when he found a loose one in the back right corner.

Cole dropped to one knee as Gomez removed the board. Haley bent forward to see an old, gray steel safe, face up, hidden under the floor.

Cole passed her the letter. "Read me the combination?"

"24–82–16."

The tumblers clicked and Cole snapped open the safe, reaching inside, taking out a money bag, handing it to Haley.

"Is that all?"

He aimed his flashlight over the dark open safe. "That's it."

Haley set the letter on the workspace next to Cora's picture, then unzipped the bag. Peering inside, she laughed, glancing up at Cole. "Money. Cash."

"You're kidding."

Haley held up the bills, hundreds and a few thousands, her heart running. This was unbelievable. "There's a note. It says, 'Twenty thousand. The amount of Aunt Jane's money lost when Daddy's bank closed.'"

She peered at Cole, then Gomez, the three of them staring in stunned silence.

Then Cole wrapped her up with a shout, swinging her around. "You got your money."

His arm felt right around her. Like she fit with him. She could breathe in his embrace. "Wait, wait," she said, pressing down to the floor. "Technically, this is Mom's. I need to show it to her."

"She'll give it to you, Haley," Cole said. "I know she will."

Gomez stared at the hole in the floor, tapping more floor boards. "I never saw anything like this. Thirty years I been in this business."

"Cole?" A male voice called from the stairs. "It's me, Mark Blanton. I've come to inspect the third floor." His footsteps echoed up to the mezzanine. "You said someone wanted to move in?"

"In here, Mark." Cole kissed Haley's forehead, backing toward the door. "Get ready to move in upstairs."

Gomez moved to the door after Cole, chuckling, scratching his head. "That boy's *enamorado*. Ain't seen him like this in long time. What'd you do to him, Haley?"

She tried to hide her grin, tried to cap the bubbling emotions in her own heart. "Nothing. And don't go telling people we're in love."

Gomez held up his hands. "Folks are already figuring it out. Especially after he sold that guitar of his."

"W-what? The Stratocaster?"

"Didn't he tell you? Linus held up the permits to pressure Cole into selling his guitar." Gomez shook his head. "I'd have told him to go jump in the river. That man? *Que sinvergüenza*. But Cole, he didn't want to waste no more time."

Cole appeared in the door. "G, Mark has a question for you, but so far so good." He pushed past Haley to the boxes of photos. "I was thinking we could frame these, well, select some, hang them around the shop. A pictorial history. I can make frames—"

She jumped into him, flinging her arms about his neck, raising up on tiptoe, her lips finding the soft, wet feel of his lips on hers, watering her desert heart.

Falling against the wall, Cole brought her with him, sliding down to the floor, cradling her in his lap, slipping his hands about her back, drawing her to him, his kiss, his passion taking over hers.

When he pulled away, he shook his head. "Girl . . . I'm afraid to ask what that was about."

"You sold your guitar for the permits."

A dark glint shadowed his eyes as he turned for the door. "G, you big mouth."

"No, no, Cole, I'm glad he told me. I can't believe you did that for me. Do you really love me that much?"

"I didn't know I did until the guitar was on the line, but yeah, I love you that much."

"You're pulling me in, Danner. It's hard to resist someone who loves you like you're loving me."

Gently, he held her face in his hands, kissing her, his sweetness filling every empty crack Dax left in her soul.

So this is why she came home. For the shop. For Cole. For love.

CHAPTER THIRTY

From the time Haley opened the storeroom, a river of favor rolled over her.

She'd moved into the third-floor apartment in March, setting up house, keeping company with Cole most evenings, her heart falling into him more and more.

He was everything Dax wasn't. Everything she needed. When she was with him, all was right in the world.

The wedding shop remodel concluded on time, including the new roof, new sidewalks and landscaping, on budget, and had passed inspection without a hitch.

The miracles just kept on coming.

More alumni brides appeared, regaling Haley with their stories as they sifted through the photos.

She'd painted the walls a soft, dove gray and the trim in white. On weekend antique hunts, she discovered a gorgeous, multitiered crystal chandelier and hung it in the grand salon. Cole found a second one to hang in the foyer.

She also hunted down and landed a battered, long, curved divan, perfect for the era, perfect for the Hollywood retro theme. Cole connected her with a craftsman to restore it to its former glory.

Display cases, area carpets over the gleaming hardwood for a cozy feel. The downstairs pantry was set for serving tea, coffee, and pastries. Haley had on good authority that's how things worked at The Wedding Shop.

Cole framed more than a hundred of the photos with his handcrafted, amazing frames. He and Haley had hung them in the shop all day yesterday.

"I can't believe I'm sharing the same space with these women. They feel like family already."

Cole slipped his arm around her, studying the smiling faces behind the sparkling glass. "They are family. Part of why you're building this business, keeping the heritage alive."

His kiss was sweeter than the last.

She needed one more miracle. Inventory. For some strange and frustrating reason, she could not land the dresses and accessories she wanted. She was desperate.

Three days. That's all until the grand opening. So many miracles until now.

Sitting at her desk on the mezzanine, phone to one ear, finger to the other, she listened to the excuses of some Melinda House lackey.

"Yes, I know it's too late for this summer, but I talked to your designer personally. She promised to send me whatever you had in stock. It's been three months. Yes, whatever. I'm not picky . . . Yeah, well, it's the way I'm running my shop right now."

She dropped her head to the desk, the accent of the man trying to help her all the way from the Grand Duchy of Hessenberg parading through her head.

"But we have no order on file."

"Then look again, please." Haley rocked back in her chair, a wicked headache threatening. She'd met her town council requirements except opening the shop by June.

Cole and his amazing crew finished the remodel on time. People gave her things, money, labor for free. The parents kicked in for the website and advertising. Even paid Cole for a custom, vintage sign: *The Wedding Shop.*

She had Cora's twenty grand in the bank.

But less than three days away from opening and her mannequins were naked.

Opening the shop had grown way beyond her childhood dream. She was moved by the women who sat with her for hours sharing their stories, looking through the photographs with their eyes misting.

They told her stories of love and loss, of happy marriages, of sad ones. Of giving birth and raising children. Of losing them to sickness or war. Of success and failure. Of being rich and poor.

Of grandchildren. European vacations. Weekends at the shore. Retracing their honeymoon steps. Of aging. Of life's window closing. Of becoming widows.

Haley could not, would not, let them down now by

missing her grand opening date. She'd not trip on the next-to-last hurdle to winning the shop's deed. And she'd keep the shop open for a year, God help her.

"I'm sorry," the lackey said one last time. "But I have nothing with your name nor your shop's name."

"I've been checking with you for three months. Every time I was told, 'The order is on its way.'"

"I don't know what to tell you."

"Tell me you have something to send. Anything. Whatever's in stock. You don't have to make or customize anything. I'm a dream customer."

Haley glanced toward the collection of boxes stacked in the alcove. She must have thirty vintage gowns and a few going-away suits. She could open as a vintage store at least, for a few weeks. But if a bride wasn't the right size, she had no process in place for altering or remaking the gown.

She'd called Charlotte last week, who helped by giving her the name of her main designer, Brey-Lindsey, but she couldn't take any orders until the fall. Then deliver them next spring.

Ads had been run in the *Heart's Bend Tribune* and the *Nashville Tennessean*. Taylor Gillingham's husband, Jack, got her a spot on morning drive radio.

The website and Facebook pages were launched. Even getting some activity. And here she was with an empty store. Except for vintage items in need of repairs.

Oh wait, she did have ten pairs of sample shoes, five sets of gloves, and about twenty veils, along with three bridesmaid dresses and four mother-of-the-bride gowns.

Lord, what am I supposed to do?

"Haley?" Gomez's big voice broke into her prayer as he landed on the mezzanine. "Why are the mannequins naked?"

She stared at him, then laughed. Yeah, this was starting to get funny. "Haven't you heard, G? It's all the rage this year. Get married naked."

He didn't laugh. "That's not funny, Haley. My daughter wants to get married next year."

"Haley?" Cole joined them on the mezzanine. "Still no inventory?"

She shook her head, sparking to life, though, when the voice came back on the line. "Yes, we can ship you some of our stock."

"Now you're talking." Haley was on her feet. "Can you overnight it? I'll pay whatever."

"We'll need a deposit." She choked when he named the amount. "We can have it to you by the end of the month."

"But I need it tomorrow."

She went around with him for another five minutes before hanging up. Giving up. Facing Cole, she confessed, "Nothing. I have no new dresses. How could I get this far, with all the favor and little miracles, and fail?"

"You're not going to fail." Cole drew her into a hug, kissing the top of her head. "Don't give up the faith now. Haley, look at what we accomplished. Time to celebrate."

"I would love to celebrate. If only I had some inventory."

Taking her by the hand, he led her down the stairs. "Look at this place. Remember how trashed it was when we first walked in with Keith Niven?" He sat on the rich red s-curved divan. "This place looks like a million bucks."

"I know. I can't believe how great everything looks. The brides in white will stand out against the red and gold accents, and the dark wood." She sat next to Cole, head on his shoulder. "Do you think Cora would like it?"

"I think she would love it. And you."

His tone, deep and resonating, caused Haley to sit up and peer into his eyes, a shiver running through her bones.

She drew in a brave breath. "I love you, Cole Danner. God help me, I do."

His smiled popped wide as he hooked his finger under her chin, his kiss proving her confession and feelings.

When the kiss ended, Haley settled down in his arms. "Today I just knew it was true. I love you. Very much." She laced her fingers through his. "And if I lose the shop, I'll still have you. Which makes the journey for the last six months well worth it."

. . .

COLE

He woke to the sound of a slamming door, the morning sun beaming bright through his windshield.

Reaching for the seat handle, he popped it upright and sat forward, shaking off the lingering sleep. As much as he paid for this truck, he'd have thought it had one good night's sleep in it. But oh, his back cramped and his knee ached from cracking it against the steering wheel all night.

Ten o'clock. The sign on the door said Malone & Co. opened at ten. Cole ran his hands through his hair, dug a piece of gum from the pack he stashed in the ash tray, and jogged across the street to the shop.

He'd driven down last night after leaving Haley. After dinner and a movie, curled on the couch with her, their hands and legs intertwined, he knew he had to do something to help her. He was falling deeper and deeper, and marriage was all over his mind.

Then as he was driving home last night, he came up with this idea. Appeal to Charlotte Rose on behalf of Haley.

Help her!

He turned the truck south and headed to Birmingham.

A soft bell rang out as he walked into the old home remodeled into a modern wedding shop. A lean woman with striking features came into the store from the back, stopping when she saw him. "Hello, may I help you?"

Cole ran his hand over his jaw, the thick stubble sharp against his fingers. "Yeah, I'm looking for Charlotte Rose. I'm Cole Danner, Haley Morgan's friend."

A sparkle flashed in her eyes. "I'm Charlotte Rose."

She offered her hand, giving his a solid shake. "How's Haley doing? Yesterday she was panicked about inventory."

"That's why I'm here. The grand opening is on Monday and she's got nothing. Well, some vintage gowns, but that's not going to cut it. Melinda House really cut her legs out from under her. She tried your designer, who was gracious, but not able to send anything to her until spring."

"Yeah, wedding designers don't turn on a dime." Charlotte motioned for him to follow her to the back. "How did the shop turn out? Did she stick with Hollywood regency?"

"Yeah, the place looks amazing. We just need something to sell."

"Cole, this is my assistant, Dixie." Another striking woman looked up from her coffee. "Dix, this is Cole. He's here for Haley. Remember the shop owner from Heart's Bend I told you about?"

"I do. Nice to meet you, Cole." Dixie peered at Charlotte. "What's going on?"

"She needs help. No inventory. Even Brey-Lindsey couldn't come through for her."

"She was asking for anything. Whatever they had in stock. She wasn't picky."

"Know what I'm wondering, Cole?" Charlotte offered him a cup of coffee, pointing to the cream and sugar. "Why are you here? Why didn't she call?"

"She's frustrated. I'm not sure why she didn't call. Maybe she doesn't want to bother you. She says you've done so much already, but I don't care. I'm here and I'm begging." He set his coffee down, his adrenaline fired up enough without caffeine.

"Ah, love, I can't stand it." Dixie patted her hand over her heart. "We have to help her, Char."

"Of course we're going to help her. Rather, we're going to help Cole help her." She started out of the break room, again motioning for Cole to follow. "This is perfect knight in shining armor stuff." She stopped suddenly, whirling around to face him. "Do you love her? Are you going marry her?"

He balked, making a face. "Yes and yes. Well, I want to marry her. Do I pass the test? Was that a test?"

Charlotte's smile said something he could not read. "It wasn't a test, but yes, you passed. Dixie, let's pull all the summer and fall line we have. Cole, do you have a truck?"

"Yes."

"Perfect." Up the center stairs, Charlotte pulled out her phone and dialed. "Tim, babe, can I borrow you for the day? We have an emergency." Glancing back at Cole, she made a wry face. "Yes, a *real* wedding dress emergency. I'll make it up to you. Thanks, darling."

He liked this woman. A lot.

"Dix, we have a light day so let's just close up. Cole, my husband, Tim, will help carry up the stuff we'll need. Dixie and I will follow you in my car. Now, tell me what Haley does have and we can fill in the rest."

"You're a life saver." He knew it was right to drive down here. "I can pay you for the inventory, and your time."

"Nothing doing. Look, I'm generous, but I'm also

a businesswoman. I'm merely moving inventory to Haley's shop, letting my dresses be sold in Heart's Bend. She'll be working for me, so to speak. I'll run the sales through my account and split the money with Haley. That'll keep her going until her *real* inventory arrives. Dix, pull veils, shoes, gloves, hats, slips, and bras. Cole, come help me with the gowns. When Tim arrives, he can load up racks and mannequins, and oh, the display stands."

Standing in their midst, Cole barely followed the conversation after the initial plan. Charlotte and Dixie started talking wedding-gown lingo in a language he thought was English but possibly not human.

They finished each other's sentences. Spoke in code and acronyms with a frightening precision. Like a military strike force.

"What do you think, Cole? Does that sound like what Haley needs? Oh, man, should we call her? No, this should be a surprise. The man who loves her driving up with shiny white dresses."

"Um, yeah, let's go for it. But to be honest, I have no idea what you just said other than gowns, shoes, and surprise."

Charlotte laughed. "Tim is going to love you."

Dixie started off, hand in the air. "Then let's get to work."

Charlotte said, "Cole, follow me. I have a special trunk for you to haul."

CHAPTER THIRTY-ONE

HALEY

Saturday evening, the shop sat silent and dark except for the glow of the evening sun. On the mezzanine, Haley lined up the naked mannequins.

"I've called you here today because I want to know why you're naked. Where is your uniform? I can't hear you! We're a team, a unit. We watch each other's back. I've done my part, now what about you? I can't hear you, airman. We have to look sharp at the grand opening or we will all let Miss Cora down."

She boosted her general-addressing-a-military-parade voice. "We're going to have to make do with what we have. Vintage uniforms. You." She pointed to the first mannequin. "You'll be Mrs. Peabody's mother."

Haley reached for the suitcase, snapping open the locks, raising the dress from the gold silk lining. Gently she slipped the gown over the mannequin's head, setting the dress on her rounded shoulders, letting the gown slip to the floor, then stepped back.

"Mrs. Peabody's mother, you're beautiful." She

regarded the faceless mannequin with a spurt of tears in her eyes. She really did look beautiful. Haley straightened the sleeves. "Tammy, what a tale you missed. It would be more fun if you were here."

But maybe that's why she lost interest. It wasn't her inheritance. It was Haley's.

She brushed her hand under her eyes, reaching for Mrs. Peabody's mother's veil and fluffing the long layers of tulle, her fingers slipping through torn and ragged places.

She'd have to find another veil, but for now . . . what she needed was music. Haley searched the albums on her phone, stopping when she came across Bublé.

The smooth melody of "The Way You Look Tonight" filled the mezzanine.

"Mrs. Peabody's mother, you get to be in the display window." Haley hoisted the plastic woman on her hip and started down to the grand salon.

But just as she got to the window, balancing the mannequin in the center, Cole peered at her through the glass. Startled, Haley reached for the mannequin's hand, snapping it off. "Cole, what are you doing?" She waved the plastic extremity. "Now I have to call nine-one-one."

"Open the front door."

"Why?"

"Just do it."

She made a mocking face, dropped Mrs. Peabody's mother's hand to the display floor, and hurried around to unlock the door.

"What's this all about?" she said, standing aside for

Cole, who grabbed her by the shoulders and shoved her back to the stairs.

"Stay right there."

"What's going on?"

Voices rushed in from outside. "Put all the dress racks in the grand salon for now. We'll see what Haley wants to do."

And Charlotte Rose walked through the front door. "The cavalry is here. Haley, meet my assistant, Dixie. Dix, Haley. Now—"

"Charlotte, what are you doing here?"

Dixie marched up a couple of stairs, a stack of shoe boxes in hand. "What do you think of displaying shoes on the stairs?"

"Dix, what a great idea! Haley? What do you think?"

"Wait, will someone tell me what's going on?" She grabbed Cole as he passed by with an armload of dresses. "What did you do?"

"I asked for help."

Dixie set the shoes on the steps. "Nice to meet you." She offered her hand with a nod toward Cole. "He's a keeper."

"Y-yeah, sure, but what's going on?"

Dixie peered into the grand salon. "Haley, this shop is fantastic. I'm officially jealous. The Hollywood regency, the staircase . . . magnificent. Charlotte, I see redecorating in our future. Girl, you are going to knock it out of the park."

Haley ran up a couple of stairs and in her best captain's voice said, "Stop, everyone." Cole and a handsome man with an armload of dresses froze in the foyer.

Charlotte and Dixie stared at her from the entrance to the grand salon.

"Would someone please tell me what's going on?"

The room exhaled. Cole and the other man went back into motion. Charlotte roped her arm around her shoulders. "Cole drove down to see us last night. Apparently he slept in his truck. Anyway, he told us what happened with your inventory. I'm so sorry but not so surprised. Anyway, he was at our door the moment we opened. Said he wasn't going to let you fail. So we loaded up—Oh, this is my husband, Tim. Tim, did I tell you Haley rides a Harley?"

"No, you didn't. Haley, nice to meet you."

Charlotte leaned into Haley. "He sold his motocross bikes for me."

"Haley, do you want to stage some dresses up here on this fantastic mezzanine?" Dixie said, walking around with her iPad, taking notes. "Customers can roam, browse, get the full scope of the place."

"The mezz is the official changing area for the brides, but for the grand opening, that would be great."

Charlotte walked the shop, discussing staging and lighting, detailing her temporary partnership with The Wedding Shop, Haley soaking in the "wow" of wonder in her life.

When all the inventory had been brought in, she caught Cole in the pantry. "You went down to Birmingham? Why didn't you tell me?"

He shrugged. "In case it didn't work out. I didn't want you to be disappointed. If it did work out, I thought it'd be a fun surprise."

She fell into his arms. "You amaze me."

He kissed her, holding her close, cradling her heart against his. "I couldn't leave my girl hanging."

"I love being your girl."

Cole stretched out his foot and kicked the pantry door closed. Brushing Haley's hair aside, he started with her forehead, kissing her temples, then her cheeks, her jaw, and her chin.

His touch ran like warm feathers over her neck and down her arms. Roping their fingers together, his lips found hers as he raised her hands to his neck, gathering her in his arms, saying nothing. Saying everything.

CHAPTER THIRTY-TWO

HALEY

At two a.m., she stood at the top of the stairs with Charlotte on one side, Dixie on the other, surveying her new kingdom.

The Wedding Shop.

It breathed with life, a river of white, cream, and gold gowns flowing from one salon to the next.

The fun vintage gowns were spaced in between the new, like wedding gown mentors, reminders of where the shop had been and where it was going.

Cole and Tim worked outside, a last-minute idea from Dixie to trim the windows with white lights. Tim started to balk at the demanded chore.

"It's not necessary," Haley said, letting the man off the hook. He'd already worked so hard for someone he didn't know.

But when Dixie barked, "Get to it," both boys hit the door running.

Haley nodded at her new friend. "You could've been a great master sergeant."

Charlotte, the grand dame of bridal shops, viewed the salon with arms crossed, her chin raised with approval.

"You are going to have a phenomenal grand opening. I can feel it."

"What's the plan for Monday?" Dixie stood alongside Charlotte. "Sign up for a newsletter? Prizes? Music? Do you have bridal consultants? Staff?"

"Yes, a sign-up. I forgot about prizes. Yes to music and no shop staff except me, myself, and I. Haven't hired anyone yet. I was on the construction crew until a few weeks ago."

"All right, Dix, can you come back on Monday and be a consultant for a few days?" Charlotte said. "I can handle things at home with our part-time staff. Haley, get to work on hiring at least one person. Those Elnora gowns I brought are going to fly off the rack. I just know it."

"Charlotte, you don't have to loan me your best girl."

"Yes, I do." Charlotte held her arms. "We're bonded now. Besides, you have my inventory and I want us both to make money. You can learn a lot from Dix too."

"Haley, you got something going on here." Dixie rubbed the gooseflesh on her arms.

"I know. Overwhelms me at times."

Charlotte turned to Haley. "Now that the opening is settled, I have something for you."

"More than you've already done?" Haley motioned to the shop. "What else could you have? Look at all this you've done for me. I can't thank you enough, Charlotte, Dixie."

Charlotte ducked into the storeroom, tugging out

an old trunk. "Remember the story I told you about my wedding dress and finding it in a battered, ugly trunk?"

"Yeah?" What was she doing? Haley took a step back.

Charlotte knelt next to the trunk. "You were the one who said maybe I should find the next bride."

"I was just talking. What do I know?"

"But the Lord woke me up in the middle of the night a few months ago and started speaking to me about you. And this dress. Haley, you're the next bride for the dress."

"Charlotte, I-I can't. Not your special dress." She wasn't worthy. Far from it. Only recently had she warmed up to the idea of being in love with Cole. Haley stared down at the battered, beat-up wooden box, shaking, the heat of the Divine running through her.

"I'm just being obedient." Charlotte released the lock and raised the lid, removing a garment that moved with a light and grace all its own. The pure white gown emanated a gold glow through the seams, into the air, into Haley.

"Designed in 1912 by a black seamstress for a white bride in Birmingham." Charlotte held up the dress, the scoop neck falling in soft folds and the chapel train swirling over the freshly polished floor.

"Oh, Charlotte, it's the most stunning gown in the place."

She held the dress up to Haley. "At my wedding, the man who married us, husband of bride number two, said, 'This wedding gown is like the gospel of Jesus Christ. It fits everyone who tries it on. It's timeless, never wears out, and never needs to be altered, always in style and always beautiful.'"

Haley stepped back. "Truth is timeless, but, Charlotte, I can't." She retreated a little deeper into the mezzanine, a taut pull between who she was and who she was to become.

Charlotte lowered the dress, smoothing her hand over the silky bodice. "I love this dress. It means everything to me. Truth, faith, miracles, family, love. It epitomizes who I am. The people I came from. So I sealed it up. Didn't even put it in the old wooden trunk. I thought it had finally arrived home, where it needed to be. Then I met you. How could I take such a blessing and hide it away, store it for another time when the time to be worn and used was now?" Her voice wavered. Her eyes glistened. "I was holding on to something that didn't really belong to me. I have to let it go." She held the dress up to Haley again. "'Freely you received, freely give.' To you from me and Jesus."

Haley shivered with tears. Old sins took a lot of love to sink.

Dixie stepped into the mezzanine from the stairs. "Haley, I've watched Charlotte over the years, and she's not lying about this dress. The torch is passing to you."

"It's the Lord's way of showing you He loves you. Time to get off the bench of past mistakes and shame."

Charlotte looked so comical, like a worn-out cheerleader not sure her lingo was on point. Haley laughed behind her hand.

"See, joy!"

"And your goofy metaphors, Char." Dixie reached for Haley. "Come on, try it on."

Haley reached for the gown, the soft, silky material rich against her skin. "Now? I'm not engaged."

"Doesn't matter." Charlotte bent to see her face. "Try it on? For me? I'm dying to be the one to pass it on now. I want to see how God fits on you."

Haley could not deny her friend. "Fine, but if it fit you, Amazon woman, it's going to be too big for me."

"You just wait and see, Mighty Mouse."

In the storeroom, Haley shimmied from her shorts and top, stepping into the 104-year-old gown. The fabric flowed up her legs, the bodice slipping over her hips to sit perfectly on her waist as the skirt swirled around her legs, the hem stopping at the top of her toes.

Haley peeked out of the door. "All clear?"

"No men, they've gone on a food run." Charlotte waved her out, her eyes glowing like polished gems. "Oh, Haley, oh, Haley . . ."

Charlotte ushered her to the wood-framed oval mirror, squaring her in front of it. Unlike when she tried on the Snow White gown, Haley loved her reflection. The gown made her look . . . pure. Whole. Healed.

"It's amazing," she whispered with a giggle. "And it fits."

"It's the gospel," Charlotte said, working the buttons in the back. "It fits everyone who tries it on. The trick is to believe. There, all buttoned up."

Haley turned across the mezzanine, the skirt moving freely about her legs, the silk so cool on her skin. "I feel amazing. I want to cry and laugh all at the same time."

In the shop where she used to play make-believe, where she and Tammy made a pinky promise, where her heritage stayed hidden away for thirty-seven years, her life came full circle in this very real, very true experience.

Charlotte clasped her by the shoulders. "It's yours, Haley. I'm passing it on to you. Wear it on your wedding day with joy and grace and peace. But never box it up. Listen for God to tell you when to pass it on."

Haley raised her pinky. "I promise."

Charlotte hesitated, raising her hand and linking her pinky with Haley's.

CHAPTER THIRTY-THREE

ONE YEAR LATER
JUNE 10

The scent of summer laced the afternoon breeze as it shoved through trees guarding the wedding chapel.

Haley scanned the blue sky as she burst through the doors on Cole's arm, wearing *the* wedding dress, wearing Love and Truth, a bouquet of purple flowers in her hand.

The guests in the small wedding chapel flowed out with them, cheering for "Mr. and Mrs. Cole Danner."

At the bottom of the steps, Cole swept her up into his arms, spinning her through the late-afternoon light lacing through the trees. Light, everything in her was light.

The guests, about forty in all, peppered them with petals of lavender, bellflower, and catmint.

Stalking alongside them, Taylor Gillingham stealthily snapped pictures.

"Congratulations, Hal," Dad said, kissing her cheek, unable to stop smiling since before walking her down the aisle.

"Haley, my beautiful girl." Mom had gotten more sentimental since the shop opened, since she read Cora's letter, since she gave Haley Cora's money for the shop.

This past week the town council deeded the shop over to Haley while naming her businesswoman of the year.

Behind Cole, his dad came up, clapping him on his shoulder with a hearty congratulations.

She never imagined that when she responded to the tug to "go home," she'd end up here. Or that reopening the wedding shop was about family and healing, and real love would conquer her heart.

While Cora never healed her relationship with her father, Cole was well on the way to mending his. He and his dad met weekly for dinner, becoming father and son again, living in the present and not the past.

"All right, let's get to the reception." Haley's oldest brother, Aaron, herded the small crowd toward their cars. "Half the town is waiting."

The reception was to be at Cole's place, *their* place, the old Good farm where Miss Cora and Birch had lived for fifty-five years. Once the cork popped, Mom poured forth with family history.

"Wait for us." Haley's bridesmaids emerged from the church, waving their bouquets. Charlotte, Mrs. Peabody, Mrs. Elliot, and Mrs. Rothschild, sisters of the dress, sisters of the shop.

Before the wedding, Mrs. Elliot declared she was hoping to catch the bridal bouquet. "I'll give the younger gals a run for their money."

Oh, love, its desire never faded as long as there was the breath of life.

"Come on, babe. Our chariot awaits."

Climbing into the limo with Cole, Haley curled onto her husband's lap. "I think my heart might burst."

"Mine already did. A year ago."

She kissed him, brushing her hand over his hair, loving the look in his blue eyes.

"I feel so full." She kissed him again. "So this is love . . ."

"So this is love." He drew her into him, his lips fiery against hers.

"Isn't this dress amazing?"

"Very, and I love the story behind it, around it. I love the woman in it."

"The wedding chapel was so romantic and stellar. I felt like I was being married in a royal court."

"When we married before God I suppose we were."

"So what was your favorite part of the day, Mr. Danner?

He brushed a stray curl from her shoulder, his warm, slight touch giving her shivers. "Don't you know, darling? You."

DISCUSSION QUESTIONS

1. The story opens with Haley as a girl, riding her bike on a summer day with her BFF. Do you have a fun girlhood memory to share? What did you love most about summer as a kid?

2. Cora inherited her aunt's wedding shop. What do you consider the value of inheritance? What about inheritances of a different kind, like spiritual, or historical? Share something you've inherited from your family—natural or spiritual.

3. Haley's mom required the family to set goals every new year. Do you set goals? What's the value of setting goals? How did setting goals ultimately impact Haley's life?

4. We know the saying, "Love is blind." That seems to be the case with Cora. Why do you think she loved Rufus so much? Why cling to him for so long? Have you been "love blind" before?

5. Haley also experienced a bit of "love blindness." Did you see that parallel with Cora? Seems kind of obvious now but I didn't start out with that in mind! Books have a way of taking on a life of their own.

6. Cole was wounded by his father's actions. As kids, we don't have control over what our parents choose to do. But we do have control over how we respond. What's the Godly way to respond to the wounds of our past? What truth did Cole come to?

7. The Wedding Shop became a sort of anchor in Heart's Bend, a desired destination for the young women. Is there such a place in your life or past? Maybe in your hometown?

8. Sometimes the best thing to happen to us is right in front of our eyes! Cora couldn't see Birch for looking. Talk about how to recognize the good that's in front of us right now. How can we be "present" in our lives?

9. Charlotte Rose believed the wedding dress belonged to her. But the Lord revealed she must pass it on. How can we have an open hand with the things God has given us?

10. Cole sold his rare electric guitar to help Haley and his father. The situation with Linus was unjust. But Cole's sacrifice brought a sort of humble justice. Jesus's sacrifice is an unjust justice. Talk about how we can surrender our wants and desires to the Lord, letting Him bring justice.

11. What did you think of the women bringing the money to Haley? What was going on there?

12. Haley's mom was an achiever but part of her edge stemmed from losing her father when she was

young. She also struggled with Cora's rejection. How do we overcome rejection and the pain of the past?

13. A lot of the story line deals with generosity—people freely giving, even the town was generous. Where do you stand on the generosity scale? Can you improve your aspects of giving?

14. What was your favorite part about the story?

ACKNOWLEDGMENTS

I'd like to thank the Internet and YouTube and all the people who load up seemingly pointless and uninteresting information. Thank you, from the bottom of my heart, and from probably every writer's heart, who's searched for information in your cyber mine and found a nugget of truth. Your videos of a boat docking blessed me.

Otherwise, let me shout out to my writing partner Susan May Warren. We're going on book 17 together and, as always, you keep my writing straight and sane. I'm still waiting for your genius to rub off on me but I'll take your love and ideas in the meantime. Give your son David a pat on the back for me too. I'm still smiling over the time I called for help and asked for him instead of you. Ha! You trained him well.

Beth Vogt, my FaceTime partner. Your insight and suggestions helped to make this book better. I appreciate you, friend.

Special heart emoticon for my editors on this book, Becky Philpott and Karli Jackson—the dynamic duo. I appreciate you both so much. Thank you for all of your patience, help, insight, and guidance—for being a phone call away, and for laughing with me on said phone! You are the best!

Gratitude to my publisher, Daisy Hutton, who is a joy to know, let alone work with. I love walking this writing journey with you.

A million heart emoticons to the entire Thomas Nelson/Zondervan team who do so much behind the scenes. I'm thankful! Feel my love coming YOUR way. You know who you are!

Big bear hug to my buddy Jim Bartholomew for details on construction and renovations. And for lunch. Any and all mistakes are mine.

Hugs and kisses to my husband who puts up with a writer in the house—late dinners, deadlines, and constant questions about minute plot points. "Is that plausible? Do you think that will work?"

Love and devotion to my mom who reads every book and shares them. And to her friends who pray for me. I am blessed by you, Mom, and by the encouragement of your friends.

Shout out to my church family for the rousing cheer when the pastor announced I'd hit the *New York Times* bestseller list. Mostly, I love that you are a people who worship, and who love Jesus, and that we fellowship in His friendship.

At the end of it all, this journey is about Jesus. I do all of this for Him. Not in a religious, platitude kind of way, but in a "You-stole-my-heart" kind of way and "I want the world to know You." He gave his life for me, so now I write for Him. Jesus, thank you!

ABOUT THE AUTHOR

Rachel Hauck is the *New York Times*, *Wall Street Journal*, and *USA Today* bestselling author of *The Wedding Dress*, which was also named Inspirational Novel of the Year by *Romantic Times* and was a RITA finalist. Rachel lives in central Florida with her husband and two pets and writes from her ivory tower.

Visit her online at rachelhauck.com
Facebook: rachelhauck
Twitter: @RachelHauck